A SEA UNTO ITSELF

i

A SEA UNTO ITSELF

A NOVEL OF THE NAPOLEONIC WARS

BY

JAY WORRALL

Fireship Press
www.FireshipPress.com

A Sea Unto Itself by Jay Worrall

ISBN-13:978-1-61179-273-7: Paperback
ISBN 978-1-61179-274-4: ebook

BISAC Subject Headings:

FIC014000FICTION / Historical
FIC032000FICTION / War & Military
FIC047000 FICTION / Sea Stories

Cover Work: Christine Horner

Address all correspondence to:
Fireship Press, LLC
P.O. Box 68412
Tucson, AZ 85737
Or visit our website at:
www.FireshipPress.com

FOREWORD

THE LONG WAR BETWEEN THE United Kingdom and republican France entered its sixth year in 1799 with both sides finding reasons for optimism. January found the French in firm control of present day Netherlands, Belgium, Switzerland, and Italy (excluding Sicily). A large French army under the command of General Napoleon Bonaparte had recently established itself in Egypt, a strategically valuable country with extensive coastlines on both the Mediterranean and Red Seas. Communications and supply from Europe, however, were severed by Admiral Horatio Nelson's fleet, which had not only decimated the Republic's naval power in the Mediterranean at the Battle of the Nile the previous August, but also held Egypt's principal port at Alexandria under close blockade.

The United Kingdom, for the moment, reigned almost supreme on the high seas, while French armies remained dominant on the European continent. A so-called Second Coalition—made up of Britain, Russia, Austria, the Ottoman Empire, and others—was formed at the behest of, and heavily subsidized by, London. The wealth that made these subsidies possible came from England's widespread and vastly profitable trade, a large portion of which derived from her troubled colonies in India.

Direct invasion of the British Isles by France remained impossible. As an alternative, in 1798 the young General Bonaparte suggested to the Directory in Paris an expedition to the east "to drive the English from all their oriental possessions." It was this plan, subsequently adopted, which led to the invasion of Egypt. It also envisioned cutting a canal through the Isthmus of Suez and obtaining control of the Red Sea. This would make French military and commercial access to the subcontinent much more direct than England's, which required sailing around the southern tip of Africa and back up the other side; a journey of some six to nine months.

Assessment of this threat by Pitt's government in London ranged from sober consideration to a more generally held incredulity that any such effort could seriously be contemplated. In July, 1798, a small squadron consisting of a fifty-gun warship, two frigates, and a sloop of war under Rear Admiral John Blankett was dispatched by the Admiralty for the purpose of sealing the exit to the Red Sea and preventing any French passage to India. In January, 1799, the thirty-two gun frigate Cassandra, under the command of junior Captain Charles Edgemont, sailed from Chatham with orders to provide reinforcement and to assist in certain intelligence gathering services. Unknown to Captain Edgemont, who in any case had more immediate problems to overcome at the time, the responsibility for thwarting French ambitions would come to rest on his shoulders and his shoulders alone.

A NOTE ON MEASUREMENTS
AND VALUES

Money: It is not possible to directly equate the purchasing power of currency between the late 18th and early 21st centuries. It has been suggested, however, that the value of an English pound in 1790 might be multiplied by a factor of 70 or 80 to give an approximate equivalent for the year 2000. From pounds in 1790 to American dollars in the year 2000, the ratio might be 1:100–110. English pounds were divided into shillings, pennies and farthings: 20 shillings to a pound; 12 pennies to a shilling; 4 farthings to a penny. A full loaf of bread cost about 4 pence.

Distance: Units of measurement for distance at sea were not always standardized. The author has used:

1 league = 3 nautical miles = 5.6 kilometers

1 nautical mile = 6076 feet (1.15 statute miles) = 1.9 kilometers

1 cable length = about 200 yards (1/10 of a nautical mile) = 185 meters

1 fathom = 6 feet (1/100 of a nautical mile) = 1.8 meters

Time: Time on British naval ships was measured in watches and bells. The day officially began at noon and was divided into seven watches, five of four hours each and two of two hours:

Afternoon:noon to 4pm Middle:midnight to 4am

1st Dog4pm to 6pm Morning:4am to 8am

2nd Dog:6pm to 8pm Forenoon: 8am to noon

First:8pm to midnight

The ship's bell was rung in cumulative half-hour intervals during each watch so that three bells in the afternoon watch is 1:30 p.m. and four bells in the middle watch is 2:00 a.m.

CHAPTER ONE

5 JANUARY, 1799
LIVERPOOL, ENGLAND

"Look, here is Mary Elizabeth," Mrs. Penelope Edgemont said to her husband. The two were strolling, arm in arm, along Liverpool's harbor so that he could show her the seagoing traders tied up along the quay. A gust of cold wind blew across the waterfront, kicking up swirls of dust and debris and rattling the blocks in Mary Elizabeth's rigging. Gangs of roughly dressed workmen moved around them, loading cargos from carts and barrows onto the merchantmen to be transported abroad, or offloading the same to be put into warehouses. While Charles Edgemont had anticipated a flood of questions about the different types of craft and the intricacies of their masts and sail arrangements, Penny seemed more interested in the names they had been given.

"Yes, Mary Elizabeth," he said dutifully, reading from the weather-beaten red lettering across her transom.

"We have also seen the Alice Harding, Diana, and Elizabeth Bea. Canst thou tell me, are all ships named for women?"

Charles searched for an answer that would please. "Many are, especially traders. They are away for such lengths of time that it reminds their crews of wives and loved ones at home." There was more to it than this, but it would be too complicated to explain. Most seamen, from captains to ship's boys, firmly believed that the name given their craft, and her fate, were inextricably linked. Women's names were always comforting, conveying a sense of hearth and home. Discovery would be apt for a vessel on a voyage of exploration. For warships, Ajax would naturally be formidable in battle; Centaur, a terror to its enemies; Hero, Intrepid, and Victory spoke for themselves. A captain had a natural advantage with a command named like that.

Penny squeezed his arm more tightly against her side. She was covered in a gray woolen cloak fastened with buttons in front up to her chin. In her free arm she held an oblong package, carefully wrapped in oiled paper and bound with rope yarn. Her eyes glistened and her cheeks were reddened prettily from the cold. Silken strands of fawn-colored hair escaped from the edges of her bonnet, teased by the wind. Charles had decided on the cloak himself and given it to her as a present. He remembered ordering it from the finest (or at least the most expensive) tailor in Chester soon after he had returned shipless from the Mediterranean, his precious frigate Louisa—herself with a woman's name—now charred and broken on the seabed in a bay off faraway Egypt. Penny had reprimanded him about the buttons for her cloak as an extravagance, but then wore it anyway and seemed pleased. The bulk of the mantle also concealed the fact, growing more obvious daily, that she was moderately advanced in her expectancy, the culmination of which event was anticipated for the middle of March. The object she carried in her arm was a gift she had ordered for him in return from a shop specializing in nautical instruments. They had collected it earlier that morning: a beautifully made collapsing telescope with the finest hand-ground lenses from London in its own highly polished wooden case.

Charles and Penny had traveled to Liverpool in hopes of having a little time together before he was required to take up a new command waiting at the Royal Dockyard at Chatham. For the occasion he was dressed in civilian clothing, over which he wore an outer coat. He was without his sword, which as a gentleman and naval officer he was entitled to wear, but out of deference to his wife's Quaker sensibilities had agreed not to. The absence of its familiar weight on his hip left him feeling vaguely naked.

"Tell me again," she said, looking up at him. "What is the title of thy new boat?" This was a painful question for her, he knew. She seldom spoke about the necessity of his leaving again for the sea, and then only to address concerns about what clothing and other effects he should provide himself with.

"Cassandra," he answered. He thought it a not particularly auspicious name for a thirty-two-gun frigate. At least it was feminine and derived from Greek mythology, which provided a little substance.

"Cassandra," she repeated thoughtfully. "'Tis a pretty name. She hath the gift of prophesy, I recall, but no man shall heed her. I find it is oft so with men."

Charles grinned. "No it isn't. I listen to you."

"Thou dost not," she answered. "Else thou wouldst remain at home."

"Penny," Charles began. "You know that I must . . ."

"Oh, stuff," she said, then tilted her head to one side. "Shhh, listen."

"Ye denizens of Liverpool," a high-pitched voice sounded from across the square. "See what poor souls as suffer from yer iniquitous trade. Come forward and observe for yerselves the fruits of this ill-gotten, pernicious profit!" Charles looked to see a scruffy man in a threadbare coat and broad-brimmed hat mounting a box to address the passersby. Beside the speaker stood two black Africans in ill-fitting clothes, barely sufficient to preserve them from the chill. They were a man and a woman, and from the look of them seemed uncomfortable, whether from the climate or from being the objects of such scrutiny he could not tell.

"Gather 'round," the speaker shouted. "Cast yer eyes 'pon these miserable wretches what have only newly escaped from the most cruel enslavement on American plantations, and what have only just regained their natural freedom that YE have aided to deprive them of."

Charles knew himself to be no friend of slavery or slavers, but if the man wasn't careful he would get his ears boxed for him, or worse. Liverpool was a port city notorious for its toughs and heavily invested in the transport of captured humanity to the Americas. There would be many in Liverpool who would not take kindly to his words. He glanced at Penny, her eyes on the speaker now risen to his full height on the crate. Charles knew from experience that his wife could become righteously indignant in her opposition to the institution of enslavement and even attended the meetings of a women's committee in Chester dedicated to its abolition. It would be better if they moved along before some kind of trouble broke out.

"May we move closer?" Penny said, pulling on his arm. "I wish to listen."

A crowd was already beginning to collect around the speaker. "I don't think it such a good idea, my dear," Charles said. "It would be better if we kept our distance."

"Stuff and nonsense," she replied. "He is making a testimony against slavery and we must display our support. Besides which, there are those wretched Negroes by him. Perhaps we can assist them in some way."

Charles looked again at the reputed African slaves, or ex-slaves. They did indeed appear uncomfortable. Penny seemed to consider it her duty to intervene in the lives of everyone she came across who suffered from some inequity or another.

"Please," she said. "This is England after all. Surely there can be no danger."

Against his better judgment, Charles allowed himself to be led to the edge of the growing audience. He noted that it was mostly made up of the kinds of people one would expect along the waterfront: fish mongers, teamsters, a few shop clerks in their aprons, idle seamen, and other sorts of layabouts. Some were very rough looking indeed.

"The evil practice of slavery is the very antithesis of civilization itself." The speaker gestured toward the sky with his finger. "It is abhorrent to the One True God for a man to enslave another. It is Satan's own work to succor such trade in human flesh by transporting these poor souls from the comfort of their natural homes in Africa to harsh and penurious labors in the Americas." He paused to add emphasis to his words. "The profits thus gained are the very wages of sin!"

Someone standing nearby yelled back, "Get ye down off that box, old bugger. Ye can bend over and I'll show ye the wages of sin." There was a good deal of laughter at this.

Penny turned to glare at the man who had called out. "I do wish he would not say such things," she said primly. "Everyone knows that slavery is an evil practice."

"Yes, my dear," Charles said, his attention on the crowd. Still more people were emerging from the shops facing the square, and even off some of the long, sleek merchant ships moored farther up the wharf, to see what the fuss was about. Those ships, he knew at a glance, were termed 'blackbirders,' specially built for rapid transit of the Atlantic with highly perishable human cargos. He had crossed wakes with the foul-smelling transports on the high seas more than once.

The speaker seemed undeterred by the interruptions and continued his harangue on the errors of Liverpudlians' ways. Charles' focus turned to the two blacks standing by the man's feet as if they were on exhibit. It must be difficult for them to be the subject of such hostile display. The male was large, heavily built, with skin as dark as ink. Charles wondered about him. He guessed that as a runaway slave he had experienced some frightening things in his life, perhaps more frightening than the crowd jeering sporadically at the speaker on the box. The man seemed to be surveying the assembled onlookers cautiously. For an instant their eyes met. Charles nodded reflexively in acknowledgement. The black tilted his head in return; his gaze moved on.

At that moment another man, a seaman by his appearance, shouldered his way past Penny and shouted through cupped hands, "Shut your fuckin' gob, you nigger-lovin' son of a whore, or there's some of us that will shut it for you."

The speaker on the box shouted ever louder over a rising chorus of derision. Penny, Charles saw with alarm, immediately turned to confront the offending seaman. "I will thank thee not to speak such rude and hateful things," she said to him, clutching her package against her chest. "I think thou art not a loving Christian person."

"Penny," Charles said, trying to gain her attention before she went further. The burley, unshaven seaman scowled back at her. It was time to move his wife away before things got out of hand. The crowd had grown increasingly hostile and it wouldn't take much to spark trouble.

"And I'll thank you to tend to your own goddamned affairs, lady," the man answered harshly. Charles could smell the waft of rum on his breath. He took his wife's arm with the intention of leading her away.

Penny jerked herself free. "Thou art a rude, uncivil person," she said with growing indignation to the seaman. "I do not abide that thou canst countenance this traffic in human flesh. It is a most despicable and hateful form of commerce and anathema to all Christians." She looked to Charles for support.

"You will please mind your language in the presence of my wife," Charles said firmly, more to appease Penny than to intimidate the seaman. He reached again for her arm. "We must leave now," he said urgently.

The seaman glared back in response. Several people around them had switched their attention from the speaker to the more interesting confrontation between the seaman and the young woman.

"I think thou a pernicious, ill-natured, uncouth, callous lout that doth prey on the misfortunes of others," Penny continued, resisting the pressure on her arm, her voice rising.

Charles thought that these were probably the severest insults she knew. He doubted that the seaman comprehended the exact meaning of much of it, but he would get the drift. "Penny," he said to regain his wife's attention. He forcefully pulled her arm to turn her away.

"So she's your Poll, is she, Jack," the seaman sputtered, turning on Charles. "You should teach her to shut her gob."

This was too much. 'Poll' was a term for a common dockside whore, although he doubted his wife would know this. "I will not have my wife addressed in such fashion," he growled, taking a step toward the man.

"Go bugger yourself," the seaman responded. He placed his hands on Charles' chest and pushed.

Charles staggered backwards then, despite Penny's pulling on his coat to restrain him, lunged forward and pushed back. "You will mind your manners when addressing me, cully," he said menacingly, "or I'll mind them for you." He found the man surprisingly difficult to budge. He was about to follow up with the potentially significant revelation that he was a captain in the Royal Navy and that the seaman had better be careful or he would find himself in serious difficulties. He didn't get beyond the introductory, "Do you know to whom you are speaking?" The seaman's fist pounded into his solar plexus like the kick of a horse. The force of it took his breath away and doubled him over. Before he could react a second fist hammered against the side of his head.

Charles found himself on the cobblestones gasping for air in a sea of pain. He heard Penny shriek. He saw the seaman's foot draw back and start forward. Charles rolled sideways as the boot shot past. He sensed more than saw that a general tumult had broken out with an uproar of shouting. Struggling to his elbows and knees, he saw the man step forward, preparing to kick at him again. Inexplicably, the foot jerked upwards, swinging harmlessly above. Charles found this unusual in an academic kind of way. He was additionally puzzled as the other foot that the man had been standing on also rose magically into the air.

His wife knelt on the pavement beside him, still cradling her package. "Charlie, Charlie," she said. "Art thou injured? Canst thou rise?"

With her help he managed to push himself to his knees. His breath came in gasps and the side of his face stung painfully. It took a moment for him to collect his wits before he saw the seaman that had struck him dangling helplessly a full two feet off the ground. Holding him by the collar and the seat of his pants was the very large black man Charles had noticed standing by the anti-slavery speaker. He looked even larger close up.

"You keep afussin' like that," the man said to his flailing burden, "an' Augustus gonna drop you on your head." The seaman became still.

Charles managed to gain his feet. "Art thou damaged?" Penny said, holding onto his arm and helping him rise.

"I'm all right," he answered, taking a deep breath. He turned toward the African. "I am in your debt," he said.

"What do you want me to do with this one?" He shook the dangling seaman like so much loose clothing.

"Put him down, but keep hold of his collar." He turned to face the seaman whose expression was now more one of contrition than hostility. "I've half a mind to see you swing for striking a king's officer," he began harshly.

"Oh, no," Penny interrupted. "Thou canst do no such thing. Too terrible a punishment for such a petty crime wouldst be against God's law."

Charles looked at his wife in annoyance. "That's easy for you to say; you weren't injured."

"Whoever shall smite thee on the right cheek, turn the other also," Penny said primly. "So sayeth the Bible. In Matthew, I think. Revenge be sinful, forgiveness devi . . ."

"Yes, yes," Charles said impatiently. "I wasn't going to have him hanged. It was only a manner of speaking. But there must be some consequence if one man strikes another in a public square. What should it be?" He noticed that the seaman was following the exchange with an expression of interest, his head turning in one direction and then the other as each spoke.

Penny pursed her lips in contemplation. "He may apologize for the hurt he has caused thee, and promise to foreswear all violence in the future."

Charles began a laugh that he quickly changed to a cough when he saw that she was serious. It would be better to have the thing over and done with, he decided, without a lot of chatter about fighting. He turned to the seaman. "Do you apologize for what you've done and promise to go forth and sin no more?" He said it with only modest sarcasm.

6

"What do ye mean?" the seaman answered, either not following or not believing what he was being asked. He cast a nervous glance at the black man still holding firmly to his collar.

"For Christ's sake," Charles snapped. "Just say you're sorry and be on your way."

"Aye, I'm regretful for smackin' ye," the seaman said readily. "Can I up me anchor now?"

"You must also apologize to my wife," Charles said to make sure everyone was satisfied.

"I'm sorry fer callin' ye a whore, missus. It's fer certain yer not," he said with some sincerity. Charles nodded to the African man to release him, and the seaman immediately edged away.

"Didst that man ever say such a thing?" Penny asked, staring at the retreating form.

"He did," Charles said. "Don't forget the 'forgiveness is divine' part." He looked around him to see that the crowd in the square had largely dispersed and the speaker gone. He turned to the black man, now standing awkwardly with his arms at his sides. "I am Charles Edgemont. May I ask your name?"

"Augustus be what they call me, sah," the man answered. A cautious smile showed white teeth against very dark skin.

Charles extended his hand. The African carefully wiped his own against his jacket before accepting it. "Is it true that you are recently escaped from slavery, Augustus?"

"Yes, sah." The man's eyes narrowed in suspicion and the smile vanished.

"I repeat that I owe you a debt of gratitude," Charles said quickly. "I'm certainly not going to send you back. You were a free man once you touched English soil anyway." This Charles knew to be true. Owning slaves had been abolished in Britain for some decades. By law, any setting foot in the country were automatically free. The institution was still practiced in the colonies, however, and Parliament had passed no law prohibiting the lucrative trade in slaves, still continued by too many Liverpool, Bristol, and London merchants.

Penny brushed at some dirt on Charles' coat, then tilted his head with her free arm to examine where he had been struck. "Tisk," she chided, releasing him. "Thou wilt certainly be bruised. Thou shouldst never have provoked such a rude person. See what thou hast wrought."

"I didn't. . ." Charles began, but she had already turned her attention toward Augustus.

"I wish to say my thanks to thee for rescuing my husband," she said. Looking out at the nearly empty square, she added, "Where hast thy companion gone?"

Charles looked around him. The crowd had entirely disbursed. Only the box the speaker had stood on remained, and sitting alone on that was the African woman he had noted earlier.

"I don't rightly know," Augustus answered slowly, rubbing at his chin. "Mebby Miss Viola can say."

Charles drew his watch from his pocket, flipped open its cover, and saw that it was nearly noon. "If you would be so good as to introduce us, the least I can do is to provide you both with a good supper, if you are free, of course."

"We free," Augustus answered with a small frown. "Mebbe too free."

The woman rose as Charles, Penny, and her companion approached. "Be you fit, Mr. Augustus?" she called out.

"There weren't no real difficulty," the man said. "Where be Mr. Willard?"

"I can't say," the woman answered, her eyes studying Charles for a moment, and then settling on Penny. "He lit out with some white folk hot after him. He already long gone to my thinkin'." Charles thought she didn't seem particularly concerned.

"Who is Mr. Willard?" Penny asked.

As Augustus spoke, Charles took a moment to study the pair. The man, he decided, was likely in his mid-twenties. He was tall, taller than Charles, and heavily muscled, but in an oddly proportioned sort of way. His shoulders seemed unnaturally large with no discernible indentation around his middle between chest and hips so that he looked something like a section taken from the trunk of a good-sized tree. The woman seemed a little younger, although it was hard to be sure. She was diminutive by comparison, with slender features, alert black eyes that gave her a kind of calculating look, and black hair bound up in a scarf. Her skin was the color of lightly creamed coffee, which made her a mulatto, he assumed. She held herself stiffly, almost defiantly, erect.

"Dost thou not agree, Charlie?" Penny said.

"Dost I not agree to what?" Charles answered.

"Dost thou not agree to sup at our hotel?"

He took a moment to consider this. Their lodgings were booked at the Prince Regent on St. Bridget Street, a respectable establishment catering to ships' officers, bankers, insurance brokers, and other moderately well-heeled travelers in the mercantile trade. He suspected that the management would be reluctant to welcome two shabbily dressed blacks, indeed any black Africans, as guests in their establishment. They would just have to adjust their way of thinking, he decided. "Fine," Charles said. "What an excellent suggestion." With that, Penny took up his arm and the four set off across the square.

"Oy, you there!" the hotel clerk shouted as Augustus and Viola tentatively entered into its spacious foyer. "Get you back where you came from. We won't have your kind in here."

"They are with me," Charles said firmly. "I have invited them to dine with Mrs. Edgemont and me."

"Oh, I am sorry, Captain Edgemont," the clerk apologized. "But this establishment does not permit blacks, and certainly not in the dining room. It's a long standing rule."

"I insist that you make an exception in this case," Charles said in his best quarterdeck I'll-brook-no-argument voice. When the clerk hesitated, he added more menacingly, "I wish to speak with the owner, Mr. Carthwright." Mr. Carthwright quickly agreed to a private room where their meals were brought and the door kept tightly shut.

"Tell us," Charles said to his guests after they were settled, "how you two came to be in our fair city of Liverpool."

"How much do you want to hear?" Augustus said cautiously.

"All of it," Charles answered.

Augustus cast a glance at his female companion. After she nodded, he spoke, reluctantly Charles thought, as if it were a closely held secret. "Miss Viola and me both be at this place in 'Ginia. Mostly I work in the rows, Miss Viola in the house. One time she say she is decided to run. I allow I am partial to go along. She hear of a way, a place we could go on a certain night, and there was some what would help us. We slip away in the dark and sure enough there be two men there, a black and a white that put us up in a hayloft in an old barn with some others." He stopped for a moment with his eyes fixed as if on some distant object.

"Why didst thou decide to run?" Penny asked, directing her question to the girl.

"I don't want to say, missus," Viola answered, her face coloring. "Everyone want to run. But for me it was just some attention I was getting."

Charles could guess what that meant, with white owners and supervisors feeling themselves naturally entitled to the favors of slave women. "Go on," he said.

"Yes, sah," Augustus nodded, and then spoke in a faster tempo as if he wanted to be done with it. "We move every night. There always be a rick or cellar to put up in, and a little food, and then someone come to show us the next place. After a time we come to a city, the largest place I ever seen. Philadelphi, it were called. Straightaway, Miss Viola and me be put into a ship by some what was guiding us. Then we were sailed to here. We only come just this mornin'."

"Philadelphia!" Penny exclaimed. "Philadelphia is a Quaker city. Who was it that helped thee?"

"I don't rightly know, missus," Augustus answered. "A white man, a gen'leman like your husband."

9

"Were they Quakers?" she persisted.

"I don't know, missus," he said again, clearly trying to be helpful. "But I didn't see them shakin' or quiverin', nothin' like that."

"I see," Charles said with a smile. "One last question, who is Mr. Willard?" He had missed that part.

Viola answered. "Him who fetched us from the boat," she said. "He brought us direct to that place and started into speaking."

Charles nodded. It wasn't a very helpful answer. He was beginning to think about what he should do for them. They couldn't just be turned back onto the street; he owed them some consideration. It was obvious they knew no one besides the vanished speaker. Out of the corner of his eye he saw Penny watching him intently and knew what she was about to suggest, if "suggest" was the correct term. She would want him to give them employment or some such. But what if this Mr. Willard had already made arrangements for them? What if he were out searching the streets at this very moment? Charles didn't think it likely, but he wanted to be sure.

"Charlie," Penny said, touching his sleeve. "We must . . ."

"Yes, of course," Charles said. "Just one minute more." To Augustus and Viola he said, "Do either of you know what you were to do when you reached England? Did this Mr. Willard say anything?"

"No, sah. Nobody didn't say nothin'," Augustus answered. "But the gen'leman in Philadelphi, he gave us a paper." Augustus reached inside his jacket and came up with a somewhat soiled envelope addressed "To Whom It May Concern."

Charles took the object, opened it, and removed a single page. To Whom It May Concern, the salutation repeated.

> I commend into thy care these two souls, Augustus and Viola, recently emancipated from the iniquitous practice of slavery, which is out of harmony with the teaching of Our Lord Jesus Christ, who doth instruct us to love all His Creatures, that thou take them under thy protection so that they might secure sustenance and succor adequate to the requirements of their persons and spirits.

Peace be among thee,

Richard Pemberton

Pine Street Meetinghouse

Philadelphia, in Pennsylvania

"This is more in your line," Charles said, handing the page to his wife. He turned back to the two. "Is either of you in need of employment? I mean a regular position, with wages. If my wife agrees, I am sure that we would be pleased by your presence."

*****

"They're coming, sir," Tom Pearson called down from his bench at the front of the carriage. "I can just see t' lanthorns round yonder bend." The one-legged former seaman was Charles' driver on this occasion, one of the former crewmen he had brought to Tattenall to recuperate from disabling injuries, and who had stayed as an employee on his estates.

Charles lowered the curtain over the window by his side and looked out through the falling rain into the dismal light of the new day. He picked out the twin lamps of the post coach in the distance as it hurried along on its scheduled two-day journey from Chester to London. The lanterns seemed ethereal flickers, suspended unmoving in the distant gloom, but he knew they would be up to them all too soon. He had reserved space inside for two persons, with the instruction that they would board at Handley, on the King's Highway a short distance from Tattenall.

"Thank you, Tom," he said, unlatching the door and stepping out from the shelter of the carriage into the weather. "Come along, Augustus. I'll give you a hand with the luggage."

"Yes, Cap'n," the black man answered, squeezing his frame through the restricted exit. He had taken to addressing Charles as 'Captain' after Charles had explained his profession and offered Augustus a position as his steward. The two men turned toward the foot of the carriage and began loosening the straps securing their sea chests.

The London coach clattered loudly to a halt, its six horses snorting and steaming from exertion. The chests were quickly handed up and lashed in place beneath a tarpaulin on the roof.

"Thank you, again, Tom," Charles said. "And mind that everything stays shipshape at home."

"Good-bye," Pearson answered, touching his hat. "I wish you easy seas and a speedy return, sir."

Charles pulled open the door and heaved himself up. There were four passengers already present, three men in overcoats and top hats, and a rather richly dressed woman of middle age wearing an elegant chapeau and a pelisse trimmed in fox. Her maid, he had noted, rode on the carriage top, out in the weather.

"Your pardon, madam," he said as he eased by the woman. The matron nodded her acquiescence and shifted her knees to make room for him to pass. Charles said his thanks as he settled down beside the far window. She gave him a half-smile in acknowledgement, then turned to stare open-mouthed as Augustus followed, dropping his bulk into the only remaining space next to her. Immediately the coach lurched and resumed its jolting progress onward.

Charles exchanged the obligatory 'good-morrows', and observations on the weather with the other passengers. Then he arranged his sword and scabbard between his thighs and settled back, hopefully to compose himself for sleep. He had parted from Penny in the parlor of their home barely an hour earlier, dreading the moment of separation and hating himself for causing her anguish. She had cried, then wiped at her tears. "Goeth where thou must, Charles Edgemont," she said sternly. "And may God watch over thee, for I cannot." They held each other tightly before she pushed him away. The collection of such servants as they had lined the hallway as he passed by: Timothy Attwater, his wife and two of his daughters; two more of Charles' former crew, both missing arms; and Viola, the newest and already, to Charles' mind, the most useful of the lot. Holding Viola's hand stood a very sleepy Claudette in her nightcap and bed clothes, disordered curls of dark hair around her face. He'd bent to stroke the child's cheek and received a dutiful kiss in return. "Gud-bye, Misseur Charle," she'd said.

Only Attwater, his wizened and, if nothing else, faithful steward for the past two years, had protested at being left behind. "Ain't you sure you won't reconsider, sir?" he'd said as soon as a fit of coughing had allowed him to regain his voice. "It ain't right you not being tended to by someone what don't know your needs like I do."

No one knew Attwater's exact age, not even the man himself, but Charles guessed that he must be well past sixty. This winter he had been seized by a persistent cough, which made him seem frailer and older than ever. "We have spoken of this before, Timothy," Charles said gently. "Augustus will learn well enough as he goes along. I am the poorer for losing your services, but you know that I shall rest more comfortably knowing that you are here to look after Mrs. Edgemont, especially in her current delicate condition."

"Yes, sir, of course," Attwater had replied, at least partly mollified.

In her current delicate condition. The phrase echoed in Charles' mind as the coach rattled and swayed along the highway. It weighed on him that he would not be present when Penny bore his child. But the war continued unabated, although there was increasing talk that it must end soon. It was widely known, or believed, that republican France had exhausted herself after six years of revolution and conflict. As a king's officer, Charles had argued with himself, he must do his duty, especially with the end so near. The birth of a child was insignificant compared to the clash of nations—wasn't it? His honor demanded that he sacrifice personal considerations out of loyalty to king and country—didn't it? That he knew himself to have doubts deepened his feeling of having betrayed his wife. Still, other ships' captains must have faced similar conflicts and opted to serve. Common seamen were never given any choice in such matters; they went where ordered without complaint, at least no complaint that anyone listened to. If others were obligated to put aside personal considerations in order to do their duty, then he was as well—wasn't he?

Such thoughts brought a melancholy to which there was no bottom. To force his attention elsewhere, he reached inside his uniform jacket to extract an envelope with its Admiralty seal. It had arrived at Tattenall nearly a month before, and he had read and reread the document so many times that he could recite it by rote:

Whitehall, London
10th December 1798
To Captain Charles Edgemont, Esq.
Tattenall Hall, Cheshire

Sir, you are hereby directed and required to report onboard His Majesty's Frigate Cassandra not later than the Fourteenth Day of January, in the year of Our Lord 1799. You will thereby take command of said frigate, requiring her officers, warrants, and men to act in strict accordance to your orders, and in accordance with the Admiralty Regulations and Instructions, and the Articles of War. Said frigate is to be found in His Majesty's Dockyard at Chatham, on the River Midway, where she is completing fitting out in anticipation of a voyage to the northern limit of the Arabian Gulf.

It is further directed and required that in good time prior to assuming said command, you shall call upon the First Lord, or his deputy, and from him receive further orders, intelligence and instructions as shall be deemed fit to be provided.

Not you, nor any of you, shall fail in the execution of these orders except at your peril.

I have the honor of being,
Evan Nepean,
First Secretary to the Board

Charles rubbed the sheet absently between his forefinger and thumb as he attempted to discern its deeper implications. It was interesting, he considered, that it had come directly from Whitehall, rather than from Lord St. Vincent or some other fleet admiral, and hinted that he might be operating independently under Admiralty instructions. There was the mention of the Arabian Gulf—the Red Sea as it was more generally known, a fourteen-hundred-mile-long indentation of water between Abyssinia and the Arabian Peninsula—but no indication of why or what he was to accomplish there. He supposed that he should be grateful that any destination had been mentioned at all. It was not unheard of for a captain to prepare his wardrobe on the assumption that he was intended for the waters of the Mediterranean only to be sent north into the Baltic in winter.

But why the Red Sea? Charles knew that the French had established themselves in Egypt the year before; he had been directly involved in the destruction of the fleet that had carried them, but that expeditionary force, large though it was, was bottled up by Nelson's squadron on blockade off of Alexandria. His orders did mention "the northern limit" of the gulf, which would include the Red Sea coast of Egypt, but why that was important was not revealed.

Cassandra was less of a mystery. He knew that she was a twelve-pounder frigate, built in the years following the American War and in the process of completing a refit to make good the wear to her structure, rigging, and fittings. She was considered a promotion where he was concerned. At thirty-two guns, Cassandra was a fifth rate warship, while his previous command, Louisa at twenty-eight guns, had a sixth (and lowest) rating. Charles' pay would be increased a step to reflect his greater responsibilities.

He had also discovered the barest description of her particulars: 140 feet along her gun deck, sixteen feet of draft, and a burthen weight of eight hundred tonnes. Her compliment would be 220 officers and men with an additional thirty-six marines. As the commander of a fifth rate, he was also entitled to three lieutenants, instead of the two he'd been authorized on Louisa. Since Charles was determined to put off his departure from home to the last possible moment, he had requested Daniel Bevan, Stephen Winchester, and Isaac Beechum, known and trusted officers from his previous command, and arranged that they report ahead of him so that any last-minute difficulties in preparing for sea should be well in hand.

Outside the coach window he noticed that it was now broad daylight and the morning overcast had given way to sunshine, turning the passing fields and pastures a brilliant rolling green. They were somewhere in Shropshire, he supposed. Augustus slumped against the coach bench, snoring rhythmically. Charles again settled back and crossed his arms over his chest in an attempt to imitate him. Again his thoughts turned back to home, keeping sleep away. In the very best of circumstances, he realized, he could not return to England for at least a year, more likely a year and a half, very possibly longer. During that time no mail might reach him. There would be no word that a child had been born, whether it was a boy or girl, healthy or sickly, or even if the infant or its mother had survived. The thought settled like a stone in his breast and would not go away.

*****

At long last, the coach reached the outskirts of the great city of London, galloping past Regent's Park to much honking of its horn, scattering foot traffic and farm carts alike. Its progress slowed in the thickening congestion of Tottenham Court Road, although the incessant blaring of the horn did not. The two men finally climbed down close by Covent Garden in the late afternoon. Charles found himself shaken and stiff and happy to have his feet once more on unmoving ground. Augustus stared around him at the streets crammed with buildings. There were peddlers loudly hawking everything from puddings, sausages, and cheeses, to live chickens, or cut flowers. Unceasing crowds swirled past. Charles handed a gratuity to the coachman and postilion. With his new steward sitting on the sea chests, he went to find a hackney to carry them to Lothian's Hotel on Albemarle Street where he had arranged lodgings. Here he found no difficulties with the management, who were accustomed to a broad range of naval clientele and their sometimes unique servants. Charles was shown to a spacious room on the second floor, Augustus being directed to the servant's dormitory in the attic. In the morning, well rested, bathed, and breakfasted, he dressed in his best uniform to call upon the Admiralty. Preparing to leave, he found his servant pulling on his own outer clothing as if to go outdoors. "It's not necessary for you to accompany me, Augustus," he said. "I expect to be back in time for supper."

"I'll just follow along, if I may, Cap'n," Augustus said.

"It's not necessary," Charles repeated. "I assure you that I can manage on my own."

Augustus stood firm.

Charles had a suspicion. "Did Mrs. Edgemont put you up to this?" Penny had a habit of requesting his seamen to look after his wellbeing as if she thought him incompetent to get by on his own.

Augustus nodded. "Afore we went off she asked me to set my eye on you, no matter what. I give my word on it."

Charles sighed. "In that case I suppose you had better obey orders. I assure you that it will be quite safe where we are going though."

"It don't matter, Cap'n. She say you be reckless. One never know what can happen."

"I see," Charles said doubtfully. With his servant following, he went out to find the carriage he had reserved. He felt a little like some Eastern potentate with his own immense bodyguard following on his heels.

The hansom from Lothian's trotted briskly down Albemarle and then St. James's Street with its exclusive clubs and gaming establishments. Augustus stared from the window with intense curiosity as they passed. In front of St.

James's Palace they turned left along Pall Mall, past Queen's Chapel, and through Charing Cross. Angling southward along the Thames, the driver soon swung his conveyance into the center of the roadway and then hard right to make the sharp turn under the archway into the forecourt of Whitehall itself.

Charles and Augustus climbed down. After paying the fare, Charles dismissed the driver. "You may come along, but you'll have to wait in the foyer while I do my business," he said to his servant.

Augustus nodded his agreement and the two mounted the steps onto the portico where a doorman made way for them to enter.

"May I help you, Captain?" a liveried attendant asked, approaching from near a fireplace to the left and casting a suspicious eye at Augustus.

"Edgemont," Charles answered, removing his hat and pulling off his gloves. "I have an appointment with His Lordship. My steward will wait by the fire, if that is agreeable."

"Of course." He gestured for Augustus to seat himself on a bench by the wall. "I am to inform you that the First Lord, the Earl of Spencer, is detained on other business this morning. Captain Millford is a member of the board. He and the Viscount Effington are expecting you. If you will come this way, please."

Charles knew of Captain Millford, a senior officer with a reputation for competence. The Viscount he had never heard of. "Who is Effington?" he asked as they started down the hallway.

The attendant hesitated as if unsure how much he should reveal. "The Viscount is not a standing member of the board," he said finally. "I believe him to provide certain ancillary services on the occasion."

"I see," Charles said, not really seeing at all.

The attendant approached a door to their left, turned the latch, and opened it. "Captain Edgemont," he announced.

Charles stepped into a brightly lit, high-ceilinged room with a long table placed in the middle. On the far wall was a globe of the world and above that a curious device with a face like a clock and a single hand, which apparently indicated the direction of the wind, currently wavering between south-by-east and south-by-southeast. Eight upholstered chairs were arranged around the table. This was the famous room, he realized, in which the board of the Admiralty met daily to decide the composition and disposition of the far-ranging British navy. From here, orders were issued for every decision, from promotions and appointments for commissioned officers, to the movement of great battle fleets. At present only two of the chairs were occupied, one by a middle-aged man in the undress uniform of a navy captain, the other, younger, in soberly tailored civilian clothing. Both stood as he entered. Charles heard the door latch softly behind him.

"Captain Edgemont," the naval officer said, coming around the table and extending his hand. "I am George Millford, and this is my associate, his Lordship the Viscount Effington. I am pleased to make your acquaintance."

"The honor is mine, sir," Charles said and shook the offered hand. Millford was tall and gray haired, with a weatherbeaten face and firm grip. The Viscount presented severely lean, angular features. Charles thought he had hard eyes and a secretive look about him. He did not offer his hand, although the eyes measured Charles closely. "Your Lordship," Charles said, bowing slightly from the waist.

Millford cleared his throat. "We shall get down to business, shan't we? If you would please seat yourself."

Charles moved to a chair at the middle of the table opposite the others, adjusted his sword, and sat. "It was I that requested this meeting," the Captain continued, "so that, on behalf of the board, I may convey to you something of the nature of your orders and to emphasize the gravity of your mission."

Charles nodded his comprehension.

"There are delicacies involved which may require both judgment and diplomacy on your part. I will be honest when I say that the board would have preferred a more senior officer, but none suitable was available."

Charles nodded again, tight lipped. This was not exactly a flattering revelation.

Millford held up his hand. "No one doubts your abilities, young man. I have made inquiries as to your career. I find you to be more than generally competent, though on the occasion you have shown a disposition to act in a, shall we say, independent manner. I have read Admiral Nelson's report on your actions immediately preceding the Battle of the Nile, for example."

"Sir," Charles protested, even though he knew Millford to be at least somewhat justified. On that occasion he had ignored his admiral's signals for hours, and in the end did not obey them at all. "I have always acted in what I considered to be the best interests of the service," he said strongly. "If Admiral Nelson has suggested . . ."

"Quite," the captain said dryly. "I should say that Nelson has expressed himself admiring of your initiative. It is among these qualities which I find may recommend you for the task at hand."

"I see," Charles said doubtfully, not at all clear on what that meant.

Millford fingered an envelope on the table top by his elbow then pushed it across. "These are your written orders. You needn't open it now; I'll tell you what they say. Afterward, Lord Effington will provide additional background so that you may better understand some of the difficulties, if not the uncertainties, involved."

Charles glanced at the Viscount who was fidgeting impatiently with a pencil in his hand. The interview was beginning to strike him as somewhat unusual.

"Captain Edgemont," Millford said formally, "you are to proceed the instant your ship can be made ready to the port of Mocha at the foot of the Red Sea. There you will find a squadron under the command of Rear Admiral Sir John Blankett. Blankett's purpose is to prevent the French in Egypt from transiting to India and fomenting insurrection there. I should stress that this is the fundamental intent of your own instructions as well. On no account may any French force be permitted to reach the subcontinent. The situation in India hangs on a knife's edge as it is, with local uprisings an ever present threat."

Millford coughed into his hand and then continued. "You will also call at Cape Town, in the course of your journey to take on board a certain agent employed on our behalf. You are ordered to provide transport to the head of the Red Sea, and afterward render such assistance as may be required. Is that much clear?"

Charles hesitated. His orders were straightforward enough, so much so that he didn't understand why the Admiralty felt it necessary to explain them in person. He did have one question: "Am I to be under Admiral Blankett's orders, or the Admiralty's?"

The Captain steepled his fingers in front of him, then spoke with what Charles took to be unusual care. "The board has considered this very question at length. The answer is that you will be under Admiralty orders until such time as the agent mentioned has completed his mission. When that is accomplished, you will place yourself at Blankett's disposal. As he is the senior officer on the scene, it is felt that it can hardly be otherwise." Millford leaned forward, resting his hands on the table. "If I may speak with the utmost confidence, some feel the Admiral may at times prove—what should I say? — cautious. You will find nothing in your written instructions, but it is anticipated that you may determine, under exceptional circumstances, it to be necessary to act on your own initiative. It is my great hope that no such occasion will arise, and that in any case you will not be reckless in your judgment. But if you do find independent action to be absolutely necessary, and if you are successful as a result, I will press the board on your behalf that no disciplinary proceedings go forward."

Charles assumed that he was being told that he had some uncertain amount of leeway as long as he was successful. But what if he was not? The arrangement made him decidedly uncomfortable. "Why not send a replacement to command the squadron?" he said. "Surely that would be satisfactory?"

"I am not at liberty to answer beyond that the board has decided against it," Millford said.

"Frankly," Viscount Effington interrupted, his patience apparently at an end, "Admiral Blankett hasn't the imagination of a pencil case and everyone knows it. I find it indefensible that he has been allowed to retain his command."

Millford sighed. Charles thought there must have been a split among the board and the compromise had been to send a junior captain with some undefined element of independence instead. Or, perhaps the split was serious enough that the board as a whole was not privy to Charles' verbal instructions. Before he could ponder this further, Effington continued. "The very possibility, if not the certainty, that the French will attempt to intervene militarily against our position in India is of such magnitude that the Crown's ability to prosecute the war may depend on it. The French, particularly under this General Bonaparte, have proven themselves both resourceful and innovative—two things which Blankett is not."

"I see," Charles said tentatively. He meant the remark as a polite statement that he was paying attention.

"I very much doubt that you do, sir," Effington said flatly. "That Tippu Sahib, the Sultan of Mysore, is on the verge of yet another war to drive the British out of India is well known. Less publicized is that he is substantially better armed and in greater strength than before and that the Directory in Paris is known to have committed itself to aiding him. At any cost—I repeat, at any cost—this must not be allowed to occur."

This was all well and good, Charles thought, bridling at the condescension in Effington's tone. He had heard these arguments before. "I understand the importance of what must be accomplished," he answered. "But so far, aside from being less than respectful to Admiral Blankett, little light has been shed on how I am to accomplish it."

"I recognize that," the Viscount said with perhaps a touch less acid in his voice. "The situation in the Red Sea basin at this moment is largely unknown to us. From what gleanings I have been able to come by, there are indications of preparations at one or more locations. The French are undoubtedly aware of our interest, and some of those preparations may be ruses. It is to address this deficiency of information that I have arranged for the agent mentioned earlier. Mr. Jones and his wives have provided useful service in the past. I am confident of their diligence in the present instance."

"Jones?" Charles said. "Mr. Adolphus Jones?"

Effington raised his eyebrows. "Do you know him?"

"Our paths have crossed twice. He was instrumental in the discovery of the French fleet at Egypt." Charles had another thought. "Did you say wives?"

19

"Yes, two," Effington said offhandedly. "Didn't you know? Jones is a Mussulman. He is entitled to four. It is an excellent religion on many levels. I recommend it to you."

"Thank you, I find one wife more than enough," Charles answered.

Captain Millford cleared his throat. "I may tell you that we have prevailed on Trinity House to appoint a sailing master familiar with the Red Sea, and he has been provided with the latest chart for the region. If we are down to discussing wives, I may assume that our business is now complete. Have you any questions?"

Charles searched his mind. He had a great many concerns that were unanswered. Aside from transporting Jones, he still didn't know precisely what he was to do. But then, it became clear, neither did either of the men across the table from him. At least it would be a help to have a master experienced in local waters and up-to-date charts. He would doubtless learn more about the situation when he reached Mocha. "No, sir," he said.

"One last piece of advice," Effington offered stiffly. "There are too many that doubt it, but be assured that the French will make the attempt. It may not be by the most obvious method. Be wary. You may find that things are not always as they first seem." He fell silent, signaling that the interview was at an end.

Charles picked up the envelope containing his orders and rose from the chair. The interview struck him as very peculiar indeed. He realized that he had learned little that he had not known before entering the room. "Thank you for your confidence, sir. Your Lordship." He shook hands with Millford across the table, bowed again to the Viscount, and turned to leave. As he was passing out and the door closing behind him, he heard Effington say, "This is pointless. This Edgemont is too inexperienced and a single frigate certainly insufficient." Millford's voice responded: "You know my feelings. He is all we have available. The political . . ." The latched clicked shut.

CHAPTER TWO

In the cold dawn of the following morning, Charles and Augustus went by hackney to the Whitehall Stairs on the Thames embankment in search of transport to Chatham. The Royal Dockyard lay on the River Medway, a tributary to the Thames, thirty miles downstream. "That's the Admiralty barge there, sir. She's for the yard with dispatches," a seaman at the head of the steps informed him. "Jeffers is the mate in charge. It's fer certain he'll give ye passage if ye tells him."

Charles saw the thirty-foot, ten-oared boat at the foot of the steps, snubbing gently at her lines, and started down. The high water and absence of any movement on its surface told him that the tide was at flood, almost on the turn. He guessed her crew would want to shove off with the ebb so that the current would help speed their progress down the river. "You're Jeffers?" he said, approaching the man who had been pointed out to him.

"Aye, sur," the mate answered, seeing Charles' uniform and touching the brim of his hat.

"I'm told you're bound for Chatham. I would be appreciative if you take my steward and me along."

"Be pleased to, sur," Jeffers said. "We might be delayed a spell though."

"Is there a difficulty?" Charles saw eddies starting along the edge of the steps as the flow of the river began its turn toward the sea.

Jeffers wiped the back of his hand across his forehead in a gesture of frustration. "It's Clive and Wickers," he said. "I don't know where they be, but they ain't 'ere. I don't fancy trying the passage with only four pair oars. It'll be a hellish pull if we miss the turn of the tide at Sheerness to push us up to the yard."

Charles wanted to take up his command without unnecessary delay. He didn't want to spend the chilly morning waiting on the steps for the two missing oarsmen to appear. "Perhaps I could be of assistance," he ventured.

"You, sir?" Jeffers said, dismissing the notion. "I couldn't ask one as yerself to do any such thing."

"I'm offering," Charles insisted. He nodded toward the large form of Augustus. "There're two of us, my steward and myself."

The mate's eyes took in the black man. "'As 'e any experience pulling an oar?"

"No," Charles admitted. "But he's a quick study. I would be pleased to man the tiller." He thought the offer a generous one.

Jeffers hesitated while he considered this new arrangement. He was not a particularly quick-thinking person, Charles realized. The current began to run strong past the steps. "I suggest we push off while we still have the tide."

"I don't know, I'm sure," the mate said. "It ain't regular."

Charles decided to make up his mind for him. "Augustus, please see that our sea chests are placed onboard." To the barge's mate, he said, "Mr. Jeffers, if you would be so good as to board, we will be off. You may take one stroke oar, my servant the other. You can show him what to do as we go." To settle the matter, he stepped across the gunwale and settled in the stern beside the tiller.

Jeffers shrugged. "Don't I appreciate your assistance, sur," he said, evidently resolved to make the best of the situation. He took his place at the rearmost port side oar, gesturing to Augustus to take up the one to starboard on the thwart beside him.

"Cast off forward," Charles called. He slipped the knot on the stern and tossed the line onto the steps. The current quickly caught the craft, pulling it forward. "Shove off all," he ordered, taking the tiller in his hand and moving it experimentally from side to side. It had been years since he'd steered a small boat. The port side oarsmen pushed their blades against the stones; the barge glided away from the shore. "Mr. Jeffers," he said, "she's your craft. You will give the orders. Please think of me as one of the crew."

"Aye, aye, sur," Jeffers said. Then, "Out oars, lads. Pull hard." He turned to Augustus who was watching him closely. "Like this," Jeffers said. "Just you do what I do."

The barge spread its oars and soon fell into steady rhythm as it started down the Thames. Charles held the tiller firmly in both hands and stared forward over the bow in search of any hazards on the water that he would be expected to avoid. He noticed that Augustus very shortly picked up the intricacies of manning an oar in concert with the others, which was no small accomplishment.

"Ease 'er toward the middle, sur," Jeffers offered. "The current runs faster there."

"Aye, aye," Charles said with a grin. It wasn't often he took orders from a petty officer. He pushed gingerly on the bar, unsure of how much rudder to apply. He saw little result for his effort.

"Begging yer pardon, sur. You'll have to steer large. She's a long boat."

"My apologies," Charles answered. He pushed the tiller boldly over and the bow angled gratifyingly toward the center channel. Ahead he saw that the traffic on the river had begun to increase along with the appearance of a sliver of the sun on the horizon over the south bank. The Savoy Palace and then Somerset House—where the Navy Board Offices were housed—passed to port. The seemingly endless expanse of the city spread out along both banks, the smoke of wood and coal fires rising from countless chimneys, then uniting in a dark stream eastward under scattered orange-bellied clouds.

Charles swung the tiller to steer behind a lighter crossing. Blackfriar's Bridge showed ahead, the first of two they would pass under. He found himself unreasonably pleased to be back on the water's surface and began to relax as he felt more comfortable managing the boat. The span soon loomed over them, then fell behind. Below the bridge, the thickening congestion of river boats, lighters, and wherries threatened to clog the waterway. Charles refocused his attention as he maneuvered the barge through the constantly changing obstructions, occasionally taking an opportunity to shout a warning or even an obscenity at some particularly obdurate craft impeding their progress.

The towering mass of London Bridge filled the skyline ahead, its closely spaced arches and huge abutments holding back the receding tide. He could feel the barge accelerate as the flow quickened, hurtling them irresistibly toward a narrow gap between two of the stone supports. He saw that the river churned white around their bases then fell abruptly in elevation as it passed through.

"Boat yer oars," Jeffers announced calmly as the span approached.

"What do I do?" Charles said in alarm. The tiller swung almost without resistance under his hand. He had no control over their direction.

"Hold 'er midships or let go altogether, sur," Jeffers replied. "It don't matter now, the current will carry us through."

The barge shot into the restricted channel. In the darkness under the span they dived over the swell at exhilarating speed, dropping a good three feet, then spilled out into the sunshine on the far side.

"Out oars," Jeffers ordered as the barge began to drift sideways in the swirls and eddies below the abutments. Immediately as the oars bit she gained way, the rudder took hold, and Charles steered to point the bow once more downstream. It took several moments for his heartbeat to return to normal.

"Boat oars," Jeffers said again after they had gone a scant cable's length from the bridge. In response to Charles' questioning look, he added, "We'll step the masts now, sur. The wind's fair and there's no more bridges 'tween here and Chatham." The two masts, one forward and one aft, were hoisted into place with practiced ease. Equally quickly the sails were bent on; the canvas snapped then filled as a firm westerly breeze pushed them over the water at a quickened pace.

"I can take the tiller now, sur," Jeffers said, coming aft. "Don't I appreciate yer help."

"It was my pleasure," Charles answered. He turned over control of the bar and made his way to the center of the boat to seat himself on one of the now unoccupied rowers' benches across from his servant. Augustus sat staring out at the river traffic and the enormous city around them.

"It's a very large place, isn't it," Charles said.

Augustus grinned. "I never saw such a thing."

"It's bigger than Philadelphia for a fact," Charles said. "London's the largest city in the world, I'm told."

Immediately to port rose the stark, block-like enormity of the Tower of London, King William I's principal fortification for the domination of his newly conquered kingdom, built more than seven hundred years before. Below lay the Pool and the London Docks, the immense port from which the great city's wealth derived. Charles himself was impressed by the forests of masts crowding both banks, ships of innumerable types and nationalities, from Ramsgate trawlers, colliers, and coasters to bulky Indiamen, snows, cats, pinks, brigs, brigantines, and even the sleek schooners from America. The Indiamen—large armed merchant ships of the Honorable East India Company with their distinctive horizontally striped ensigns—stood out. There were more than a dozen of them waiting to unload their hugely valuable cargos. It was to preserve this trade, Charles knew, that was the underlying purpose of his orders. Just below the Pool he noticed three slavers moored stern to bow. He saw Augustus looking through narrowed eyes at the black-hulled craft, but his servant remained tight lipped and silent.

As they progressed down the river, the commercial shipping began to thin and men-of-war to predominate. Charles studied the naval craft with professional interest as they swept past. They were mostly seventy-fours, a few larger and a number smaller. The majority had their topmasts struck down and were undergoing overhauls, from replacing frame members to coppering. In slips along Deptford Creek on the south bank were the rising skeletons of a number of new two-deckers under construction, and what looked to him like one that might be a first rate—a warship of one hundred or more guns on three decks. This was the Royal Dockyard at Deptford, he knew. There were five such major naval dockyards in England: three along the Thames below London, Deptford, Woolwich, Chatham, as well as Portsmouth and Plymouth on the Channel coast. In these yards the great power of the royal navy was largely built and maintained. A wooden warship, no matter how well constructed, required constant attention to the wear of wind and weather, and a thorough overhaul in a well-equipped yard every two or three years.

The sight of so many navy ships brought him back to the interview at the

Admiralty the day before. It was clear that at least some on the board felt a French attack on India to be a credible possibility. But was it really? It would require a fleet of nearly a hundred transports to carry a force of ten thousand with their horses, artillery, and stocks of supplies. There was a relatively small French harbor with some supply facilities at Mauritius in the Indian Ocean. Could they manage such an expedition? He doubted it; troops and transports would have to be brought all the way around the mass of Africa from Europe. Perhaps this General Bonaparte, of whom everyone spoke so often, would rely on commandeering such craft as were to be found locally. Charles had no clear knowledge about what types or how many Arab merchantmen might be available, but he supposed it was a possibility.

One thing became increasingly evident as he thought about it. Despite Captain Millford and Viscount Effington's assurances, no one really knew what French intentions were, the strength they might employ, or the methods they would use to employ them. If there was an invasion attempt, and if he were somehow to help thwart it, there would be little praise for preempting an emergency that never came to pass. If he were to fail, he might well become the nation's scapegoat for the loss of her most precious colonies.

Beyond Deptford the river widened and slowed. While they were rounding the broad horseshoe bend at the Isle of Dogs, Charles noticed that Augustus had switched his attention from the surrounding countryside and was now studying the barge's sails and rigging. Of course, all this would be unfamiliar to a newly escaped slave from the plantations of Virginia. "It's like magic, isn't it?" Charles said. "I mean skimming along the water with no effort on our part."

"I know how the wind can push a stick across a pond," Augustus answered seriously. "What I be trying to figure am how they can turn this boat so that with the wind commin' from the side they can still go straight ahead."

Charles tried to think how he could explain this to someone who knew nothing about ships. "You see," he said, "there's a long board along the bottom which we name the keel. This keeps a craft running forward because it's the easiest direction for it to go. At the back end, the stern as we call it, is the rudder which presses sideways against the water. The rudder obliges the boat to turn on the keel, which otherwise it doesn't want to do. This forces the front part, or bow, around to the direction you want to go in. The canvas does pretty much the same. The foresail catches the wind to drive her forward, while the mizzen uses the same breeze to push the stern one way or the other." He looked to Augustus to see whether any of this had penetrated.

The black nodded thoughtfully. "You mean, it be like usin' a bar to lever out a stone," he said after a moment. "The block what you put under the bar be your keel; it stay put, but the stone move."

Charles had not thought about the forces operating on a boat's hull in terms of a lever and fulcrum, but it made sense. "It's a little more complicated in actual practice," he said with a smile. "But I think you've got the main point."

Just for a moment Augustus turned to study the barge's canvas, particularly the set of the mizzen, now swung out over the gunwale to port. He nodded again, "There be one more thing I've been hopin' to inquire on, Cap'n, if it ain't a bother."

"Of course it's no bother," Charles said. The question, when it came, was unexpected.

"Be it true that I'm a free man, just like that?"

"Just like that," Charles answered.

"And Miss Viola be a free woman?"

"She can stay on with Mrs. Edgemont, or go elsewhere, as she pleases," Charles answered. "I hope she decides to stay."

"And the masters can't come to take her back?"

"Not as long as she is in England," Charles said. "No court here would allow such a thing."

"It be a wonder," Augustus said. "I don't rightly know how to fasten my mind on it." He fell silent.

Charles thought it curious that Augustus seemed more concerned about the girl's status than his own. He wondered, not for the first time, about the relationship between the two.

The river widened still further, to a half a mile or more, with broad expanses of marshland on either bank. Occasional merchant shipping passed on the opposite tack, and once a single navy frigate. The warship was one of the newer thirty-sixes with an eighteen pounder cannon on her main deck, and Charles studied her with envy. As the frigate neared he saw that her sides were freshly scarred and she had jury repairs to her masts aloft. The strakes along her gun ports were stained black by burnt gunpowder. She had clearly been in a scrape and must be on her way to Deptford to have it repaired. The crew of the barge stood and gave a cheer as she passed. The frigate's captain came to the rail and raised his hat in acknowledgement. Charles responded in kind.

The sun continued its steady rise until it hung nearly overhead. Beyond Gravesend the tang of clean salt air began to replace the mixed smells of the land. Charles felt a growing sense of anticipation despite his misgivings. He wished he were on board, with his own deck beneath his feet. Wherever he was going, he would be free of the land and on the unbounded sea. There the requirements on him would be simple and direct. He enjoyed the life of a sea captain, with his relatively spacious private cabin and the familiar routine of shipboard life. There might be dangers to be sure, but with capable officers and a willing crew all things were possible. He would be in his element with its comfortable sameness and familiar challenges. There were worse things than that.

Past Lower Hope and the Blyth Sands the river began to open to the North Sea. The tide was on the turn, beginning to run against the breeze, and starting up a sharp chop over which the barge gently bucked, kicking up small bursts of spray as it went. At last, Sheerness showed ahead and just before the town a broad opening that was the mouth of the River Medway. As he watched, two seventy-fours exited the inlet, and then wore in succession to the east and the open sea beyond. They had most certainly come from Chatham. Only seven miles up the inlet lay the sprawling complex that was His Majesty's royal dockyard where his own ship lay.

*****

"That's 'er there," Jeffers said, pointing with his arm toward a frigate moored fore and aft in the basin a cable's length off the victualing wharf. Charles studied the ship with an experienced eye. She was freshly painted black with the strakes along her gun ports picked out in a band of white. It was a style that had become increasingly popular among captains in the British navy, emphasizing the sleek lines of their vessels. He found the effect pleasing. Closer inspection told a different story. Between the paint and the waterline lay a broad streak of bright copper which meant that she was riding high and not yet laden with her full requirement of stores and supplies. Her yards were up and crossed, although in a haphazard fashion, the canvas sloppily furled. He could only guess what that implied.

"Ahoy. What boat?" a voice from the frigate's quarterdeck called as it became evident the barge intended to come alongside.

"Cassandra!" Charles shouted back, announcing that the ship's captain was approaching and intended to board.

The familiar figure of Daniel Bevan, his friend and first lieutenant, appeared almost immediately at the railing. "Hello, Captain Edgemont," he called down through cupped hands. "I suggest you come aboard as quick as you can."

This was not the welcome Charles would have expected. He had a premonition that all was not well on his new command. The barge hooked onto the main chains. "See that the chests are swayed up if you will, Augustus," Charles said. Turning to Jeffers, he extended his hand. "You have my thanks for an agreeable passage." He reached into his pocket and came up with an appropriate number of coins. "Something for you and your men's efforts." So as to cut short any prolonged good-byes, he took hold of the manropes on the frigate's side and started to climb the sidesteps. Just before the tumblehome

27

he glanced upward and saw three topmen on the mainsail yardarm eying him narrowly.

Charles climbed up through the entry port and looked around him, taking in as much as he could. Two marine privates with bayonets fixed to their muskets stood at attention on either side. Bevan's sturdy form hurried toward him from the quarterdeck with a noticeable limp, a reminder of an encounter the previous summer. Additional marines with their red coats and black-lacquered hats stood guard at the ladderway to the gundeck and at intervals along the gunwales. In the waist he saw a body of men along with a half dozen or so women staring up at him warily. There was none of the busy work of men preparing a ship for sea. The stationing of so many marines was peculiar; the presence of the women—'wives and sweethearts' as they were loosely termed—was not. There didn't seem to be very many though. From the look of them he guessed they might be actual wives, or something close to it. There was none of the drunken whoring that was common enough when a ship was in port. It was possible, he supposed, that the men had already exhausted their pay and the prostitutes had gone away.

"Welcome aboard, Charlie. All is well at home, I trust?" Bevan said. His expression was not one of happy reunion.

"Hello, Daniel. Penny sends her affection," Charles said curtly, not wanting to be reminded of the parting from his wife. "What ... ?" he began, intending to ask about the presence of the marines and the lack of working parties, when he noticed a commotion at the head of the ladderway from the waist. One of the women, being prevented from entering the quarterdeck by a marine guard, called out to him. "Captain, Captain. Please, sir."

Bevan frowned. "For Christ's sake," he said angrily. "You there, get back down to where you belong."

Charles looked more carefully. She wore a patched shawl over a threadbare dress, frayed at the hem. "I'll hear what she has to say," he said. The marine stood with his musket across his body pushing the woman back so that she nearly stumbled and fell on the ladderway. "You there, stand aside and let her pass."

With some trepidation the woman pushed past the marine. She was no longer young, Charles saw, but not yet old. Her eyes widened with respect or fear as she stopped in front of Charles with his tailored uniform, its glittering gold epaulette and trim. "I do beg yer pardon, sir," she said with an effort at a curtsy. "But it ain't right, what my Tom bein' just back from one cruise and now to be away on another wif nary a day's leave nor a farthin' paid." Her lips quivered; her courage nearly spent. She continued in almost a whisper, "Us what's left behind, we ain't got nuffin'. My little ones, they'll starve. Please, sir."

"Do you mean to tell me that your husband hasn't been paid off from his last commission?" Charles asked. He was dismayed by this, but not entirely surprised.

"No, sir. Not a bit of it. And now them's sayin' yer to sea again afore it can be done. I'm at my wit's end, and t'other wives what have families too. What shall become of us?" This last came in a choke of desperation. Charles turned to Bevan. "Is this true? The men haven't been paid?"

The lieutenant nodded. "I've been to the clerk of the cheque, twice. They weren't helpful."

Charles thought it scandalous how the navy sometimes treated its seamen. The annual allocation from parliament was never sufficient to cover costs, and the answer was to push payment of the men's salaries further and further into the indefinite future whenever they could. After all, the crews were kept on board under conditions approaching imprisonment, and flogging was always available to keep them in line. It was a wonder that mutinies were not more common than they were. He looked down into the waist and saw that a sizable crowd of men had gathered, glaring up at him defiantly. The woman had begun sobbing into her hands. Charles felt embarrassed for all their sakes. "There, there now, Missus . . . Missus . . . ." he said.

"Twilly," Bevan prompted.

"Mrs. Twilly, I will look into this personally to see what can be done. I promise you that we shall not leave Chatham before the men are paid. I give you my word on it."

Mrs. Twilly looked up with a crooked, red-eyed smile. "Thank you, sir; thank you," she burbled, taking his hands and kissing them in her gratitude.

"You're welcome," Charles said, awkwardly attempting to pull himself free. "Now if you will . . ."

"Could ye also find it in yer heart to give my Tom leave to come home?" she said more boldly. "It'd be for just a week. He ain't seen his little ones in near four year, the youngest he ain't seen never."

Charles extricated his hands. "No, I can't, Mrs. Twilly. I'm sorry. Now you must go back down. You may tell Tom that he will receive his pay as soon as I can arrange it." He turned the woman by her shoulders and guided her back to the ladderway. When she was safely on the other side of the sentry he took a deep breath and turned back. "What the hell is going on, Daniel?"

"We have an unhappy crew," Bevan answered. "It's not exactly a mutiny, but they've made it clear they won't work or allow us to sail unless their grievances are met. I haven't informed anyone in the dockyard yet of our situation. I thought it best to keep it under my hat until you arrived."

"I appreciate that," Charles said. "There must be some way to fix this. I'd be angry myself if I weren't paid."

"It's not just that, there's more."

"About leave to go home, you mean?" Charles said. "You know that we can't do that; none of them would come back."

Bevan shook his head. "You've heard of Captain Edward Bittington?"

"I think I read he's recently been given a seventy-four," Charles said, wondering at the connection.

"May god help one and all who serve under him. He did not transfer his old crew to his new command when he moved on. We've been given them. He'd striped almost all their backs more than once over the past couple of years. Captain Bittington is one of those officers who considers himself a strict disciplinarian."

Charles had a sinking feeling. "How bad is it?"

"Worse than you might imagine. They had been at sea without a break for nearly three years. I feel badly for the poor buggers. Most of them tried to jump ship as soon as they came aboard. I've put a stop to that with the marines."

Charles' unease turned to anger. The last thing he wanted was to embark on a long cruise with a crew full with pent up hostility from probably justifiable grievances. The fact that they had been abused by a captain too free with the cat was bad enough. That they had been turned over directly from one ship to another, while a common enough practice, would add to their discontent. Some among them wouldn't have set foot on their native soil or visited families and loved ones since the war began six years before. All of this a seaman might adjust to—life in the British navy was known to be harsh—but to be deprived of their wages at the end of a long commission was beyond any excuse. Small wonder there were no whores aboard; the men had no money. For those with wives and families to support it would be intolerable. "You've been to the clerk of the cheque about their pay? What do they say?"

"A lot of rigmarole about the crew being turned over from one ship to another, in which case they aren't due to be paid off as they would be at the end of a commission. I think this is sheer evasiveness on their part; it's possible there isn't enough cash on hand to do it. A number of seventy-fours have come into the yard for refits. I expect they'll be settled first."

"What about tickets?" Charles asked. To his mind this was not an acceptable alternative, but it was something. Tickets were vouchers normally issued to seamen transferring from one ship to another. They were no more than paper promises for payment of wages, sometimes years in arrears, with stoppages and purser's charges, and the last six months earnings withheld to discourage desertion. They could not be cashed at Chatham and only promised a specified sum at some future date. In order for them to be drawn up, their previous ship's muster book and purser's accountings would have to be sent to the clerks of the navy board for the sums to be calculated. This, itself, could take months before the paperwork was done and the vouchers issued. And even then there was nothing the men could do except sell them to brokers at discounts of thirty percent or more.

Bevan scratched at his chin uncomfortably. "They allowed that tickets might be issued, eventually. They wouldn't say when."

"Wonderful," Charles said."Have you disciplined anyone since you've been on board?"

"No, I haven't. It isn't like I haven't considered it. I thought it best to wait until you arrived."

"Good," Charles said. He disliked public whippings with the nine-tailed cat, each strand knotted at close intervals so as to tear the flesh off a recipient's back. Thus far in his career he had never ordered one of his crew to be flogged —which Bevan well knew—relying on withholding spirits, disratings, or unpopular duties instead; he did not think that imitating Captain Bittington was the solution to his problems. Punishments that were too severe did more harm than good.

"You can't go easy on this," Bevan insisted. "Once they get it into their heads that they can do as they please, there'll be no end to it. You should take them firmly in hand now to put a stop to this nonsense."

"Do you mean that I should pick out a few of the leaders and have them flogged to set an example?"

Bevan nodded. "I'd do it."

Charles expelled his breath in frustration. "Well I won't, Daniel. Not right at the start. I want to go easy with the punishments for a time."

Bevan looked at his friend with a dubious frown. "You know, Charlie, sometimes you trust people too much. You don't want to see trouble when it's coming."

"If something happens, we'll deal with it," Charles said firmly. "In the meantime, I don't want to make life aboard any harsher than it has to be. You know my feelings on this."

"Aye, I do. You're as soft as warm butter. I will admit that it's a hell of a thing for the Admiralty to put this on your plate as soon as you come aboard, though."

"I doubt the Admiralty is aware of our problems," Charles answered. "They probably assume that we've been given a ship and a crew and we'll go merrily on our way in blissful contentment." With the tightest of smiles, he added, "I suppose we should be thankful; it could always be worse."

"Ah, oh yes," Bevan answered. "Just to complete your day, we're fifty hands, more or less, short of our complement, content or otherwise."

CHAPTER THREE

Charles stood on the forepart of his quarterdeck deep in thought. He was conscious that others of his officers had collected a respectful distance away, waiting to welcome him on board. Despite his words to Bevan, he didn't know what to do. There was justice in the men's complaints, but his lieutenant was correct in one respect—he must gain control of his ship and establish his authority. How? One misstep and the crew might erupt into open mutiny. One misstep . . .

He glanced down into the waist and saw that a crowd had gathered around the plaintive Mrs. Twilly, doubtlessly listening to her retelling of his promises. He had blithely sworn that he would see that they were paid. It had been a mistake to make such a rash pledge. The clerks at the payment office would laugh at him if he walked in and announced, "I'd like my men's wages, if you please." He should have agreed to "try," or "do my best." The men might be satisfied with that—no, probably they would not. The crew might even have other grievances that he was not aware of. Damn Bittington for mistreating his crew, he thought, and damn the Navy Board for not promptly seeing to their payment. Damn the whole goddamned Admiralty for sending him halfway around the world to cover its political backside and giving him a rebellious crew. On top of that, he had to find fifty additional hands from somewhere. That would be nearly impossible in the middle of Chatham Dockyard with dozens of more senior captains clamoring to complete their own ships' companies. And, since his own crew had decided to stop their work, his ship was still not fitted out or supplied for sea.

"Don't you think you'd better read yourself in?" Bevan prompted. Charles looked and again saw Lieutenant Stephen Winchester and Midshipman Michael Sykes, whom he recognized; along with a few others he did not, standing near the wheel. All were looking at him with concern. It crossed his mind that they would be as worried as he about the difficulties they found themselves in. One step at a time, he decided. The first thing would be to at least appear as if he had some confidence in what he was doing. He took a last look down at the men on the gundeck and saw that the crowd had mostly disbursed, although a few of the seamen stared sullenly up at him. Bevan wanted him to read himself in. That would make him legally Cassandra's commander, with every one of the considerable powers and responsibilities implied. All that was required was to read his orders aloud in front of the crew. Well, he wouldn't—not yet. He wouldn't give anyone the satisfaction of seeing him hurry. The men would be anxious about his appearance and how he would react. He would let them brood on it. It was the kind of thing a confident captain would do.

Charles pulled his watch from his coat pocket, flipped open its cover and saw that it read two thirty-five. "No," he said to Bevan. "I'll read myself in at three bells in the first dog watch. Everyone's supper will be afterward." He made an attempt at a smile. "Come along, I haven't yet spoken to the other officers." With that, he pulled on the lapels of his coat to straighten them and started aft.

"Hello, Stephen," he said to Winchester and extended his hand. "I'm to tell you that Ellie sends her love."

Winchester touched his hat and grinned. "Welcome aboard, sir," he said. Serving as second, he was also, by chance, married to Charles' younger sister. The two Winchesters lived with a newborn son just by the village of Tattenall, and Charles had seen his brother-in-law off on the coach to London only two weeks before.

"Good day, Mr. Sykes," Charles said to his senior midshipman. "You are well, I trust?"

"Oh yes, sir," Sykes answered happily. "If I may say, it's good to have you back. I'm sorry about the difficulties with the crew, sir." The young man had served for two years on Louisa, first coming onboard at the awkward age of fourteen. Charles had developed a certain fondness for him. Sykes looked more grown now, his features beginning to fill out and a hint of blond fuzz on his chin.

"Thank you, Mr. Sykes. I'm sure we will have the situation in hand presently."

Two additional boys wearing midshipmen's jackets fidgeted anxiously to one side. Charles assumed them to be the 'young gentlemen' he had agreed to take on board. Neither looked old enough to be allowed far from their nanny's skirts. They were ushered forward to be introduced as Thomas Hitch of Yorkshire and Horace Aviemore, from the west of Scotland. Charles recalled both names, as their fathers had written him to request that he take each under his tutelage in the hope that their sons would establish themselves on the way to honorable careers in the navy. The regulations only stipulated that such young gentlemen be at least thirteen years of age. Charles guessed that Hitch probably met this criterion, if only just. Aviemore, however stood in an oversized jacket whose sleeves reached past his fingertips. "How old are you, son?" he asked.

"Eleven and a half, sir, almost," Aviemore squeaked in a thick Scottish burr.

Charles sighed. The boy's father had assured him otherwise. Oh well, it would be a larger inconvenience to arrange to send the child home than to keep him onboard. He'd decide later. He had enough problems for the present. "I am pleased to make both your acquaintances," he said evenly. "You may return to your duties."

"Where is Beechum?" Charles asked. Lieutenant Beechum, the senior midshipman on Louisa, had been provisionally raised in rank the year before. The Admiralty had since confirmed the promotion and Charles had requested that he be posted with him as Cassandra's third lieutenant.

"Asleep below," Bevan answered. "I've kept the lieutenants as watch officers because of our situation. He was up all night." Then he added, "Who's this?"

Charles turned and saw Augustus carrying one of his sea chests toward him. The other lay on the deck boards by the entry port. As there were no hands to sway them aboard the man must have hauled the things up the side himself. Charles introduced his steward to the assembled officers. Augustus answered seriously as each name was spoken with a nod of his head. "If you would be so good as to take them to my cabin, I'll be along presently," Charles said.

Augustus looked around him. "Where be your cabin?"

Charles realized that he had no knowledge of the frigate's arrangements. There would be a lot that would have to be explained. "Aft on the gundeck," he said patiently.

"Yes, Cap'n," Augustus answered. "What am the gundeck and where be aft?"

"I see. Mr. Sykes, would you be so good as to show the way?"

"Of course, sir," Sykes said.

"Afterward, perhaps you could acquaint him with the general layout of the ship. Take your time; it's a lot to learn if it's all new."

"Yes, sir," Sykes answered. Turning to the black man and arching his head back, he said, "Augustus, is it? If you would accompany me, please. You ain't small, are you? Mind your head." Winchester also took the opportunity to be excused.

Alone with Bevan, Charles looked around him once more, attempting to take in the details of the ship. The contrasts to his previous command were immediately apparent. There were gangways running above both sides of the gundeck connecting the fore and after castles and providing some protection for the gun crews below. She was longer by about fifteen feet to accommodate the four additional twelve-pounder cannon that were her main armament and proportionately wider in the beam. An evident Englishness stood out, whereas Louisa had been originally French. He could see that she was of heavier construction and, because of her increased size and sturdier frame members, would displace a greater weight of water. His mind turned irresistibly to how she might run with the wind on her quarter or how handy when tacking. He decided that she would probably not be as fast as some, due to her greater weight, but she would hold her own in rough seas, and he saw no reason she might not be as quick as any in the stays. This led him to thoughts of putting out to sea, and to the state of her fittings, armament, and supplies.

"What still needs doing before we are prepared to sail?" he asked.

"You mean aside from finding a crew that's willing to actually work?" Bevan answered. "Let's see, we've yet to receive our powder and shot. That's the biggest thing. I've had to put the deliveries off since we've no one to stow them. I did manage to complete our stores of water, victuals, and wood. Told them they wouldn't be fed otherwise. There's some small rigging work still to be done aloft, and a few other odds and ends, but we could attend to that as we go. We'd be ready to weigh most any time after we find some additional hands and the ones we have get over their current fit of pique."

"We'll see what we can do," Charles said. "In the meantime, I am going to my cabin. If you would please send someone for me when it's time." He turned and made his way below, trying to take in the details of the ship. She was untidy with unsecured falls and carelessly placed gear, but her line and cable work were all new and freshly tarred against the weather. At the base of the mainmast he took a moment to collect a loose signals halyard that particularly offended him. He looped the excess around his hand and elbow, tied it off, and hung the line in its proper place.

Once down the ladderway to the gundeck he paused to examine the freshly painted twelve-pounder cannon neatly aligned on their carriages, thirteen to a side. They were the newer Bloomfield pattern guns. The Ordinance Board must have ordered them to replace the outdated Armstrong models. This pleased him. He was aware that a number of the crew were watching him warily from across the deck; indeed, some had removed themselves from the pathway to his cabin to give him a wide berth. He did not acknowledge their presence, but noted that most were able seamen, the older, professional, highly skilled men who knew the ropes and the accepted customs of shipboard life. Most had been at sea all their lives and tended to be conservative in their outlook and expectations. In the normal way of things, nothing happened without their consent and they had their own methods of enforcing discipline below decks, almost none of which ever reached a captain's ears. If there were to be a real mutiny, it would only be with their blessing. If the crew were to return to their work, it would be because the able seamen said so. In whatever they decided, the ordinary seamen, landsmen, and ship's boys usually followed.

The marine sentry at the door to the captain's cabin came to attention as he approached, then stepped aside for him to pass through.

"Thank you, Private," Charles said. "May I know your name?"

"John Smith, sir."

"How long have you been posted on board?"

"'Bout a week, sir," the sentry answered, still standing rigidly erect, his eyes fixed on some point over Charles' shoulder.

"And how do you find life aboard?"

A flicker of curiosity passed over the marine's face, but he answered formally, "I find it agreeable, sir."

"Truthfully," Charles said. "Have you no complaints?"

"Well, sir," the man's eyes settled on Charles momentarily before looking away again. "The victuals ain't too special, if you take my meaning, sir."

"Thank you again, Private Smith. I'll look into what can be done about that. Pass the word for the ship's cook and purser to attend to me, if you will." Charles pushed open the door and entered his cabin. He found it a relatively large room, at least larger than he'd had on Louisa. A desk set against the forward bulkhead and a table with six chairs midships close to the stern windows were the only furnishings. The deck beams were just high enough for him to walk upright beneath them, and there was a raised skylight cut into the quarterdeck above. The canvas-shrouded forms of four cannon projected into the space, two on each side. When cleared for action, the forward bulkhead to the cabin and all his things would be struck below, the guns uncovered, and his quarters would become an indistinguishable part of the gundeck running the length of the ship.

Charles hung his hat and sword on pegs fastened near the door. The sea chests lay on the deck in the center of the room, which meant that Augustus was still being shown around the ship by Sykes. He crossed to the table and sat; steepled his fingers, and attempted to decide what he should do next. A knock at the door interrupted him. "Mr. Burton and Mr. Wells are here, sir," he heard the marine private announce. Charles assumed this would be the cook and the purser.

"Come," he called back.

The door swung open; two men entered. One was rather short, wearing a stained apron and a wool cap. He had a cheerful look about him aided by a certain ruddy tint to his cheeks. The other was of average height, somewhat elderly, and more presentably dressed. He carried a ledger tightly under his arm. Charles stood and gestured for them to take chairs opposite him at the table.

"Which of you is the ship's cook?" he said as soon as they were seated. He knew which was the cook by his dress, of course, but he didn't know which name belonged to whom.

"Peter Burton, sir. Pleased to meet ye," the pink-cheeked man said affably.

"What are your intentions for this evening's dinner, Mr. Burton?" Charles asked directly.

"Dinner, sir? For the crew?"

"Yes, Mr. Burton. For the crew. Not, for example, the populace of China."

"The usual, sir," the cook answered, any sarcasm evidently lost on him. "I've salt beef, fresh from the cask, ship's bread, and sauerkraut. The kraut's good for the scurvy, I hear."

"You've no vegetables, fresh bread, flour for gravy, anything like that?"

"I ain't got stores for provisions like that," the cook protested.

"We are in harbor, Mr. Burton. Provisions like that can be obtained from the victualing wharf."

"Well, yessir, but . . ."

Charles cut him short. "These are my orders, Mr. Burton. "It is too late to change tonight's supper, although you may send someone on shore for fresh bread."

"Yes, sir," the cook said doubtfully.

"I further require that in future, dinner and supper will include fresh vegetables, soft bread, fresh meat if you can get it, and the like. It is my wish that it be palatably cooked. This will be the rule whenever we come into a port or harbor where local provisions can be obtained. Is that understood?"

The cook nodded.

"Good. Don't forget about the bread, and add some fresh butter while you're at it." Mr. Burton pushed back his chair, rose, and started toward the door.

Charles turned to face the purser who eyed him cautiously. "Do you have a concern, Mr. Wells?" he said.

The purser laid his ledger book on the table so that it was exactly centered in front of him and precisely squared to its surface. "I am not authorized by the victualing board to expend unlimited sums on independently procured foodstuffs, sir," he said tightly. "I am required to draw provisions from the yards whenever possible."

Charles understood that pursers were at least in part independent contractors who were expected to enhance their minimal salaries by economizing on provisions and through the sale of certain "necessities" such as tobacco, candles, and clothing to the ship's company. There was ample room for corruption in this system and some pursers amassed small fortunes at the expense of their crews' comfort. On the other hand, there were those who overspent their allowances and were bankrupted when held responsible for the deficit. A ship's captain was officially responsible for reviewing his purser's accountings and checking for any malfeasance. Some were diligent in this tedious task, others scarcely bothered. Pursers were rarely beloved figures by a ship's crew, who universally assumed they were being cheated, real or not.

"I am aware of the requirements of your position, Mr. Wells," Charles said. "I know, for example, that when in an English harbor you are entitled to draw fresh provisions from the victualing wharf."

The purser did not apologize. "I have only come onboard these three days past," he said. "I have not yet had the leisure to attend to it."

"I trust you will find the leisure for it the first thing on the morrow," Charles said.

"If that is your wish," Wells answered pertly.

"It is my wish to have a healthy and happy ship, Mr. Wells," Charles answered. "I may tell you that we are about to embark on a prolonged cruise into potentially hostile waters. Neither you nor I would wish the temper of the ship's company to be otherwise."

The purser nodded noncommittally. He was a close man with his feelings, Charles decided, and had probably been caught making a few extra shillings by keeping the crew on seagoing rations. Wells would bear watching in the future.

"Is that all, sir?" the purser asked.

"That is all for now, Mr. Wells," Charles said. "Thank you for attending me so promptly. I will be pleased to review your ledgers regularly on Wednesdays. I trust you find that agreeable."

When the purser had gone, Charles looked once more at his watch. He needed to come to a decision on what to say to the crew when he read himself in. The thought of it stirred up the bile in his stomach. He would be expected to speak about their pay and what he would do about it. But what could he do about it really? He must make no more empty promises. It would be important to set the right tone, to reassure the men that he would be a fair commander, that he believed in a disciplined ship, that he expected hard work from them and their best efforts at practice with the guns or aloft. He could appeal to their patriotism, or even religion—the French were after all known to be Catholic. He considered this for a time, then decided that it wouldn't do. They would have heard it from every captain assuming a new command. In fact, he wouldn't give any speech at all beyond the briefest reading of his orders. Instead, he would have them speak to him.

Augustus soon returned. Charles busied himself with showing his steward how to arrange his belongings and explaining in general terms what his duties would be. He was considering where to hang a framed pen-and-ink drawing of Penny, a memento of his last cruise, when a knock came at the cabin door. The ship's bell rang three times. It was time to be on deck. "Yes," he yelled at the door.

Isaac Beechum, Cassandra's Third Lieutenant, entered. "Hello, Captain Edgemont. Welcome aboard, sir. Lieutenant Bevan's respects. He says the ship's company are assembled as requested."

"Yes, yes," Charles said. Now that the moment was upon him he felt unsettled and unprepared. "Hello, Beechum. How are you?" Without waiting for a reply he turned to Augustus. "My dress uniform coat and hat, quickly please." To Beechum, "My regards to Lieutenant Bevan. I will be on deck presently."

"Aye, aye, sir," Beechum said, and departed.

Charles slipped his arms into the heavy garment, then buckled on his sword and took up his hat. As he gained the quarterdeck he saw the marines, drawn up in a neat line, snap to and present arms. Bevan stood at the base of mainmast. Below in the waist, the crew milled in an undisciplined mass. He noticed that the senior seamen mostly collected around the edges in groups of three or four. There were probably about seven or eight score present in all, Charles guessed, which was probably right if they were fifty short of a complement. His nervousness increased. Their eyes were turned on him as he passed behind the line of redcoats. What would they see? That he was a junior captain from his single epaulette, that he looked young. What would that mean to them? From what he could tell, none exhibited any indication that he was especially welcome in their presence.

He stopped beside Bevan and removed the envelope from his pocket. "All right," he said.

"Off hats," the lieutenant bellowed in a voice that could be heard in the tops. Before Charles could unfold his document, Bevan signaled to the marine lieutenant standing behind his men.

"Atten-shun!" the lieutenant barked, and simultaneously the drummer began a long rat-at-at-at roll. The marines loudly stamped their boots on the deck and came to a rigid parade-ground attitude.

Charles frowned. He guessed that Bevan had arranged the ceremony in order to impress the crew. It was not the tone he wanted to set at all. "Stop the drummer," he said. When the noise ceased he pointedly turned to the lieutenant of the marines. "Stand your men at ease." He said loudly enough for those in the waist to overhear.

"I beg your pardon, sir?" the surprised lieutenant answered back.

"Stand your men down," Charles repeated. "I do not wish to give the impression that I take up this command by right of military force. I have been appointed by the King to this position. I am sure that is sufficient for every man on board."

"Aye, aye, sir," the lieutenant said in a surprised tone. He then ordered his company to parade rest. Charles had not yet been introduced to him; he would have to make amends later. With barely a glance at the men below he unfolded the paper and read. "To Captain Charles Edgemont, Esquire. Sir, you are hereby directed and required . . . " He finished the page barely having taken three breaths. Charles raised his eyes to look out over the men that were legally under his authority now. He knew it, and they knew it. There was an expectant silence followed by a commotion of exchanges from below.

"What have you to say for yourselves?" Charles said in an almost normal voice. The mutterings died away. "Come now, why are you refusing orders?"

"What 'bout ar pay?" a voice shouted up almost immediately.

Bevan shifted uneasily beside him. Charles knew that he did not approve of seamen speaking directly to their captain, particularly in that tone of voice. "Leave it be, Daniel," he said. He saw that the speaker was a hard looking man with a golden earring and his hair tied back in a club—an able seaman if ever he'd seen one. He was sitting on the first reinforce of a gun with two of his mates, all had quids of tobacco in their mouths and a bucket on the deck between them to expectorate into. "I am aware that your pay is in arrears and I will do my utmost to address it before we sail," he answered.

"Wif all respect, zur," the man shot back, spitting a gob expertly into his receptacle, "Ye tol' Mrs. T ye'd do it, not look into it."

Charles saw the other seamen perched on the cannon nod in agreement. An angry murmur started up again from the crowd. He knew he was on thin ice, but it was best to be truthful whether they liked it or not. "It was a mistake for me to have said that. I can't force the navy to deliver your pay. I will promise you that I will do everything that is in my power to see that it is done as quickly as possible."

Another seaman lounging against the bulwark on the other side of the deck pushed himself to his feet. He was of indeterminate age with deeply weathered skin, eyes narrowed to slits. "We ain't sailin' wifout our wages. It be our money what we earnt it. Ye got that, captain?"

Charles took a deep breath. He felt his fingers tapping against his thigh and balled the hand into a fist. "Yes, I got that. Thank you," he said. "I will make this bargain. You will come under orders and return to your duties. I promise that we will not sail until you are paid. We will sit in this stinking harbor until hell freezes over or the paymaster comes, whichever is first." He saw heads nod in tentative approval, particularly among the older seamen.

41

"That's not good enough," another voice shouted out from somewhere in the middle of the company. "Back pay be only one of our demands." Charles searched the faces until he saw a red-headed man, his hair cropped short. The speaker waved a sheet of paper in his hand. There was a commotion of agreement, mostly from those close by him. The older seamen watched from the edges with interest.

Charles' heart sank. He thought he'd made an offer they could accept. It was as far as he could go—farther than he should have gone. "Who's that, Daniel?" he asked under his breath.

"Dick Stimson," Bevan answered. "Rated as a landsman. Was a clerk of some kind, I think. He fancies himself a regular shipboard barrister. I've had words with him before."

Charles held up his hand for silence and faced Stimson. "Fine," he said, biting off the words. "I'll listen."

The man held his page before him and read. "The first is, we want our back pay before starting any labor, and full in cash, no tickets." He had six demands, which he had evidently spent some care thinking through. The others were: 2) no floggings or harsh punishments, 3) better food, 4) leave at every port, 5) the redistribution of all prize money so that one-half would be divided among the crew instead of the established quarter, and 6) pardons for everyone who had participated in the work stoppage. "We ain't lifting a finger lest you agree to all of it," he concluded.

It was strange, Charles thought, that he had sympathy for most of the demands; but he couldn't do it—not unless he wanted to hand the running of the ship over to the crew. "I'll grant pardons to any man who hasn't committed a more serious crime. That includes you, Stimson, on your promise of good behavior in the future. As for the rest, I won't agree to any of it. I've made my offer and I'll honor it. This ship will be run under the same rules as every other in the navy."

Stimson moved to protest, but Charles decided the man had said enough. It wouldn't do for him to stand on the quarterdeck arguing back and forth. He took a breath. "It is my wish that you come under orders immediately. If you refuse, I will take whatever steps are necessary to make it so, bargain or no bargain." He said it flatly, he meant it, but he did not relish the prospect of making it so.

A confusion of exchanges broke out in the waist. "Then we ain't none of us returning to work," Stimson shouted up.

Charles turned to the lieutenant of the marines. "Form up your men, if you please." When he turned back he noticed that the man on the cannon, the one who spoke to him first, had gotten to his feet and was shouldering his way through the crowd along with his mates. A few of the older seamen were also moving quietly toward the center. Mostly the men moved out of their way to let them pass. He wondered what they were doing.

"A-ha," Bevan said.

Four senior seamen arrived without a fuss around Stimson with his page of demands. For a moment they blocked him from Charles' view. Quite suddenly the mass began to break apart, the men drifting or hurrying away. Stimson was revealed sitting alone on the deck boards, blood running from his nostrils onto his shirt.

"Beg pardon, zur," Charles heard a familiar voice speak to him from just below on the gundeck. He looked and saw the earringed man from the cannon who promptly knuckled his forehead. "We're under yer orders, zur."

"Thank you," Charles said, unable to think of anything else.

"Mind that ye live up to yer end."

"I will." The man turned to leave. "Wait," Charles said. "May I ask why . . ?"

The seaman pushed his tobacco into his cheek, pulled a filthy piece of cloth from his pocket, spit into it, then put it back. "I saw as you tied orf that halyard at the mainmast all nice and neat. I reckoned ye might be a fair captain if ye'd do a thing like that. We'll see though, won't we."

"We will that," Charles said. He turned to Bevan. "You may dismiss the hands below."

"Who was that?" Charles asked after the men had started toward their messes.

"Able seaman Thomas Sherburne," Bevan answered. "He's a hard case."

That evening Charles received an invitation from his officers to share their supper. The wardroom occupied the after third of the mess deck below Charles' own quarters and was reserved for the ship's lieutenants, senior standing officers, and warrants. Individual cabins the size of large closets lined both sides of the space. Between was a low-ceilinged room with a long table aligned fore to aft where they did their paperwork and took their meals. Charles was introduced to the men who would be responsible for Cassandra's administration, navigation, maintenance, and the health of its crew. He shook the offered hands and attempted to fix names to faces: Mr. Silas Cromley, the sailing master whom he had been assured was specially selected for his knowledge of the Red Sea; William Owens, surgeon; and Lieutenant Thomas Ayres, a Scot commanding the marines, he managed to place firmly. Wells, the purser, he had already made the acquaintance of. He found himself too tired to form an impression of them except that the master took an unusual amount of time to answer a direct question. Ayres seemed decisive enough. They would all sort themselves into their places as he heard their reports in the coming days.

43

The atmosphere during the meal turned convivial. Everyone expressed relief that the problems with the crew were finally over. The courses came and went, the wine passed from setting to setting. Charles struggled to be attentive to the conversation but found that he could barely keep his eyes open. It had been a very long and eventful day. As soon as he decently could, he excused himself and trudged up the ladderway to his own cabin and to his cot.

*****

Charles did not immediately call on the clerk of the cheque to see about the men's pay. Instead he set about to have Cassandra prepared for sea. He sent Winchester with a small party of marines in the ship's launch back up the Thames to call on the Impress Service headquarters in hopes of securing additional seamen to complete his crew. Beechum was dispatched to the gun wharf with a request that their supplies of powder and shot be brought out for loading at their earliest convenience. Next he met with the ship's officers one by one: the master, quartermasters, boatswain, carpenter, gunner, the lieutenant of the marines, surgeon, purser, cook, armorer, cooper, master at arms, and so on. From each he received a report on their particular responsibility, was introduced to their mates, and led around for him to inspect their efforts. He noticed as the morning progressed that the hands worked steadily if unenthusiastically under the watchful eyes of their petty officers. This satisfied him for the moment, aware that it could all come to nothing if he could not secure their pay. Ideally, he would like to have it done immediately after Cassandra had completed her fitting out. He would allow them one night to spend some of it, and not have to wait until they recovered to complete their lading. Late in the afternoon he went to call on the pay office. He did so with some trepidation and his own purse augmented by an extra one hundred pounds.

"I am Captain Edgemont of the frigate Cassandra," Charles announced himself to the first person he encountered inside the large, overheated room that housed the bookkeepers of the Bureau of the Clerk of the Cheque. "Are you aware that the men under my command have not yet been paid off since their last commission? This is scandalous, sir. I demand to know the why of it."

The functionary appraised him, unimpressed. He had doubtless encountered many captains with similar demands. "You'll have to speak with the senior clerk, Mr. Wallbottom. He is to be found at the rear of the room. I'm certain he will be pleased to receive you."

"I see. Thank you," Charles said, at least some of his carefully prepared indignation spilling from his sails. He picked his way among the dozen or so desks with their accountants toiling over ships' muster books, pursers' reports, and dockyard indents. He saw a larger table piled high with stacks of paper at the room"s far end. A somewhat elderly man with spectacles clamped to his nose and garters holding up his sleeves frowned as he approached.

"I am Captain Edgemont of the frigate Cassandra," Charles said, attempting to resurrect his outrage. "The men under my command have not been paid off since their last commission."

"Yes, it's scandalous how the pay office keeps the wages of the hard working crews of His Majesty's navy in arrears," Wallbottom said, completing Charles' argument. "I suppose you would demand this to be rectified immediately."

"I would," Charles asserted, struggling to maintain his indignation. "I cannot sail otherwise." He took a breath preparatory to informing the man in the strongest terms that he had recently been instructed at the Admiralty, by members of the board in person, as to the urgency of his weighing anchor without delay.

Wallbottom held up his hand. "Of course, captain," he said evenly and turned to pick through several of the ledgers by his elbow. "Let's see, let's see . . . Cassandra, is it? Ah, here we are. Your men were only turned over a week, no, eight days ago. I believe your lieutenant has already been here to complain. You do know that these things take time, don't you?" He closed the folder and replaced it. "The tickets will be available on Friday. Is that acceptable?"

"The timing of it is acceptable," Charles answered in as firm a voice as he could manage. "But tickets are not. The men believe themselves to have completed their previous commission. By rights they should be paid off in full."

Wallbottom steepled his fingers in contemplation. "Yes, I can see your point," he said agreeably. "Unfortunately, I am only authorized by the navy board to issue tickets. But you can always appeal their decision. If you will write out your protest I will be more than happy to send it on. I will hopefully say that we may expect an answer within three or four months, although it sometimes takes longer."

Charles leaned confidentially over the table. The offer he was about to make was distasteful to him but he had learned that such things were sometimes necessary. "Surely, between gentlemen, there must be some way around this, some discretion at your disposal. I well understand that it may require an additional effort on your part. I am prepared to offer a gratuity, a contribution of a generous nature, to help the process along." He thought it wise to leave the actual sum to be negotiated.

The clerk smiled. "A gratuity of any amount would always be welcome, I'm sure."

"And what might I expect in return?"

45

"The men's tickets to be delivered on Friday," Wallbottom said flatly.

"I see. Thank you. I suppose that will have to do then," Charles said, accepting the finality of it and departed the office.

Winchester returned the following morning with eight additional men, three of them able seamen, for which Charles was thankful. He himself called on the port admiral to beg for hands and was grudgingly given four landsmen, then told in so many words not to return.

On Tuesday, in the forenoon watch, a gun wharf powder hoy came across. All fires were extinguished, smoking prohibited, and the entire ship's company ordered to go barefooted or in felt slippers. Only then were the five tons of gunpowder in hundred-weight kegs lovingly hoisted aboard and tenderly stored in the magazine below. In the afternoon, round shot was ferried out to be swayed up in nets and divided into shot lockers fore, midships, and aft. This operation was overseen by the sailing master, Mr. Cromley, as a part of his normal responsibilities. The distribution of their twelve tons would have a large influence on Cassandra's handling qualities at sea. Cromley, a painfully spare man in his middle forties and nearly bald, proved meticulous in the performance of his duties. Charles watched almost in amusement as he hurried fore and aft, and back again, checking the quantities in each locker. Charles could almost hear the man calculating whether this end was too much, or that not enough, or vice-versa. He wondered if Cromley had ever been solely responsible for balancing the trim of a ship before.

When the loading was finally completed, Charles approached. "I trust the shot has been stowed to your satisfaction, Mr. Cromley. If I may ask, how long have you served as a ship's master?"

"This is my first as actual master, as it were," Cromley answered. "I been a mate for over a score of years though."

"I see." This would account for his carefulness. "I am pleased that you have received your step at last. I'm sure it was long overdue. Could you tell me the extent of your experience in the Red Sea?"

"Yes, sir," Cromley frowned as if reliving an unpleasant memory. "Back in '77 on the schooner, Betsy. We was months sailing up and down. Hot as all Hades as I recall."

"But you are familiar with the region?"

"Oh yes, sir. I think on it often. And the hydrographer's office has sent along the latest chart. I took many of the soundings on it myself."

"Thank you," Charles said. It was clear to him that the sailing master was not exactly as advertised, but at least he had a map; an old map, but normally the seas didn't change all that much.

Charles' main worry remained the manning of his ship. He now had a crew of one hundred and eighty-two, still well short of his allocated complement of two hundred and twenty. As usual, the greatest need was for topmen, the younger, agile men who worked high in the yards, setting, reefing and taking in the sails. The following morning, in an act of some desperation, he sent Lieutenants Winchester and Beechum, each with a party of marines, in the ship's launch and one of her cutters down to the Noire in the mouth of the Thames. There they were to board merchantmen returning to port, and take off whatever excess seamen they might contain, either by financial inducements to come willingly, or by force if necessary. It was a proposition for which he had scant hopes. Other ship's captains, and the Impress Service itself, would already have visited almost all of these hapless craft before they reached the anchorage.

For himself, Charles decided he could use the morning to accompany Augustus into Chatham's civilian harbor to purchase supplies for his larder. He had entrusted this task to Attwater in the past, despite sometimes haphazard results, but realized his new steward would have little experience dealing with shopkeepers or bargaining over prices. The one bright spot in his existence was that Augustus rapidly proved a more than agreeable steward. He was quick to pick up new tasks and unfailingly good natured as he performed them. For their first stop he chose a wine merchant located in a brick-fronted shop along the quay.

"Six cases of claret, if you please," Charles told the shop's clerk. "Two of your best and four of middle quality."

"Very good, sir," the clerk responded, jotting a note on a scrap of paper. "And what else?"

"Do you see, Augustus," Charles said, "with wine it's wisest to order the bulk of average quality. The best is frightfully expensive."

"Yes, Cap'n," Augustus answered carefully.

The clerk: "Will there be anything else, sir?"

"Yes. Four of port," Charles answered. "Portuguese, if you have it."

"Best or middling?"

"Something in between." To Augustus he explained, "Cheap port can be disgusting."

Augustus nodded.

"Anything else, sir?"

"That will be all, thank you. If it could be delivered to the frigate Cassandra this afternoon. She"s moored in the number two basin."

The clerk's pencil moved across the paper. Looking up, he said, "That will be seven pounds, fourteen and six in all, sir."

Charles opened his purse and began to count out the correct amount. He noticed Augustus watching him intently. "Do you see what I'm doing?" he said.

47

"No," Augustus said promptly. "Well, I see but I don't. . ."

"Look," Charles said. "This is a pound note. These are shillings. This one is two . . ." He stopped. "You've never seen English money before, have you?"

"I ain't never seen much of any kind," Augustus said doubtfully. "I had a copper coin once."

Charles thought that his steward seemed troubled by his lack of experience with money. "Ah," he said. "We will have to do something about that."

He paid the clerk, then led Augustus from shop to shop where they purchased jams, preserved fruits, several wheels of cheese, a quantity of fresh potatoes, a dozen hams, a half a hundred-weight of coffee beans, a machine to grind them, a dozen chickens, a goat, three sheep, a pair of swine, and all the other items which would be his own personal supplies while at sea.

Back on board in the afternoon he left Augustus to deal with the purchases as they were delivered onboard. The wine and foodstuffs went into the captain's pantry, the livestock to be penned in the manger by the bow, along with other animals purchased in shares by the officers in the wardroom. Charles sent for Midshipman Sykes.

"Sir?" the midshipman said as he arrived on the quarterdeck.

"I was hoping you would do me a favor of a personal nature," Charles said. "You are under no obligation to do so."

"Of course, sir," the boy said. "What is it?"

Charles asked if he would take an hour a day or so over the next few weeks to instruct Augustus in his sums and to explain the mysteries of pounds, shillings, pence and farthings. In return Charles promised to see that the midshipman would be excused from his normal duties for an equivalent amount of time. To this Sykes readily agreed.

Winchester and Beechum returned after dark with seven newly conscripted hands, four of whom actually had experience in the tops. Three, Charles was told, had accepted the two-pound bonus he had offered and were enlisted as volunteers, but only after being informed they would be brought along whether they did so or not. The others had been too busy cursing their fate to focus their minds on it. Charles decided that this would bring his crew close to the bare minimum he might sail with. Cassandra would still be thirty-one short of her allocation, but with care they might manage. It was not impossible they would find more along the way or at Cape Town.

Early the next day a harbor boat came out with the men's tickets as promised. The crew were assembled on deck and given their paper as their names were called, then checked off in a ledger. Before the process was completed, a full half-dozen boats carrying "agents" and "brokers" had arrived to wait alongside, ready to convert the payment slips into hard cash at a steep discount on the spot.

Charles carefully watched the proceedings for signs of trouble. There were sour looks from some of the crew when they learned that they were to be issued tickets instead of cash. The older seamen didn't seem to care. For most, their life was on the waves and they had little concern for accumulating money for its own sake. If they had enough for something to send home, and their tobacco and the occasional binge on whores and liquor ashore, they tended to be satisfied. He noticed Stimson circulating among some of the crew, stopping to speak in animated terms to them in small groups. Charles thought to stop this before it went too far. "Mr. Beechum," he called to his nearest lieutenant. "Please send someone down to inform Stimson that I request the pleasure of his company."

Close up, Stimson appeared older than he had from a distance. There was a slyness about him that Charles did not like. It was clear from the list he'd presented when Charles took command that he could read and write, unusual enough for a member of a ship's crew. He wondered how he'd ended up in the navy. His guesses were paternity suit, bigamy, or skimming money from his employer, and he'd accepted a turn in His Majesty's service rather than gaol.

"You sent for me, sir?" Stimson said. There was a hesitation before he knuckled his forehead.

"I take it you are dissatisfied with the men receiving tickets."

"I'll lose a third of my pay to some broker. There's many of us what's not satisfied."

"Tickets are what the navy saw fit to issue; I suggest you make your peace with it. I'll not tolerate any more trouble. If it comes, I'll know who started it."

"Yes, sir, I understand," Stimson answered, his face set in a frown.

"Good. Then you are dismissed, but remember that I will have my eye on you."

The moment the pay office accountants went down the side, the brokers came up, usually with an assistant to carry the satchels of gold and silver coin and to stand guard while it was being dispensed. Immediately behind came a third armada of small boats, "bumboats" as they were called, crowded to the gunwales with all manner of merchandise for the newly moneyed seamen, from sausages and cheeses to pipes and clothing, but mostly liquor and freshly painted prostitutes for whom the bum-boats were named. Charles agreed to allow them onboard for one night of seamless debauchery.

In the morning he ordered Ayres's marines (many of them the worse for wear) to sweep the ship from stern to stem, rousting out women and men alike. The women—wives, sweethearts, and professional sweethearts of the moment—were firmly escorted to the entry port and over the side. As the women went down, a water hoy came out from the port to refill the few empty casks. Next a lighter with firewood and another with hogsheads of salted beef and pork, casks of dried vegetables, and bags of hard bread to top off the last corners of the hold with provisions.

At four bells, under watery morning skies, Charles stood on his quarterdeck beside the harbor pilot, an overly jovial man named Thompson. Both were intently judging the state of the tide.

"The bower's hove short, sir," Bevan informed him.

"Thank you," Charles answered. After a moment he saw what he had been watching for. The river's surface turned from slack water to the barest eddy starting down the river. "You may weigh and cat home, Daniel," Charles said. "Mr. Thompson, the ship is yours until we clear Sheerness."

Cassandra fell off with the quickening current, her bow angling into the River Medway. On the shore a small cluster of newly off-loaded women waved handkerchiefs to husbands, brothers, lovers as they glided past. Penny had stood in such a group once, Charles remembered, waving her handkerchief from the Point in Portsmouth as Louisa had glided past in the early dawn on her way to the open sea. He clenched his jaw, determined not to show any outward sign of sentiment.

CHAPTER FOUR

An incessant hammering came from somewhere. Charles' mind refused to accept it. The sound became regular, a loud knocking. By degrees he pulled himself to wakefulness. "Sir, sir," he heard a voice call—Beechum's voice. He heard Augustus moving through the outer cabin. Grudgingly he pushed himself to a sitting position and swung his legs over the side of the hammock. Something must be wrong somewhere to have him called in the middle of the night.

Charles forced his senses to work. It wasn't for a change in the weather. From the pitch and roll of the ship he determined that Cassandra sailed on the same easy seas and moderate westerly breeze that she had when he'd gone to bed. Two weeks out of Chatham, they were in open seas well off the North African coast with no navigational hazards. There was none of the shouting or even musket fire that might signal a mutiny in progress. In fact, aside from the gentle groaning of the ship's timbers and the wash alongside, it was deathly quiet, as would be expected at this time of night—whatever time of night it was. His feet rubbed across the floor until they found his slippers.

"It be Mr. Beechum, Cap'n," Augustus announced, pulling back the curtain to the sleeping cabin. He held a candle in its holder, casting a dim glow into the room. "He say he must speak to you urgent."

"I'm coming," Charles said and stood upright. Beechum, he knew, was scheduled as deck officer for the middle watch.

"I'm sorry to wake you, sir," Beechum said as Charles emerged.

"What is it?" He stretched his arms, trying to shake the torpor of sleep.

"It's Stimson, sir." The young man looked genuinely upset. "He was found in the hold forward, under the orlop."

"What was he doing? Who was with him?" Charles came fully awake, angered but not completely surprised that an obstinate Stimson might have continued with his schemes. At least he had been discovered in time.

"No, sir. He's alone. He's dead."

"Dead?"

"Dead, yes, sir. I'm certain of it."

It took Charles a moment to digest this. "Wake Mr. Owens, the surgeon," he said. "Tell him to meet me there, and Lieutenant Ayres with a few of his marines. You might get Lieutenant Bevan out of his cot as well. Is there anyone with the body now?"

"Just Sykes. He's midshipman of the watch. I told him to stay until you came."

"Let me put on some clothing; I'll be there in a moment."

"Aye, aye, sir," Beechum said as he started toward the door.

Charles found his breeches and pulled them on, tucking his nightshirt into the waistband. It took him a moment to find his shoes, then he slipped into them without bothering about the stockings. He buckled on his sword as he passed out the door.

The hold of any ship of war is a dank, airless place below the waterline. As Cassandra was newly overhauled and only a few weeks from port, hers smelled sweeter than most. He climbed down by the forward ladder-way, holding a lantern before him, and hurried along the narrow aisle between the casks, barrels, hogsheads, and crates stacked to the deck beams and wedged tight on either side. The space was eerily silent, his light casting patterns of constantly transforming shadows as he passed. Ahead he could see the platform for the orlop. "Mr. Sykes," he called out.

"Here, sir," the boy answered. "You'll have to come under."

Charles saw the light of Sykes' lantern and ducked low under the beams. The midshipman sat cross-legged on a looped section of cable. On the floor in front of him lay the red headed Stimson. The body lay stretched out on its back, the arms straight on either side, legs slightly splayed. There was no blood that Charles could see as he drew near; no obvious bruises or scrapes. Stimson's head was twisted at an unnatural angle so that he appeared to be examining the deck boards at close range.

"Christ," Charles muttered. He looked at Sykes, who seemed calm enough. "How long have you been here?"

"It might be ten minutes," Sykes answered.

"How did you find him? I mean, how did you know to look here?"

"One of the men, Roberts I think, told Mr. Beechum. We came down to find him just like this. We ain't touched nothing."

Charles wondered what one of his seamen was doing wandering around below the orlop in the middle of the night. Probably searching for rats. Some liked to make sport with them in their idle hours. He patted his pockets in the vain hope of finding his watch. Stimson's death had clearly been no accident. There would have to be an official inquiry; he needed facts. "Do you know what time it is?" he said.

Sykes scratched his chin. "Sometime between four and five bells in the middle watch, I think. Least, I remember hearing four bells just before we came down."

"Thank you," Charles said. "Do you have any idea how it happened?"

"No, sir. I can guess though."

"What's your guess?"

"Some of the older able seamen don't like Stimson much. They thought he was a trouble maker."

"That's a good guess," Charles said. He heard the sounds of footsteps coming toward them. "Charlie," he heard Bevan's voice. "Are you under there?"

"Yes," Charles answered. There was no more room in the cramped space so he crabbed back out into the hold where he could stand upright. He saw Bevan, Owens, and Ayres with two marines trailing behind.

"Stimson's dead?" Bevan said.

"It looks like someone's broken his neck for him," Charles answered. He turned to the ship's surgeon. "If you would be so good as to examine the body and establish the cause of death. I will require a written report on it."

"Yes, sir," Owens replied. He bent low and entered the space.

"Lieutenant Ayres, you will post sentries at both the fore and aft ladderways to the hold. No one is to enter or leave without my permission."

Ayres nodded his comprehension and spoke to the marines behind him. "Anything else, sir?"

Charles tried to think of what he would need to do in order to find the perpetrators. "Yes. If you would please detach sufficient of your men to search the hold from stem to stern for anyone who might be hiding. They'll have to check the carpenter's walks as well. I would appreciate it if you would supervise this personally." The carpenter's walks were the space kept free along the inner sides of the hull so that leaks or shot holes could be detected and repaired without having to shift the stores. He doubted that anyone would be there, but it was important to be sure.

"Yes, sir," Ayres said.

"And one more thing," Charles said, beginning to think of the possible repercussions of Stimson's murder. "I want all of your men to turn out at the change of the watch to keep order. That is all for now."

"You're expecting trouble over this?" Bevan asked.

"I don't know, Daniel, but think about it. Stimson was a spokesman, maybe a leader, among the lower ratings. They may decide that it was the senior seamen who did him in and attempt some kind of retaliation. I won't have it."

Owens and Sykes sidled out from under the orlop. "What have you found?" Charles asked.

"He's dead, that's a fact," Owens said, brushing at some grit on the knees of his breeches. "His neck was broken. Someone twisted his head clean around.

He must have died suddenly. There were no signs of a struggle."

"There's no possibility he injured himself, hit his head on a deck beam, tripped and fell, anything like that?"

"No. There'd be bruises around the head or face somewhere. The man didn't even fall; he was lowered to the deck and then dragged under there."

"I see. Thank you," Charles said. "Are you finished with the body?"

"You may do with it as you please."

"Thank you again, Mr. Owens." Charles turned to Bevan. "Have someone sew Stimson into his hammock and we'll bury him this afternoon. I will begin an official inquiry into who did this immediately after the men's breakfast." He paused for a moment in thought. "We'll start by questioning some of the able seaman, and then the others. Somebody must have seen something."

*****

Jason Harley appeared promptly and respectfully in Charles' cabin when sent for. Charles sat behind his table, the able seaman standing easily across from him. After Harley was sworn in, Lieutenant Winchester laboriously wrote down the questions and replies for the record from the table's end. He wrote:

Captain Edgemont: Do you know that seaman Stimson was found dead last night?

Able seaman Harley: Yes, sir, I heared of it. Busted his fool neck, he did.

Capt: Do you have any knowledge as to who might have done it?

Harley: No, sir. I thought it must of been some kind of accident. Those things happens all the time.

Capt: At any time during the middle watch did you observe or hear anything out of place?

Harley: No, sir. I were asleep in my hammock. I didn't see or hear nothing.

Capt: Do you have any personal feelings about the victim?

Harley: Yes, sir. Dickie-boy Stimson was a little sh. . . , person what didn't know what was good for him or how to treat with his betters. (more in this vein, but irrelevant to inquiry)

All of the half-dozen able seamen Charles interviewed gave much the same story. Others of the crew, those known to be the man's associates or mess mates, were called next. None could, or would, shed any light on the matter. None saw Stimson or anyone else go below to the hold, heard any commotion, heard any rumor of any commotion, or expressed anything but cautious respect for the deceased. Charles learned that his entire crew, at least on the word of those he interviewed, spent their nights in the undisturbed repose of the truly innocent and never stooped so low as to pry into the concerns of others or to indulge in idle gossip.

All except possibly one. Last, Charles called Jeremy Roberts—a harelip in his forties, covered in tattoos, with a lazy eye and wildly disheveled hair—who had found the body.

Captain Edgemont: When did you discover Stimson and where?

Landsman Roberts: Don't know the time. It were dark. Might have been nighttime. I were in the 'old under the orlop.

Capt: Did you touch or move the body after you discovered it?

Roberts: Oh, no, sir. I only tripped and fell on it like. I knew it were a man though, it were soft.

Capt: Didn't you have a light?

Roberts: Of course not. A lanthorn scares away the spirits.

Capt: Spirits?

Roberts: The spirit of John Trambor for one, sir. 'E's got my wife in the hold, do you see, to 'ave 'is way with 'er. I search real quiet when I can. I'll catch them at it yet.

Capt: Your wife?

Roberts: Yes, Aggie. We been married these two hundred years and more, since the time of 'Enry the Eighth. She was married to 'im too. At first I thought she might have been fornicatin' with Stimson, but I told you he were soft, so I don't think so now. She were always free with her favors. Bless 'er black 'eart.

Capt: King Henry the Eighth?

Roberts: 'E were a lustful man, don't you know.

Capt: Yes, I do. Thank you Roberts, you've been most helpful.

Charles ordered that Stimson's body be consigned to the deep immediately after the men's dinner. The crew were called to stand in their divisions, the marines aligned on the quarterdeck, and a pulpit rigged by the mainmast for the ceremony. He watched carefully for signs of dissension as the men sorted themselves into their places. Some among the able seamen shouldered their way roughly past the younger men, receiving angry looks and words in return. Inevitably, one offended topman, younger and fitter, shoved back. The two men quickly faced off with supporters for each gathering around.

"Avast, there!" Charles shouted. "Belay that. Petty officers, you will keep order among your men, or I'll know the reason. Get them into their places." The sergeant at arms, the boatswain, and his mates waded into the knot, separated the antagonists, and pushed them along. An uneasy quiet settled.

Charles hurried through what was in any case to be a brief ceremony—a few lines from the Book of Common Prayer and a single sentence about departed shipmates. When he was done, the plank on which Stimson's hammock-shrouded body lay was tilted toward the sea. The form slid down and over the side with a splash.

A single snicker sounded out from somewhere among the men in the waist.

All heads turned, looking for the offender.

"Silence!" Bevan bellowed, already embarrassed by the earlier disorder on the deck and furious at the disruption. "I want that man's name." None of the petty officers had seen who'd done it, and no one else would admit to knowing.

Charles decided it was best to end the ceremony quickly. He did not think that it was the time for a speech on comradely shipmates. He did think he should say something. "There will be no further outbreaks or altercations on this ship. Any persons involved in quarreling or fighting will be answerable to me." He knew it was a weak gesture. Some captains would have promptly selected a few possible ringleaders or persistent trouble makers and ordered each thirty lashes to set an example. Charles did not believe that minor pushing and shoving warranted laying a man's backbone bare. "You may dismiss the men," he said to Bevan.

The incident angered him. The whole situation with his crew was frustrating. On Louisa, his only other real command, there'd been little trouble, and now he felt himself ill prepared to deal with the problem. He would have to devise a plan to establish discipline, but he was damned if he knew what it should be. He watched the hands milling about on the deck below, some returning to their duties, others to go below. Out of the corner of his eye he noticed the topman that had been involved in the pushing incident angling across the deck with two of his fellows just behind. As he watched, the younger man bumped intentionally against the back of the able seaman he had scuffled with before. The older man spun around. A fist was thrown, then a flurry. Additional men rushed to join in the growing brawl.

"Goddamnit to hell." Charles spat out the words as he raced past an astonished Bevan. He threw himself down the ladderway three steps at a time and ran across the deck, furious that the orders just given had so blatantly been ignored. "Get back," he shouted at a man just entering the fray. He grabbed the man's jacket and pulled him aside. "Stand down! Stop it!" He forced himself between two more men, pushing them apart. He saw the topman who had started it grappling with the able seaman at close range, exchanging blows. "You will cease fighting immediately," he roared at them, grabbing the younger man by his wrist with one hand and pushing against the seaman's shoulder with his other.

The two men paused, surprised at their captain's appearance. "Stand back," Charles snarled. "Stand back, or by God you'll wish you had. Put your hands down and step back this instant." The men grudgingly separated. Charles was aware that the marines from the quarterdeck were hurrying toward him, pushing men to one side or the other with the butts of their muskets. Ayres, Bevan, Winchester, Beechum, even Sykes had waded into the mass, pulling men apart.

"You, what's your name?" Charles said to the topman.

"Andrew Nicols, sir," he answered reluctantly.

"When I ordered that there be no further fighting, was that unclear to you?"

"No, sir."

"Your spirits are stopped for one week. You will go below to your mess table to await Lieutenant Bevan's displeasure. He will doubtless have further punishments." Both Bevan and Ayres arrived to stand beside him.

"But, sir," Nicols protested. "He murdered Stimson."

Close up, Charles recognized the able seaman as Thomas Sherburne, one of the men he had interviewed earlier in the day. "Is this true?" he demanded.

"Not me, sir," Sherburne answered indignantly. "This little shit . . ."

"Shut up," Charles said. "You may speak only when spoken to, and then only a direct answer." To Nicols he said, "Do you have any evidence of this?"

"Well, no, sir. But if it weren't him it were one of his like."

"I'll not have any wild accusations of that kind. Go to your mess and stay there. Lieutenant Ayres," he said, "send one of your men to accompany Nicols below and see that he stays put." He turned on Sherburne. "Your spirits are stopped as well for starters. Go to your mess and wait until Lieutenant Bevan sends for you."

"He bumped me on purpose, he did. Nicols started it." Sherburne seemed genuinely aggrieved.

"The same as you did to him before the burial. I'll not have it. I don't hold with floggings unless they're necessary, but by God, Sherburne, you're pushing me. Now go below." To Ayres, he ordered that another marine be sent to accompany him.

The remainder of the crew stood in a large circle, watching. "This must stop now," he said in a loud voice, turning as he spoke to include all of them. "Do you hear me? If there is one further incident of fighting or provocation I'll stop the entire ship's company's grog until we reach Cape Town. That's two months at least. And I'll put the offenders in irons on bread and water until we get there as well. If you don't think I'll do it, just try me."

In the following days, Charles remained acutely aware that he commanded a tense, unhappy ship, riven with conflicts. Watch and work bills were adjusted to keep quarrel-prone men apart. The petty officers responsible for maintaining discipline were ordered in the strongest terms to prevent arguments and fisticuffs and to report offenders to the captain. He felt himself to be responsible. They should have been an experienced, capable crew. Instead, they were inattentive in their duties, sullen, and resentful toward one another and their officers, with frequent contemptuous looks and harsh words just short of coming to blows. Practice with the guns or aloft in the yards was equally unsatisfactory. The men walked through the evolutions with the barest minimum of effort, gibing at each other as they did so. Charles ordered that the guns be run in and out only; there was no point in wasting good powder and shot. He hoped upon hope that in time the situation would work itself out. So far it hadn't.

His other concern was the overall shortage of men. This made for more work for each watch and undersized gun crews. He ordered an eye kept out for any passing merchantmen off of whom he might press additional hands, but the seas remained empty. He wrote in his report on Stimson's death, that the seaman had been murdered by a person or persons unknown and left it at that. He would forward the document to the Admiralty when they reached Cape Town.

*****

Charles lifted his sextant to one eye and leveled its scope on a clear stretch of horizon. He found the sun in its smoked mirrors and swung the index arm to bring the reflected image down until it exactly overlapped the line between sea and sky. He tightened the clamp screw on the arc. Satisfied, he lowered the device and glanced at its vernier scale. There had been a sea fog earlier in the morning which still lingered in patches, particularly to the north. The sky was overcast, though thinly so, and the sun shone through hazy and indistinct. These were not ideal conditions for a noon sighting, but it would be a good experience for his younger officers to practice under varying conditions.

Around him on the quarterdeck the others stood in a similar pose with similar instruments to their eyes, except for Mr. Cromley, who preferred to employ an older quadrant for his navigational sightings. Charles raised his instrument once more and saw that the sun's reflection had separated from the horizon as it continued to rise. He loosened the screw and re-adjusted the arm to bring the points together again. He watched carefully for any further movement, but saw none as the light hung briefly motionless in place.

"There," Winchester announced. "I make it to be noon."

Charles re-tightened the clamp screw and lowered his sextant. He nodded to a master's mate by the binnacle who immediately turned the half-hour glass then loudly rang the ship's bell eight times to announce the official beginning of a new day. "Now, where are we?" he asked, looking at the others. In particular, he was interested in the progress of the three "young gentlemen"— his midshipmen—already busy studying their vernier readings and chalking calculations on their slates. Charles quickly made his own jottings to determine that Cassandra was at twenty-six degrees, forty-five and a half minutes latitude, which was about what he would have expected. At this time the day before, they had been approaching the Canaries, its westernmost island of La Palma almost indistinguishable on the horizon. In twenty-four hours they had gained about a hundred and fifty-five nautical miles southward in a moderate northeasterly breeze. That was about the same distance they had managed daily since departing Chatham dockyard three weeks before. It was a respectable distance, but it had become clear that Cassandra was not as fast as he might have hoped.

"May I see your computations, Mr. Sykes?" Charles said. Receiving the slate he saw that the mathematics were neatly and accurately done. Sykes' result matched his own, close enough, at forty-five minutes even. "Very good," he said. "I judge that to be acceptable. Mr. Hitch?"

Thomas Hitch held out his slate with a confident smile. "Here you are, sir," he said. "I think you'll find it satisfactory."

Charles saw that the results were indeed satisfactory. Hitch had not only reached exactly the same result as Sykes, but the calculations had been made in an identical fashion down to the spacing of the figures on the board and a double underlining before the final expression of their latitude. He remembered that Hitch had been standing just behind Sykes as the work was done. He made no immediate comment on this.

"Mr. Aviemore?"

The very young midshipman was still struggling with his numbers. He hurriedly wiped at a spot on his slate with his sleeve then chalked a new figure. With his tongue pushing out the side of his cheek, he handed his effort over.

Charles took the merest glance at the jumble of scribbled digits. "There is no 5,283rd parallel on this earth, Mr. Aviemore," he said patiently. "You will please attend to your text on navigation once more. I shall expect a better result tomorrow."

"Aye, aye, sir," Aviemore answered with an unashamed grin.

Charles turned to Hitch, standing idly with a superior smile. "And tomorrow, Mr. Hitch, you will place your person next to Mr. Aviemore in the event he requires assistance."

Hitch's smile faded.

"If that is all, gentlemen," Charles said, "I suggest we may return to our duties." He noticed that Aviemore had become distracted with his sextant and was peering absently through its scope at random objects—that moment at a bird that had lighted on the taffrail at the stern end of the quarterdeck. "Mr. Aviemore," he said sternly. "I will thank you to attend to me when I am speaking."

"Sir," the child said excitedly as he lowered his instrument. "I seen something what's there."

"Terns are of no particular interest to us at the moment," Charles said.

"Your attention to your captain is."

"No, sir, I seen something other, afar on the sea."

"No, you didn't. All right, what?"

"I dunna know. A speck yonder, just on the edge of that cloud like."

This made no sense to Charles, but he saw that Beechum had snatched up a long glass from its place at the base of the mizzen and was training it toward a low-lying bank of mist in the far distance to windward. "There is something on the horizon," the lieutenant said. As Cassandra's stern rose on the crest of a swell he added, "It's someone's royals, I think."

At that moment a shout came down from the mainmast tops, "Sail ho, north by northeast out of that fog. There's two of them." Charles looked up angrily. The lookout should surely have reported the sighting before Aviemore.

"Mr. Beechum, if you would take your glass up to the mizzen tops and report back what you see."

"Aye, aye, sir."

"And tell the lookout that I expect him to keep a sharper eye out in the future. No, on second thought, send him down to me."

Beechum touched his hat and departed for the shrouds.

Charles went to stand beside Bevan. "What do you make of it?" he said.

"The sails? I don't know, could be anything—Indiamen, men of war, slavers, or just your average merchant bottoms. I'd guess Indiamen outward bound, so you can't press any men off of them, if that's what you're thinking."

Charles knew that any ships of the East India Company or other friendly merchant shipping would be making to round the Cape of Good Hope, the same as he. British captains were strictly prohibited from enlisting, by coercion or otherwise, men off them when they were in transit. Once they returned to home waters, however, they were fair game so long as enough were left on board to make port. Slave ships, to his mind, were another matter. He would have little hesitation about taking what men from them he wanted. It would be a long time before he returned home, and any complaints their captains made would receive no great sympathy at the Admiralty in any event.

He saw that Beechum had reached the tops, and watched as the seaman stationed there swung out onto the futtocks and started down.

"What are you going to do with that one?" Bevan said, nodding toward the descending lookout.

Charles frowned. "I'll know the reason he was late in reporting. I can't just let it pass. This kind of sloppiness has gone on too long. "Hell," he said in frustration, "I should flog him. I should flog them all."

"Yes," Bevan said. "But you won't."

"No." Charles fell silent as the man crossed the quarterdeck toward him.

"You're Jenkins, aren't you?" he growled.

"Yes, sar." He touched his forehead.

"Tell me, Jenkins, why you failed to spy that sail aft before I saw it from the deck."

Jenkins did not seem particularly cowed. "She must of just emerged from that bit of fog, sar. One minute there was nothing there; when I looked back again, I saw 'em." It was a plausible explanation, and Charles' anger drained away. "Thank you for your report. Keep me informed," he said. "You may return to your station."

"There's one thing more," Jenkins said.

"What is it?"

"Them's Frenchies, sar. Both of 'em,"

"I beg your pardon?"

"Them are two warships to windward, sar," Jenkins repeated. "One larger than t'other. Mebby a frigate and a ship o' the line. I could see them's French by the roach in the cut o' their sails. I made 'em out just afore I came down."

"Christ." Charles glanced up at the mizzen shrouds where Beechum was just beginning to descend. He had enough problems without having this put on his plate. Something like twenty miles to windward of him were two enemy ships on a detached mission to somewhere. Where? It didn't matter. The French, and whatever their intentions might be, were no concerns of his. He immediately dismissed any notion that he might engage them. Even if it were a lone frigate he would not entertain it. It was no part of his orders and his crew were not sufficiently practiced—not even near to sufficiently practiced. He also knew too well that the relatively frail Cassandra was no match for a line of battle ship with thirty-six-pounder cannon on her lower gun deck.

Beechum arrived breathlessly from his hurried descent of the shrouds. "There's two, a frigate in the fore and a bigger one following about a mile or two behind. They've seen us by now, I'm sure of it."

"I imagine they have, Mr. Beechum. What can you tell me of the battleship?"

"Don't know for sure, sir. She's hull down, a two-decker I should think. Possibly a seventy-four from the size of her masts."

That seemed probable. It made little sense to send a lumbering three-decker far from home in the company of a single frigate. A seventy-four-gun warship would be powerful enough to deal with anything they might be likely to encounter, but with sufficient speed to almost keep pace with a swift-running frigate. "Thank you," he said.

It would be safest, he decided, to move out of their way so that they might pass him by. He didn't want to take any chance of being overhauled in the dark. "Make our course due west, Daniel," Charles said. "We will resume southward when those two have moved on."

Bevan passed the order to the quartermaster at the wheel, then sent the men to brace the sails around. As Cassandra settled on her new course, Charles went to the binnacle and took up his personal long glass that he kept housed there. Training the telescope aft, he soon picked out the dot on the horizon that was the enemy frigate's upper sails clear in the lens. As the stern rose on a crest he saw her royals and a sliver of the topgallant beneath. He could see no sign of the second Frenchman from the deck. He was about to lower the glass when he thought he saw the attitude of the sail alter. Immediately a call came down from Jenkins, now back in the mainmast: "Deck! T' Frenchies' changing 'er course towards us. She's 'anging out her stuns'ls."

Charles' first reaction was annoyance. Surely the French had something better to do than chase a solitary English frigate across the high seas. There was no cause for alarm. He didn't need to outrun them, only to be sufficiently ahead when darkness came so as to lose them in the night. "Daniel," he said, "we will hang out the studding sails as well. There's no point in encouraging false hopes."

"Aye, aye," Bevan answered. He went to bellow the orders.

Charles turned to Cromley standing near the wheel. "What do you figure is our best point of sailing?"

The master cast his eyes at the set of the canvas aloft and the long pendant fluttering toward the southwest. "I figure it to be three points on either quarter, near enough, sir," he answered, giving the conventional response.

"We will take the wind three-points off the starboard quarter then, if you please," Charles said. He tilted his head back and watched with disapproval as the topmen started up the shrouds of the fore and mainmasts to put out the booms at the ends of the yardarms to extend their reach. There was the barest appearance of hurrying aloft, enough to avoid a reprimand, but no real urgency about it. The studdingsails would be hung from the booms extending the yardarms and alongside the leeches of the main and maintop sails, increasing their surface. It should give them another knot or two.

Hour by hour he could see more of the distant frigate's masts despite the addition of the studdingsails. All too soon the Frenchman's topgallants had shown clear, then glimpses of her topsail. There was no doubt she was the faster ship. By late evening, in the last of the dying light, he climbed into the mizzen ratlines with his glass. From this vantage he could see the masts of the frigate nearly down to her deck and guessed that she would be about fifteen miles behind. For the larger warship he had to scan the horizon for several minutes before he picked out the tip of her uppermost sails, a tiny dot of lighter gray against the increasingly overcast sky. "In two hours, Daniel, wear ship to put the wind on the port quarter," Charles said as soon as he returned to the deck.

"You hope to lose them in the dark?"

Charles nodded. "With any luck at all they will give up and go on their way. I'm thinking to loiter a bit before taking up our course again. We should be well to windward by then."

"Aye, aye," Bevan said. "In two hours."

The lookout shouted down: "I think the big Frenchie has sent up signal flags, sir. It's hard to be sure in this light."

Charles assumed that the captain of the larger ship was recalling his frigate lest they become separated during the night. Satisfied, he made his way below to his cabin. He allowed Augustus to bring his supper, found he had little appetite, and returned to the quarterdeck where he stayed until Cassandra wore to take up her altered course.

*****

""Tis a half-hour to the dawn, Cap'n," Augustus' voice spoke from behind the small circle of candlelight at the curtain to Charles' sleeping cabin. "Here be your coffee."

"Bless you," Charles said. For an instant he had a lingering sense that he could feel the warmth of Penny's breath against his neck and smell the scent of her hair as if she had just been under the bed linen beside him. The image faded quickly. He pushed himself into an upright position and took the offered mug. With the first sips of the heated liquid inside him, he pulled on his clothing and left to go on deck. Passing along the darkened gun deck, he heard more than saw the crews gathering around their weapons and speaking in low tones as they prepared to run them out. This they were required to do when greeting every dawn at sea, in the case they should find themselves in proximity to an enemy warship. He heard less grumbling about it this morning and guessed that the appearance of yesterday's enemy might have sparked some interest in them.

Emerging from the ladder-way onto his quarterdeck he felt the breeze against his cheek. It had freshened during the night, he decided. Looking up, he saw neither moon nor stars, only the black void of what must be a still overcast sky. Low on the horizon to the east lay a band of light, or at least less dense blackness, signaling the coming of the day.

"Good morning, Mr. Cromley," Charles said to the sailing master, dimly illuminated by the lantern shielded in the binnacle near the wheel.

"Good morrow, sir," Cromley responded formally. "There's a blow coming, less I miss my guess."

Charles sniffed the air. He could feel the beginnings of long rollers passing under the ship's hull. But he wasn't thinking about the possibility of a change

63

in the weather. He wanted to be comfortable that he had shed the French during the night. "I expect you're right," he said absently.

"The barometer's falling," Cromley persisted.

"I expect so," Charles answered. He stared intently over the rail, but the darkness obscured anything on the sea's surface.

"With the wind picking up we should take in the stuns'ls. They'll be blowed out otherwise."

Charles knew this to be sound if conservative advice. The studdingsails on their undersized booms were for light and moderate airs only. The breeze came strong enough to think about taking them in; if it strengthened they would have to. "I'll have them stay as they are for now, Mr. Cromley," he said. "I'll think on it again when it becomes light."

"Yes, sir."

Bevan came aft from the ladderway. "The men are at their quarters," he reported.

"Very good." He looked again at the widening streak of gray. He waited. Soon he could make out the base of the mizzenmast and the boom of the spanker above, washed in the palest of light, then the foot of the mainmast forward. The sea surface slowly revealed itself, undulating, hard and dark. Nothing had been reported from the mastheads. He began to relax.

"Deck there!" The cry came down from high above. "I see a ship two points to port over the stern."

"Damn all," Charles muttered, more to himself than anyone nearby. He stared into the indistinct darkness aft. Almost immediately he found the pyramid of sails, black against the lightening sky. She was the French frigate without a doubt; not more than two miles to windward.

"How did they . . ?" Bevan began.

Charles knew how. He'd miscalculated—he'd been careless. The French had turned back to southward, but there must have been some delay about it, or perhaps the seventy-four was slower than he'd imagined. He should have waited longer to resume his own course. Instead of allowing the enemy to pass him by, they were still to windward, only closer. The French commanders must be delighted.

He tried to think. This was not a situation he wanted. If the frigate took up his wake again, he would be forced to engage, and that might not be long in coming. Cassandra had all the sail aloft she could carry in the stiffening wind, maybe more than she should. It would be an hour or more before the frigate would close to within range. He turned to Bevan. "House the guns and send the men to their breakfast. They'll have to be quick about it. Afterwards have the ship cleared for action."

Charles stood alone for the moment on his quarterdeck looking out at the French ship. She was a dark menace with all her sails aloft, long and sleek with twin pale waves curling back from her bow—a thing of beauty for whom his own ship was not yet prepared. From her size, he guessed she was a thirty-two, almost certainly with twelve-pounders on her gundeck—the same as his own ship. He was reminded that Cassandra remained undermanned, enough so that he doubted he could effectively maneuver and fight at the same time. And he had no confidence in the capabilities of the crew that he did have. The men might rise from their lethargy at the appearance of the enemy, but they were still slow in carrying out their duties and completely unpracticed at firing the guns. They would probably do more damage to themselves than the French if it came to a broadside to broadside fight.

He heard a shout come down from lookout: "Deck! I seen the second ship. She's signaling something. I can't make out what." He glanced upward at the masthead, annoyed at the distraction. He looked back at the frigate to see flags run up her mainmast, then back down again.

A gust of wind came across the port beam causing the sails to volley loudly. "The stuns'ls, sir," Cromley said plaintively, reminding him that he had a dangerous spread of canvas aloft. A glance told Charles that the Frenchman still flew her own studdingsails. He did not answer; instead he tried to sort through the options available to him. He could continue on as he was. The faster Frenchman would continue to run down the wind on him, luffing to fire her guns into him as he fled, or overhauling to force battle. Or, he could do the unexpected—tack suddenly across the wind, throwing Cassandra in front of the enemy and firing into her as they passed. If he caught her unprepared, she would be forced to bear up to avoid being raked. He could then turn away and flee to windward. He could expect to gain a mile, or even two. The more he thought about it, the more it appealed. With luck they might even damage a spar or a mast. It all depended on surprise and a precise execution of the maneuver. He searched the sea surface to the north. It took him a moment to find the second set of sails against the brightening horizon that would be the ship of the line. Twelve miles, he judged; that was far enough.

"Sir. Sir!" the sailing master intruded.

Charles looked upward and saw that the studdingsails were severely strained in the strengthening wind, their booms bowing under the pressure. He also noted that the French frigate, a mile or a little more behind, had sent men into her shrouds to shorten her own canvas.

"Yes, Mr. Cromley, the sails. I apologize for my inattention. I will see to it immediately." To Bevan he said, "Send the men up to take the studdingsails off. I want them to remain on the yards. We shall come about shortly."

"You're going to attack the frigate?" Bevan asked doubtfully.

"I think it's our best chance," Charles said. "Just the single broadside and then we'll run. Having the topmen already in place may disguise our intention."

"You're sure about this?" Bevan said.

"No, I'm not," Charles answered. "Just send the men into the yards and keep them there."

The sea surged with the rise of the wind, the wave crests white at their tops, traces of spindrift blowing from the tips. The French frigate plowed resolutely across, kicking out bursts of spray from her cutwater as she came. She had closed with alarming speed. "Find Lieutenant Winchester and say that I request his presence," Charles said to Aviemore, standing nearby to carry his orders.

"Aye, aye, Captain," the boy responded, cheerfully unconcerned as to any approaching danger, and scurried away.

The men aloft had almost completed gathering in the studdingsails when Winchester arrived from the waist. "Stephen, we shall tack to confront the Frenchman in a few moments time. I expect to engage with our port side battery. You may run out after we have completed the turn."

Winchester, who would command the gun deck, gave a sour expression. "These men couldn't hit a three-decker if they were moored close alongside."

By this Charles took his lieutenant to mean the gun crews were not particularly proficient with their weapons, which he already knew. "I"m sure their performance will be improved in the face of an enemy," he said.

He saw no point in waiting any longer; at that moment it seemed possible. "Haul the braces," he said to Bevan. To Cromley: "Put the helm over, if you please." Cassandra's head soon began to turn toward the wind. A sudden gust, stronger than before, came across the beam, snapping the canvas loudly. These were not ideal conditions for tacking, Charles realized, but the gust passed and he decided to carry through with it.

"Let go the foresheet and foretop bowlines!" Bevan bellowed through his speaking trumpet. "Brace around there, smartly now." The execution of it was anything but smart. The men were making an effort, but were not together. Since leaving England they had largely following winds and no reason to tack. Their practice aloft had been casual and half-hearted. Now it showed. A halyard to the foretopsail kinked, jamming its block. It seemed to take forever to be unstuck.

The foremast sails began to shiver, then flog, as Cassandra reluctantly neared the eye of the wind, the bow heaving and plunging on the wave crests. The line of a squall enveloped the French frigate, the dark band rushing onward like a shroud. Their momentum further slowed. Curtains of rain pelted down as the line found them, then lightened as it moved on. Charles realized with alarm that they might miss stays as a second gust pushed strongly against the port side bow. He stole a quick look at the enemy, again visible over the beam. He saw men hurrying up her shrouds and her head beginning to angle windward, mirroring Cassandra's maneuver. She was only a half mile to the north, close enough so that he could see the gun ports opening along her side. Forward he saw that the foretopsail and topgallant were finally backed against the mast to push the bow across. The wind strengthened and became contrary, coming from the north. Cassandra hung in stays almost motionless, the pressure of the elements beginning to force her sternward. "Helm alee," Charles shouted urgently at the two quartermasters at the wheel, hoping the rearward pressure on the rudder might move the stern to starboard. The canvas aloft flogged convulsively, volleying and snapping in confusion in the howling wind.

"She's in irons, sir," Cromley shouted at him. "She won't come across."

"Give her a minute, damnit," Charles snapped back, but he knew the master to be correct. He watched, his frustration building, as his ship's head began to fall off the wind, turning irresistibly back in the direction from which she had come. A rogue wave smashed against the bow, sending a cloud of scud across the deck. Cassandra staggered, heeling from the force, rivers of seawater streaming from her scuppers. "Damn all," he muttered to himself. Now what was he going to do? It wasn't as if he had an abundance of choices. To Bevan he said, "Gather her back up; we will wear."

The French frigate smoothly continued her turn into the wind, taking in her main and mizzenmast sails as pretty as you please, her foresails neatly braced and hauled. Charles' face reddened at the thought that her captain had witnessed his own ship's sloppy performance.

Cassandra struggled sluggishly to regain headway as the wind pushed on her bow and foresails, the hull heeling under the pressure. "Brace up tight there!" Bevan boomed out as the canvas filled. "Handsomely for once, damn your eyes."

Cromley approached. "What course?" he shouted anxiously.

Charles' eyes barely left the frigate. He had also caught a glimpse of the second French warship, farther away, topsails only on the horizon. He could still run to the south or west. Cassandra had gained a little ground by aborting her turn, while the frigate continued through. There was no point to fleeing downwind; he would soon be overtaken again. If he wore all the way around to the east, he would effectively reverse his course to press toward his opponent on opposite tacks. There would be an exchange of broadsides, but once past the Frenchman would have to turn again to take up his wake. That would give him additional distance, and he might yet hope to do some damage. He had little choice.

"The course, sir?" the sailing master prompted.

"Bring her around to put the wind on the port beam." He stared intently at the frigate and gauged the distance. "Once she's settled, put her on a line for that ship's bow, if you please." Charles moved to the fore of the quarterdeck for a better view. The frigate's masts came slowly into a line, her sails pivoting to catch the wind. Cassandra bore up, her own yards braced tight, her bowsprit pointing directly at the French ship as if they were both on a string, racing at each other from opposite directions.

"Steady as you go," Charles said to Cromley. He thought for a moment to force the frigate to veer off in a game of bluff, but knew there was no benefit to it. If the French captain miscalculated, or his own crew were slow in their performance, the two ships could well come aboard each other with catastrophic results. Still, he should make it close—the closer the better. With the smallest margin in distance between them, the frigate would be unable to elevate her main deck guns enough to fire high into his rigging. At that moment, Cassandra's masts and spars were the most valuable assets he possessed.

"Double shot the guns and run them out," he called down to Winchester in the waist.

Winchester raised his hat in acknowledgement.

One cable's length separated them; even that diminishing rapidly. "Two points to starboard, Mr. Cromley," Charles said. "Steer to shave her."

Cassandra fell imperceptibly off the wind as the wheel came over, then steadied as it eased back. The enemy frigate loomed ever larger, combing white at her bows. Her bowsprit angled to pass Cassandra on her port side, the French captain luffing toward the wind to gain distance and to maintain the weather gage. Along her side, a line of black muzzles projected outward. "Close on her," Charles shouted. "Don't give her any space." He stared at the vanishing gap. The bowsprits crossed, the two ships hulls passing at barely twenty yards, yardarms within a hairsbreadth of overlapping. The French cannon roared out in a measured, disciplined string of explosions, deafening at close range. Round shot repeatedly smashed against Cassandra's side, accompanied by screaming and buzzing sounds as ordinance hissed overhead like a thousand angry wasps. That must be langrage, Charles decided. Despite the narrow range, the Frenchman's forecastle and quarterdeck guns had still fired high, employing the sprays of irregular metal shards in hopes of slicing his lines and cables. Cassandra's own guns replied in a disjointed, uneven outpouring, the last of which trailed away after the enemy had passed.

Charles saw a number of dangling lines and halyards, but no real damage to the more critical supports for the masts. "Set the boatswain to splicing those immediately," he said to Bevan. "Sponge out!" he heard Sykes yell shrilly to the gun crews on the quarterdeck. There was mayhem around the cannon, with over-eager men getting in each other's way, or tripping over lines as they attempted to reload. Someone dropped a cannonball, then went scurrying after it as the thing rolled across the deck. "Jesus Christ," Charles breathed.

He saw the French ship, already a quarter-mile down wind, her rudder hard over and beginning to wear around. It was a moment's grace. If he could manage to have Cassandra tack successfully on her second attempt, he would gain both sea room and the advantage of being to windward. A chase into the wind would be a drawn out affair. With any luck he would still be ahead at nightfall. After that anything was possible, but should he risk it? He ground his teeth at the thought of the inept performance of his crew at the first attempt. If they failed again, the frigate would be on them before they could recover. He bridled at the thought of his crew and their lubberly petulance, the sloppiness of his ship's performance in full view of the enemy, and at the humiliation of being forced to run.

"Mr. Cromley," he called across the deck. "We will tack presently. When that is accomplished, you will steer as close to the wind as she can hold." Without waiting for a reply, he hurried down the ladder-way in a cold fury.

"What the hell kind of seamen are you?" he shouted angrily as soon as he reached the gun deck. The men standing by their guns looked at him in surprise. Charles kicked at an overturned bucket, sending it skittering across the deck. "I have never in my life seen such a goddamned abysmal performance. You are the sorriest excuse for a crew in the King's Navy. Women and children would do better." He glared at the men around him; his frustrations boiling to the surface. "I have gone easy with you out of consideration of your previous captain and for your being turned over from one ship to another. This is the goddamned thanks I get—a slovenly mob of sullen, self-pitying, over-indulged, lazy, undisciplined malcontents. Your king would be ashamed. I am ashamed that it has been my dishonor to command you. That Frenchman is at least manned by seamen who know their duty."

He paused to think of what he could say next. Some looked back at him sheepishly, others frowned. At least he had their attention.

"We could still fight 'em," a man nearby said. "She ain't beaten us yet."

"You couldn't fight off a bumboat," Charles snapped. "Where are the topmen? Step forward, all of you." Tentatively, the men assigned to work high in the masts left their guns to move toward the center of the deck. "We will attempt to tack again," he said. "If you fail this time you'll have plenty of leisure to reflect on it in a French gaol. Get yourselves aloft and put some effort into it." He turned and made for the ladder-way without a backward glance.

Bevan met him as he stepped onto the quarterdeck.

"We will put the ship about," Charles growled, barely trusting himself to speak. He then moved past to stand by himself beside the weather rail. Only then did he look upward. He saw the men already on the yards, genuinely hurrying out to their places. The wheel came over. He listened as the orders were bellowed out and relayed upward. Cassandra's bow turned toward the wind once again. The yards for the foresails braced around, the sails handled and hauled with reasonable, if not exemplary, competence. The bow hung momentarily as it pointed dead into the eye of the wind, then pushed reluctantly across. Charles allowed himself a breath. He looked to port to see the French frigate, having completed her turn, on an eastward course a half-mile away and falling downwind. She had no men on her shrouds or in her yards that he could discern. He breathed again. Someone pulled on his sleeve. He turned to see that it was Midshipman Hitch trying to get his attention. "What?" he snapped.

"Begging your pardon, sir. Lieutenant Bevan's respects. He says to tell you the frigate's been called off, he thinks."

"What do you mean?"

"She was signaled back by the bigger Frenchie. I seen the flags myself, sir," Hitch said with a large smile.

"I see," Charles said, the message sinking in. "If you will come with me." Still seething, he moved to the fore of the quarterdeck and looked down at the men securing the guns. Every eye turned up toward him; some who had seen the frigate's departure smiled. "Don't you dare be pleased with yourselves," he said loudly. "It was through no effort of yours. I assume that the Frenchman passed on after witnessing your performance and was troubled that you would lower the standards of their prisons." He turned back to the midshipman. "My respects to Lieutenant Bevan. Tell him to reduce the canvas aloft; topgallants and topsails only until the rigging is repaired." Hitch touched his hat and hurried off.

Bevan himself approached a few moments later. He did not speak.

Charles looked down at the men in the waist again and fumed. "We will resume practice with the guns immediately the rigging is spliced. In the mornings we will exercise the topmen aloft. See that they put their backs into it. We will continue day by day until they know what they are doing. I'll tolerate no further slackness. If they don't improve I'll stop everyone's spirits, their food if need be. By God, I'll never have another performance like this one."

"Aye, aye, Captain," Bevan answered. He gestured toward the taffrail and over the stern.

Charles saw the departing frigate, close hauled, a mile and a half away. Beyond her, just on the horizon, the larger French two-decker sailed purposefully southwards. "Why do you think she was called off?" he asked.

"I don't know. The captain of the seventy-four must have grown unhappy at the length of time it was taking, or that it was drawing him too far off course. It's just possible he just didn't want to expend powder unnecessarily or be burdened with a prize. Depends on what orders he has, I guess."

As Bevan left to attend to his duties, Charles leaned by the rail looking out at the receding French warships. What orders could they have that called them so urgently southward?

As a sure sign that there was a God that looked out for ships and seamen, a clear streak of blue sky showed on the horizon to the north in the early afternoon. The winds fell away to a steady northeasterly breeze and the sea surface tamed itself on the long Atlantic swells—all to the sounds of the rumble of the gun carriages as their crews labored to run them in and out, and in and out again.

*****

"It ain't too bad in all, zur," Aaron Burrows, Cassandra's carpenter said, holding his lantern so that Charles could inspect the repairs to the hull where French shot had penetrated. "That's the last. They wuz all above the waterline, do you see."

Burrows was a stump of a man with muscular forearms and an even-tempered, agreeable way about him. After giving his report on the damage sustained, he had virtually insisted that Charles personally see that the repairs had been done properly. As one of the standing officers, he remained on the frigate from commission to commission and probably knew her peculiarities better than anyone else.

Charles dutifully bent to stare in admiration at the carpenter's handiwork. "It seems very well done to my eye, Mr. Burrows," he said. "I can hardly tell where the boards have been joined." He said this even thought it was obvious enough where new wood met old.

"Thank you, zur," the man said proudly.

There was another issue which nagged at him, and upon which he thought the carpenter might shed some light. "Tell me, how long have you been posted on board Cassandra, Mr. Burrows?"

Burrows scratched behind his ear. "Neigh on five years, I think. Since ninety-four anyway. Why would you be asking, zur?"

"I was wondering, has she always been so slow a sailer?"

"Oh no, zur," he said with a look of puzzlement. "Well, she were never what you'd call real fast, but faster than now. I can't figure what they did to her in the yard that changed her so."

Charles was pretty certain that they had done nothing in the yard, besides applying new copper sheathing, and that should have helped, not slowed her down. "Thank you, Mr. Burrows," he said. "I am appreciative of your efforts." He was also certain as to whom he should speak with next. It was something he should have looked into long before.

"Mr. Cromley, a word with you please," he said as he regained the quarterdeck.

"Sir?"

"Might I inquire as to how you have decided on Cassandra's trim?"

The master nodded seriously. "About even fore and aft, maybe a trifle down by the head. It takes away a little of her speed, but I find most ships hold better than way."

"I see," Charles said. "Would it be agreeable to you if we transferred some weight aft? I am in hopes that lightening the bow will improve her way through the water."

"I don't know, sir," Cromley said with a frown. "It might give her a tendency to gripe."

"Then I shall have to insist upon it," Charles said. "You will please see to the shifting of one-half ton of shot from the forward locker to the aft most. If that gives a beneficial result we may try an additional amount. I trust you will inform me if she shows any undue inclination to fall off in a forewind."

"Yes, sir," Cromley said, tight-lipped.

Cassandra did improve her speed almost as soon as a bucket brigade of men began passing nearly a ton of round shot, ball by ball and hand to hand, from the bow to the stern. She was still no race horse, but eventually gained two knots under all plain sail, by the casting of the log. Charles took a great deal of satisfaction from this, which he was careful to keep from the master.

*****

Early in the afternoon watch on the fifth day since their encounter with the French, Charles watched Lieutenant Beechum exercise the gun crews on the quarterdeck cannon and carronades with a critical eye. The open deck baked under the midday sun, and the men worked shirtless, heaving on the relieving tackle to run the guns in and out, their progress measured by the Beechum's stopwatch.

If not exactly enthusiastic, his crew had adopted a seriousness toward their work, perhaps a grudging acceptance that they were where they were, and any further grousing might get them killed. Cassandra plowed resolutely across the sea, propelled by the steady northeast trades. They had rounded Cape Vert, the westernmost extremity of Africa, two days before. Their noontime sighting revealed that they had already crossed the eighth parallel and might reasonably expect to make the equator within a further week. With any luck they could raise Cape Town in a scant month and a half. At present their course roughly followed the coast of the continent, just visible as an indistinct line on the horizon to port.

"Hoy, the deck there," a familiar cry came down from the lookout posted in the mainmast tops.

"What's your report?" Charles heard Winchester call back up.

The voice came down clear enough. "There's a barky off the port beam, mebby five leagues. She's schooner-rigged, like. Yankee, I'll wager."

Moments later, Midshipman Hicks mounted the ladderway and crossed the quarterdeck. "Mr. Winchester's respects, sir," he began, touching his hat.

"I overheard, Mr. Hicks," Charles said. "My thanks to Mr. Winchester. We will take no action." The schooner would in any event be too fast for them to catch, even with Cassandra's increased speed.

Cromley, standing nearby, observed conversationally, "Bound for the fort at Bunce Island most likely."

"You think she's a blackbirder, Mr. Cromley?" Charles asked. He remembered hearing that the island in the mouth of the Sierra Leone River was a common port of call for the slave trade.

"Aye," Cromley said, a wistful tone in his voice. "Probably on her way to the Bight of Biafra to take on a cargo. Bunce is the first place after crossing the Atlantic to refill the water casks. "Or," he added, still slowly thinking the possibilities through, "she might be calling on the fort itself, if she's a trader out of Charleston or Savannah. It's the rice plantations, you see."

Charles knew that this stretch of the African shoreline was sometimes referred to as the Rice Coast, and that the grain was also grown in South Carolina. He reflected that he still had a deficit of more than thirty in the makeup of his crew. "You have called at Bunce Island, Mr. Cromley?" he asked with new interest.

"Oh, yes sir. More than once or twice. I was a mate on several slavers in former times. It lies just over to the east there."

This was an aspect of Cromley's experience of which Charles had been unaware. "And how many blackbirders do you figure might be found off the island this time of year?" he said.

Cromley squinted in concentration. "Could be any number, if I recall. Sometimes one or two; others mebby a half score. 'Tis a fair busy place. Why do you ask, if I might inquire?"

"We will alter our course to the east, if you please," Charles said. "I have a notion to see the island for myself."

CHAPTER FIVE

A shimmering glare reflected off the broad waters of the mouth of the Sierra Leone River under a sweltering noonday sun. Cassandra glided easily through the entrance under her topgallants alone. The seemingly lifeless village of Freetown squatted above the mud banks to starboard. Despite the lush jungle crowding the water's edge, the place had an air of desperation and abandonment. Near the center of the inlet lay a small finger of an island with a low rectangular fort at its western end. The fecund odors of the land and the heavy, sultry air overwhelmed the cleaner scent of the sea. Below the fort four sleek merchantmen rode at anchor.

"Hoist the colors, Daniel," said Charles. "You may run out the starboard battery. We will come to anchor between those vessels and the sea. May as well not encourage any false hopes."

"Aye, aye," Bevan responded. He nodded to Sykes to send the ensign up its halyard and shouted for Winchester on the gun deck to set the cannon crews into motion.

Charles watched as three of the ships, all schooner rigged, hurriedly sent up the peculiar red and white striped flag of the new United States, with its blue square in the upper corner and white stars. The forth, a brigantine, flew the familiar union flag of Great Britain. One of the schooners, more alert than the others, immediately began to heave her anchor cable short. "Fire off a gun," Charles ordered.

Bevan spoke to one of the gun captains. A single six-pounder cannon exploded inward on the quarterdeck, its smoke drifting lazily forward. The ball sent up a spout a hundred yards from the schooner's bow. All movement on the schooner ceased.

As Cassandra came about and hove to a half-cable's length from the slave ships, Lieutenants Bevan, Winchester, and Beechum collected on the quarterdeck. The marines had gathered in the waist under the watchful eyes of their officers. One by one, the launch, both cutters, and the jollyboat, were hoisted out and lowered into the water. "I'll have eight seamen off of each of those ships," Charles said firmly. "Mind you, I want prime seamen, no lubbers or ship's boys."

"What if they resist, sir?" asked Beechum, fingering the hilt of his sword.

"Surely, some may not come willingly."

"I doubt any will come willingly," Charles answered. "You will each have a detachment of the marines to keep order. It shouldn't be difficult. They'll only have crews of twenty or so. Ask for volunteers first. You may offer the king's guinea as an inducement. No one will accept it, of course, but make the offer anyway. You have my authority to take anyone you like who cannot produce a certificate of exemption from the Admiralty in London."

"Even if they claim to be American citizens? None of them will have that."

"Mr. Beechum, if they are older than sixteen years of age they were born as the king's subjects, and the king's subjects they remain. Besides, a goodly number are probably British deserters, no matter what they claim."

"Yes, sir," Beechum said. "I got it."

"You have your assignments?" Charles said, looking at his officers one at a time. The boats' crews, he saw, were settled at their oars and the marines preparing to climb down. The three men nodded. Winchester and Beechum started forward while Bevan hung momentarily behind.

"You do know that you'll be leaving them with barely enough of a crew to make it home, don't you?" he said.

Charles met his friend's eyes. "Barely enough is still enough, Daniel. It's more than they've a right to."

Each lieutenant was to call on one of the American schooners. Charles had reserved the British flagged ship for himself. "You are in command until my return," he said to Sykes, standing stiffly self-important by the wheel.

"Aye, aye, sir," answered the midshipman.

"Keep them under your broadside. If I am needed back on board, you may fire off one gun. Don't hit me with it."

"Yes, sir. I mean, of course not."

Charles made his way forward to the entry port, then down into the waiting jollyboat. The boat already held six red-coated marine privates and Lieutenant Ayres in addition to its regular crew. Augustus had taken up his usual place at his oar, seated rearmost to larboard.

"Shove off," Charles said to Malvern as he settled himself in the sternsheets.

"Out oars," the coxswain ordered. The jollyboat pushed off from Cassandra's side and started toward the brigantine. Approaching her stern, Charles saw that she was Amelia Jane, out of Bristol.

"You needn't come aboard if you don't want to," he said to Augustus as they glided to a stop alongside. Charles assumed that being onboard the slaver would be unwelcome for his steward.

"I'll just follow anyway," Augustus said, his eyes narrowed. Charles nodded his assent. "As you wish."

A man of middle age with long strands of wispy gray hair protruding from under his hat stood at Amelia Jane's entry port. "What's the meaning of this?" he demanded as Charles gained the deck. His focus switched to Augustus as he came onboard and then the marines with their muskets much in evidence.

Charles did not answer until Ayres had his men lined up smartly on the deck. "May I know to whom I am speaking, sir?" he asked politely.

"Owen Harris," the man answered. "I'm the master." The sailing master on a merchant ship effectively served as her captain.

"Your certificates please, Mr. Harris," Charles said, "registration, bill of lading, and muster book."

Harris quickly produced several papers from his pocket and held them out. Charles unfolded the documents and saw that they were the brig's registration and manifest, showing that she carried mostly rum and bolts of cloth from Liverpool and was bound for Lagos in the Bight of Benin, where the cargo would almost certainly be traded for newly captured slaves. These were the papers usually requested when stopped by a British naval vessel, and the master had them ready to hand.

"Your muster book, please," Charles said.

"What do want me muster book for?" Harris said suspiciously, but Charles could tell from his eyes that he knew. In a last-minute attempt to stave off the inevitable, the man added, "Besides, in a barky this small we ain't no need for such a record."

"Augustus," Charles said, "in the master's cabin aft, you will find a desk. Bring me all the papers you find in its drawers. Do you have a knife?"

"Yes, Cap'n," Augustus answered, touching the handle of a blade tucked into his belt.

"It's possible you will find it necessary to force the drawers. There may even be an axe about somewhere. You needn't worry if you have to break something."

Amelia Jane's master looked around him in dismay. "All right," he said. "I'll send for it." He turned toward a seaman standing beside the ship's wheel. "Huggins, go below and fetch the roster, do you hear?" He produced a key from his pocket and held it out.

"But, sir, he means to. . ." the man began.

Charles noticed that the master nodded his head ever so slightly to the seaman in a conspiratorial kind of way. He would have none of that. "Augustus, you will please accompany Mr., er, Huggins. You may assist by carrying the muster book back in your own hands. Lieutenant Ayres, if you would be so good as to send one of your men along to keep them company." As the men started toward the ladderway, Charles spoke to Harris. "You will be pleased to assemble the crew on deck." The master shrugged and did as he was told. Charles watched as the odd assortment of Europeans, two Lascars, and even a number of blacks tumbled up from below. Some regarded the naval captain and the marines with curiosity, others with hostility; still others would not look at them at all. Charles counted their number at twenty-two. "Is this the entire company?" he asked.

Harris studied the group sullenly. "Aye, it's all of 'em. You have my word on it."

Charles accepted the statement for the present. The party dispatched below soon returned. Augustus held out a slim ledger, "That be it, I'm told, Cap'n."

Charles opened the book and soon found the correct page. He counted twenty-four names, which, including Harris and Huggins, matched the number on the deck. Four were entered as having American citizenship. He called out their names, then added, "You will collect your sea chests and go down into the boat alongside."

"I ain't going," a man who had answered to the name of Peterson said defiantly. "I ain't no British subject. You can't . . ."

Charles put his finger on the ledger by the name. "It says here you were born in Alexandria, in Virginia, in 1775. At that time Virginia was a colony to the crown, was it not?"

"Yesser, it were, but today it ain't. It's part of the United States; everyone knows that."

"I'll grant you that it is," Charles answered. "But you are a citizen of where you were born, and always will be. Everyone knows that. You were fortunate enough to be born English. Lieutenant Ayres," he said, bringing the debate to an end, "this man is a duly pressed subject of the King. You will please see him over the side." The American swore under his breath but went uneventfully, if unhappily.

Muster book in hand, Charles called out the names of the English seamen and demanded from each their certificates of exemption. Two lacked such protections entirely and a third presented such a crude forgery that it made him laugh. "Did you make this yourself?" Charles asked. When the man nodded, he said, "Next time use a pen and ink. Nobody at the Admiralty writes official documents in pencil." Those three, the remaining Americans, and the larger of the two Lascars, a subject of colonial India, he allowed to collect their sea chests before going down into the jollyboat.

"I find your papers to be in perfect order, Mr. Harris," Charles said, returning all of the documents to the m. "I thank you for your cooperation. You are free to go on your way."

"You have ruined me," Harris said plaintively. "I haven't enough men left to manage a load of blacks. I shall have to go back direct."

"You should have chosen a different cargo to trade in," Charles said curtly, then swung out over the side and went down.

On board Cassandra, he watched with satisfaction as his boats returned from the American schooners. Generally, the seamen taken off scowled in anger as they came upon the deck, much to the delight of his own crew who gathered round cheerfully at the sight of the newly pressed men. It was an old adage that a British tar, pressed himself, loved nothing more than seeing another suffer his plight. That many were Yankees only sweetened the experience.

With Lieutenant Bevan returned, Charles ordered the newly pressed men taken below and read in. He decided that it would be preferable if they departed before the American ships' masters decided on some course of action. "Heave the anchor short and weigh, if you please," he said to Winchester, now at his station as officer of the watch. "I believe we may have already overstayed our welcome."

"You've left it too long," Winchester answered, nodding over the starboard beam.

Charles looked and saw a ship's longboat pulling across from the nearest schooner. A black-coated man stood midships waving his arms at the frigate. He supposed it was unreasonable to expect that there would be no protest. "Prepare to weigh in any case," he said. "We will sail as soon as this gentleman has his say."

"I object to this foul act in the strongest possible terms," shouted the red-faced American master as soon as his head showed above the level of the deck. "I have never experienced such bald thievery." Seemingly without pausing to take a breath, he launched himself the three paces across the deck to stand toe-to-toe in front of Charles. "This is a most serious breach of the law, sir. Mine is an American ship. I have my cargo only half loaded, and you have enslaved a goodly part of my crew."

"Enslaved?" Charles said, interrupting the flow. "That's a hypocritical charge, isn't it?"

"What do you mean?"

"I mean, sir, what is the nature of your own cargo?"

The man hesitated, then gathered himself. "That's nothing to do with it. Trade in niggers is a legal enterprise. Impressing American citizens on the high seas is an act of piracy, pure and simple. I demand that you release all of my countrymen you have taken." He added reluctantly, "The others you can keep."

"I won't release anyone," Charles said, irked at the man and his manners. He noticed additional boats being lowered from the other schooners. "As much as I have enjoyed your company, I suggest you return to your ship."

"There will be an official protest," the man persisted, "a diplomatic protest at the highest levels. You may be assured of it. I am not unknown in Washington."

"I see," Charles answered. He turned toward Winchester who had been watching the exchange with an amused expression. "You may weigh the bower, Stephen, and sheet home." Touching his hat to the schooner's master, he said, "Good day to you, sir."

"I ain't yet finished."

"Fine, I have all day," Charles answered. He heard the anchor cable's rasp as it was heaved up through the hawse and saw the topmen on the shrouds, for once smartly climbing aloft. "You'd better hurry though, or your boatmen alongside will have a long pull back."

With the indignant American returned to his boat, Cassandra began to gain way, listing gently to seaward as the breeze off the land pushed against her sails. There was little that worried him with respect to any official protest. It was a common enough practice to press Americans off their own ships. To his knowledge, no British captain had ever been reprimanded for it. In any event, it would be a long time before the slave runner returned to his country, managed a hearing in its capital city, and any diplomatic exchange passed from Washington to London. He was also comfortable that, given the state of less than happy relations between the two nations, London would not bother to respond. He'd gained a score and a half prime of seamen; it was a bargain he would take any day.

Later that evening, Charles sat at the table in his cabin with quill and paper before him, adding to the growing letter it was his custom to compose for his wife. He wrote several paragraphs most nights and would post the accumulation of his efforts whenever he came into a suitable port. He was in the midst of describing his encounter with the slave ships and his "recruitment" of some of their crews (in addition to slavery, Penny also did not approve of impressment), when Augustus silently placed a small glass of claret next to his elbow on the table. This was his servant's signal that it was time for Charles to prepare for bed. Charles had learned that Augustus could move very quietly for a man of his size.

"Thank you," he said, laying down the quill and stretching his arms. "I was just writing Mrs. Edgemont about our visit today."

"Yes, Cap'n . . . ," Augustus said hesitantly.

Charles guessed there was more, but his steward remained silent. "Out with it," he said finally.

"Well, I was just wonderin', if it weren't no trouble . . ."

"Would you like me to write something for you?" Charles prompted. "I would be pleased to do so."

Augustus smiled.

"A letter to Miss Viola?"

The man's face turned even darker, something Charles would not have believed possible. "Oh, no, Cap'n, I could never. But mebby if you could just pass a word to her for Missus Edgemont to read out."

"I think that could be arranged," Charles said with a small laugh. "Tell me what you want to write."

Augustus pursed his lips in concentration. "Just say that I be fit. I wish she be fit too."

"That's all?"

"That all I dare, Cap'n," Augustus said solemnly.

Charles knew very well that Penny would relay everything that he wrote which even touched on Augustus' situation. When he was alone again he revised his letter to add a few details, such as how "Augustus heroically accompanied the seaman below to fetch the muster book, and bravely returned."

*****

Charles Edgemont stood on his quarterdeck under a blazing sun next to Daniel Bevan. Both men's eyes fixed on the canvas aloft, currently hanging lifeless like sagging window curtains in an airless room. Five days from Bunce Island, Cassandra made to the southwest dressed to her studdingsails and royals in hopes of picking up the Brazil Current to carry them south to the westerlies and thence on to Cape Town. For the moment she made no progress. The blue-gray sea lay smooth as a table top, quiet for the moment, vast and empty in every direction.

Charles placed his sextant carefully back into its case and snapped the latches closed. The noon sighting had shown them to be at the second degree of latitude north of the equator, near enough. The Brazil Current could not be expected until seven or eight degrees south, a distance of something like six hundred miles. A puff of a breeze started from the north, causing the sails to ruffle apathetically, then passed away as if it had never been.

"I do believe we've found the doldrums at last," Bevan observed dryly.

"You've been this way before, haven't you?" Charles asked. He himself had never crossed into the southern hemisphere, but often heard tales from those who had.

Bevan nodded, rubbing thoughtfully at his nose. "Once as a youngster in old Ajax. We called on Bombay. Took us weeks to get through as I recall. The return went easily enough though."

Charles knew that crossing the doldrums—a band of often windless, but always unpredictable, seas reaching around the globe several degrees north

81

and south of the equator—was an uncertain business. Hot, humid conditions predominated, sometimes overcast, sometimes in bright sunshine. It could be dead calm for days or weeks, pouring rain or stifling haze, or sudden squalls and violent wind shifts. He had heard it said that hurricanes were born in the doldrums.

"As we may be here for a bit," Charles said, "I want to increase the time the men practice at the guns. Once each day, I should think. They still have a long way to come."

"It'll be hot work," Bevan said.

"Increase the water ration. You may start after their breakfast. It'll at least be a little cooler then."

Bevan nodded and went forward.

Charles stayed where he was, watching a small knot of seamen on the forecastle in their off time. They were smoking pipes and talking among themselves. Cassandra was a crowded ship now that she had been brought up to her full complement. Every inch of berthing space below decks served for the men to hang their hammocks and there was no empty seating at the mess tables. It was a peculiar logic that governed their mood. The Americans proved a stubborn, defiant group determined to show they were the better seamen, and damn all to the others. The British, in their turn, would not be shown up. They left off quarreling among themselves and fell to their tasks aloft and at the guns with a will heretofore unknown. There were angry words between the two groups, as would be expected, and an incident or two of pushing. Charles ordered the sergeant at arms and boatswain's mates to keep a tight rein, and handed down swift if, in Bevan's estimation, relatively light punishments. His first thought had been to distribute the newly pressed men randomly among the gun crews to bring all up to strength. On second insight, he selected four of the guns with the slowest times, redistributed their crews, and assigned them to the Americans. The result gratified him. The two groups eyed each other closely, each determined to achieve a better performance than the other. She was not a happy ship, he knew; there were plenty of tensions, but so long as the men focused on their internal differences it was less likely they would turn on their officers.

Looking outward, Charles watched a stream of wind as it crossed the almost glass-smooth sea, ruffling its surface a pale matted blue as it passed. The track of the breeze was clear enough that he could predict to the moment when the sails cracked and bellied. Cassandra reluctantly gained way, her timbers groaning gently as she glided forward. Within the half hour the breath died away.

One watch had gone below to their dinner; the other lazed about on the deck in the waist or on the forecastle. Charles glanced upward to see if the single lookout posted in the mainmast tops was attentive to his duty. To his satisfaction, he saw that the man was standing erect on the platform, staring intently forward—not that Cassandra was in any danger of having an enemy warship swoop suddenly down on them. Unexpectedly, the sentry reached out for the topmast shrouds, then began to climb upwards. Charles watched curiously for a moment. He looked around the deck for someone he could send up to find out what had excited the lookout's interest. His eyes settled on Aviemore. He didn't want to send the youngest of his midshipmen aloft. The child capered around high in the rigging with such distracted abandon that Charles was sure he must eventually fall. He saw no one else suitable. "Mr. Aviemore," he called.

The boy left off his daydreaming by the wheel to approach. "How may I be of assistance to you, sir?"

"A simple 'yes, sir' is sufficient, Mr. Aviemore. Where is Mr. Sykes?"

"I dunna know."

"Mr. Hitch?"

Aviemore's eyes brightened. "At his supper, I think," he said, smiling triumphantly as if he had just passed some important examination.

Charles decided that the boy would have to do. "Get you carefully up the mainmast to inquire of the lookout if he has seen anything of interest. Take note of what he says. Afterward you will equally carefully return to me and report."

Aviemore turned to run almost before Charles had finished speaking. The child scurried up the ratlines like a monkey, heaved himself out over the edge of the tops and onto the topmast shrouds. It made Charles tired just to watch. Near the crosstrees the youth encountered the lookout beginning to descend. The two, a hundred and twenty-feet above the deck, appeared to converse for the briefest of moments before the midshipman launched himself downward, hooking a leg and an arm onto the mainmast backstay to slide at breakneck speed to the deck. Charles was impressed in spite of himself.

"Sir, he says he seen two sail," Aviemore squealed excitedly. "He says they're the . . . , the . . ."

Charles could guess what they were. "French?" he prompted.

"Aye, the two same Frenchies what we done with t'other time. Eight leagues to the south; they've gotten afore us."

"He's certain that they are the same French frigate and line of battle ship?"

"I told you what he said," Aviemore insisted impatiently. "The same what we saw t'other time."

"Thank you," Charles said. "Go sit down somewhere and catch your breath."

"I ain't lost it."

"Go sit somewhere anyway."

Charles leaned against the railing, tapping absently on its cap with his fingers. He found it interesting that the two French ships of war were following the same course as himself. That they had come this far south ruled out most destinations on the Atlantic coasts of South America or Africa. The Indian Ocean seemed most likely, probably to join the French squadron at Mauritius, but it was just possible they would continue due south to make for Cape Horn and the Spanish waters of the Pacific. If he could keep them in sight until exiting the doldrums he would know for sure and be able to report the fact at Cape Town.

It came to him that he might use the presence of the French, however distant, to his advantage. The minute the lookout went below, every man jack on board would know that the enemy, the same they had encountered south of the Canaries, lay just over the horizon. It was not impossible they had heard already. Scuttlebutt-- fact, rumor, or purest invention spread like lightening below decks, often sparked by fatuous speculation. The simple fact that he had sent a midshipman aloft had probably started tongues wagging. It would be the most natural thing in the world for him to work them at the cannon and aloft in these circumstances. In fact, they would expect it. There was that, Charles reflected, and the unhappy experience of their earlier encounter with the frigate; the memory of it gnawed at him. He would like to even that score if the opportunity arose—it was now personal. He stopped his tattoo on the rail and crossed to speak with his first lieutenant. "Daniel, we will clear for action and exercise the men at the guns as soon as both watches are on deck. I expect to keep them at it for the remainder of the afternoon. We will begin again in the morning."

Before long the deck sounded with grunts and shouts from the gun crews, the deep rumble of carriage trucks, and squeals of the axles as the two-ton cannon ran in and out the gun ports, and in and out again. Charles watched with satisfaction. The men swarmed around their weapons shirtless and barefoot, glistening with sweat as they struggled with the tackle. Some of the crews, he noted, were finding the knack of heaving together on their gun captains' commands, while others remained uncoordinated and slower. The practice continued, with measured pauses for water and rest, until the top of the first dog watch, when he ordered the men released to their supper. In the evening, a relatively constant breeze started out of the west. The lines were immediately taken up and the sails braced to their best advantage. As the last of the daylight died, so did the wind.

The next day, and the day after, and the day after that were much the same.

The men struggled with their ponderous weapons for two hours after their breakfasts and two hours again before the evening meal. Each crew went through the motions of cleaning, loading, running out, and simulating firing a half dozen repetitions, timed by a stopwatch. Then they were given leave for a drink of water and a short rest before doing it again. Slower and less adept gun crews were singled out for Beechum or Winchester to pace them step-by-step through the evolutions until each member understood when to pick up the relieving tackle, which hand to place over which, where his feet should be, and to anticipate the exact instant to throw his full weight in concert with his fellows. Charles set himself the task of observing the captains of each of the gun crews, ordering three to be replaced by more promising candidates.

The air tended more hazy than clear under increasingly overcast skies. Odd pieces of wind came over the water at disparate intervals and from unpredictable directions. The breezes were universally, and sometimes loudly, welcomed by the men on the gun deck for cooling their skins and because practice was interrupted while some were called away to tend the sails. Usually sluggish, sometimes brisk, the wind pushed Cassandra ever farther southward. On the third day, a blue-black storm reaching from sea surface to the heavens passed several miles to the north, of which only the muffled rumble of thunder, like a great ship's distant broadsides, reached them.

Day by day, more of the two French warships' masts became visible from the mainmast tops. Charles climbed to Cassandra's masthead himself and judged that they were not more than twenty miles away. It did not surprise him that his ship was closing. The English and French frigates could be expected to make about the same progress in the light intermittent airs, but the seventy-four, with all her mass to move, would be slower.

That night a gusting wind came up from the southeast. By morning it had steadied, shifting easterly, and held all day. At latitude eight degrees south Cassandra exited the doldrums.

*****

"Stop!" Sykes called, holding the fourteen-second sand glass up before his eyes and watching carefully as the last grains had dropped into its lower chamber. The seaman in the forechains pinched off the log line, stopping it from running out freely to the southeast, then studied the knots tied along its length. "Two knots, one and a half fathoms, I make it, sirs," he reported.

Charles, Bevan, and Cromley stood together near the bow. The foretopsail above had been backed against its mast, causing the ship to lay to, resisting the force of the wind. That the log line ran forward indicated that only an ocean current could have carried it along.

"What is your opinion, Mr. Cromley?" Charles asked.

The master shifted uncomfortably. "It might be the Brazil Current."

"What else could it be?"

"Well, it probably is the current," Cromley asserted. "I think."

"Thank you," Charles said. "We are agreed." He turned to Bevan: "We will brace the foresail around to resume, if you please."

As Charles started back toward his quarterdeck he paused on the gangway to consider his circumstance. The French frigate and her larger consort lay just over the horizon in front of them. More significantly, after passing the Trindade and Martin Vaz Islands off Brazil, they had turned their course toward the southeast, the same as his own. This indicated an intention to make for the strong westerly winds near the fortieth parallel to carry them beyond the southern tip of Africa and into the Indian Ocean. Where they might be bound beyond that he could only speculate.

A source of irritation was that the French ships, or at least the seventy-four, now impeded his progress. Charles had ordered that the royals, studdingsails, and even the main course be taken in to avoid overhauling them. He might bend southward and go past, but he disliked having the frigate to windward. He also disliked the idea of following patiently behind while the enemy went on their way unmolested. He began to think whether there might not be some way he could prick at them, if for no other reason than his own satisfaction. There was the previous meeting south of the Canaries to atone for. His crew had improved their performance at the guns. They still lacked experience firing for accuracy, but something could be done about that. Actually firing into an enemy would be a welcome change from hours of dry practice. With Cassandra solidly established to windward, he had the initiative as to how and where any engagement might take place. If there were damage, he could make repairs at Cape Town; the French would have to continue all the way to Mauritius in the Indian Ocean. The more he thought about it, the more it appealed. He decided that the first thing he should do was to announce his intentions.

Charles resumed his way aft. He found Winchester standing officer of the watch near the binnacle. "Stephen, pass the word for the carpenter to make up a raft with a small mast to hang a flag from. For this afternoon's practice we shall attempt a target with powder and ball."

Winchester nodded his head toward the horizon forward of the bow. "The sound will carry, you know."

"I'm sure their lookouts can see us as well as ours can them. I want to remind them we have teeth."

"May I ask why?"

"I am considering running down on them," Charles answered, still working the plan out in his head. "In the morning we will move two of the six-pounders forward and have at them from long range. Then we'll see what they do."

"What they'll do is send the frigate back to settle our porridge," Winchester said.

"They probably will. Have you an opinion as to how we should respond?"

"Attack her," the lieutenant said without hesitation. "The men are up to it now."

"And, if the other, the seventy-four, comes to her assistance, what do we do then?"

Winchester hesitated. "We could draw the frigate away, then attack her," he said.

Charles shook his head. "I think it would be better if we kept our distance. If either of them turns back, we will stand off to windward." It was not a plan he was altogether happy with, but at the moment it seemed the most prudent.

Winchester nodded his acceptance, if not his agreement. Excusing himself, he went to find the carpenter to have the target for the day's gun practice prepared. Charles stood where he was, still thinking. What if the French frigate was ordered back to confront him? It could be an opportunity. Perhaps Winchester had a point; what if he could draw her far enough from the protection of the seventy-four? He would have to wait and see what situation presented itself.

The afternoon rang with the explosions of the twelve- and six-pounders, singly and in pairs, as the gun captains laid their cannon carefully, adjusted the quoins, then pulled the lanyards to spark the powder. As the guns leaped inward, all eyes turned outward to mark the fall of the shot. Sudden geysers spouted up around the bobbing raft that was being towed well behind the jollyboat, a cable's length to starboard. Some skipped along the water with a diminishing series of splashes like a stone cast across a pond. More were long or short than significantly wide. It was easier to peer along the barrel to sight the guns than to judge the elevation for distance. Charles found himself pleased with the two hours of effort and several hundred shot expended, despite that the raft was hoisted back onboard as undamaged as when it had first been put into the water. After the sun had set he ordered the main course sheeted home, but not the studdingsails or royals. He hoped to increase their speed sufficiently to close during the night, but not so much that he might run aboard one of the French ships in the dark.

Charles and Bevan stood together in silent anticipation on the forecastle in the last minutes before dawn the next morning. Both men stared intently at the growing hint of gray to the east.

"Deck there!" the call came down from the tops as he knew it would. "Both t'em Frenchies, dead on the bow." It was almost an unnecessary announcement. Within minutes he could see the silhouettes of the warships' sails against the edge of the lightening sky.

"Can you tell which is closest?" Charles asked.

"The seventy-four," Bevan answered promptly. "I'm thinking she's not more than five miles. The frigate's almost hull down, say, two more."

Charles thought that looked about right. He guessed that he would be close enough to begin in about two hours. "Send the men to their breakfast. Afterward we will clear for action." The first sliver of sun showed above the line of the sea, illuminating the distant sails a brilliant white.

The crew came up from their morning meal to begin preparing the ship for battle. Everything unessential was struck below, the decks cleared, wetted, and sanded. The sun had by now fully risen. The enemy seventy-four lumbered onward over blue-gray seas two and a half miles ahead, seemingly disdainful of the smaller enemy following in her wake. With his glass Charles could easily make out the name Raisonnable across her transom. He saw a cluster of officers looking back at him with their own telescopes. On an impulse, he raised his hat in greeting. No one on the French quarterdeck returned the gesture.

"Mr. Beechum's compliments, sir. The forward six-pounders are prepared as you requested," Sykes reported, appearing at his elbow.

"Thank you," Charles answered. "If you would be so good as to run up our colors." It would be a breach of the etiquette of war to fire on an enemy without showing one's own national flag first. In this circumstance it was also an announcement that Cassandra intended to open with her guns.

Almost as soon as the union flag broke out aloft, the red, white, and blue tricolor of France showed on the warship's mizzen peak. The distance between them had shrunk to a mile and a half, with Cassandra closing. The maximum range of the six-pounder guns was just under a mile. At that distance Charles knew that he would be lucky to hit anything, and if he did it would be a miracle if they did any real damage. But he wasn't hoping to cripple the two-decker, only to irritate her captain and redeem his own ship's honor. Charles thought he saw some activity at her stern. Raising his glass he saw two gun ports below the taffrail open and the barrels of cannon emerge.

"I am going forward," he said to Bevan. "Take the courses in when we begin firing. Mind that we don't get up any closer than necessary. I wish to stay at long range. If she shows any sign of heaving to we will bear away."

"You can be assured on that score," Bevan answered.

At the forecastle he saw Beechum standing with the crews to the two six-pounder long guns, now moved into the bow to fire forward. The French seventy-four appeared larger from this vantage—large enough that she might be just within range. As he watched, twin gray-black clouds bloomed from her stern. An instant later two geysers spurted upwards on the surface of the sea, followed closely by the reports of the guns. Both splashes were to port, one even with the bow, the other a hundred yards short.

"Good morning, Mr. Beechum," Charles said. "As you command the forecastle, you may do the honors."

"Aye, aye, sir," Beechum responded with a grin. "On my command," he said to the two gun captains, standing well behind their weapons with the lanyards to the flintlocks in their hands. Charles could see that the quoins for both guns had been entirely removed for maximum elevation. Cassandra's bow rose as her cutwater breeched a wave.

"Fire!" Beechum shouted.

The two guns exploded inward, their smoke joining into a single cloud as it trailed forward.

"Sponge out."

The balls arced across the water as diminishing black specks to splash down in a direct line with Raisonnable's rudder, forty yards short. "That was good shooting," Charles said.

Beechum grinned in response. "Load with cartridge," he ordered to the gun crews. "Wad and ram home."

"Home!" both captains shouted almost simultaneously, feeling with their wire pricks into the touch holes for the felt powder cartridges.

The French warship fired her stern chasers again. Charles guessed they were nine-pounders from the size of the splashes alongside, one about thirty yards off, the other twice that. "Run 'em up," Beechum ordered. He paused waiting for the bow to rise.

"Fire." The cannon jumped back, their muzzles smoking. Immediately the crews fell to work on them. One ball landed close alongside Raisonnable's quarterdeck with enough spray that it might have doused her officers. Charles smiled. He looked farther forward to see that the French frigate maintained her station two miles ahead.

Comfortable that all was in good hands on the forecastle, he interrupted Beechum long enough to say that he was returning to the quarterdeck. Halfway back along the gangway he heard the guns boom out again, followed by a cheer from the bow. He turned to look.

"We hit her with one!" Beechum yelled happily. "Square on the poop." An angry buzzing screech passed close alongside to port, the splash coming fifty yards forward of the stern. He looked and saw signal flags running up Raisonnable's halyards. Before he reached the quarterdeck, a shout came down from the lookout aloft, "T' frigate's falling off with the wind. She's wearing 'round!"

"You heard?" Bevan said.

Charles nodded. "Maintain our course for the present, but begin to shorten the sails. If the seventy-four shows any sign turning back, we will do the same."

The forecastle guns sounded again. Charles decided he'd made his point. It was time to break off. He looked around for Sykes, didn't see him, but noticed Hitch watching expectantly. "Run forward with my compliments to Lieutenant Beechum," he said. "Tell him I would be pleased to cease firing and to have the guns replaced as they were."

Charles looked for the frigate and saw her head on, her sails braced tight as she came into the wind. Through his glass he could see her men aloft on the yardarms taking in the courses. She was readying herself for battle. Within the half hour she would pass the seventy-four, still holding to her original course. He'd accomplished what he'd wanted—firing into the line of battle ship and actually hitting her. He should be satisfied, even pleased with himself. He could turn away and allow the French ships to continue eastward as they pleased, but he wasn't satisfied. He recalled the earlier encounter with the frigate, how smartly she had handled her sails and guns while his own has floundered in confusion. If he wore around to escape it would appear to all the world—at least to the enemy and to his own crew—that he was running away, afraid of a ship no larger than their own. He looked once more at the two French men of war. The seventy-four showed no sign of turning. By the time the smaller one was up to him, the larger would be five miles or more down wind. That was good enough.

"Lay the foresail against the mast, Daniel," Charles said. "We will come to and wait."

"I thought we were going to turn away," Bevan said.

"I've changed my mind."

"You're sure?"

"I'm sure."

"You're daft," Bevan said, but went to give the orders.

Charles moved forward to call to Winchester in the gundeck. "You may man the port side battery," he shouted down. "Do not run them out until my order."

Winchester smiled broadly as he lifted his hat in acknowledgement.

Cassandra hove to and backed her foretopsail, her broadside toward the advancing enemy. Raisonnable and her frigate passed in opposite directions a mile and a half and more ahead. The frigate came on, straining into the wind, kicking puffs of white spray from her bow as she breached the crests. Charles wondered what her captain was thinking. Surely he remembered their previous encounter where Cassandra could have been taken easily, had the weather cooperated and he not been called off. He would probably still be angry about it, and confident of success. He had no reason not to be confident, even overly so. Charles watched the approaching ship carefully, particularly for any change in the angle of her sails. He guessed that the French had expected him to turn away and run as he had before. Soon it would be clear that he intended to remain as he was. What would her captain decide then? With the wind firm from the north he could only continue on or fall off to the southwest to meet Cassandra beam to beam. If he was cautious he would make the maneuver early; if he assumed Cassandra's handling to be as lubberly as before he might wait until the last moment. Charles hoped he attempted the bolder plan.

The enemy warship continued steadily closer—eight hundred yards, four hundred, her hull cleaving the sea. Charles could see that she had run out her guns on her starboard side. She was within range of his own cannon, but too far away to for the kind of certainty he wanted. The first broadside should come with as much shock as possible. He would wait until he could expect every shot to tell. Charles realized that he was not as assured as he had felt only moments before. His stomach tightened. Despite all their practice, the crew were untested in any meaningful way. For an instant he thought that if he were to be killed he would leave Penny widowed and their child fatherless, never having known him. With an effort he forced the thought away. He judged the frigate to be at a half-cable's distance. "We will present, Daniel," he said.

Bevan relayed the order. Gun ports flipped upward and the rumble of trucks growled in the air. Charles could feel their vibrations through the deck. How would the French captain react to the appearance of Cassandra's guns? The answer came immediately; the frigate's mizzen boom came over and her yards began to brace around. "Fire!" he shouted.

The cannon roared in a single gratifying explosion, the smoke swirling across the bulwarks and out to sea in a low, drifting cloud. Charles saw only one or two waterspouts as the barrage pounded into the frigate's bow. Her bowsprit jerked convulsively near the beak, then angled sharply downward, throwing the jibs into confusion. "You put it off too long," he muttered, as if speaking to the frigate's captain. "You thought we'd be easy, didn't you?"

"Sponge out," Sykes screamed excitedly at the quarterdeck gun crews. Charles heard a call come down from the tops, unintelligible in the shouted orders and struggling seamen on deck.

"Mr. Aviemore," he said without hesitation, "get you up the mainmast." The boy left at a run before he had finished.

The frigate continued her turn, bringing her broadside to bear. Both ships fired together. Round shot screamed across Cassandra's decks. A number crashed against the hull, others struck the sea or flew through the rigging. Charles judged his own salvo had told to better effect. The men swarmed over their weapons with a will. The quarterdeck carronades barked first, soon followed by a half dozen of the twelve-pounders on the gundeck leaping inboard on their carriages. After the briefest of intervals the six-pounders and the remainder of the main armament loudly emptied themselves.

The Frenchman's more disciplined broadside exploded outward in an eruption of black smoke, orange tongues showing through, as the last of Cassandra's died away. Six or seven of the French round shot, he thought, struck home. A loud crack came from close over his head where a ball found the mizzen boom, snapping the spar midway along its length. The mizzen sail bellied loosely, spilling its wind. "Trim the foresails to keep her balanced," Charles said to Bevan.

In threes and fours the faster guns fired again in their deafening roar. Charles noticed that those manned by the Americans were among the quickest. Unaccountably, this pleased him. He studied the French frigate with care. There was noticeable damage to her bulwarks and railings. He was almost certain that one of her main deck twelve-pounders had overturned or been otherwise damaged, and had not run out with the others the broadside before. On the other side of the coin, Cassandra was also knocked about, both to her hull and rigging. He had surprised the Frenchman with his improved gunfire, but the enemy showed no sign of distress. She was well fought, he decided. Having begun, he very much wanted to finish the thing quickly.

Aviemore appeared suddenly beside him, pulling on his sleeve. He had almost forgotten all about the boy and the message from the lookout. Before the midshipman spoke he looked beyond the enemy frigate and knew what it was. "T'other warship's hauled her wind," Aviemore squeaked out, his voice rising ever higher in pitch in his excitement. "She's turned back toward us."

Bevan, who overheard the report, cleared his throat. "We'd best leave it go, Charlie," he said. "We've made our point."

In the distance, through the frigate's tangled rigging, Charles again saw the seventy-four's full length, in the process of wearing around. Signal flags flew from her masts. He didn't want to accept it. "Not yet," he answered. "The seventy-four won't be up to us for almost an hour. The frigate might strike before then."

"No she won't; not with the bigger one coming up. Even if she did there'd be no time for us to board her. And, if we lose a mast in the meantime, the other will run us down at her leisure."

The French frigate enveloped herself in smoke as all her guns fired together. The tops in the mainmast lost half of its deck in a shower of splinters as at least one ball struck it, severing a number of the futtock shrouds. The main topmast promptly canted to port, but thankfully did not fall. That was enough. Charles knew Bevan to be right. He'd wanted to contest the frigate, he'd done it, and the result was a draw. It would be foolish to try for more. "Damn all," he said under his breath, then reluctantly to his lieutenant, "All right, we will break off." He tried to turn his mind to the new problem—disengaging from a close-fought gun duel was no easy thing.

"Wait," Bevan said. "Look."

With smoke still clearing across the frigate's decks Charles saw her yards come around and her topmen scrambling up the shrouds to loosen more canvas. She had also decided, or been ordered, to run. Her head fell off with the wind as she wore back toward her companion. As the stern showed, he saw her name: L'Agile. Cassandra's cannon fired off a final broadside in a prolonged tearing series of explosions. A number struck the frigate's after structure, smashing in a pair of the windows across the stern, others sending up spouts of water close alongside. The gun crews then stood by their weapons and cheered.

"Cease firing," Charles said. He knew he should be satisfied. Cassandra had acquitted herself well enough; the French had turned away first. He had made his point; his honor and that of his ship had been redeemed. He looked around him at his quarterdeck to survey their damage. Some railing and hammock netting had been beaten away, and an off-side carronade lay broken, its slide shattered and the barrel upset on the deck. He saw two men lacerated by flying splinters sitting propped against the binnacle, waiting to be taken below. He turned back to Bevan. "The butcher's bill?"

"I'm guessing it's not too bad. A half-dozen or so injuries; Mr. Owens will say for sure. The lookout in the tops had a near religious experience when a goodly piece of his platform disappeared, fortunately not the bit he was standing on."

"House the guns and stand the men down," Charles said. "Start the repairs immediately. I'll hear the carpenter's, boatswain's, and surgeon's reports as they have the time. For the moment, I think it best to stay where we are until we see what those other two decide to do."

If the larger French warship continued to beat into the wind toward him, Cassandra would have to turn and run. But Charles doubted she would. The seventy-four had never shown any special interest in the smaller English ship. Still, he watched with relief as Raisonnable took the frigate under her lee, and then wore again to resume her former course.

Mr. Burrows approached after a time with a lengthy list of needed repairs, the most serious of which were shot holes in the hull between wind and water, and the mainmast tops which would have to be replaced before the topmast shrouds could be repaired. Similarly, William Baker, the boatswain, presented a seemingly unending enumeration of cut lines and cables which he insisted on going through item by item. The main thing Charles took away was that a suitable replacement for the cracked mizzen boom could not be obtained until they reached Cape Town; sistering a smaller spar along its length would do for now. The surgeon's report confirmed what Bevan had told him earlier. In all, Charles considered, he had gotten off relatively lightly. It could have been very different if he had come under the guns of the seventy-four.

Late in the afternoon Cassandra resumed under easy sails, keeping the French in sight, their hulls just over the horizon. In the morning the enemy had vanished, even to the lookouts in the masts. Consensus among the officers on the quarterdeck was that the pair had turned south during the night in order to shake Cassandra from their wake. Charles had no argument with this. He wondered again where the French warships might be bound that the senior captain in the seventy-four would keep the frigate on such a tight leash. There must be some urgency about his orders. For the first time he considered the possibility—just the possibility—that their destination was the Red Sea to aid this General Bonaparte's supposed conquest of India. It seemed to him improbable. There were a dozen more likely places they could have orders for, but it was not impossible.

CHAPTER SIX

"You may begin the salute, Mr. Sykes," Charles said, pleased in spite of himself at the growing extent of land off the starboard bow. Cassandra passed Green Point, her ensign streaming from the main peak, her recognition signal and number on the signal halyards. The forts and settlement of Cape Town revealed themselves in a low line beneath the forbidding slopes of Table Mountain. She sailed large, under all plain sail, on a tack that would easily clear the headlands at the entrance to the harbor.

"Fire the first," Sykes ordered gravely. The near most quarterdeck six-pounder boomed out its powder charge, the sound echoing back from the heights beyond the bay.

"One . . . , two. . . , three," Charles heard the midshipman count out under his breath. At "five," he announced, "Fire number two." The gun captain yanked the lanyard to the flint lock and the next gun jumped inward. Coincident with the third gun firing off, an embrasure of the closer fort emitted a cloud of smoke, beginning its return of the ceremonial greeting. Charles saw a number of John Company ships, the large armed merchantmen of the Honorable East India Company, moored in the harbor. It being March, a late-summer sun shone down, pleasantly warming the afternoon air. Raising his long glass, he watched the pilot boat push off from the waterfront to guide them to their anchorage off the port. It was an agreeable little place to make landfall, he decided. The Dutch buildings seemed somehow both familiar and strangely foreign with their narrow fronts and curiously embellished gables. The colony had been taken from Holland four years before after the Low Countries had fallen under the dominion of France.

Charles noticed that a number of the crew had gathered along the lee rail of the gangway in their best clothing in anticipation of leave to go on shore. He wasn't comfortable about this and had not decided whether to allow them to do so. The men had behaved themselves reasonably well over the past weeks and had shown marked improvement during the most recent encounter with the French. The bickering and arguments had trailed off—or at least he thought it had—there had been few incidents reported to him in the interval. It would be appropriate, expected even, that he reward them with time ashore. There would be some who would take the opportunity to run, he was sure, especially among the Americans. It would be awkward to search them all out and escort them back to the ship. He looked again at the men by the rail, talking among themselves while staring at the port. It wasn't a particularly large place, he decided; rounding them up shouldn't be too much trouble.

The harbor cutter approached and Charles ordered that the courses be taken in and the ship heaved to so that the pilot might safely board under their lee. There was some grousing among the topmen sent aloft, a number of whom had to be called away from the railing. Cassandra drifted a little past the cutter, which had to reverse its course to catch them up. Charles frowned at the lapse. He was embarrassed at this new display of inept seamanship, but decided not to make an issue of it. Bevan could apply minor punishments as he saw fit; no real harm had been done, aside from inconveniencing the pilot.

"I do most sincerely apologize, sir," Charles said as the man climbed through the entry port. A number of the topmen, British and American alike, were descending the mainmast shrouds a few feet away.

"Got lubbers for a crew, have you?" the pilot answered testily. "I've seen better ship handling on scows."

Before Charles could answer, one of the topmen, just having reached the deck, cast his eyes upward at another. "It's you Yanks what done it, you know. Ye'r all as slow as Boston whores."

"Shut your fuckin' gob, Limey, or I'll shut it for you," the American replied. "It weren't me gawkin' over the rail."

"Belay that kind of talk," Charles snapped at the two. They were being closely followed down the ratlines by a dozen more. He turned back to the pilot. "It's been a long voyage, and a trying one," he said. "It'll be a blessing to be in port."

"All right, then. We'll get underway, shall . . . " The pilot stopped in mid-sentence, his eyes wide, staring over Charles' shoulder. "My God," he uttered.

Charles turned. At the head of the ladderway to the gundeck a knot of topmen returning below were pushing and shoving. One threw a fist. The recipient tumbled bodily down the stairs while others rushed up from below to join in the confrontation. In an instant, half the crew were wrestling and punching in a disorganized, seething mass. Charles looked on in disbelief.

"Avast there!" Bevan bellowed, hurrying as best he could on his gimpy leg toward the growing disturbance. "Sergeant at Arms! Where are the marines? Stop that; I'll have order, do you hear me?"

None of the words made much impression that Charles could tell. His first thought was to stop it, with force if necessary. Then he decided not to. Afterward he would show them that he would tolerate no more. "Excuse me for a moment, if you will," he said to the astonished pilot. He then started back toward the quarterdeck. "Lieutenant Bevan," he shouted over the melee.

Bevan looked up, his eyes wide in frustration. "I've sent for Ayres to fetch his marines," he sputtered. "We'll have order restored one way or another in a moment."

Charles shook his head. "Let it go. This has been building since we left Chatham. Maybe a good fight will help to get it out of their system."

"Do you think so?" Bevan said, unconvinced.

"Maybe," Charles answered. The men were packed so tightly in the still growing fracas that there was little room to cock an arm or deliver a blow. Most of the conflict appeared to involve grappling at close quarters. There would be scrapes and bruises aplenty, he thought, the odd broken nose, and any number of lost teeth, but few serious injuries. He saw Baker and his two mates approaching from forward along the gangway, staring incredulously at the uproar. "Clear the ladderway, if you please," Charles ordered as two men spilled onto the quarterdeck. "Do not intervene otherwise."

Baker nodded with a grim smile and touched his forehead. "Aye, aye, sir," he said. The three petty officers moved to the head of the stairs, picked up the first seaman they came to and pushed him back onto the heads of the men below. A second quickly followed as Charles noticed Lieutenant Ayres, his sword drawn, at the head of a file of red-coated marines hurrying aft.

"Your orders, sir?" Ayres said, his eyes on the confusion in the waist.

Charles scratched his chin. "Line your men along the break of the quarterdeck," he said. "We will do nothing for the moment. Once they have worn themselves down we'll sort them out." He glanced again at the struggling mob below, then decided he should return and speak to the harbor pilot before the man gave up in dismay and left.

"It's a fine day, isn't it, Mr . . . , Mr. . . ," he spoke to the pilot, still standing with a disbelieving expression at the place where he had come on board.

"Barkley," the man answered, then stared at Charles. "Is this a normal occurrence?"

Charles grimaced. He wasn't answerable to the harbor pilot but he had to say something. "There are some hard feelings among the crew. We will be ready to proceed as soon as they are finished."

"You're going to tolerate this?" Barkley asked. To Charles it sounded like an accusation.

"Until they're done," Charles answered tersely. "Then I'll deal with it."

The brawl continued for a relatively short time, a broiling mass of forms. Charles didn't think they knew who they were fighting—landsman, seamen, Americans, British—all seemed to be working out their discontent on whomever was closest. He pulled out his watch and looked at it. He would give them a quarter of an hour—if it lasted that long. After five minutes he thought he detected a flagging in their enthusiasm. Individual seamen began to stagger out from the midst of the fray to collapse on a clear space on the deck, more from exhaustion than injury; nose bleeds seemed a common ailment, although some might be more serious. Charles turned to Midshipman Hitch, watching the contest with considerable enthusiasm. "My complements to the surgeon, if you please," he said calmly. "I would appreciate his presence on the gundeck as he has the leisure. Ask that he bring a goodly supply of dressings and unguents."

"Aye, aye, sir," Hitch responded and hurried along the gangway toward the bow, where he could descend in relative safety to the surgeon's quarters by way of the forward hatch.

Charles checked his watch again. There was more moaning and gasping for breath than cursing coming from the waist. The men lay mostly in an undifferentiated heap on the deck. Here and there an effort was made to strike a blow or simply to clear some space. "Lieutenant Ayres," he called. "If you would be so good as to send your men down to separate the combatants."

"Yes, sir," Ayres answered. He gave the necessary orders and the marines started down the ladderway, collecting bodies and dragging them without ceremony to the unoccupied parts of the deck. Owens arrived with his case of supplies, and began moving from man to man in search of the more seriously injured.

"Daniel," Charles said next. "We'll give them a few moments to catch their breath. Then I want them on their feet, those that are able, and aligned in their divisions."

"What are you going to do?" Bevan asked, visibly furious at what had happened.

Charles frowned. "There'll be no shore leave, that's a fact. I intend to lay down the law."

"Floggings?" Bevan prompted. "You can't let this go with a slap on the wrist."

"You can't flog the whole crew," Charles answered evasively. He had yet to come to a final decision on what he would do. Bevan was right in at least one respect: He could not overlook it. He watched with as much patience as he could muster as the men were sorted out. A number, having recovered some of their strength, pushed themselves into sitting positions. A few were ordered below by the surgeon where he might better treat broken bones or dislocated fingers. Soon, Bevan sent Winchester and Beechum, the midshipmen and petty officers down to get the men to their feet and into some sort of order. They were a sorry mess with torn clothing, missing hats, some with only one shoe. Any number had blood down their fronts from bleeding noses or minor cuts.

"The men are all present and sober," Bevan reported when he was satisfied that the crew were assembled in as orderly a fashion as they were going to get. "Except for those with the surgeon, of course." Their sobriety was not Charles' greatest concern.

Charles nodded and stepped to the forward edge of the quarterdeck where everyone could see and hear him. The faces below, bruised and scuffed though they were, mostly looked up dully, some sheepishly, a few with some satisfaction. He spoke loudly: "If you poor sods fought half as hard with the French as you do against each other, the war would be over by now." There were a few grins at this, as he knew there would be. Now he resolved to wipe them away. "Do you want to fight with your own shipmates?" he went on. "Fine. Fight to your hearts' content. But if anything like this occurs again, not a man jack of you will set foot ashore at any port of call so long as I am captain of this ship."

The grins vanished, as did any expressions of satisfaction. "What about Cape Town?" a voice shouted up.

"Silence there," Bevan growled.

Charles lifted his hand in forbearance. "There will be no shore leave in Cape Town," he answered. "I had planned to allow it, but you have scotched that." The seaman opened his mouth to protest. Charles spoke first. "It is not a question that is open for discussion. I will not have this kind of behavior on board my ship. In the future, any man caught taunting or fighting will receive a dozen lashes for the first offense. There will be two dozen for the second, three for the third, and on, until you get it into your heads that I won't tolerate it." There, he'd said it. He hoped that the threat would be sufficient. "If you expect liberty in port in the future, you will have to earn it by your good behavior. Is that understood?"

Bevan looked at him with a surprised expression. "Do you mean it?" he said.

Charles nodded reluctantly. "Yes, I mean it. Now, if you please, we've still to make port. Set the men--those that are able--to trim the sails. I will go and apologize to the pilot for the delay."

"Hoist out the jollyboat, if you please," Charles said. "See that the mail is passed down. I'm to call on the port admiral; be back by suppertime, I expect." As soon as the boat went down over the side and its crew had settled in, Charles climbed down. He seated himself in the sternsheets, two satchels—one with dispatches he carried from England, the other with the ship's mail to be returned there—lay at his feet.

Cassandra had finally come to rest in the Cape Town roads almost a half mile from the harbor front. It was not an ideal anchorage since it left them exposed to the steady westerly winds and steep rollers sweeping across the Atlantic, but the increased distance and rough seas would discourage most from jumping ship to attempt the swim ashore.

"Out oars," Malvern ordered. "All pull." The boat started across the chop for the long row into the port. As they neared, Charles saw that a party had gathered at the end of the closest pier. A welcoming committee of some sort, he assumed. Since the pilot boat had returned earlier, word of the activities of his crew would have long since spread up and down the waterfront. He was already in a sour frame of mind and did not relish having to explain why there had been a riot on his ship in the very mouth of the harbor.

"Boat yer oars," Malvern snapped at the boat's crew. "Smartly now, damn yer eyes. Dick, get a hook on that ladderway." At least the coxswain was making an attempt to show that Cassandra was a capably manned and disciplined ship. Of course, the large black bruise around one eye, already swelling shut, went some way to counter the impression. The boat pulled alongside the ladder; Charles stepped across and climbed upward.

The first person he encountered on the surface of the dock greeted him warmly. "Captain Edgemont, what? May I welcome you to the Cape Colonies? I am Samuel Cobbham." The speaker was a middle-aged man with a round face and a comfortable paunch. He wore the undress uniform of a vice admiral in the Royal Navy. "It's a pleasure to greet a real navy man for once, eh? Mostly we get those John Company duffers; not real captains, if you take my drift. The Admiralty has informed me that you"d be passing our way, don't you know?"

"Thank you, sir," Charles answered, touching his hat carefully and looking for something solid to hold onto. He found himself unsure of his balance on the rigidly unmoving surface of the wharf.

Cobbham laughed. "Been at sea long, what?"

"Eighty-one days from Chatham, sir. I expect it will take me a time to find my land legs."

"Eighty-one days, eh? Long enough for your lads to work up some raw feelings, I do hear." The admiral's eyes narrowed a fraction. "Is everything shipshape where your people are concerned, or do you require some assistance, eh?"

Charles hesitated. He could fob off any excuse to the harbor pilot, but he didn't want to lie to the Admiral. He didn't want to admit that he couldn't control his own crew either. "It's not as serious as it might have appeared to the pilot," he said carefully. "Just at present I have factions among my crew. We recently pressed a number of Americans at Bunce Island and they haven't adjusted to their role on board as of yet. I expect to have the matter in hand before long."

Cobbham glanced reflectively at Cassandra, absurdly small in the in the distance, then back at Charles. "I see," he said easily. "It doesn't do to pry too closely into other officers' methods is my rule, but if you're to require resupply, she's going to have to come into the harbor."

Charles said nothing to this.

"If you're worried about your men running," the admiral continued gently, "I'd be more than pleased to post sentries for any strays that find their way ashore. I wouldn't be concerned if I were you, it happens more often than you'd think, don't you know?"

"Thank you," Charles said. "That would be welcome."

"Otherwise, an uneventful voyage, eh?" the admiral said, seemingly unconcerned as to Charles' other problems. As he spoke, Augustus climbed up onto the pier with the mail bags and stood behind Charles in an expectant attitude. "Collect that if you will, Peters," Cobbham ordered an assistant standing close by.

"We encountered a pair of French warships along the way, a frigate and a seventy-four, sir," Charles answered, thankful at the change of topic. "I am certain they will pass by the Cape into the Indian Ocean."

If he thought the admiral would be alarmed by this, he was mistaken. "There's always some going back and forth to Mauritius. It's a damned nuisance. Still, a ship of the line is somewhat unusual, what? But enough of this chit-chat is my thought. Come along to my office and we'll make quick work of whatever official business there is. You'll be staying to supper, of course. Mrs. C. will be dying for the latest news from home, don't you know?"

"I'd be honored, sir," Charles said. He noticed that Augustus was still positioned resolutely behind him. He guessed that his steward wouldn't know what he was supposed to do and so naturally stayed where he was until instructed otherwise. "You may go back to the ship," he said. "I'll return later this evening."

Augustus stayed in place, looking uncertainly around him. "I'll just follow with you, Cap'n, if I may," he said.

"Whatever for?"

The man's eyes narrowed and his face assumed a serious expression. "In case somethin' were to happen, Cap'n."

"What could . . ." It came to Charles that Augustus was concerned that some harm might come to him in a foreign port, English governed or otherwise. He remembered that Penny had appointed him as a kind of bodyguard, and while thoughtful, it would be awkward to have the man trailing him everywhere he went. "This is British soil," he said. "I'll be as safe as in my own home. You may return to the ship with an easy mind. In fact, I insist on it. I'll be back later in the evening."

Augustus looked doubtful, but went down into the boat. Charles told Malvern to inform Lieutenant Bevan that he would return later than he'd expected.

A mercifully short walk took them to a low stone building that was the Port Admiral's headquarters. Cobbham ushered him through a small anteroom with a pair of clerks at their desks and into a spacious, well-lit office furnished more like a parlor than a place of business.

"Sit, sit, Captain. We don't stand on formality in this far outpost of the Empire, what? Will you take some refreshment?"

"Coffee, if you have it," Charles said, removing his hat and seating himself in a cushioned chair.

"Coffee? You're sure? The navy isn't what it used to be, eh?" Cobbham summoned a servant and gave instructions for a mug of coffee and a glass of sherry. "To business then," he said, easing himself into an adjacent seat. "I find it's best get the preliminaries out of the way in the beginning, don't you think? We are reasonably well stocked for victuals, water, firewood, that sort of thing. You have only to supply me a list. Is there anything else you require, what? Anything, anything at all, eh?"

Charles found the admiral's manner of speech somewhat difficult to follow, but the fellow seemed genuinely pleased for company and was certainly amiable enough. "In addition to the normal kinds of supplies, I would appreciate the opportunity to top off my powder and shot, and the replacement of a mizzen spar."

Cobbham raised his eyebrows. "What?" he said.

"I mentioned that Cassandra encountered two French national ships on our way south. We engaged the frigate on two occasions. My report on both incidents is in the mail satchel."

"Damages? Outcome? Eh?"

"Aside from the mizzen, there's nothing we haven't been able to replace ourselves. The results of both engagements were inconclusive."

"I see," Cobbham said thoughtfully. "Inconclusive, was it? Well, I'm sure we can provide satisfaction where your needs are concerned. That's why we're here, don't you know."

"I have two additional items, if I may."

The admiral nodded happily. "Of course, of course."

"My orders are that I am to take onboard certain passengers at Cape Town, to carry them into the Red Sea. I am also instructed to call on the governor for any recent intelligence he may have for that region."

"Yes, yes. I have already sent word to the residence that you might be calling on His Excellency in the morning. Time enough for that, I do think. I am also familiar with Mr. Jones and his—what should I say?—party. They've lodgings in the town, don't you know? If I may take the liberty, I find them passingly odd. Very secretive, don't socialize at all, no matter how many invitations are sent out. There's something strange afoot there to my mind, what?" He took a sip from his glass, sighed in appreciation, then replaced it on the table. "So you're bound for the Red Sea, are you? Bit of a red herring, that." He chuckled to himself. "Do you follow? Red Sea, red herring, what?"

Charles smiled politely.

"Admiral Blankett's station, don't you know? You'll find no joy there; hotter than the embers of hell itself. Frightened to death in India that the French'll come down from Egypt to join with Tippu Sahib, the Sultan of Mysore, and toast their muffins for them. Of course, no such thing will happen. Can't, there's no transport for that kind of thing, what? Besides which, Blankett's got the exit to the sea corked up with his frigates; besides which, the governor-general in Bombay just recently declared war on ol' Tippu, don't you know? That'll be settled soon to my thinking."

"No, I didn't know," Charles said. "About the war against Mysore, I mean. Have they begun an offensive?"

"Oh, no," Cobbham said, dismissing the idea with the wave of his hand. "There's plenty of time for that. Still searching about for the right officer to lead them. I hear tell it might be young Colonel Wellesley put into command, that's the scuttlebutt, don't you know?"

"Yes, er, no," Charles answered, thinking that a question may have been asked. Any news Cobbham would have from India would already be months old. Anything or nothing could have happened since then. One thing was clear, that the port admiral at Cape Town, considerably closer to the area in question than the Admiralty, had few worries about a further French excursion from Egypt toward India.

"Oh, my! Look at the time!" Cobbham exclaimed suddenly. "Mrs. C. will be sorely disappointed if we are late to sup. We must be off." The admiral rose, leaving his half-full glass on the table. "We shall walk, eh? It's only just up the hill."

Charles followed as Cobbham passed through the anteroom to the out of doors. From what he could tell, the building was now entirely empty, without clerks, laborers, or servants. Activity along the waterfront had also largely ceased. The Cape Town dockyard was not a twenty-four-hours-a-day concern, he decided.

As they climbed a winding cobblestone drive up the hillside, the admiral asked, "You're not married by chance, are you?"

The question brought Penny's face before his eyes. If all was well she would have birthed by now. Perhaps at this very . . .

"Eh?"

Charles pulled himself up. "What? Yes, I am, sir. Very happily so, if I may say. Why do you ask?"

Cobbham clicked his tongue several times as he huffed his way up the lane. "My daughter, Arabella, will be pleased by your presence, don't you know? Comely enough, but too clever for her own good, if you ask me. Too clever for the local lads anyway, what? There's plenty of dead wood around here, I don't have to tell you, I'm sure. Mrs. C. and I are ever hopeful of finding someone suitable. I suppose we'll have to arrange something back home." He fell silent for a moment, then laughed. "If you mention to Arabella I said that, Captain, I'll court martial you, eh? She's an independent thinker, that one." Then he laughed again.

The admiral's house, when they came to it, was a comfortable place and reasonably substantial in appearance. Charles noticed several native African groundsmen working in the gardens. At the entrance they were greeted by yet another black servant in livery who took his hat and sword.

"There you are, Mr. C." A cherubic, middle-sized woman swept into the foyer. She was pleasantly, if amply, proportioned, with an irresistible smile. Charles guessed she would be Mrs. Cobbham. The two even resembled each other. He could only imagine what their daughter's appearance might be and why there was such difficulty finding a match for her.

"My dear, this is Captain Edgemont of the frigate in the harbor. Just arrived, don't you know?" the admiral announced. "Captain E., Mrs. C., eh?"

"Ain't I pleased to meet ye, what?" the woman dipped a curtsey and held out her hand to be kissed.

Charles obliged and then said, "It is my honor, madam," which seemed appropriate in the moment.

"Don't I want to hear everything from home, don't you know?" Mrs. Cobbham said cheerfully, taking his arm and leading him to a too colorfully decorated parlor off the hallway. As soon as Charles had been seated and offered refreshment she launched into a series of observations and inquiries focused on the latest gossip relating to the lives of the much-admired King George and his somewhat notorious offspring. It was a subject about which Charles had little knowledge other than hearsay, but he answered politely where he could and expressed regret for his ignorance where he could not. Either response seemed to please equally.

After a time in this occupation he heard the admiral, who had largely left the floor to his wife, say, "Ah, there you are, my dear."

Charles turned to acknowledge the new presence. His heart stopped. Framed in the doorway stood a slender young woman of considerable beauty.

She wore a low-scooped gown with a tight bodice and long blond hair pulled back from her face so that it fell in ringlets on bare white shoulders. A high forehead, bright blue eyes and a wide smiling mouth completed an appearance so closely resembling Penny that for an instant he thought it must be her.

"Are you well, sir?" Arabella approached, concern on her face.

Charles was cast into confusion as he stumbled to his feet. "I'm sorry . . . I apologize." He struggled to regain his composure. The woman awakened such a yearning that he did not trust himself to speak.

The admiral saved him. "Arabella, this is Captain Edgemont. Fresh from home he is, what?"

"I'm very pleased to meet you, captain, I'm sure," the girl said, still looking at him doubtfully.

"I do apologize. I am honored to make your acquaintance," Charles said, his heartbeat returning to almost normal. He carefully shook the offered hand instead of kissing it. Arabella seated herself on a sofa near him and began a new interrogation on the various intrigues surrounding the royal family. "I want to know everything there is, don't you know?" she said happily. Charles found his composure returning by degrees as he watched her and answered her questions. She was not the twin of Penny, he realized, and any resemblance was superficial. The thought crossed his mind that any young woman he encountered during this long separation might remind him of her. Fortunately, where he was going, any such occasion would be rare.

Late in the evening, following a leisurely and surprisingly enjoyable supper, Charles begged to return, asserting that pressing duties awaited him. Cobbham insisted on providing a carriage to convey him back to the waterfront, and the admiral's barge was rousted out to carry him to his ship.

"Has there been any further trouble with the men?" Charles asked Beechum as he climbed onto Cassandra's deck.

"No, sir. All's quiet. How was your time ashore?"

"About as pleasant as could be expected, what? eh? don't you know?" Charles answered, then made his way below.

In the morning he spoke with Bevan about moving into the harbor, then met with Mr. Wells to review with him the list of foodstuffs, water, and firewood required to replenish their supplies. That completed, he sent for the ship's gunner to obtain an accounting of their expended powder and shot, and then for the boatswain about the replacement of the mizzen boom. By nine-thirty he had changed into his best shirt and breeches. He allowed Augustus to help him into his full-dress frock coat with its heavy bullion lace and trimmings, which he wore only for the most official of occasions. An interview with His Excellency, the Honorable Sir Horace St. Legier, the British governor for the Cape Colonies, was clearly such an event. He noticed that his steward was also clothed with unusual care, with a short jacket, hat, and neckerchief over clean trousers made of sailcloth, and newly blacked shoes. Augustus looked quite presentable, Charles thought, and he knew why. "It's not necessary for you to accompany me, you know," he said.

"I'm thinkin' I should come, Cap'n. Just in case." Augustus answered with his usual fixed expression.

Charles knew that sooner or later he was going to have to put a stop to this. There was no harm to it, but it was embarrassing, as if he needed protection. "All right, this time if it pleases you. But be assured, I can manage on my own."

"Yes, Cap'n."

At the dockside, Charles hired a glorified farm cart with two aging dobbins that passed as a carriage. The thing jolted along on its unsprung axles through the town's market square and up a broad cobbled way to the residency. The building stood as an imposing structure on the crest of a low hill with a panoramic view of the harbor. It took him only a moment to pick out his own ship, small in the distance, an oblong black and tan form surrounded by dark blue waters. She had evidently pulled her anchor and was even then dropping her topgallants to move closer into the port.

"Captain Edgemont of His Majesty's Frigate Cassandra," Charles announced to the corporal of the guard at the arching wrought-iron gates.

"Sir." The red-coated soldier saluted, touching the back of his open hand to his forehead, in the army fashion. Two privates opened the barrier, and the carriage passed into the courtyard. Charles ordered the driver to wait, and then stepped down. Augustus immediately moved to follow. "You will have to stay with the carriage," Charles said firmly. "I hope not to be long." Without waiting for an objection he turned and started toward the entrance.

"May I know your business, sir?" another uniformed attendant inquired as he stepped inside.

"Captain Edgemont to see Sir Horace. I am expected." Charles looked around him with some curiosity at the high-ceilinged hall with its marble floor and oddly foreign ornamentation.

"This way, if you please," said the attendant, indicating a side door which led into a small anteroom. "His Excellency will be at his leisure presently. Please make yourself comfortable." He left, closing the door firmly behind him.

Charles made himself comfortable for two full hours. After a half an hour, he rose to examine the oil paintings hung from the walls. They were in the Dutch style and tended to be portraits of men with beards in black suits against dark backgrounds. One was of a woman with deep eyes and a small mouth that reminded him of Lady Hamilton, whom he had met in Naples the year before. When he finished the portraits he examined a large globe of the world with interest, even though all of the place names were in Dutch, some of which he could not read. A case of books against one wall housed texts in Dutch, French and German. He found one, however, that was a leather-bound atlas, which he had open on his lap when finally summoned.

"This way, sir. Sir Horace will see you now. You may have a quarter hour of his time."

St. Legier was a tall, formally dressed man with a superior, suffer-no-fools look about him. As Charles entered he rose from behind a highly polished desk bare of any papers or implements or objects of any kind. "Captain Edgehill, I apologize for keeping you waiting." He extended his hand.

"Edgemont," Charles corrected. The two men shook.

"Edgemont," St. Legier repeated. "Please be seated. I assume you are on your way to Bombay to join the East India Fleet?"

"No, sir. My orders are for Mocha on the Red Sea to join Admiral Blankett's squadron. I had hoped you might have some recent intelligence on the situation there."

"Do you mean the rumor of the French coming down from Egypt?" He scowled. "Has Whitehall nothing more pressing to worry about? I have heard no credible evidence of such a threat. Dreamed up by a gaggle of Admiralty clerks in petticoats, I'll wager. Frankly, it is a fantastic notion to begin with, and I can tell you on some authority that the government on the subcontinent are taking steps to settle this Tippu Sahib business for once and all. That is serious; this other about the French is nonsense." His face changed expression. "Mocha? Are you connected with that American group in some way? I seem to remember that Araby was mentioned in connection to them."

"I'm to provide transport. Why do you ask?"

"Why? Because I ordered the lot of them arrested this morning. That's why."

Charles held his breath. "Arrested? On what charge?"

"On the charge of bigamy." St. Legier assumed a look of moral indignation. "Do you know that this man Jones has been living openly with two women? One is young enough to be my daughter. He has not denied it. The courts will make quick work of this case."

Charles' heart sank. Christ, what else could go wrong? Already he had been sent into distant waters for what in all probability was no purpose, he had a bullheaded crew, and he'd had to contend with two French warships just to get as far as he had. Taking Jones to gather his intelligence was most likely the only useful thing he would accomplish. "But, sir," he said, "I'm told Doctor Jones is a follower of Muhammad. Multiple wives are usual among them."

"An American and a Mussulman? I don't believe it. Doesn't matter in any event; the laws are clear."

Charles had some difficulty with this concept as well, and he chose not to argue the point. Jones, if that was his real name, was clearly a very odd bird. He didn't really know if the man was American, a doctor of antiquities as he had once claimed, a Mussulman, or if he was in fact married to anyone. All he knew for certain was what was in his orders. "When do you anticipate they will come to trial?" he asked.

"In a month, not more than two," St. Legier answered. "The formalities must be observed, you know. I promise to see they receive their punishments immediately they are convicted so as not to detain you needlessly."

Charles felt a rising sense of alarm. He could not possibly sit in Cape Town harbor with his crew confined on board for a month, or two, or no one knew how long. There would hardly be any point in going on after that. "Sir, if I may speak in confidence," he said, struggling to keep any note of desperation out of his voice. "Jones and his, er, companions are charged by the Admiralty with a mission of the utmost delicacy regarding French intentions in Egypt. My orders are to carry them into the head of the Red Sea without delay. Surely you have some discretion to release them."

St. Legier did not hesitate. "No, I will not do it. Bigamy is a serious crime, sir; it's in the Bible. They must stand trial and have their punishment. As for the other, I am certain the situation with the French will be the same in a month or two, or even a year, as it is today. There's no urgency there."

If a sense of urgency was required, Charles knew that he would have to supply it. "I should inform Your Excellency of more recent intelligence that I conveyed to Admiral Cobbham only yesterday. Intelligence which I trust you will find changes the situation significantly."

St. Legier straightened in his chair. "What intelligence?"

"Off Cape Verde and again in the southern latitudes, we encountered a force of French warships on the same course as our own. I have followed in their wake long enough to determine that they have passed the Cape, very possibly on their way to aid in the attack on India. The Joneses must be taken to Egypt to do their work before it is too late. The future of India, no, even of Britain itself may depend on it." Charles was surprised that the tale came out so easily. Once he'd said it though, it didn't seem so preposterous. It wasn't true, or it probably wasn't true, but it could be. "Time is precious, sir," he continued. "I must sail, with the Americans, the moment we are reprovisioned. On behalf of the Admiralty, I must insist on it."

The governor hesitated, but maintained a firm scowl.

Charles decided he would have to come up with something more. "What kind of punishment is normal for bigamy?" he asked.

"A public whipping for all concerned and banishment," St. Legier answered thoughtfully. "It's not in my power to brand people any longer."

"Would it be possible to release them into my custody? In that way, they could do their work and I can see them brought safely back to Cape Town on my return."

St. Legier stroked his chin in contemplation. "You will guarantee their presence at trial?"

"I must of necessity put them on shore in Egypt, otherwise there is no point. It is always possible they will be captured or even killed. I cannot be responsible in that event."

"But what it they decide to take the opportunity to run?"

Charles allowed himself a small smile. "In that case they have banished themselves. None of them could ever return here. Your problem would be solved."

A door opened and an attendant, the same that had called Charles in, half entered. "Heer Johannes de Groote and his delegation are arrived, sir," he announced.

"Damned Dutch farmers," St. Legier muttered under his breath. "You'd think they'd be grateful the French don't occupy the Cape Colonies. A more obstinate bunch of ingrates I never saw."

Charles rose from his chair. "And the Americans?"

The governor assumed a displeased look. "Oh, all right, since you insist. Just a moment, I'll write you a note to the jailer."

Charles found Augustus standing patiently with his arms folded across his chest, leaning against a pillar, just outside the entrance to the building. "Come along, we've an errand to run," Charles said as he passed.

They found the driver laid out on one of the benches in the back with his jacket covering his shoulders and face. "Wake up, it's time we were off," Charles urged, pulling the covering away.

The man blinked, than sat up and rubbed his eyes. "Back to the waterfront, sir?"

"No." Charles pulled himself on board over the tailgate. "To the jail. Do you know where it is?"

"Aye," the driver climbed forward to his bench. "Why would you want to be going there for?"

"The governor has been gracious enough to give me my pick. Hurry, I want to arrive before all the good ones are gone."

Cape Town's gaol proved a dingy, low stone building with a single door and no windows. An imposing gallows stood in front. The smell of the place was evident from a distance; even the horses shied at it.

Charles recalled that he had encountered Doctor Adolphus Jones twice, both times during the previous year. The first was off Cadiz in Spain. Dressed as some sort of academic, the man had convinced a Spanish port official to carry him and his two women out from the harbor to the English frigate Charles commanded. On that occasion he had brought the intelligence that a large French fleet was preparing to sail from Toulon. The women, Charles thought he remembered, had been introduced as his wife and a niece. The second time was at Acre, at the far end of the Mediterranean. There, in Arab dress, he informed Charles that the French had landed at Alexandria, in Egypt, information which ultimately contributed to Nelson's victory at Abukir Bay.

"I do not expect to be long," Charles said to the driver. He dismounted the carriage, signaling Augustus to follow, and stepped to the heavily studded wooden door. The nearer he came, the more noxious the odor that swept over him. The door would not budge so he banged loudly several times. As he was about to knock again a panel opened and a pair of eyes peered out.

"What d'ye want?"

"I am a king's officer," Charles said. "I have come to collect three of your prisoners. If I may enter, please."

The panel closed. Charles heard a bar slide back. The door opened just enough for him to see an unshaven man in soiled clothing standing with a ring of keys on his belt. The stench of feces and sour body odor from within was almost overpowering.

"Lemme see yer paper," the man demanded.

Charles took the note from St. Legier and handed it over. "I am in a hurry, if you please." He thought the foul emanations from inside would make him retch.

He held the paper in front of his eyes. "It ain't the proper form," the man said firmly. "You have to have to proper forms—one for each."

"I'll have them sent around later," Charles growled. He pushed on the door to open it wider. The man pushed back. Charles nodded to Augustus. "If you would, please."Augustus stepped forward, put his shoulder against the wood and the portal swung back.

Charles forced his way inside and instantly regretted it. "How do you breathe in this place?" he said. "The smell is atrocious."

"What smell?"

"Never mind," Charles said, wanting to get the thing done without delay. "Release my prisoners and hurry about it." He looked around him and saw a small, unlit space with a table and a single chair. The floor was bare earth. Barred doors revealed two holding cells, neither with any furniture or sanitation facilities. He tried not to breathe. The larger of the cells held something like a score of men with the familiar Jones standing in the fore, his hands on the bars. The others were mostly blacks in rags. In the second cell were two well-dressed white women whom he also recognized immediately.

"We keep the men from the women when we can, you see," the jailer explained. "It leads to trouble otherwise." He made no move to open the cells.

"How civilized of you," said Charles, and reached for the man's belt to snatch up his keys. These he tossed to Augustus. "The two women and the white man," he said.

"But I ain't been paid for them," the jailer protested.

Charles wanted nothing more than to be out of this stinking hellhole as quickly as possible. "How much do you get for three prisoners a day?"

"A quid each." The reply came quickly.

"No you don't," Charles said. "I'll give you six-pence for the lot and call that generous."

"Two shillings," the man insisted. "I got expenses."

"One shilling, and if you argue with me any further I'll lock you in with them when I go." When he saw that Jones and the women were free, he tossed the man a coin, and hurried outside. In the sunshine, he took several deep breaths to cleanse his lungs.

"Captain Edgemont, as I recall," Jones said, brushing at some filth on his jacket. "Did the Admiralty send you? What the hell took so long? I've been waiting a month already."

The American was a dark-haired, rugged-looking man of middle height whom Charles guessed to be in his late thirties or early forties, although it was difficult to be sure. "My ship has only just arrived. I've orders to provide transport for yourself and your companions to the Red Sea," he answered. "The idea may have originated with a certain Viscount Effington I met with in London."

"Ah, Freddy," Jones said, apparently more concerned with the state of his clothes than anything else. "I do odd jobs for him on the occasion. Somewhat nervous in temperament, but the only one worth a fig in London."

"And how did you find yourself in prison? Really, bigamy?"

"An unfortunate misunderstanding," Jones answered offhandedly. "The authorities hereabouts are a gaggle of crab-assed, myopic, puritans. Beside, I've been in worse places."

The older of the two women, whom Charles had understood to be the only Mrs. Jones, stood disapprovingly silent. The younger, an attractive, delicate-looking brunette he remembered as Constance, spoke indignantly. "If that sodding turnkey came in to paw me one more time I was going to hand him his balls." She lifted her skirt and petticoats above her knee and came up with a slender nine-inch dagger. "I need to pee," she added.

"There are facilities on board ship, I'm sure," Jones said. "Cross your legs." He turned to Charles. "We must hurry; there is not a moment to lose. You are prepared to sail? We must be away on the tide."

Charles opened his mouth but Mrs. Jones spoke first. "You are always in such a rush. We shall proceed to our lodgings for the luggage, Adolphus. Constance may attend to her wants there. Then we can sail."

This was agreed to. The carriage clip-clopped off in the direction indicated by Mrs. Jones with repeated urgings to hurry from Constance.

"Why such an urgency to depart?" Charles asked as they rattled along. "I've spoken to the port admiral and the governor. Neither considers the French any threat to India. Even the Admiralty is divided on the subject."

Jones looked at him incredulously. "No threat? Of course there's a threat, a deathly serious threat. That the dim thinkers of Cape Town find the notion inconvenient does not mean that it will not be attempted."

Charles remained skeptical. "But why?" he said. "This General Bonaparte has only just secured Egypt. The door to any reinforcement from France has been shut by Admiral Nelson. He has not only destroyed their fleet but now blockades Alexandria. Why would the general, as intelligent as he is said to be, further extend himself to India? I should think he has enough on his plate where he is."

"Think, man," Jones goaded impatiently. "Use your head for once. You ask why Bonaparte would attack India. Ask yourself this, why did he invade Egypt: For the sand? For the trinkets of the Pharaohs? There is nothing in Egypt of the slightest interest to Paris. But India is different. The loss of the colonies on the subcontinent would cripple your government and destroy the economy. The value of Egypt, the only value of Egypt, is as a stepping stone to India."

"Still," Charles argued, "there's no point to it. Bonaparte could have no hope of supply apart from what he might capture or loot. Even if British forces were defeated he couldn't hold the place. Why would he make such an effort with no hope of success?"

"What is success?" Jones said patronizingly. "The French, I am sure, have no intention of occupying anything as large and fractious as India. They have no need to; success is throwing the English out. The place can go to hell after that for all they care. I doubt this little man Bonaparte seriously intends remaining in Egypt once the greater object is accomplished. You must think strategically. It's not winning every battle that matters; it's which battles you win. Even the complete loss of their expeditionary force in exchange for cutting away India would be considered a capital bargain in Paris. A general as capable as Napoleon understands this; the pooh bahs in London do not."

Reluctantly Charles had to admit that Jones's argument carried weight if one looked at it that way. He had a further objection. "It is well known that Tippu Sahib would be France's strongest ally. The governor-general in Bombay had decided on war against Mysore. Surely that changes everything."

"It changes nothing," Jones snorted derisively. "I doubt the army in India has a competent general among their ranks. But, I grant you, suppose by some miracle they were to suppress Mysore. If not Tippu, it will be someone else. There is little love for the British Empire anywhere in that region. I tell you, even five thousand veteran French grenadiers would make hash of your colonial forces. Mark you this," he said firmly, "whatever General Bonaparte does is planned to the last detail. The man is a genius; his methods are always well considered. Of course the French will attempt India, and they will do so sooner rather than later, you may count on it. There is no time to lose; we must sail immediately."

"We will have to complete our revictualing first," Charles answered dryly. "It is a little known fact that navy ships require food and water for long cruises."

They came to a halt in front of a nondescript building along a narrow dirt side street. With Augustus' and Charles' assistance, a small mountain of trunks and other baggage were carried out and heaped onboard. With just enough space for the women, the carriage started again, groaning its way toward the waterfront. The men followed on foot.

Charles had asked Sykes to bring the jollyboat and its crew to the dockside at noon, the hour at which he expected to return. It now being mid-afternoon he found the midshipman sitting on a bollard whittling on a stick, but saw no sign of his boat, or Cassandra, either at her former anchorage or closer to in the harbor.

"She's been moved to the victualling wharf, sir," Sykes explained. "It's only just around that bend yonder. As you can easily walk, I thought it best to send the boat back."

Charles introduced the midshipman to Jones and the two women. Sykes, he noticed, eyed Constance admiringly and greeted her with sputtered enthusiasm. Good luck to you there, Charles thought.

A short way, with the carriage following, brought them to his ship, moored fore and aft to bollards on the dock. Charles was pleased to see numbers of Cape Town's marines lined along the wharf to prevent desertions. Hogsheads of foodstuffs, livestock, and casks of fresh water were being assembled alongside, there to be swayed across. They boarded by means of a gangway. He repeated the introductions to the other ship's officers. The elder of the Mrs. Jones promptly announced, "I am fatigued and wish to retire. If you would show me to our cabin, please."

Charles had considered this problem earlier, without reaching a conclusion. There were, of course, no spare cabins on Cassandra. Indeed, there was hardly any free space between decks even to swing a hammock. There was the women's privacy to be considered and, where Constance was concerned, the safety of his crew. The most suitable accommodation on board was his own quarters. He hated to give it up. The only real alternative being to turn over two or even three of the wardroom cabins. That would mean displacing a similar number of his officers to the already cramped gunroom where they would have to berth with the midshipmen.

"I'm sure the captain's cabin will suit, my dear," Jones announced airily. "It will be a little cramped, but we must all make sacrifices."

Charles racked his brain one last time to find an alternative, without success. He observed Bevan grinning at his discomfort. "Of course," he said, surrendering to the inevitable. "Mr. Sykes, if you would be so good as to show the way."

The moment the Jones' departed, he turned to his lieutenants. "Daniel, I will be pleased to accept your gracious offer of the loan of your cabin. You may have Winchester's smaller one. Stephen, you are awarded Beechum's palatial accommodations; and you, Mr. Beechum, have the honor of berthing with the midshipmen." No one seemed pleased with this change of arrangements, which gave Charles some small satisfaction.

The supplies of water, firewood and foodstuffs were completed by midmorning the next day. The damaged mizzen boom had been quickly replaced and re-rigged. Only then was Cassandra kedged back into the harbor where the required powder and shot were lightered out and stowed away. Late in the afternoon, as the last of the shot were lowered into their lockers, Admiral Cobbham had himself ferried out and climbed aboard.

"I want to express my thanks for the promptness with which our needs were attended to," Charles said sincerely.

"Only too pleased, don't you know?" Cobbham answered. "I've only come over to wish you luck and a speedy voyage, eh? Mrs. C. and Arabella were hoping that you'll call to dinner when you're next back this way. Perhaps you'll bring along your officers, what? Any single?"

"I would be honored, sir, and I am sure I speak for my two unmarried lieutenants as well. Please convey my fondest regards to your wife and daughter."

Midshipmen Hitch and Aviemore, who had overheard this conversation, stood smartly by the entry port as Cobbham descended. They passed the remainder of the evening with an 'eh,' or 'what,' or 'don't you know' at the tail of every sentence until Charles snapped at them to stop it.

At dawn the next morning, at the start of the run of the tide, Cassandra weighed her anchor. A brilliant late-summer sun warmed the air, the barren crags at the tip of southern Africa receding over the aft port side quarter. With an increasingly brisk beam wind they weathered the Cape of Good Hope before noon and Cape Agulhas, the true southernmost extremity of the continent, by nightfall.

Charles spent the day pacing the quarterdeck, unwilling to return to the closet-sized space that was now his cabin, attempting to untangle what he might actually find when he arrived at the mouth of the Red Sea.

CHAPTER SEVEN

Captain Charles Edgemont stood on the windward side of his quarterdeck looking out at the rugged heights of the mountains of Yemen, hard and deeply ravined, on the southern tip of the Arabian Peninsula. At their base, almost as if resting on the sea, he could just see the port of Aden. If he used his glass, he could make out the shapes of the whitewashed, flat-roofed buildings in the town. The sky stood an unbroken expanse of deep blue, shaded darker in the east, a blaze of blood-orange sun settling into the horizon off the bow. A golden highway reflected across the wave tops in a line, as straight as any rule, connecting living ship and dying light. He felt a twinge of anticipation that the end of the long voyage lay just a day ahead.

Fifty-one days from Cape Town, he calculated. Cassandra had made good progress northward following the so-called 'inner channel' between Madagascar and the African mainland in order to avoid any possibility of running afoul of French naval forces based at Mauritius. More particularly, it was one hundred and thirty-three days since they had weighed anchor in Chatham dockyard, and eleven more-as if he hadn't counted them-since he had parted from Penny at their home in Tattenall. Four and a half months had passed since he had heard anything of her. She must have given birth by now. He found it troubling that he could no longer see her face before his eyes or hear her laughter whenever he chose to do so, but the image would come to him unbidden when his mind was elsewhere, sometimes with startling clarity, leaving a void as it faded. He had learned not to dwell on the subject unduly, else there was no bottom to the well of self-pity he would fall into. He forced his attention on the sails, full bellied, and braced around sharply to catch the wind. He saw nothing amiss that he should call to Bevan's attention, so he decided to speak with the master instead. "Mr. Cromley, a word if you please," he said crossing the deck.

"Sir?" Cromley answered from his customary place near the binnacle.

"How long do you reckon before we try the straits?" Ninety miles farther along the coast, the Gulf of Aden narrowed like the waist of an hourglass at the Straits of Mandeb, the entrance to the Red Sea. Mocha, his rendezvous with Admiral Blankett's squadron, lay only fifty miles or so beyond on the Arabian side. He expected to encounter one or more of Blankett's force on patrol well before reaching the port.

Cromley answered without hesitation. "It'll be too late to make the passage tonight."

"I see," Charles said. "I take it you do not wish to try the straits in the dark?"

"No, sir, not even with a full moon. It's not more than fifteen mile across, and that with Perim Island and the Seven Brothers islands and plenty of shoals. It might be attempted for good reason. I wouldn't advise it unless there were urgent cause."

Before Charles could respond to this he heard the lookout in the mainmast tops shout down, "Deck! Sail ahead, direct on the bow." He looked forward, only to shield his eyes against the glare of the sun.

To Winchester, doing his turn as watch officer, he said, "Stephen, who is the sentry at the masthead?"

"George Crowe, I believe."

"Send up a replacement and have him report on deck, if you please."

Within moments the seaman Crowe, a deeply tanned man, thin as a stick, with a bowlegged gait, came onto the quarterdeck. He cautiously approached and pressed the knuckles of his fist against his forehead. "Yer sent fer myself, sur?"

"I did. You must have uncommon eyes. How could you see anything into that sun?"

"It weren't direct in t' sun, sur. It were just ofter t' side. If'n yer peer through t' gaps in yer fingers, yer can see fair keen. 'Tis a trick I learnt."

"And very useful it is. What can you tell me about the craft?"

Crowe pulled on his lower lip, then caught himself and scratched at his nose instead. "Well, I'd say they be about as far as yer can see, mebby ten league. T'were only a touch o' t'eir t'gallants I saw, sur."

"They? Were there more than one?"

"Might o' been a pair. I only seen one fer sure. Her masts in a line, braced up tight, bearing away like."

Charles smiled his appreciation. "I thank you for your alertness, Crowe. You may have the remainder of the watch at liberty as a consequence."

"T'ank yer, sur," the seaman knuckled his forehead again and backed away.

"What do you make of it?" Winchester asked. He had been standing nearby, listening intently.

"I'm sure it's Admiral Blankett's frigates patrolling the exit to the Red Sea. They seem a fair distance afield though."

"I would have thought they might have signaled, or run down on us to see who we are," Winchester offered.

Charles pondered this for a moment. "Possibly we're at such a distance they didn't see us." He had an uncomfortable sense that, with the last of the sunlight before them, Cassandra's sails should have stood out in bright contrast against the darkening sky behind.

*****

Bevan and Charles stood by the rail of the quarterdeck, the day lit by the just-risen sun. Even in the early morning the heat intruded like an unwanted blanket. The two looked out to where the coastline of the Arabian Peninsula turned away toward the north, the small lump of Perim Island, and the faint line of the African continent hazy in the west. The deep channel into the Red Sea lay on the far side of the island, Cromley had informed him. The entirety of the sea around them, and as far as the lookout in the crosstrees could see, was bare of any shipping.

"Whoever we saw yesterday, they've gone on," Bevan observed. "Up through the straits, most likely."

Charles thought that much as clear. "Yes," he said. "But in the night? I would have thought them to lay to and wait for daylight."

"Maybe they had some pressing need. Could have been in a hurry."

"What kind of hurry? They're most likely bound for Mocha. They would have arrived in the middle of the night. There's no need to risk running upon a reef for that."

"I don't know, Charlie," Bevan said easily. "But it's clear they didn't care to dawdle."

"I suppose so," Charles said. His feeling of discomfort did not leave.

Cassandra soon came about to put the wind on her beam, her bow cutting through the moderate chop northwestward into the channel. The low, arid form of Perim Island passed to starboard, the desert plateau of Somalia to port. Charles studied the occasional villages along the shore as they passed, miserable mud-and-wattle places with reed roofs set among scrub and palms. Rough fishing smacks lay where they had been pulled up on the beach. As the sun climbed, the air became oppressively warm with a stultifying humidity that brought rivers of sweat at the smallest exertion. He ordered lookouts in all three mastheads to keep a sharp eye for any ships of war, in particular English warships that would be Admiral Blankett's frigates watching the entrance to the sea. He had even spoken with Sykes about the appropriate salute when this occurred. It did not occur; no ships of any kind were encountered.

Early in the afternoon watch, a substantial walled town, its battlements and towers salmon pink in the shimmering haze, came into view along the Yemeni coast. It the midst of its tightly packed buildings rose a slender minaret and the glistening golden dome of a mosque alongside. Behind, a dun-colored plain stretched eastward to the sharp peaks of mountains in the distance. To Charles it was fantastic, a mysterious scene straight from the Arabian Nights. Of more immediate interest were four European warships at anchor in the roads a mile and a half off the port. They were soon revealed as a two-decked, fifty-gun ship, two frigates, and a brig-sloop. From each of their mizzen peaks fluttered the blue ensign of the British navy. The fifty, the smallest two-decker in the navy's arsenal, showed a broad pendant trailing languidly from the main.

"Am I correct in assuming that to be Mocha, Mr. Cromley?" Charles asked.

"Aye, sir," the master answered. "Famous for its trade in coffee, but you can get almost anything in the suq—that's what the locals call a market. They'll have all manner of merchandise: gold, pearls, hashish, girls, young boys. Whatever it is suits your fancy."

"I thank you for the information," Charles said. "I do believe I'll settle for calling on Admiral Blankett at the moment. Mr. Sykes!"

"Yes, sir." The boy came hurrying up.

"You may send up our colors and recognition signal. If you would be so good as to begin the salute afterward."

"Aye, aye, sir."

The flags ran up Cassandra's halyards and guns boomed out, soon to be answered by the flagship. Charles turned his mind to the things he needed to accomplish while in port. In addition to the resupply of water, foodstuffs, and firewood, there was the question of leave for the crew. From what he observed, and his officers reported to him, their temper had improved. There had been no further outbreaks of fighting, or even the generously shared insults that had been common enough before. Still, the men went through their work with a certain grimness, he thought, performing their assigned tasks readily enough, but without enthusiasm. He put this down to their having been denied leave or even visitors from the bumboats while at Cape Town. He could make up for that now and allow them ashore. He glanced once more at the heat-soaked jumble of mud-brick structures and wondered what delights the men might find there. He imagined some would be unusual indeed. At least it would be a change for them, and he was comfortable that few would choose to desert in such an isolated and inhospitable place. He saw the signal flags as they rose the flagship's mast.

"Anchor to leeward," Sykes reported, the signal book open in his hand.

"Thank you," Charles said. "Mr. Cromley, we will come to anchor as ordered, if you please."

Cassandra glided past the other warships, taking in her topsails and courses as she went. He identified them as Hellebore, the brig-sloop; Daedalus and Fox, smart thirty-two-gun frigates; and the flagship Leopard. He thought it a light force for protecting against something potentially as important as the

French entering or leaving the Red Sea. In all likelihood there would be others on patrol beyond his sight.

A half cable's length beyond the flagship, Cassandra's foretopgallant braced around to lie against the mast. "Let go!" he heard Beechum's voice forward, and the anchor cable begin to run out through the hawse. The hands aloft fisted in the remaining sails and tied them off. Cassandra snubbed once at her anchor and stilled, swinging slowly on the barely existent current. Charles ordered the jollyboat hoisted out over the side and waited for the signal calling him to report on board. The satchel of mail and dispatches for the squadron was passed down, followed by the boat's crew. No signal showed. The five warships lay quietly at anchor in the glaring heat of the bay as if forgotten toys in a pond. He waited by the entry port for ten minutes, fifteen, with Bevan standing beside him. The ship's bell dinged out four times, marking two hours into the afternoon watch.

"Maybe Blankett's learned of your reputation and is just hoping you'll go away," Bevan offered. "Can't say as I'd blame him."

"I'm going across anyway, invitation or no," Charles said, growing impatient at the lack of communication. He swung out and climbed down into the boat. Augustus had taken his place on the stroke oar, he noted, more carefully dressed than was usual in anticipation of Charles' going ashore and requiring protection. He almost regretted disappointing him. "The flagship," he said to Malvern. The climb up Leopard's sidesteps brought pools of sweat under his uniform coat.

"The admiral is ashore, sir," Edmund Danforth, the Leopard's too carefully dressed first lieutenant, said. "I am sure he will call for you on his return." Charles noticed that the flagship was in perfect order—her decks holystoned pristine white, the brightwork glistening, her yards perfectly squared, and the falls flemished down. She looked as if she had been prepared to receive an inspection from the king himself.

"When will that be?" Charles asked.

"When his business is completed," Danforth answered pertly. "I suggest you employ the time smartening your ship. The admiral expects a shipshape appearance."

Charles took this as an implied insult, but ignored it. "What is the strength of the squadron?" he asked. "How many are out on patrol?"

"Come now, captain. This is the foot of the Red Sea, the closest place on earth to Hell. Nothing happens here. We are not conducting the blockade of Toulon." He chuckled at his joke.

Charles decided that the lieutenant was being intentionally unhelpful. "How many ships?" he repeated.

"The squadron is just what you see," Danforth answered finally. Charles recalled the sails he had seen making for the Straits of Mandeb. "Do you tell me that there is no one on patrol to look out for ships passing into or out of the sea?"

Danforth smiled knowingly. "Patrol? Of course not. You've only just arrived, or you'd know there is no need for it. Daedalus was out a week ago. She reported nothing, as you would expect. The Admiral considers it a waste of time."

"No one's come or gone from this anchorage since then, no one at all?" Where were the two ships that had passed the straits immediately before him?

"No," the lieutenant answered flatly. "Now if you will excuse me, I have . . ."

"Where in the town is Admiral Blankett," Charles interrupted. "I insist on reporting to him at once."

"I told you, it would not be convenient. He is involved in negotiations with the local authorities. He cannot be . . ."

"I do not care whether it is convenient or not, Lieutenant," Charles snapped. "You will provide someone to take me to the admiral at once, or I will go with my marines and turn Mocha upside down until I find him."

Danforth assumed a displeased expression, then sighed in resignation. "He is at Mr. Underwood's residence. Mr. Underwood is the British commercial agent in Mocha. He trades in coffee and such, I believe."

"How do I find him?"

"I will send Midshipman Palgrave to show the way. But I warn you, Admiral Blankett will not be pleased at the intrusion."

"Admirals are seldom pleased, I find," Charles replied.

The sixteen-year-old Palgrave, perfectly attired in his uniform jacket buttoned up to his chin, tumbled down into the jollyboat, closely followed by Charles. They began the long pull into the port.

Mocha's harbor consisted of a pair of sandstone jetties projecting into a shallow bay. At the northern and southern ends were long abandoned, crumbling forts on points of land, which presumably had once protected the entrances to the port. The sea, Charles noted, was shallow to more than a mile out, with frequent coral reefs just beneath the surface, over which waves washed with a gentle froth. Numerous small, shallow-draft sambuks, with single masts for their lateen sails were pulled up on the beach. A half dozen more sizable vessels known as baghalas, some as large as several hundred tons burthen weight, lay at anchor a mile or more from shore. These would be sea-going trading ships, easily capable of journeys as far as the East Indies or the Philippines. All were double-ended affairs, often with large eyes painted on the bow, and not dissimilar to some he had seen in the eastern Mediterranean. The jollyboat grounded on a glistening white sand beach before the walls. The oarsmen jumped into the water and hauled the craft onto land. Charles rose from his place in the sternsheets, went forward, and stepped out. Immediately he was assaulted by an army of flies swarming at his eyes and mouth and any bare skin, no matter how persistently he brushed them away. "Rest the men in the shade of those palm trees," he said to Malvern. "Keep an eye on the boat. I'll return as soon as I can."

Augustus immediately moved to stand beside him, his mouth set in a determined line. Charles looked up at the town, then at a number of the local inhabitants watching cautiously from a distance. All were men or boys, deeply tanned to the color of weathered oak. The men were a hard-looking lot, mostly dressed in loose-fitting turbans and gowns with large curved daggers tucked prominently into belts over their bellies. "All right, this time you may accompany me," he said to his servant, and felt the better for it. He turned to Palgrave. The boy was swatting ineffectually at the flies competing for the trickles of moisture running down his face. "Lead on," he said with some sympathy.

Charles trod laboriously over the loose sand, sweat collecting anew under his open uniform coat. The buttoned up midshipman soon had the appearance of having stepped out from under a waterfall. The air cooled noticeably once they reached the town. Four- and five-storied, mud-brick buildings crowded against unpaved streets. The fronts of the structures, often with a workshop of some kind at the ground level, were overhung with awnings and balconies, shutting out the direct rays of the sun. The roadway was shared with lumbering camels, heavily laden donkeys, goats, chickens, and crowds of men. Few women were to be seen, and those completely covered except for their faces, and sometimes only their eyes. No breath of air stirred to disturb the flies or to relieve the robust odors of milling animals and crowded humanity.

"This way, sir," said Palgrave, who seemed to know exactly where he was going. They soon turned into a narrow alleyway completely shaded with reed mats, then into another so constricted that Charles had to follow in single file, scraping against the building sides whenever someone passed in the opposite direction. After several turnings, which left him completely without any sense of direction, the midshipman stopped and knocked loudly on a nondescript wooden door set into the peeling wall of a three-story building. The door swung back revealing a large black man, almost as large as Augustus, in a yellow turban, bright blue vest, and baggy trousers of the same color gathered at the ankle. A familiar curved dagger with a fabulously decorated scabbard and hilt was tucked into his belt.

"Mr. Underwood, please," Palgrave said.

The servant, if that is what he was, glanced suspiciously at Charles, then with something bordering on respect at Augustus. Then he stepped out to look up and down the alley. Satisfied, he spoke in oddly accented but otherwise perfect English: "Enter, gentlemen. Mr. Underwood and Admiral Blankett are in the courtyard. Your name, Captain?"

"Edgemont," Charles answered, stepping cautiously into a darkened room. As his eyes began to adjust he saw another similarly proportioned and uniformed retainer behind the door. The second man closed it and slid a heavy wooden bar into place. Charles felt the thick texture of a carpet beneath his feet.

"Follow, if you please," the doorman intoned, and started toward an arched passage at the room's far end. As Augustus moved to follow, the second man barred his way. "Not this one," the first said firmly. "He will wait here."

"Cap'n?" Augustus protested.

"It's all right; do as he asks," Charles said. He followed the doorman and soon came to a cloistered walkway surrounding a courtyard with a running fountain, flowers in profusion, and several date and orange trees. Intricately decorated rugs overlaid a flagged surface beside the fountain. On these, two men reclined on thick pillows. They were in the midst of being served a dark liquid in tiny cups by an exotically attired young woman. Another, similarly dressed, plucked at a stringed instrument off to the side. One of the men wore Arab dress, including a long flowing head cover; the other wore white European breeches and a silk shirt of the same color. Charles took the second man to be Admiral Blankett, his new commanding officer. "Mr. Midshipman Palgrave and Captain Edgemont," the doorkeeper announced. He took up position with his arms crossed immediately behind Charles.

"What is the meaning of this?" the admiral said in an irritated voice. "Mr. Palgrave, I left distinct orders that I was not to be disturbed."

"I know, sir. I'm sorry. But the captain is newly arrived. He insisted."

"Well then, what have you to say for yourself?" Blankett said, transferring his gaze from the midshipman to Charles.

"I have only just arrived . . . ," Charles began.

"I know that."

". . . from England." He looked meaningfully at the Arab man. "I have important recent information."

"This is Mr. Gladfridus Underwood," Blankett said. "He represents His Majesty's government in this region. He can hear anything you have to say."

Charles studied the oddly dressed figure more closely. His features were darkened by the sun, but softer than those of most natives he'd seen. The man might be European, he decided, or of mixed blood. He shrugged. "Yesterday evening as Cassandra approached the Straits of Mandeb, we sighted two unknown warships off our bow. It is likely they passed by here during the night."

"Cassandra is your ship?" Blankett asked.

"My frigate, sir. Thirty-two guns."

"And you did not discover the nationality of these two warships?"

"No, sir. To be truthful, I cannot swear they were warships, but they were ship-rigged. I imagine there are few European merchantmen in these waters."

Blankett frowned to show his displeasure and pushed himself to a sitting position. "Captain Edgemont, I very much doubt this concerns me in the least. My orders are to prevent the French, should they incredibly decide to attack India, from exiting through the mouth of the Red Sea. This I am well able to do. A brig of war, now three frigates, and a fifty-gun ship of the line are more than sufficient to destroy any number of dhows, baghalas or any other bottoms available along this godforsaken waterway. Do I make myself clear?"

"Yes, sir," Charles said. "But . . ."

"No buts," the admiral snapped impatiently.

"Yes, sir. But the sails, sir."

Blankett frowned. "I see that I will have to spell it out for you. Really, I don't know why the Admiralty foists such unimaginative officers on me. You have allowed yourself, sir, to become twisted into a pretzel about some hypothetical ship, or ships, that may, or may not, have sailed past Mocha and up the sea. Mind you, I have no orders regarding any craft entering, only those attempting to leave. I will also enlighten you to the extent that we do indeed see the occasional European merchant going back and forth." He turned momentarily to Underwood. "Where is it they do their trading?"

"Massawa," Underwood answered. "Those Italians."

"Oh yes. They have some legitimate business there, I believe."

Charles stood rigidly erect. None of the customary courtesies, such as inviting him to sit or offering any refreshment, had been extended to him; now he was being condescended to. He clenched his jaw to keep from saying anything that could be taken as insubordinate. It did not ring true that the sails his lookouts had seen were ordinary merchantmen, not passing through the straits at night.

"Let us assume the worst, shall we?" Blankett continued. "Supposing that these ships were French. Most likely it, or they, would be transports. That's what would be needed most. Even at that, only two would be sadly insufficient. Just possibly one of them might be a frigate. It's unlikely but possible. It might even be that both are frigates. This borders on the unbelievable, of course, but I still have ample force should they attempt an exit. You do understand that, don't you, Captain?" Possibly to mitigate the harshness of his tone, he added with a small chuckle, "It's not as if they'd be ships of the line."

Ships of the line. Charles felt an itch crawl up his spine. What if the two sets of sail his lookouts had glimpsed were the same frigate and seventy-four he had encountered in the Atlantic? It was not impossible. A single seventy-four would make short work of Blankett's tiny squadron. He wished he had been closer so that he could be sure. He had nothing concrete, only supposition. He sensed that if he pressed the issue, the admiral would dismiss him as one of those officers who see terrors in every corner. Charles made an effort to compose himself. "With all respect, sir, you have no patrols out," he said carefully. "I'm not suggesting it, but you wouldn't know if the combined fleets of France and Spain have passed this way." He smiled as if he'd meant it humorously.

Blankett did not take it as humor. "There is no need for patrols just now in any event."

"Why is that?"

"The wind's wrong, that's why. Do you think me a fool?" The admiral glared at him impatiently. "During this season it blows to the north, up from the Horn of Africa. Won't start southerly for another month or two. If the French intend to come down, that's when they'll do it, not before. And, sir, that's when I intend to put out active patrols."

Charles knew he should tread carefully, but something had to be done. "Wouldn't it be useful at least to know what forces have progressed up the sea, if for no other reason, to know what to expect when they come down?"

"If they come down," Blankett emphasized. "It's a poppycock notion to begin with." The admiral's expression cracked into a smile. "But all right, since you are so concerned, I'll send Cassandra out to patrol. Perhaps that will calm your nerves."

Charles felt his anger rise to the surface at Blankett's sarcastic tone and rigid thinking. "The man hasn't the imagination of a pencil box," he remembered Effington saying at the Admiralty months before. "I am sorry, sir," he said, controlling his tone. "I would be pleased to do so were it possible. I am under the Admiralty's orders to make for the head of the sea. I am not to join the squadron until my return."

At this the second man, Underwood, raised his eyebrows. "Are you really?" he said. "Why?"

Charles looked to Blankett, uncertain of how much he should reveal. "I'm sure this is explained in the dispatches I brought from London," he said.

"Doubtless," the admiral observed dryly, "these same dispatches will inform me of your anticipated appearance. But do tell, why are you being sent north?"

Charles glanced uneasily at Underwood in his Arab dress. For the first time he noticed the man was missing three of the fingers of his right hand. Who was he anyway? "I have orders to land certain persons there," he said carefully.

"Who are you intending to put ashore?" Underwood asked. Blankett nodded in agreement at the question.

"I do not think I should say," Charles answered firmly. "The admiral will learn of it in his written orders."

"Then let me guess," Underwood said with a wry smile. "You are Captain Edgemont: I recall the name in connection with the affair at Abukir in the Mediterranean. Or was it at Acre? Could it be your passenger is a certain Adolphus Jones?" Charles wondered at the man's knowledge and knew that no answer was required. "I am sure you will be at Mocha several days to renew your water and such," the agent continued. "By all means, invite Jones and his party on shore. We are old acquaintances."

"I will mention it," Charles said. He sensed that there was a history between the two that he did not understand.

Underwood rubbed his jaw thoughtfully before speaking to Blankett in an undertone. "I believe there may be some benefit to watching for who enters the sea," Charles heard him say. "It's a small thing, but best to err on the side of caution."

The admiral nodded sagely. "You will inform Commander Griffiths of Hellebore to make ready to sail," he said to Charles. "Tell him his written orders will be prepared this evening. If that is all, you may return to your ship."

Charles was as anxious to be away as the admiral was to see him gone. He had a great deal to think through. There were only a few administrative details while he had Blankett's attention. "Yes, sir," he said. "I take it that we may begin the resupply of my ship in the morning? I expect to sail as soon as that is complete." As an afterthought, he added, "And, it is my intention to allow Cassandra's crew leave to go on shore, with your permission, of course."

Blankett's glare expressed annoyance that Charles had not already left. "No," he said in a barely interested tone. "Your men are to be confined on board. Those are my standing orders for all the ships of the squadron. Watering parties and the like are excepted, of course, but keep them about their duties. I have enough problems with the damned natives as it is."

Charles wasn't prepared for this. He knew that the crew would be expecting leave and would be disappointed if it were withheld. "But, sir," he began.

The admiral scowled, his patience apparently exhausted. "You are dismissed, Captain Edgemont. That is an order. Do you require it in writing?"

"No, sir," Charles said, his face rigid. "I thank you for your time. Good day, sir."

Charles followed Palgrave back through the dwelling whence they collected Augustus and soon found themselves in the foul-smelling alleyway once again.

Charles, with Augustus following, obediently stayed on the midshipman's heels as the boy turned from alleyway to alleyway, leading hopefully back to the waterfront. Was it possible that the French ships had entered the Red Sea on their way to Egypt? Might the sails they had sighted really be the same L'Agile and Raisonnable he had encountered in the Atlantic? Would that mean that an invasion of India was certain? It all seemed fantastic, but then everything in this part of the world seemed fantastic, from the determined clouds of flies to the unmoving British squadron in the port, while their admiral idled his time away in secret luxury on shore. And, who was Mr. Gladfridus Underwood? He seemed a most peculiar creature indeed. The only thing that Charles thought certain was that Underwood exercised some undefined influence over the admiral. He also was keenly aware that he would have a potentially far larger problem when his crew learned that they were to be restrained on board.

They came at last to the beach in the sweltering heat of the late afternoon. Charles quickly found his boat's crew lounging in various attitudes of ease under the cluster of palm trees. Someone had obtained a goatskin of water which he had passed around.

"Would you care for a sip, sir?" Malvern offered as they approached. Charles took a deep drink. He looked at the assembled seamen, most in their jersey shirts, although some had removed them. Then he glanced at young Palgrave, still in his buttoned up uniform and hat with sweat running down his cheeks. There were limits to maintaining dignity, he decided, and slipped off his jacket, removed his stock, and unbuttoned the top of his shirt. The effect was instantly gratifying. "You have my permission to open your upper clothing," he said to the midshipman. "You'd best put it back before we reach Leopard, though."

They soon re-launched the jollyboat, and with the breeze coming off the land, set the fore and aft sails to carry them out. A huge sun lay just above the horizon, its reflection sparkling across the gentle chop. Penny would love to see this, he thought; she would enjoy the strangeness of it all. Then he remembered that she would have recently been in childbirth and might at that moment be nursing their infant—or she might be dead. Women dying from the complications of birthing was by no means uncommon. That was just one additional uncertainty among the many others which were visited upon him. His mood darkened. For the moment he didn't see how he could overcome any of it.

After hastily re-buttoning himself, Palgrave was deposited back onboard the flagship. Charles ordered Malvern to steer for the Hellebore so that he could convey Blankett's orders. The brig-sloop rode placidly at her anchor a cable's length away. "I'll only be a moment," he said as he climbed up over her side.

"Welcome aboard, sir," Hellebore's first lieutenant said, greeting Charles as he pulled himself onto the deck. The officer was probably in his middle thirties, he guessed, a lean man of average height with the prominent white line of a scar down his otherwise deeply tanned left cheek. Charles' first impression was of a thoughtful, steady man, probably capable of dealing with most problems put before him. "I am Nathaniel Drinkwater. I see you've only just arrived."

"Charles Edgemont of Cassandra, fresh from Chatham," he responded with a smile and extended his hand. "Pleased to make your acquaintance." The two men shook. "Is this all you do, sit in the harbor?"

Drinkwater's mouth tightened. "We serve at the Admiral's pleasure," he said carefully.

"Then perhaps I bring a welcome change. Is Commander Griffiths available?"

"On what passes as our quarterdeck. This way, if you please."

Charles saw an elderly, grizzled figure seated in a chair aft, with one leg propped up on a stool in front of him.

"Captain Edgemont; Commander Madoc Griffiths," Drinkwater announced, making the introductions.

"Bach, my pardons if I don't rise, Captain," Griffiths said with a thick Welsh accent. "It's the gout, you know. Still, I'm pleased to greet you. You've met Nat here, I take it."

"I have," Charles said, taking an instant liking to the older man.

"He's been as grumpy as a puppy who can't find a teat these past weeks," Griffiths continued sympathetically. "His lady back home is in an expectant way and he'd rather be there than here. Am I right, Nat?"

The lieutenant colored at this intimate revelation about his personal life.

"Du," Griffiths said with a grin. "If you can't take the pressure then you shouldn't have done the deed." At this Drinkwater blushed a still brighter shade.

Charles laughed out loud. "Really?" he said. "I find myself in similar circumstances. It's the very devil not knowing, isn't it?"

"It is that," Drinkwater admitted.

"But enough of this," Griffiths said, turning serious. "You've been on shore; to see Blankett is my guess. Is this a social call, or do you have some word?"

"I'm to tell you he's decided to put out a patrol," Charles said. "There's reason to believe the French may have already entered the sea. You are to make preparations to sail."

"And you, sir?" Drinkwater asked.

"I'm going north," Charles answered. "We should be back to join the

129

squadron in a month or so."

"It's about time he put some ships out, to my thinking," Griffiths offered. "Past time. There's no arguing with the man, though."

Charles returned to Cassandra in a brighter frame of mind, satisfied that there was at least one other person who shared his misery over the unknown condition of his wife. The sun dropped into the sea; in these latitudes night followed swiftly. His sense of wellbeing did not last long. "Assemble the men on the deck, Daniel," he said almost before he had fully passed through the entry port.

"May I enquire as to why?" Bevan asked.

"They will be expecting to be permitted leave ashore. Blankett has forbidden it."

"Hell's embers," Bevan said. "Pardon my French, Charlie, but they aren't going to like it."

"I don't expect they will."

Bevan relayed the order and the boatswain's calls summoning the hands sounded the length of the ship. In the gathering darkness Charles stood beneath a lantern hung from the mainmast as the men tumbled up the hatchways fore and aft. He could make out the forms as they found their divisions, but not see the faces except for those just below him. An expectant silence fell over the ship.

"I have called on the admiral commanding this station," Charles spoke loudly, "to request permission for leave ashore." There was a murmur of whispered conversation at this from below. He wished he could make out their expressions, but he knew well enough.

"Silence on deck!" Bevan bellowed, as usual.

"It's all right," Charles said, also as usual. He wanted to hear their reaction. Taking a deep breath, he spoke again. "The admiral denied the request. There will be work parties only. I am personally sorry for this. I thought it best if I told you myself."

"Bloody 'ell," an angry voice immediately shouted back. "We ain't any of us 'ad a minute of liberty since Chatham."

"Since afore that," shouted another. "Us was turned over to this scow direct. I ain't been ashore in more 'n a year! It ain't right." An uproar of protests broke out.

Charles let it go on for a few moments. He felt badly for them. They did deserve leave; they'd earned it, but there was nothing he could do. Finally, he held his arms up for silence. The noise tapered away. "It happens that I agree with you," he said when he had their attention. "I promise to make it up at the first opportunity." He doubted that his words would satisfy. "You may dismiss them," he muttered to Bevan. "I'd keep a careful watch over the next several days if I were you."

Charles looked on unhappily as the hands milled about on the dimly lit deck, grousing and complaining as they made for the hatchways and below. He thought to go down to the wardroom for his supper when he saw Midshipman Aviemore lounging against the binnacle. He was reminded of one final detail he should attend to. "Mr. Aviemore," he called.

"Sir?" the boy inquired.

"You will be pleased to go down to my cabin to inform Mr. Jones that I would appreciate a word with him."

"Which cabin, sir?" Aviemore asked. "The captain's cabin or Lieutenant Bevan's cabin which be also your cabin?"

Charles decided that he would be very pleased when Jones and his entourage were finally put on shore so that his life could return to normal. He would also be pleased when Aviemore reached the age of about forty and might be expected to reason as a normal human being. "Whichever you might the most reasonably anticipate finding him in," he offered. Aviemore actually skipped across the deck to descend the ladderway.

"What do you want?" Adolphus Jones growled. He appeared with a napkin still tied around his neck and had apparently been disturbed at his own meal.

Charles pushed down his annoyance. "I have been into the port this afternoon," he said. "There I met with an acquaintance of yours. Underwood is his name. He has extended an invitation for you to visit."

"Ah," Jones said.

"Ah? Is that all you have to say: Ah?"

"I believe it best to decline," Jones elaborated.

"May I ask why?"

Jones stood silent for a moment, then said, "Mr. Gladfridus Underwood is indeed an acquaintance of some duration. A trifling misfortune befell him several years ago, over which he has adopted an unforgiving attitude. In short, he has sworn to have me murdered should I set foot in Mocha. I would prefer to reminisce with him in a more neutral setting."

"His fingers?" Charles asked.

"It seemed appropriate in the spirit of the moment."

"Ah," Charles said. "In that case we may allow the invitation to lapse."

*****

The next days passed in a flurry of activity under an intemperate sun. Cassandra's boats plied to and from the beach, returning laden to the gunwales with filled water casks, bawling bullocks, sheep, goats, and scrawny chickens. There were great sacks of millet, wheat and peas, dates, lemons, limes, and a towering pile of firewood. All were swung up by sweating, shirtless seamen, and tucked into their places in the filling hold. The cattle and sheep were butchered on the forecastle as they came aboard, cut into mess-sized chunks, and stored in salt-filled barrels. The hands, Charles observed, labored steadily if unenthusiastically under a blistering sun, which he found understandable; but there was something in their attitude that had changed—an increased distance, resentment. He couldn't put his finger on it. Was he measuring the temper of the crew, or were they measuring him?

Charles watched as Hellebore sailed on the second day to begin cruising back and forth between Mocha and the African shore. He also took the opportunity to pay social calls on Captains Harry Bell of Daedalus and Dante Sugden of Fox. Bell proved a not quite piercing officer who expressed himself content to sit in the Mocha roads "until hell froze over," if his king commanded it. "At least it would be cooler then," he said. Sugden's diversion was endless games at whist, to which Charles was invited but declined.

On the fourth day Cassandra pulled her anchor from the sandy bottom of Mocha Bay and started northward under fitful southerly airs. Cromley's chart informed that it would only be 1,400 miles or so to Cape Muhammad on the tip of the Sinai Peninsula. He stared at the paper until he had memorized what little information it contained. Despite himself, he had an intense curiosity and no small apprehension about what they might find there.

CHAPTER EIGHT

The long columns of crabbed figures on the page refused to stay in focus. Charles sat on the cot in Bevan's cabin, his back propped against the bulkhead and his stockinged feet drawn up so that he could more easily read the purser's ledger, open across his thighs. A dim lantern swung from the beam above his head, the flame adding unwanted warmth to the musty, close space. The room was cramped, eight by six feet, containing the cot, a tiny table, and a single chair. A door, louvered for ventilation, opened onto the wardroom. And if the wardroom itself had been in any way ventilated, Charles might have been pleased. Excepting her captain (normally), all of Cassandra's officers and senior warrants had similar though less spacious cabins partitioned against either side of the hull in the aftermost third of the mess deck. On a two-decked ship of the line these accommodations would be shared with a hulking thirty-two-pounder cannon, which allowed less floor room but at least provided a gunport to open for light and air. A frigate's mess deck was at the waterline and, aside from the hatchways, unpierced by any opening its entire length. It was a dark, airless expanse lit by occasional lanterns and perfumed by the too infrequently washed bodies of hundreds of seamen and marines who berthed forward and the still more malodorous delights of the bilge below.

"Purchased in Mocha, 30–31 May, 1799," he re-read the heading at the top of the page. "Oxen, one score; sheep, two score and six; millet, five hundredweight; peas, six hundredweight; dates, two hundredweight . . ." What the hell did Wells want so many dates for? Charles struggled to keep his mind on the list in front of him. If the wind held it would only be three weeks to a month before he could reasonably expect to put Jones and his women ashore somewhere along the Gulf of Suez at the head of the sea. He was anxious to get the thing done, not just so that he could be rid of his passengers and have his own cabin back, with its operable gallery windows and gun ports, but because it would take him one step closer to the completion of his mission. Once Jones had discovered the true intentions of the French—whether or not they were intending to come down the sea—all Charles had to do was inform Blankett. It would be the Admiral's responsibility to decide how to confront the situation— if there was indeed a situation to confront. He ached to have it settled so that he might be able to retrace his course back to England to see Penny, or even to make Cape Town or Gibraltar where there would be letters with word on the outcome of her pregnancy, and with news about her health and that of their child. There were times when he didn't care whether the enemy landed in India or not. He wished it were finished and he could go home.

He fingered the thick paper of the ledger and stared at the list of supplies again with renewed determination. "Lemons . . ." The seasonal shift in the direction of the prevailing winds from southward up the sea to down the sea from the north would be essential to any French calculations. If they intended to come down, it could only be done with favorable winds. How would such an effort be organized? If it were up to him, he would collect whatever transports were available at some convenient Egyptian port on the Red Sea—Koessir, which was shown on his chart, for example, or possibly Suez—load them with troops and supplies, then run south as soon as the wind allowed it. That had the advantage of being the most straightforward approach. The disadvantages, as he saw it, were two: It was a long sail from Egypt to Bombay, a month and a half at the least, even with the best of winds. And the British squadron at Mocha would have to be somehow defeated or avoided. He was certain that the French would be aware of Blankett's presence and strength; local traders passing up and down the sea would long since have informed them.

There was another disadvantage, Charles reflected: Massing the transports at a port in Egypt was the most obvious thing to do, and left them vulnerable to attack—should they be discovered and should Blankett be so inclined. He remembered the viscount at the Admiralty telling him to be wary of the obvious. What in God's name did that mean? If not the obvious, what—the obscure? Maybe Blankett and all the others were right; there was no French intention to invade India, and his whole goddamned mission was a goddamned waste of time.

Charles muttered an obscenity under his breath. All he had to do was force his attention until he finished with the purser's report, then he could sign the damn thing and go on deck. "Lemons . . ." He remembered that he was also arrears in his log-keeping. That could wait until another time. It was uncomfortably warm in the cramped cabin. If he listened he could hear Beechum, Sykes, and Aviemore playing at cards on the wardroom dining table and the footfalls of seamen on the gundeck above. There was little talk at the game which had been going on for hours, but the shuffling and slapping of the cards was clear enough. He could not hear anything of the activities on the quarterdeck, two decks above, which he would have followed easily were he in his own cabin. His ears picked up when he heard the door from the crew's mess to the wardroom open, then slam loudly shut. "Slow down, Hitch," Beechum's voice commanded. "And keep it soft, the captain's working."

"It's the Frogs!" Midshipman Hitch chirped breathlessly, then the tap-tap-

tap of a pair of feet hurrying across the floor.

Frogs? What frogs? What could frogs possibly have to do with anything? It came to him—not frogs, Frogs! He dumped the ledger on the cot and swung his legs over the side to search for his shoes as the knock came at his door.

"Come."

"Lieutenant Bevan's respects, sir," Hitch said formally. "The lookout's seen a Frenchie. The same, he says, what we did with before."

"Thank you, Mr. Hitch," Charles said, attempting to suppress his excitement. "You may tell Mr. Bevan that I shall be on deck presently."

He quickly slipped his feet into his shoes and buckled them. Without bothering with his coat he took up his sword and hat. "Come along, gentlemen," he said as he passed the card game, exited the wardroom, and made for the ladderway.

Cassandra sailed a course north-by-northwest in deep water up the center of the long, narrow sea with a following wind. Two days from Mocha, they were giving the reef-strewn Dahlak Archipelago a wide berth to port. At the noon sighting their latitude had been fifteen degrees, forty-five minutes north.

"What has he seen, Daniel?" Charles said as soon as he came onto the quarterdeck.

"Two sail off the larboard quarter," Bevan said. "One of them is square-rigged. The lookout swears she's the same French frigate we encountered in the Atlantic, although that seems a bit hard to swallow. The other's some kind of local dhow, I think, double masted with a small mizzen aft, all lateen sails."

"What course do they have?"

"The dhow's running to the southwest; it's possible the frigate is in pursuit."

"Mr. Sykes," Charles called. "You will be pleased to take a glass up to the mainmast crosstrees. Make careful note of every detail you can, then report back what you see. I am particularly interested in the identity of the frigate. You might also make a careful scan of the horizon to be certain there are no other sail in sight."

"Aye, aye, sir." Sykes took up a telescope from the binnacle and started toward the mainmast shrouds.

"Mr. Cromley."

"Sir."

"Steer west-by-southwest, if you please."

"Yes, sir. We'll be heading into shallow water amongst those islands, you know."

"Thank you, Mr. Cromley. I am aware of that."

Charles rubbed a hand across his forehead. If the lookout was to be believed, the sighting confirmed that at least one of the French warships had

entered the Red Sea. Where was the two-decker—what was her name?—
Raisonnable. If there was one, the other would probably have accompanied
her. He thought it a good wager that the big seventy-four was somewhere
farther north. The frigate—L'Agile, he remembered—had likely been detached
to collect suitable transports as she came upon them. In this instance, he did
not pause to consider whether or not he should give chase to engage. It was his
duty to do so. The presence of the two ships of war would seriously
compromise Blankett's ability to blockade the sea's exit. Capturing or crippling
the frigate would help to redress the balance, leaving only the seventy-four to
deal with. Besides, it was the first time he had come upon her without the
larger consort. As he had the opportunity, he had best take advantage of it;
there might not be a better one.

It was troublesome that Cassandra's change of course to intercept the
enemy would carry her ever closer to the Dahlak Archipelago, an almost
completely uncharted expanse of scores, if not hundreds, of small islands,
coral reefs, rocks, shoals, and shallows. The morass extended for a hundred
miles or more to the African coast. It was likely that the shallow-drafted dhow
intended to run there for her safety. For the deeper draft of the frigates, it
would be an ungodly dangerous place for a sea battle.

"Daniel, you may clear the ship for action. Don't send the men to quarters
until we are closer."

"Aye, aye," Bevan said.

"Station two men in the forechains with lead lines, one on each side. We'll
take soundings as we go. Send Beechum forward with a notebook to keep a
record. Assign Hitch and Aviemore to run back and forth with reports. Do you
have all that?"

"Aye, I have it."

The bosun's call sounded for all hands on deck. The men hurried up the
ladder-ways full of chatter. Word had apparently already passed between
decks that a French warship had been sighted, and she was the same they had
fought before. Charles watched the men carefully, attempting to read their
mood. Some at least were excited at the prospect of renewing the battle. Others
—he noted the more experienced seamen among them—moved deliberately to
their places, their eyes cautious as they glanced up at him in passing. Still, the
waisters took up their lines to brace the sails around. Others fell without
notable enthusiasm to work preparing the ship for battle. They would tend to
their duties when the guns began firing, he knew. They would have little
choice.

Cassandra heeled gently in the calm seas as she wore to take the wind on
her port quarter, all plain sail aloft. The bulkheads and furnishings of what

would normally have been the captain's cabin were struck below, as were the living animals and partitions for the manger forward. The cook doused the galley fire, raked out the embers, and tossed them overboard. The gundeck soon became a single unobstructed expanse from stem to stern, occupied by Cassandra's main armament of twenty-six twelve-pounder cannon. Six additional six-pounder long guns were shared between quarterdeck and forecastle, as were eight short-barreled twenty-four-pound carronades. The decks around the guns were sprinkled with sand to improve footing, then wet with buckets of seawater to discourage fires starting from spilled gunpowder.

Charles noticed that Adolphus Jones, Mrs. Jones, and Constance had come onto the quarterdeck to stand by the far rail, which they must have done since their cabin was now dismantled. It would not do to have any of them killed before they even reached Egypt. He thought to cross and tell them they would have to go below when he saw Sykes approaching along the gangway.

"Sir," the midshipman panted, breathless from his rush to what was nearly the very top of the mainmast and back down again.

"Take a deep breath," Charles said. There was no great urgency; he could see no sign of either ship from the deck as yet.

"I seen them clear," Sykes managed. "She's the same French frigate as before, I'm sure of it. The same number of guns and the shape at the beak. The other is medium-sized, maybe three-hundred tons. I'm not sure what she is, but she ain't no dhow like you'd find hereabouts."

"What sort of craft to you make her to be?"

"From her looks I'd say a pink from the Mediterranean," the midshipman said, scratching at his chin in thought. "I seen the like at Genoa, but I don't fathom what she's doing here. She's not armed that I can tell."

"Her course?" Charles asked. He didn't know what to make of Sykes' opinion of the smaller ship, or if it mattered. A pink was a common enough type of merchantman along the southern coast of Europe. They normally carried triangular lateen sails, which might lead to mistaking her for an Arab trader.

"I'd say to the southwest, sure enough. Into them islands forward, anyway. There's a mass of them when you look from the crosstrees. They go on as far as you can see."

"Thank you, Mr. Sykes. Have you been able to ascertain anything of their purpose? Could you tell if the frigate was in pursuit, for example?"

Sykes furrowed his brow in concentration. "It might be, sir," he said hesitantly. "The Frenchie was following by about two cable lengths. I didn't see no cannon fire though."

"I see," Charles said. He thought it unlikely the frigate would fire into anything she was hoping to capture except as a last resort. She might fire warning shots though. "Thank you. If that is all, you may assist Lieutenant Beechum forward."

"There is one more thing, sir."

"What?"

"The warship, she's seen us. She's braced her sails up tight to come into the wind. You should see her masts from the deck soon. The other has gone straight on. It's possible the frigate means to have at us, sir."

"I expect you're right. Again, thank you, Mr. Sykes."

Before Charles could seek out Bevan to speak with him, he saw the boy Aviemore fidgeting anxiously, waiting for his turn. "What have you to say?" he asked.

"Twenty fathoms, and . . ."

"Mr. Aviemore, you know how to make a proper report. Do so, please."

"Yes, sir. Mr. Beechum's respects, sir," the midshipman said laboriously. "The sea depth is at twenty fathoms and shoaling, sir."

"Very good," Charles said, feeling he had been unnecessarily abrupt. "That was nicely done. I apologize for being sharp with you. My respects to Mr. Beechum and please ask him to keep me informed."

"Oh, it weren't nothing," Aviemore squeaked and left at a run to return to the bow.

Twenty fathoms. Charles knew that it would become shallower. He remembered from the very few soundings on his chart depths as shallow as a single fathom far from any land, although five and six were more normal. Before they had turned westward, there had been no bottom on a hundred-fathom line. Cassandra's keel would be nearly three fathoms below the waves, slightly more by the stern as she was newly provisioned. The added complexity of having to fight in uncertain waters gnawed at him.

Looking forward he could see the first of several low-lying islands in the distance over the sparkling water. He saw something else as well. Picking up his own glass he found L'Agile's upper masts wavering in its lens. He opened his watch and looked at it. With the wind as it was, it seemed likely they would meet sometime in the evening and there should still be enough daylight to do his business. In all probability there would be little opportunity for maneuver. It would be best to lie close to, very close to, where superior gunnery would tell. They might even come aboard and try her by main force if the opportunity presented itself.

He went over to Bevan near the wheel. "I want all of the cutlasses, axes, and pikes sharpened."

The lieutenant nodded his comprehension. "You plan to board?" he said.

"I don't know. We'll have to see as the situation develops. I'll tell you this, I don't want a long drawn out exchange of broadsides if it can be helped. I'd rather it were over with quickly."

"Wouldn't we all, Charlie," Bevan answered dryly.

Charles ignored the comment. "In about an hour's time you may send the men below and feed them," he said in clipped tones. "Something easy—cheese, biscuits, whatever the cook has to hand. No spirits." Without waiting for an acknowledgement, he turned and hurried along the gangway to speak to Beechum in the bow.

"By the mark eighteen and a half," he heard the starboard leadsman call out loudly, repeated by the seaman in the larboard chains. From forward everything looked closer, the islands and the enemy frigate's masts.

"Mr. Beechum," Charles said, "a word, if you please."

"Sir," the lieutenant said, looking up from his paper. Charles saw that he had sketched out their course and the small islands ahead, neatly penciling in the soundings as they were given. A transit lay on the deck beside him, which he assumed Beechum was using to take bearings with which to fix the positions of the islands.

"Do you see those French masts there?"

"Yes, sir?"

"I'm thinking you might take note of her course as best you can. She has to have deep enough water under her to swim in. It may come that we will need to use the same path."

"I've thought of that," Beechum said seriously. "Here, you can see where I've made a line. She altered her course a trifle to starboard a quarter hour ago."

Charles smiled. He had a fondness for the young lieutenant, and thought him to have the makings of a more than competent officer. "Very good," he said. "Please carry on."

The boatswain's call piped the men to their supper. Charles returned to the quarterdeck to pace nervously back and forth, occasionally looking forward to judge the steadily decreasing distance between himself and the Frenchman. He did not like the situation he found himself in. There were too many unknowns. The lay of the seabed was one. L'Agile was the faster ship; why hadn't her captain decided to run? Why had he chosen to sail into the archipelago instead of the safer waters in the center of the sea?

By degrees, the base of her masts and then the line of the frigate's hull became visible over the edge of the sea. She angled obliquely toward a gap between two small islands, little more than lumps covered with low scrub, near to where the two ships' courses would intersect. Five miles separated them, he guessed, maybe less; the islands were three or four miles distant. The enemy frigate's hull appeared hard and dark between the pale blue sea and paler sky.

She flew her topsails and topgallants, bright white under the glare of the descending sun. Charles took up his long glass again. Snapping it open, he trained it on the Frenchman, forward near her bow. He saw no sign of anyone in the forechains tossing a lead to take soundings. Her captain must have better charts than his, or some foreknowledge of where the channels ran. His unease increased.

He could just hear the leadsmen in the bow calling out the depth, "by the mark ten," but Aviemore and Hitch ran back at regular intervals to inform him anyway. It had been at a more or less steady ten fathoms for the past half hour.

Augustus appeared noiselessly by his elbow. "Won't you have somethin' to eat, Cap'n? It may be a spell before the chance come again."

Charles had to think. He felt no desire for food. The muscles of his stomach were already tight from anxiety. "Bring my uniform jacket, if you would. Put a few ship's biscuits in one of the pockets."

Augustus nodded and left to go below. As Charles watched, L'Agile slipped between the two islands, spilled her wind as she hove to, and began to take in her sails. Broadside on, she came to a halt in the water only a mile or a little more ahead. He saw a small splash by her bow and then her stern.

"She's dropped anchors fore and aft," the lookout in the tops shouted down.

Charles suspected the anchorage had not been chosen at random. The positions of the islands left few options, and he would bet his eye teeth that there was an underwater barrier, a reef or a bar, between them. Possibly the French captain hoped that his English opponent would rush forward in all haste, only to run aground and rip his bottom open, all without his having to fire a shot. Charles ground his teeth. There would be no boarding, or even a gun duel at close range where the issue might be decided relatively quickly. He was not happy about it. Feeling his way around the obstruction to come up from the other side would take hours. The setting sun squatted, huge and orange, just above the horizon. No, if this was the ground the Frenchman wanted, he would have to give it to him. It was time to get some of Cassandra's way off.

The crew began to come back on deck after their meal. He spoke to Bevan, "Daniel, get the topsails in. We will proceed under topgallants alone. When that is done you may beat to quarters."

"Aye, aye, Charlie."

"Mr. Beechum's respects, sir," Midshipman Aviemore said, coming to a halt and touching his hat formally.

"Cut all the folderol," Charles snapped. "What's the depth?"

"Six and a half, sir. The bottom's rising rapidly."

"Mr. Aviemore, listen to me carefully. Go back and stay by Beechum. When the depth reaches to three-and-a-half, come running as fast as you can."

"Aye, aye, sir."

Augustus appeared with the uniform jacket, which Charles slipped into without speaking.

Cassandra slowed noticeably as her lower sails were put up in brails. The marine drummer marched stiffly to his place at the fore of the quarterdeck and raised his sticks. The long drum roll rattled menacingly across the decks. Charles raised his telescope again and stared hard at the frigate less than a mile in front. He saw that her gun ports were open and cannon extended. As he lowered the glass he again noticed Jones and his two women standing together by the far rail.

"We will employ the starboard battery," he said to Bevan. "Be prepared to come about on my command. Have the ship's boats put over the off side. We will also anchor fore and aft." Without waiting for an answer he crossed the deck to speak with his passengers.

"You must go below decks now," he said. "I suggest that the orlop is the safest place."

Jones nodded in apparent unconcern; the elder Mrs. Jones in agreement. The sound of L'Agile's broadside thundered across the water. Several balls screeched low through the rigging; a number splashed close alongside, throwing up tall geysers. At least one struck home somewhere forward. "I will not," Constance said. "I want to watch."

"If you please," Charles insisted politely. "It will be dangerous. I am ordering you below."

The younger Mrs. Jones folded her arms across her chest, eyeing him defiantly. "I won't," she repeated.

"If you do not do as you are told immediately," Charles growled, "I will have you carried to the hold and put into restraints. If you wish to be useful, you may assist the surgeon."

Constance glared at him as if she'd been insulted. "You mean that I might tend to the wounded? Me? What kind of woman do you think I am?" She might have said more but Mr. Jones took her firmly by the arm and the three started toward the hatchway. Charles looked forward to check L'Agile's position, saw that she was at almost two-cable's distance. He also saw young Aviemore racing aftward along the gangway, hatless, his coattails flying.

"Bring her to bear," he shouted at Bevan.

Cassandra slewed to port, her starboard cannon confronting the frigate. The men on the topgallant yard fisted in the remaining sails to tie them off.

"Fire!" he yelled at the top of his voice.

Cassandra's guns exploded in a single outpouring of cloud and flame, the reverberations of the guns' recoil jarring the ship. Before the smoke had blown clear, the Frenchman fired a second time. Round shot filled the air, snarling, buzzing, screaming as they passed. Several told against the hull, which Charles could feel through the timbers of the deck. In one part of his mind he heard the splashes of anchors at the bow and stern.

"Sir, sir!" Something was pulling at the sleeve of his jacket. He looked and saw Aviemore frantically trying to get his attention. "Mr. Beechum's respects, sir," the midshipman began, his eyes shining with excitement.

Charles wondered if Aviemore had any comprehension of the dangers flying all around him. "Thank you, I am aware that we have come to our assigned depth," he said. "I appreciate your reporting so promptly." He saw the quarterdeck carronades being pulled forward on their slides. Their crews seemed to be handling the weapons as well as he could expect. On the six-pounders, the wads were only just being rammed home. The carronades discharged almost as one with their high-pitched barks, at the same moment the crews serving the long guns heaved on their tackles to run them out. Cassandra trembled with the tearing broadside from the twelve-pounders in the gundeck and the six-pounders on the quarterdeck and forecastle. He watched carefully through the drifting smoke for the fall of the shot and counted only four striking the sea surface. The sun touched the horizon beyond.

As the battle settled into a steady exchange Charles paced the quarterdeck, his eyes intent on the enemy with a growing sense of unease. The distance between them when Cassandra had come to anchor was a little more than a cable and a half's length. It was an unsatisfactory distance for an engagement. At this range, the larger guns did not have the destructive power they would display at fifty or even a hundred yards. Most shots told, of course, as both ships were stationary, and he could see evidence of damage on L'Agile, a section of broken railing, scars to her sides, trailing rigging.

L'Agile fired off her guns as one, clouding herself in gray-black smoke, an orderly row of angry orange sparks showing through. A section of hammock netting burst inward between two guns, hurling a seaman backward across the deck. Two others writhed in pain, pools of red on the deck boards. Bevan quickly ordered the men taken below. The carronades again jerked back as they fired, their crews already moving to sponge out and reload. Before Charles could take a full breath, the remaining guns discharged in a drawn out series of rending explosions as the quicker crews fired before the slower. Again, he counted four splashes close alongside the enemy hull. It became clear to him that the whole thing was a waste of time and powder. Nothing was going to be decided while the light lasted.

Charles found the fingers of his left hand tapping impatiently against the hilt of his sword. To still them he slipped the hand into his jacket pocket where he discovered the ship's biscuit Augustus had placed there. He raised one of the biscuits to his mouth and began to chew. L'Agile's cannon blazed out once more. He saw two strikes to the bulwarks along the gangway and some fresh-cut rigging snapping from the impact. Cassandra maintained the faster rate of fire, he determined; probably four to the opponent's three and the Frenchman would be suffering proportionately. Still, it wasn't enough; it wasn't near enough. Charles looked out at the sun, more than half buried beneath the horizon. He began to think of options. There would be no moon until after midnight. That would help.

His own increasingly ragged broadside sounded out, first the carronades, then the easier to manage sixes. The gundeck armament exploded in a satisfying roar, only two or three trailing afterward. A small cheer went up from forward and Charles saw the main topsail yard crack on L'Agile, the yard arms dangling at an awkward angle from their stays. He took another bite of the biscuit. A silence came from the frigate as she reloaded, then both ships' guns boomed out together. He thought he noted a gap in the otherwise orderly row of fiery tongues from her side. That was promising, he thought, but nothing that couldn't be repaired overnight. The sun dipped lower, a golden sliver on the sea. He knew that darkness would follow quickly.

As the long-range fusillade continued, Cassandra sustained added damage to her hull and bulwarks. A twelve-pound cannon on the gundeck dismounted with a loud clang, its carriage shattered. From reports he received, ten men had been taken below to the surgeon, three were dead. He ordered Hitch and Aviemore, who held no particular duties except to carry his messages, to collect buckets of fresh water to carry from gun to gun so the men could refresh themselves. Charles noted with little satisfaction in the last of the daylight that the enemy's main topgallant mast had cracked at its step to hang upside down beside the broken yardarms. It was a hell of a weight of round shot for so small a result, he thought.

The French ship's form became indistinct against the darkening sea and sky. L'Agile's position soon revealed itself only when she fired, and then as a line of yellow-white flashes in the distance.

"Cease firing, Daniel," Charles ordered, satisfied that both ships were now firing blind.

Bevan bellowed out the order several times before the cannon fell silent. Men, spent from their exertions, sat on the deck, their backs propped against bulwarks and gun carriages. "Christ," the lieutenant said in frustration. "This has been just about goddamned pointless. We'll have to find some way to close the distance if we're going to start again in the morning."

"I don't see any point to starting in the morning unless we have to," Charles said, coming to a decision. "We will attempt cutting her out in the night."

"Boarding parties?"

Charles nodded, only slightly more at ease now that he had fixed on a course of action. "Give the men a half-ration of spirits and time to rest. We will begin a little before the rise of the moon."

L'Agile's broadside flashed out of the darkness once more, to little effect that Charles could determine. The French ship did not fire again. An eerie silence descended, tainted by the acrid odor of spent gunpowder heavy in the air.

Two hours passed slowly, the sea surface as black as coal. Charles spent much of the time pacing the quarterdeck up and down, and down and up again in nervous anticipation of the event to come. He, Bevan and Winchester had worked out the plan for the attack fairly quickly. Cassandra's four boats would be filled with the marines and as many seamen as they could carry. Under the cover of the near total darkness they would row across in two groups of two boats each. The main thrust would be at L'Agile's quarterdeck, boarding at the mizzen chains. Charles would lead with Lieutenant Ayres and the marines in the launch, with Winchester commanding the first cutter. Bevan, in the second cutter and Beechum with the jollyboat would make for the hopefully less well defended bow as soon as they heard the commotion. With luck, they would catch the French unprepared, capture the quarterdeck and pinch the crew between two forces.

Charles knew that there were a hundred things that could go wrong. The French captain might well guess his plan and have his men prepared and waiting; one or more boats might run upon a reef, or get lost, or simply arrive too early or too late. He did not want to contemplate the implications of an unsuccessful attempt. Cassandra would be stripped of almost all of her crew and the French might well launch a counter attack of their own. Charles gave Cromley strict orders to cut the anchor cables and sail for Mocha as best he could if no lantern signal was received confirming the frigate's capture within an hour and a half of the boats' departure.

The time, when it arrived, seemed to have come too quickly. At seven bells in the first watch, the men were assembled with their weapons in the waist, under orders to maintain silence. Augustus brought Charles his pistols, which he stuck in his belt. He then stood silently by with his hand resting on the handle of his cutlass. Charles spoke one by one with his officers to make sure each understood his part in the assault and the importance of the two sets of boats boarding in close sequence. The seamen and marines went down first, on netting fastened over the side, then Beechum, Bevan, Winchester, Ayers, and

Charles himself.

He was committed now, Charles thought, as Malvern gave the order to shove off. The thole pins to leverage the oars had been wrapped in cloth to soften their grinding as the blades dipped and pulled. He soon lost sight of Bevan's boats as his own circled to the left, lit only by a universe of stars. It would be a row of fifteen or twenty minutes before they would come up to L'Agile's stern. Charles could not read his watch no matter how closely he held it to his eye and he dared not strike a light, so he began counting out the seconds in his head. Ten minutes passed. They should be able to make out the French ship's masts before long. Cassandra was already an invisible shadow in the darkness behind. Fifteen minutes. He felt his heartbeat quicken in anticipation. She must appear soon. It was unnerving that he saw or heard no indication, not even muffled speech or work to repairs the damages from the day's carronade. The launch's oars dipped into the water with the smallest of splashes, the wash chuckling along her side.

Charles stopped counting at twenty-two minutes. A softening of the darkness announced the imminent rise of the moon. There was nothing, no sound, no looming hull, no slap of waves against a ship's planking. He swore under his breath. He must have miscalculated the distance, or the direction, or the current. No, he couldn't have; it wasn't that far. He thought he heard the smallest of sounds off to starboard.

"Over there, sir," Malvern whispered, indicating with his arm.

"Put the rudder over," Charles said softly. He held his breath, his eyes and ears straining for the slightest indication. He noticed as the rising moon cracked the horizon.

The noise became more distinct. It sounded for all the world like a boat's oars pulling in the water straight toward them. "Be ready men, it may be the French rowing guard," he heard Bevan's muted voice.

"Is that you, Daniel?" Charles called out. It wouldn't do to be fired upon by one's own boat.

"Charlie?"

"Come along side," Charles spoke in a normal way. To Malvern he said, "Show a lantern."

A ship's boat appeared from the depths, ghostly in the slowly increasing moonlight. "Boat yer oars," Malvern ordered as the cutter glided alongside.

"Where the hell are they?" Bevan asked.

Charles looked around him in all directions. With the moon half up, he could just make out Cassandra in the distance and, after a moment, the low forms of the two islands between which L'Agile had anchored herself. The second cutter and jollyboat soon closed around them. There was nothing else.

"She's cut her cables and left," Charles said. "She's not here."

CHAPTER NINE

"What can you tell me of this bay, Mr. Jones?" Charles asked. The two bent over the chart spread out on the binnacle, Charles' finger on the mark for a small village on an island in a bay against the African coast some twenty leagues to the southwest. The place lay behind the maze of islands and shoals that made up the Dahlak Archipelago. It might provide a haven in which L'Agile could carry out repairs after the encounter the day before. There was also the question of the European pink and where she had run to. He remembered Underwood mentioning some trade in a place he called Massawa. The name for the village given on the map was "Matzua."

Dozens of Cassandra's ratings were aloft splicing lines and cables at the direction of the boatswain, or forward scabbing a splint to the bowsprit, which had been damaged in the battle. The two cutters had been sent out at dawn under Winchester and Beechum to take soundings of the seabed to satisfy Charles' curiosity as to whether or not there was an underwater barrier between the two islands and if there might be some channel through it. Charles could see them scuttling to and fro off the starboard beam, dropping the leads and taking the readings.

"Matzua?" Jones said with a frown. "They've got the name wrong. The place is Massawa. Those as pass for cartographers in London must be addled."

Charles had long since decided that the American (if he was American) would never be admired for his congeniality. Halfway through the forenoon watch, the heat of the day had already become suffocating beneath an unmerciful sun. Even the light southerly breeze seemed to increase their discomfort rather than bring relief. "Massawa, then," Charles agreed, more interested in facts than Jones's opinions of mapmakers. He already knew the chart to be sadly deficient. "Is there a harbor there, port facilities?"

Jones rubbed at the growing beard on his cheek. "Aye, there's a harbor, so I'm told. A good one, too. At least as good as any you'll find along the Red Sea. You have deep water to right up behind the island."

"How deep?" Charles asked.

To this he received a blank stare. "Deep enough for dhows. How the hell would I know?"

"Fair enough," Charles said. "What else can you tell me?"

A SEA UNTO ITSELF

"The town's on an island of the same name," Jones elaborated grudgingly. "The main harbor's tucked behind between Massawa and the mainland. It's an Arab settlement with a Turkish governor, I believe. Only local craft call there, mostly trading in coffee and civet, maybe the odd girl or boy."

Charles thought about the pink Sykes had reported being pursued by the frigate. "Might there be any Europeans there? A trading post of some sort, or an agent from Spain or Italy?"

"I've heard a rumor that there's a few Genovese on the run from the French attempting something. I doubt it's of consequence," Jones answered with some impatience. "Look, I've never been to the place and I don't care to go there. It's a godforsaken desolate little island in a sweltering bay with a stinking little Arab town. There's no goddamned good reason for anyone to call there." He looked at Charles suspiciously. "Why do you want to know? You're not still after that Frenchman, are you?"

"I am," Charles said.

"No," Jones said flatly. "You cannot do it, sir. Your duty is to take me to Egypt and put me on the coast. My work there is vital. We've already wasted a precious day exchanging bombardments with that frigate, to no particular purpose. I've no more time for such foolishness."

"I am well aware of my duty, I'll thank you, sir," Charles said, his patience at Jones' overbearing presumption wearing thin. "We will carry you to the head of the sea in good time. But if there is an enemy warship loose in these waters it is also my duty to capture or destroy her. It seems likely she has gone to this Massawa, and therefore we shall follow. I trust that satisfies your objections."

"No, it does not."

"Then I trust you will accommodate yourself to the inevitable. If you will accept my regrets, I have other responsibilities requiring my attention."

Charles' other responsibilities included receiving the reports from the ship's carpenter and gunner. Mr. Burrows allowed that Cassandra had sustained little serious damage to her hull, and none below the waterline. The French round shot had lost much of their penetrating power over the distance at which they were fired. The gunner had less welcome news: They had expended almost half of their supply of powder and ball during the ultimately fruitless exchange. While Cassandra might replenish her water and some form of food from the towns along the coast, there was nowhere within two thousand miles to procure additional supplies of cylinder powder and iron shot.

Shortly before the end of the forenoon watch, the ship's cutters returned. Charles, Winchester, and Beechum went down to the wardroom where

148

Cromley's chart of the sea and a sheet of paper were spread out on the table. Charles glanced at the smaller page with its penciled sketch of the two islands and numbers jotted all around them. On the larger chart, the islands that the French ship had used to protect herself were not shown at all, nor were nearly any of the features of the seabed except the briefest notation that it was "corally." "What have you to tell me of the depths hereabouts?" he said.

Winchester placed the page with his and Beechum's soundings on top of the Admiralty chart. "The ground's thick with coral all around," he began. "Much of it is four and five fathoms down, but there are outcroppings nearly to the surface. Almost the whole distance between the islands is high coral; you can see it fairly clear from the boat."

"What's this?" Charles said, looking closely at the islands and the depths. He noticed that the two bits of land had been given names.

Winchester colored slightly. "To be clear we thought it best to identify them. Beechum chose the labels."

Charles saw that the larger island to the south had been christened 'Mrs. Edgemont Island,' the northern one, 'Mrs. Winchester.' "I see," he said with a laugh. "For simplicity, why don't we call them 'Penny' and 'Ellie?'"

Winchester looked doubtful, but Beechum immediately took the paper, crossed out the names, and entered 'Penny's Island' and 'Ellie's Island' in his neat hand. "I was thinking that together we might term them the 'Sisters-in-Law,'" Beechum said happily.

"I'm sure the women will be pleased," Charles said. "But to business: is there any channel between them?"

Winchester nodded. "On the north side ... here." With Beechum's pencil he indicated a space nearer to the smaller of the islands. "There's a channel at three and a half fathoms. It's narrow, but if we go cautious it should be manageable. The main thing is keep closer to Ellie than P ... the other." He seemed embarrassed to use Penny's name, as if it might reflect on her personally.

"I thought you might feel that way," Charles said with a straight face. "Seeing as to which you're married to."

Beechum looked blankly at this; Winchester smiled.

Within the hour, repairs to the rigging completed and a yardarm scabbed onto the wounded bowsprit, Cassandra weighed her anchors. Cautiously she angled across the wind toward the gap Winchester had indicated. Looking over the side rail, Charles found he could see clearly beneath the sparkling water. It was an amazing sight with schools of bright-colored fish, several kinds of shark, from two and three feet to much larger. Once he saw a huge gray-white ray at least twelve feet across swimming languorously along the bottom, its broad fins undulating like the wings of a gigantic bird. With two leadsmen in the forechains on either side, they slowly crossed over the reef. Charles stood nervously in the beak, staring down as the orange fingers of coral passed just beneath the stem, blizzards of fish darting and swirling in unending streams from their path. Then the bottom abruptly fell away, the darker shades of seaweed and black sand predominating.

"By the mark, seven," the leadsmen chanted out almost together. The next throw recorded almost ten fathoms. Charles breathed easier and made his way aft where he ordered a single seaman to be left in the bow to cast the lead, and he to be replaced half hourly in deference to the leaching heat. "We will make to the southwest, if you please, Mr. Cromley," he said to the master. "Under topsails only for the time being." Cassandra would still be treading gingerly, and there was no point to hurrying upon some obstacle with too much speed to avoid it.

The archipelago revealed itself as a seemingly unbounded expanse of scattered islands, some mere specks, others several miles in width. All appeared low lying and featureless in the shimmerings of the heat rising off the water. By noon the ragged dark line of the African coast took form along the horizon to the west. Sea depths remained at a relatively comfortable fourteen and sixteen fathoms, although once going as deep as forty before coming back up again. At nightfall, Charles ordered the sails taken in and an anchor cast off to wait out the hours of darkness.

In the morning they started again. The sea soon opened to a broad uninterrupted expanse, the islands and atolls falling behind. The depth of the water beneath also increased abruptly from fourteen fathoms on one cast, to thirty-five, then forty-seven. Charles allowed the leadsman to stand down when no bottom was reached on a fifty-fathom line. By the beginning of the afternoon watch, the line of coast formed as a dark serrated mass, unbroken to the north and south as far as the eye could see. Bell by bell, as the half-hour glass was turned, the mass defined itself as a rugged chain of blue-green mountains falling to a narrow strip of desert beside the sea. There were no signs of human habitation, not even the meanest hovel along the expanse of shore. The afternoon watch turned to the first dog, then the second, the sun sinking toward the mountain crests. A thin line of white surf showed along the foot of the bluffs at the sea's edge, now three miles to starboard.

"There it is," Bevan said, a long glass to his eye, pointing southwestward toward a bluff point with an opening bay beyond. He lowered the telescope. "That's your Massawa, I'll wager."

Charles looked through his own lens, following the line of the surf until he came to a low settlement on what might have been a small island or a spit of land tucked into the northern end of the bay. It was difficult to pick out much detail in the failing light, and what there was of it was shaded by mountain scarps rising on the land behind. He made out some sort of craft there, dhows or what, he couldn't tell. He was fairly certain that he saw nothing of the towering masts of a ship of war.

"I think it would be best if we came to anchor for the night, Daniel," he said. "We will call in the full light of day. I might suggest an especially vigilant watch be kept about the ship until then."

Daybreak came as clear as crystal, the sun rising above the sea orange-red, just as it had set. The light outlined a sprinkling of islands to the east, the inner limit of the archipelago. With it, the warmth of the day announced its soon-to–be-magnified presence. Through his glass, Charles carefully surveyed the distant bay. It became evident that there were two settlements. One occupied a modest outcropping with mud-brick, flat-roofed dwellings similar to those he had seen at Mocha, only smaller. An abbreviated minaret poked above the roof lines, and there were two sambuks, probably what passed for fishing boats, pulled up on a sandy beach.

A peninsula jutted into the bay a half mile to the north, occupied by a collection of single-story European-style buildings laid out in a regular pattern with low-pitched roofs. Charles thought he made out signs of construction along the water's edge on the southern side. Three ships rode placidly at anchor in a natural harbor between the island and the point of built-up land. He studied these carefully and decided they were indeed two pinks, with their distinctive narrow sterns and lateen sails, and a larger, square-rigged polacre. From their shape he thought it likely they were of Italian construction, probably from Genoa or Leghorn. There was even a newly built and relatively small stone redoubt overlooking the anchorage at the point of the peninsula. At the distance he couldn't tell if the fortification was armed with cannon or not. Yellow and blue flags of a pattern he had never seen before flew from the redoubt as well as from the roof of the largest of the buildings. One thing was abundantly clear, there was no ship approaching the size of a frigate of war by either of the settlements or anywhere else within sight.

When Charles lowered the glass he found Daniel Bevan standing beside him. "Weigh the bower, Daniel," he said. "We'll take soundings and chart them as we go. It might prove useful to somebody."

Bevan relayed the orders to Winchester, standing officer of the morning watch; then turned back. "Do we offer a salute to the fort?"

'Fort,' was an overly generous term, Charles thought. Still, it was stone and had some sort of flag. He hated using even the minuscule amount of powder it would take for the gesture. "Five guns," he decided. "I'll be damned if I'll waste more powder than that." It was almost an insult to fire off so few, particularly if the residents were touchy about the subject, or if, on the longest chance, some royalty happened to be present; but he didn't even know whose flag it was or what authority lay behind it except for Jones's mention of Italian refugees.

Cassandra approached slowly under topsails braced tight as she clawed across the fitful morning breeze. The ship's bell rang eight times to mark the beginning of the forenoon watch. Still a mile away, Charles watched the distant settlements. He wondered about the Italians, if that's what they were, and how they had found themselves in this faraway place, fleeing the French or no. Genoa had fallen relatively easily to the advances of Napoleon Bonaparte's army, and there was said to be considerable Republican sentiment there. It crossed his mind that they might in some way be connected to France's designs on India, but it seemed a farfetched idea. In any event, he would soon know.

Raising his telescope again, he saw the figures of people—white skinned in European dress—beginning to gather at the near end of the town close by the fortification. There were a few women among them, he noted, with dresses down to their shoes and parasols for protection against the sun. He saw no one making an effort to man the redoubt. The construction along the harbor front was more extensive than he had thought earlier. In addition to a stone quay almost a cable in length, there were a number of substantial buildings rising, possibly for use as warehouses, judging by their size. What sort of trade could be carried on from this desolate part of the world that would require such facilities? A large number of native laborers were gathered at the far end of the quay under white supervisors, preparing no doubt for the day's work. The place looked to be thoroughly hot, dry, and dusty, with an expanse of desolate scrub stretching several miles to the rising massif behind.

"You may show the colors," Charles said to Sykes, already standing beside the halyard with the multi-crossed flag of the United Kingdoms of England and Scotland bent on. At once the bunting ran up the mast, breaking out to fly in the wind when it reached the mainmast truck. Charles nodded to Beechum. Simultaneously, the first of the six-pounders sounded out, the noise echoing back from the heights.

The boom of the first gun brought a flurry of activity from the settlement. Additional numbers appeared from some of the buildings, mostly men, some with muskets in their hands. A few ran toward the redoubt, but for what purpose he couldn't guess since he could now see into the empty embrasures. They must have seen that Cassandra was British and not French, but that should have been more reassuring than otherwise. As the second of the guns fired its powder charge, Charles saw the flag at the center of the fortification dip and then lift, then dip and lift again. Since there were no cannon to return the salute, lowering and raising the flag was the only form of greeting available.

"Do you think they'll send a pilot boat out?" Bevan asked with a grin.

Charles laughed. "I doubt they have a pilot, or a boat for that matter, other than what came with the ships. I think we should come to anchor at the head of the harbor about midway between the town and that Arab island. If you would have the launch prepared, I'll take Winchester, Beechum, Ayres, and a dozen of his marines across for a call. Just in case, run out the starboard guns. That should impress them."

Bevan spoke to Winchester about the orders. Charles glanced over the port rail at the little island with its sleepy Arab village. Hardly a soul stirred along its beach except for a few curious children drawn out by the sounds of the cannon fire. He saw no flag or any other sign of Ottoman authority. That was unusual, but perhaps the Turks just didn't bother for such a distant and tiny outpost.

He saw Jones come onto the quarterdeck as the men were preparing to cast off the anchor. "I am going over to pay a visit to that settlement, Italians I think you mentioned," Charles said. "I would be pleased to have you along."

"Genovese," Jones corrected him. "And, no, I can't be bothered with their kind. I require a boat to take me there." He pointed toward the Arab town. "See that it is arranged."

Charles asked Bevan to prepare the jollyboat for Jones, and then slipped reluctantly into his best uniform coat and hat that Augustus had brought up from his cabin. "Thank you," he said to his servant. Augustus would be part of the launch's crew, he knew. "I would be pleased for you to come on shore when we land, just in case there is trouble." He decided there were situations where he felt more comfortable with the man at his back.

"Yes, Cap'n," Augustus said. Charles noted that he had already armed himself with a cutlass, which was hung from his belt. Shifting his gaze, he saw that numbers of the crew were gathering in the waist in anticipation. Some were looking out over the side, others up at the quarterdeck with questioning eyes. Of course, Charles realized, they would be expecting permission to go ashore. He had promised it to them at the first opportunity that arose. He looked more carefully at the Italian settlement, then the Arab. Both were minuscule places. Such a large influx of seamen would easily overwhelm them. He also doubted that the men would find much to satisfy them in either locale. He sighed in resignation, then spoke to Bevan. "Pass the word among the hands, if you will, that I have gone ashore to request leave for them to visit. I hope that serves."

"Christ," Bevan said. "There's nothing there. Not of the sort they'll be looking for anyway."

Charles cast his eyes again with a growing sense of unease. "You might suggest that if this Massawa proves inadequate, there might be better pickings farther north."

The master, Cromley, overheard this and chuckled. "Begging your pardon, sir, but there are no ports with much in the way of those services anywhere along the Red Sea. Jeddah on the Araby side, just maybe, but that's close to the seat of their religion and they'd never allow it. Koessir and Suez is now French."

Charles grumbled under his breath. Possibly, by some miracle, the Italians would be well stocked with alcohol and whores in anticipation of a British ship of war dropping by. Genoa certainly was; at least he could ask. Maybe the crew would be satisfied with an afternoon of innocent sightseeing, a comradely stroll up and down the quay. He could guess the answer to that too. "Tell them I've gone to inquire anyway," he said to Bevan.

Charles followed his servant over the side and into the launch; Winchester, Beechum, and Ayres, with the marines, had already settled in. "Shove off," he said to Malvern. "Smartly now."

The marines filed up the wooden ladder onto the half-finished quay first, followed by the two lieutenants, then Charles, with Augustus behind. A sizable crowd greeted him as he stepped onto its flagged surface. Charles searched the faces and appearances among the women hopefully, but saw no one remotely identifiable as a practitioner of the world's most elemental profession. The marines in their bright red coats and lacquered black hats were aligned in a file, their muskets at shoulder arms, as if on a parade ground. Three formally, if hastily, dressed men and a younger woman hurried forward. The delegation came to a halt in front of Charles. The elder of the men bowed in the continental fashion.

"Siamo onorati de ricevere sua eccellenza alls nuova Colonia di Massaua. Io sono il Governatore Giovanni Bellagio. Le posso chiedere a cosa dobbiarno l'onore della suo venuta in Massaua?"

Charles recognized the language spoken as Italian, but he understood almost none of it. He bowed politely in return anyway. "What did he say?" he asked, looking hopefully to Winchester and Beechum, who between them at least spoke some French and Spanish.

Winchester shrugged. "Something about welcoming us to his dominions. He's the governor, I think." Beechum nodded sagely in agreement.

"He say that he is most honored by your arrival," the woman interjected. "He is Signore Giovanni Bellagio, the governor of this Massawa Colony. He requests to know the purpose of your call."

Charles looked at the speaker in surprise. She was a petite woman of slender frame with direct green eyes and a full mouth, probably about his own age. Strands of rich dark hair showed under a straw hat contrasting exquisitely with cream-colored skin lightly freckled by the sun. She smiled at him warmly.

Charles felt his pulse quicken in spite of himself. "Thank you, Signorina," he said, using one of the few polite Italian words he knew. "May I know your name?"

"I am Signora Teresa di Correglia, and you?" She smiled prettily, which for her was not difficult. Her voice had a husky, strangely rhythmic quality. He made note of her emphasis on the term 'signora' rather than 'signorina'-—she was, or had once been, married.

"Captain Charles Edgemont of His Majesty's navy, at your service, ma'am," he said and bowed stiffly. He wondered if he were expected to kiss her hand. He wouldn't mind.

The woman merely bobbed her head in reply. "You are English, not so?" She pronounced it "Eeenglez."

Charles nodded. He noticed that the three men accompanying her watched closely. The eldest, the one who had spoken first, coughed discreetly.

Signora di Corriglia turned and said something in her language, then introduced "Capitan Edgemont" to her companions. Bows were made, no hands offered or shaken. Bellagio, Charles recalled his name, was a stocky, muscular figure with a thick moustache and an unhappy expression. He wore a cavalry saber as his gentlemen's sword. The names of the other two were given and forgotten. They wore no swords, but each had a pistol in his belt. In all, they were a hard-looking, cautious group in their late thirties or early forties.

In his turn, Charles introduced his officers. More bows were exchanged. The woman spoke to her companions. Bellagio answered at length, somewhat insistently, Charles thought. As to what they said, he had no idea. The word "Inglese" he noticed was repeated several times, and once "Mocha," which he understood. The atmosphere appeared to lighten to the extent that the governor's expression transformed from scowl to frown. The woman nodded her head in acknowledgement.

"You would be welcome to enter our poor house to relieve the heat of the day," Signora di Correglia said, turning with a charming smile to Charles. "Regrettably, we can offer only coffee for refreshment, we have no tea. So few visitors such as yourself arrive to this place that I am afraid our manners are quite deficit."

Charles stated his acceptance. He then turned to Ayres, "Stand your men down, but keep them vigilant. I don't expect to be long." The cluster of onlookers on the quay parted as he, Winchester, Bevan, and Ayres, with Augustus following, started toward a larger building facing the waterfront. As he passed, Charles noticed that most of those in the crowd were men. The great majority were of military age, and almost all were armed in one fashion or another. They tended to keep their distance while watching intently.

The signora walked closely beside him. "You have transported all the way from England?" she asked. "Or have you come from India?"

"England," Charles answered. "We sailed almost six months ago."

She touched his arm with her finger tips and looked up into his eyes. "Such a long time. And you have a family I would think, a wife perhaps? It must be hard for you to be away so long." Not entirely against his will, the touch sent a shiver through him.

"I have family," he answered reluctantly. He knew it was an ambiguous answer and could be interpreted in different ways, but he left it at that. For some reason he hesitated to bring up Penny or their possible child. To change the subject, he said, "And you, signora? Where is your husband?"

The Italian woman's face took on a pained expression. "My Antonio died several years past. He was of the resistance to the French. We were young and not yet blessed with children. For this I will always hate the Frenchmen."

Charles' heart went out to her. It must be terrible to lose a loved one so young. He was too acutely aware that she was a handsome woman, very much in her prime. Unbidden, it passed across his mind that she must suffer certain frustrations.

The door to the building opened and they passed inside to a large room with a long table served with benches. The space was much cooler than the rapidly rising temperature outside. The English officers were shown to places at the table, the signora seating herself beside Charles. Governor Bellagio and several other Italians sat themselves near the table's head. Augustus, Charles noticed, stood against the wall between two armed Italian men near the entrance. Once seated, Bellagio clapped his hands and shouted instructions toward a back room. He turned without smiling to Charles, "Perche siete venuto qui?"

"The governor welcomes you to Massawa warmly," Signora di Correglia translated. "He asks what brings you to your happily visiting us?"

Charles was prepared for the question but unsure of how much he should reveal about his mission. He decided to tell them what they already knew. "My ship observed a French frigate in pursuit of one of the merchant ships in your harbor. We have fought this warship, but she escaped in the night. I thought it possible she had come here."

The woman spoke in a short burst of rapid Italian. Words were exchanged among the men before Bellagio spoke at length. Signora di Correglia listened carefully; when he finished she turned to Charles.

"I am most sorry, but we know nothing of the whereabouts of this enemy.

No French have come to this place as of yet. It is true that one of our innocent trading boats was chased after and almost captured by the ship you speak of." She took a deep breath before continuing. Charles stared almost involuntarily as the fabric of her blouse stretched across a surprisingly ample bosom, then averted his eyes before anyone would notice. "The governor has asked me to express his bottomless gratitude for your intervention," Teresa said seriously. "Our little colony is in constant fear that the hated French will attack us even here." She spoke so earnestly, her eyes unwavering in their focus on his, that Charles knew he must do what he could to protect her and her companions. This little outpost of civilization in an untamed land would easily be overrun by the French for use as a way station for their descent on India. He told himself that he could not imagine the outrages that might be visited on the signora and the other women of Massawa, should they fall into enemy hands. Then, in the briefest of intervals as he gazed at her, he realized that he could imagine it quite easily. He felt beads of sweat under his uniform coat.

Bellagio spoke several forceful sentences, his fingers rapping out his points on the table's top. The woman shook her head in the negative. The governor spoke again. This time she answered him tersely. Bellagio fell silent. Signora di Correglia laid one hand on Charles' arm. "The governor is grateful for your protection," she said. Charles felt his heart race. "We wish to make to you welcome here."

Several servants appeared from the back room bearing trays with steaming cups of coffee and plates with biscuits and fruit. With the diversion, questions began to form in Charles' mind, one on top of the other. How long had these people been at Massawa? Why did they come, and why to this place? He'd seen no fields for crops or pastures for cattle—all the land he could see to the edge of the mountains was desert—how did they survive? He assumed there were some sort of relations with the local tribes, since he'd seen African laborers helping to construct the port facilities, and black servants were much in evidence, but what about the Arab settlement on the island; and, for that matter, what about the Turks? Massawa was supposedly an enclave of the Ottoman Empire; what had happened to them?

And there was the woman. Who was she? How did she come to be, alone and unattached, in such a place? Did she, or had she, had a lover here? She certainly must have attracted attention. He thought this very interesting indeed.

The refreshments were placed around the table. Charles saw that the coffee was almost a light tan in color. He tasted the liquid and found it hot and richly mixed with milk. "How do you make this, Signora?" he said. He knew how it was done, but he wanted to extend his conversation with her.

She smiled at him, free for the moment from her duties as translator. "But please, you must address me as Teresa, not as Signora di Correglia. We may have friendship, no?" She emphasized this by running a fingertip across the back of his hand.

"Then you may call me Charles," he answered, acutely aware of the contact between them.

"Carlo," she said softly. "I will call you Carlo when we are speaking intimamente." She removed her hand. "But I will answer your question. This we call caffelatte. It is one part the local coffee from the mountains and one equal part of the milk. Both are made heated before mixing together. It is how we prepare this drink in Genoa. It is the one pleasure which remains of my native land."

Since she was speaking freely, Charles decided to ask about some of the other things of which he was curious. "Tell me about this colony of yours—how did you come to be here?"

"Oh, it is no secret," she said, sipping at her drink then touching her lips with a cloth. "One year ago and a half we came from Genoa in the three boats you see in the harbor. We wish only a new life with freedom from the domination of the French, and to bring civilization to the savages. We are having with them economico . . . what do you say, tradings. We are a small number of simple peoples wanting to be prosperous in peace with all humanity. This place was nothing when we came, only the few heathens on the island. After hard labors and many obstacles, we have already achieved much. The fine harbor here is nearly completed, and we have made an industry for the salt manufacture behind the town. In the hills before the mountains there is much agriculture and pastures. It is very beautiful and the air is sweeter and cool. We have great plans for our future. Already we have achieved good trade up and down the sea. Everything is possible for us."

Charles saw that she was clearly proud of what had been accomplished. It must have been a struggle against harsh odds. And now she and her companions would have the added difficulty of the arrival of their old European enemy. "Are you not worried by the appearance of the French warship in these waters?" he said. "They are in Egypt and have established a foothold at the north end of the Red Sea."

She made such a charming expression of distress that Charles smiled. "They are a hateful, low people who seek only to subjugate all the world," she said forcefully. "The French Generale Bonaparte now in Egypt is the same that ravaged my homeland. He has pillaged all he desired in Genoa as he passed across, even to the very virtue of the women. There is much fear he will come here. We have no army and no navy. We can do nothing."

"I am no friend to the French," Charles said confidently, his mind captured by the thought of the pillaged virtue of the women, or at least this woman. "I mean to fight them whenever they are. If it will reassure you, I have had some success in the past."

"I am certain that you are very capable in such things," she said, her eyes on his. "But, do you not think they will attempt to come south? Many are hopeful that they have no reason to do so." Her voice turned to despair. "It cannot happen. The malletto French would destroy everything we have built, everything we have hoped for."

The governor spoke out, interrupting their conversation. From his tone, Charles thought he was asking questions, which Teresa promptly answered in an unemotional, matter-of-fact manner. Charles watched the two and listened carefully, comprehending few of the words and none of the meaning, as the man's expression changed from inquiry to authority. The woman answered twice, once with an impatient, "Si, si," followed by a longer sentence or two. The second reply was more animated, her breast rising and falling as she spoke quickly, almost angrily. Charles wondered what the disagreement had been about.

"The governor has asked me to offer an invitation to you to dinner," Teresa said, regaining her composure. "He has also said that all the facilities of our little colony are of course available to you, such as to food and water or whatever your needs. He hopes you to call often to our harbor and asks only your protection from our mutual enemy."

Charles heard Winchester, seated on his other side, cough discreetly. He turned and asked, "What is it?"

"The boat's crew and the marines have been out in the sun this past hour," Winchester said under his breath. "Also, if you will forgive my saying so, you have no orders to protect this place. You do have orders to transport Jones and his party. May I suggest that we get that accomplished and dally later."

Charles thought Winchester to be impertinent. He saw a disapproving look as his brother-in-law glanced past him at the Italian woman. The implied accusation irritated him. There was nothing improper in his behavior toward Teresa. Any such suggestion was absurd on the face of it. But he also knew the lieutenant to be correct—he had no business remaining in Massawa any longer than necessary, no matter how pleasant it might be. Of course, he could always return, to resupply for example.

"I hope you will accept my deepest apologies," he said, nodding to the governor, but speaking to the woman. "I have orders to sail north which cannot be avoided. My mission is to prevent the French from progressing southward." His eyes met hers. "This I will do with every resource available to me, you may rest assured."

For the smallest of moments he wondered if he had spoken too freely. It might have been better if he'd left his future movements undisclosed. He looked to Teresa's smile and direct gaze. The concern left him. These Italians were his allies against a common enemy after all. If he could not confide in them, whom could he trust?

"If you must depart so quickly, then you must," Teresa said, clearly unhappy at his decision. Bellagio rose at his end of the table. He spoke a few words and accorded Charles the barest of bows. "The governor wishes you a profitable voyage and a soon return," the woman translated. "It is his sincerest wish that your mission will be blessed with every success. Come, I will accompany you to the harbor." Somehow Charles had the impression that the leader of the Italians had not been nearly so warm in his well-wishing, but he thought it unimportant. Perhaps he was one of those men who were naturally reserved in their sentiments.

.Outside, in the heat of a blaring sun now nearly directly overhead, Teresa paused by the doorway to allow the others to go ahead. When they had gained some relative privacy, the woman slipped her free arm into his.

"These times are most difficult for everyone," she said. "Signore Bellagio has many responsibilities. As a consequence he may not always express himself as friendly as he feels. Please do not yourself be offended."

"I am not offended in the least," Charles said seriously. "I feel I have been warmly received in Massawa."

"Good," Teresa said with a broad smile. She squeezed his arm tightly against her side. "It is my wish also that you have victory in your every effort. I, my personally, am much saddened that you must go. I will pray that you may return to me as soon as is possible."

Charles felt his heart pounding in his chest. The brush of her body against his side carried its own implications. He knew he must leave, he didn't want to, he had no excuse to delay his departure. He looked out at Cassandra riding at anchor in the harbor. He remembered something he should have inquired about before. It was important. It was delicate. It was something he would have to speak with a man about. It might serve to keep his ship in harbor at least another day. He should have gotten Winchester to ask discretely, but it was too late for that now. "Is there anyone beside yourself here who speaks English?" he asked hopefully.

Teresa assumed a helpful expression. "No," she said. "Why do you ask such a thing?"

Charles hesitated. He wanted—needed, he realized—to ascertain whether there might be suitable diversions available for his crew, should he allow them on shore: a brothel or drinking establishments, for example. Such places didn't have to be large; he could rotate the men in small parties. There had to be something, every port had some such enterprise to service seamen's needs. But he couldn't ask a woman, especially not this woman. "It's nothing," he said. "It was something to be discussed among men."

"Do you wish to ask the governor? I will translate."

Charles felt himself redden. "No. I'm sorry; it is in the nature of . . . It is too indelicate for a woman's ears."

Teresa's brow furrowed inquisitively, her curiosity peaked. "Carlo, you may speak anything to me. I am a grown woman, not a novice in a nunnery. I think you cannot say anything I have not before heard."

Charles decided to take the plunge for the sake of his crew. He spoke softly, lest they be overheard. "Is there a brothel hereabouts? You know somewhere . . ." His voice trailed off in embarrassment.

Her reaction was abrupt. She released his arm and stared at him wide-eyed. "Do you require such services as from a bordello?"

"Me?" Charles said, aghast. "Oh, no. Oh, good lord, no. Not for myself, of course not." His face went flush. "For the men of my ship. Some have not been on land for a year or more. I'm sure you understand. No, I'm not sure, but for me personally, no." He thought to add a few additional denials that he had any intentions in this line, but stopped when he saw she was laughing at him.

"More than a year," she said warmly. "But the prostituto would be very busy, I think." She pursed her lips. "To answer your request, I must speak that we have no such profession in Massawa."

"Any wine shops?" Charles asked, hoping for something. He began to be concerned about the reaction of his crew. "Taverns? Anything at all?"

"I am sorry, no. We are such a small place."

"Would it be possible for them to come ashore to walk up and down, if only to look around?" It wouldn't satisfy them, but at least the men would see for themselves that there was nothing for them here.

"There is little to see," Teresa said doubtfully. "But I will ask." She turned to the governor, standing a short way off with a few of his lieutenants, and spoke in her language.

"No," Bellagio answered, gruffly shaking his head.

"I must apologize," she said to Charles. "It would be inconvenient at the moment. He hopes you will return another time."

"I see," Charles said. "Thank you for making the request." There didn't seem to be any further reason to delay. He bowed to the governor and the other men. To Teresa, he took her hand and kissed it lightly. "Until we meet again," he said, then turned, almost bumping into Augustus who he realized with a start had been standing close behind him all the while. He followed his servant and Winchester down into the boat and took his place in the sternsheets. "Shove off," Winchester growled immediately. Looking back,

Charles saw that Teresa stood alone and unmoving, framed against the sky until the launch bumped against Cassandra's side. When he gained the deck and looked back, she was gone.

He turned to Winchester, waiting at the entry port and staring at him disapprovingly. "Is Jones returned from the island yet?" Charles said. The last thing he wanted was more pert criticism from his lieutenant and brother-in-law.

"The jollyboat's still out," Winchester answered, his lips pursed in a hard line.

"Then send someone to fetch him back."

Before he could turn away, Winchester spoke: "I know you don't want to hear it, but you're going to. You'd better be careful, Captain, or you'll do something you'll regret."

"I'll thank you to keep your speculations to yourself," Charles snapped.

Daniel Bevan arrived in the middle of the exchange from the quarterdeck. "What?" he said.

"Prepare to weigh the anchor, Daniel," Charles ordered. "We shall sail immediately Jones is on board. I am going below."

"What was that about?" he heard Bevan say to Winchester. Charles made his way to his cramped temporary cabin in a sour mood. My God, he would be grateful when he could be rid of Jones and his women and have his own quarters back. He sat down on the edge of the cot to think. Was Winchester right? Had he done anything improper? Of course not. He had made an ally of the Italians and secured a haven where they could water and revictual. That was all to the good. And what of the woman, Signora Teresa di Correglia? Even her name sounded desirable as she pronounced it: "T-e-e-resa." It was nothing serious, he reassured himself. She was simply a woman who'd spoken English, a chance occurrence. He had to speak through her. She was friendly and attractive—desirable even, to be sure—but no more than that. He'd done nothing improper. There were no secret understandings, no implied promises; he'd been a perfect gentleman. Winchester was out of line and intruding into affairs that were beyond his concern. Besides, if his brother-in-law kept his mouth shut Penny would never know anything he did or did not do. Not that he had the slightest intention of doing or not doing anything.

Unbidden, he could feel his skin tingle where Teresa had traced her fingers across his hand. It had been too long since he had felt a woman's touch, any woman's touch. The remembrance of her eyes, her lips, the firmness of her body against his arm made him ache. It wasn't bedding, it wasn't just bedding that he yearned for, but intimacy. Someone he could be unguarded with, familiar. Winchester was partly right, he decided. It would do no harm for him to be careful.

A knock came at the cabin door. "Come," he said.

Augustus entered, rather deferentially, Charles thought. "Be you all right, Cap'n?"

He sighed. Everyone was anxious about his deportment. Probably he should have been more guarded than he had been. "Yes, I'm fine. Everything is fine. Thank you for your concern."

"If I may say, she were a powerful pretty lady." The servant's voice was cautious.

It occurred to Charles that his servant would be as troubled as anyone about his possible wanderings. After all, Miss Viola was a member of Penny's household. "Yes, she is. But you have no need to worry on my behalf." To change the subject, he said, "What did you think of this little colony of Italians?" Charles had in mind the apparent harmony between the Europeans and the local tribe's people.

Augustus' reaction was unexpected. His expression hardened. "I saw too many blacks workin' and too many whites with muskets watchin'. I do'n like it; I do'n like it at all."

"I see," Charles said. He wished he'd paid more attention to those kinds of details.

"Afore I forget," Augustus said quickly. "I'm to tell you Mr. Jones is back on board. He wishes a word with you in your cabin. Mr. Bevan, he say he be ready to weigh in a half hour."

"Thank you," he said to his servant, then called "Mr. Hitch!" into the wardroom. He remembered seeing the midshipman leafing through his book on navigation, which was remarkable enough.

"Yes, sir?" Hitch said, appearing in the doorway.

"Get you up to my cabin and inform Mr. Jones that he will attend to me in the wardroom immediately."

"Aye, aye, sir."

"And, Mr. Hitch, if you would be so good as to ask Lieutenant Bevan to send word as soon as the anchor is atrip."

"Aye, aye," Hitch repeated and left.

Augustus busied himself brushing off Charles' uniform coat and putting his things in their correct places. Charles went into the wardroom and sat at the table to await the American and whatever news he brought back from the Arab village. Jones appeared almost immediately, still dressed in his flowing native gown. "What do you have to report?" Charles said as he came into the room.

"I don't report to you. I work for the Admiralty," Jones replied testily.

"Fine," Charles said. "What did you want to speak to me about?"

"To tell you that we must sail for Egypt immediately. I am informed the

French are scouring the sea for every transport available, and not only with the frigate we did with yesterday. I am certain they will make the attempt as soon as the wind favors it. There is no time to lose."

Charles felt he already knew or had guessed all of these things. "From where will they sail?" he asked. That was the central question. When Jones looked at him blankly, he added, "Where is all this shipping being collected and where will their troops be embarked?"

Jones rubbed his bearded chin. "The local traders think it might be at Koessir, in Egypt. They haven't seen it first hand, but it's a logical place."

"Is that where you want me to take you, Koessir?"

"Don't be stupid, of course not. We must go further north, to Zafarana. It will be easier to make our way inland to Cairo from there. You may return to take us off at Koessir."

Charles groaned inwardly. This was getting to be a complicated undertaking. What was he to do while Jones was on land? He supposed he couldn't just leave him there, tempting though that might be. He reminded himself again that he wanted to get the thing over with as quickly as possible. "When?" he said.

"When what?"

"When do you want me to arrive to take you off?"

"When we're finished. What difference does it make?"

"I can't just anchor off Koessir and wait for you to appear. Someone's bound to notice. We must set a specific day, even a certain time of day, that you will be at an agreed place. I will stand off the shore and send a boat to fetch you. We'll arrange a signal."

"That will not do," Jones said hotly. "I can't possibly know how long this will take. In any event, I've never been good at appointments. It's a lot of unnecessarily rigid thinking if you ask me."

Charles sighed in frustration. "You'd better make this appointment or you'll find yourself walking back to London. How long do you need on land—a week, two?"

Jones actually laughed. "Two months, at least."

"That's impossible. I can't sail around in circles for two months."

"Then I suggest you find something useful to do with your time for a change." On this Jones dug in his heels and would not be budged.

"All right, fine. I'll give you two months," Charles said irritably. "I'll take you off near Koessir, but you must be there at the agreed time. I'll give a day or two's grace; after that I'll sail without you."

Jones glowered at him. He had just opened his mouth to speak when Hitch raced in, slamming the door loudly behind him. "Sir," the midshipman began excitedly.

Charles could not remember hearing the capstan turn to take up the strain on the anchor cable or any of the other activity which he would have expected preparatory to weighing. "Just a moment, Mr. Hitch," he snapped. "Watch your manners, if you please. I will attend to you as soon as Mr. Jones and I are finished."

"Yes, sir," Hitch said, fidgeting nervously.

"Then we are agreed?" Charles said, turning back to Jones.

"Sir, the crew has mutinied!" Hitch blurted out, unable to contain himself any longer. "They refuse to lift the anchor or go further until their grievances are answered."

"What?" Charles said.

"Lieutenant Bevan has requested your presence on the quarterdeck as soon as you find it convenient, sir," the boy said, finishing his message.

Jones rolled his eyes heavenward in disbelief.

CHAPTER TEN

Charles bolted from the wardroom without thinking to take up his uniform coat and hat, or even his sword. "Come with me," he snapped at the marine sentry outside the door, leapt onto the aft ladderway and ran upwards. He had thought to make for his quarterdeck, but as he emerged onto the gundeck he saw the crew clustered in the waist. He could see from their attitude that it was not a mutiny, at least not in the sense that they were attempting to seize control of the ship by force. Hitch had said that they refused orders to hoist the anchor; he could guess why. Charles started forward, angry that his crew was once again disobedient, angry at the impossible situation he found himself in, and above all, angered that he had been frustrated at every turn in finding a solution.

"What's the meaning of this?" he shouted. He pushed the first man he came to aside and forced his way into the crowd, then moved to the center of the deck and looked around him. "Who's in charge here?" No one spoke or stepped forward except the lone marine from outside his cabin who had finally caught up and moved to stand nervously beside him. "Who's in charge?" he repeated loudly. "Who is your spokesman?" Still no one moved, so he said, "For Christ's sake, what kind of mutiny is this? You have to have a spokesman if I'm to hear your complaints. Pick someone then." There was a small commotion on the starboard side near the number nine gun. After a moment an able seaman Charles recognized as Thomas Sherburne was thrust to the front of the circle. Hesitantly, Sherburne knuckled his forehead. "It ain't no mutiny," he said. "We have grievances. Yer ain't goin' to flog me for speakin' out, is ye?"

"I've never flogged anyone for speaking their mind," Charles answered. At that moment Augustus made his way toward him, carrying Charles' sword and pistols. Charles motioned for him to wait. "Speak up, Sherburne; I'll hear what you have to say."

"Ye have broken yer word to us, sur," the seaman said, more sure of himself. "Ye promised us leave ashore at the first opportunity. Well, here it is," he pointed toward Massawa, "and we ain't got it." Before Charles could speak, a second man—one of the Americans he'd pressed at Bunce Island—stepped forward. "We ain't sailing nowhere 'til we get what's due us." Charles noticed

167

that all of the men in his field of vision—British, American, senior seamen and junior—nodded in agreement. He heard a chorus of "ayes and yeas," and similar sentiments all around him. He suddenly saw the irony of it. All of his efforts to stop the crew from fighting among themselves had finally succeeded. He had somehow managed to unify them in opposition to himself instead. He raised his arms for silence. "You're right," he said, leaving his hands partway up in a gesture of conciliation. "It so happens that I looked into the port here, but it wouldn't do. To be sure they are Europeans, but there are no brothels or taverns, not even a shop for trinkets or a coffee house. There's nothing you would find of interest."

"Respectfully, sir," another seaman spoke out. "You should 'ave let us ashore anyhow. There's women there, I saw 'em."

"Thank you for being respectful, Fox. I did request it, and yes there are women there, proper women, not your bumboat whores. The governor turned me down flat, and that's likely the reason."

A murmur went up around him, not an angry, defiant murmur; more one of digesting information. He felt he was making progress. "Look, I'll give you the facts and tell you what I'll do, on my word as your captain. Cassandra is ordered to sail north to deliver our passengers to Egypt to the detriment of the French forces there. It is important for king and country that we do this; otherwise the Admiralty wouldn't have asked us. Once completed, I promise to return south without delay and I'll put you ashore somewhere suitable, permission or no, but then I will tolerate no more of this nonsense. Will you agree to that?"

A second hum of conversation started as the men turned to each other to discuss his offer. Charles glanced up at the quarterdeck and saw Bevan and his other officers, as well as the marines with their bayonets fixed, aligned along its forward edge. Bevan looked at him quizzically; Charles shook his head to indicate he not intervene. While he waited, Augustus approached and wordlessly buckled his sword belt, with its sword and scabbard, around his waist. Charles stood silently, his fingers tapping a tattoo on the blade's hilt as soon as they found it. After a few moments that seemed like an hour, Sherburne came forward with two of his mates. "Aye, we find it agreeable," he said. "But I'm to say that we'll hold ye to it, just as ye spoke."

"You always have," Charles answered, relieved in spite of himself. "I have given my word. Now, if you would be so good as to come under your officers' orders again, we have an anchor to hoist aboard. The sooner we are away, the sooner we can return." As the crew returned to their business, he stayed in the waist a moment longer, thinking about what he had promised. He wondered where he could put them ashore, and what the consequences might be, then decided they were questions he could worry about later. Not entirely satisfied, he turned and made his way to the quarterdeck.

"God's bones, Charlie," Bevan greeted him. "What have you agreed to?"

"Leave ashore at the first opportunity," Charles answered, not wanting to talk about it.

"And when will that be?"

"After we return from the north."

"Where, for Christ's sake? They've been banned from Mocha and even this little place here. There isn't anywhere else."

This was, of course the single flaw in his plan, or at least he thought it was the only flaw. "I don't know," he said testily. "I'll think of something." His mind turned to a more pressing concern. "Daniel, where's the French frigate run to? She hasn't passed this way; the Italians on shore haven't seen anything of her."

Bevan shrugged. "With the wind as it is, I would think to the north the most likely. Beyond that it's anybody's guess. Another question is, where might that seventy-four have set off for, and what are her intentions?" Charles had no answer to this, or whether Raisonnable was even in the Red Sea, or whether L'Agile and Raisonnable were the only French warships present.

The capstan began to clank on its pawl as the men heaved the anchor cable short. Bevan turned away to shout out orders for the gaskets on the yardarms to be cast loose and the spars braced around. "Take her out into the bay," Charles said. "I'll speak with Cromley about the course."

"Aye, sir," the master answered after Charles had queried him. His fingertip traced a line upward from Massawa on his chart, following the coast. "There's a channel here, close in to the shore at ten and twenty fathoms. If the breeze holds, we should clear them islands by nightfall." The islands Cromley tapped at with his fingers marked the northern edge of the Dahlak Archipelago. What soundings there were on the chart showed safer seas beyond .

"Will we be able to fetch the deep-water channel up the center of the sea then?" Charles asked. He would be more than relieved to be clear of the treacherous maze of islands and shoals.

Cromley nodded. "Aye, it'll be easy sailing all the way to Koessir and beyond. Depends on where you're headed. And on the wind, of course."

"Zafarana," Charles said, remembering Jones's request. "It's north a ways past Koessir, I believe." It took several moments for the two men to locate the landing place on the chart—well up the Gulf of Suez, one of two sizable inlets at the northern end of the sea. Zafarana wasn't a town so much as a stretch of barely inhabited coast along a section of rugged Egyptian highlands. Charles' jaw tightened as he looked at the chart. It would be a long run, longer than he'd thought and longer that the crew was going to like. It couldn't be helped.

The direction of the prevailing winds would be crucial for his own wellbeing as well as for whatever plans the French might have. "Tell me, Mr. Cromley, when do you expect the breeze might shift around to from the north?"

The master pulled to loosen his stock in deference to the stifling midday heat. Even on the water it was like being in an oven. "It could be anytime now if it starts early," he said in a matter-of-fact voice. "Most likely toward the middle of the month; later if it's slow in coming. We'll know when we begin to see clouds. The northerlies bring the start of the rainy season, such as it is."

*****

Day by day, Cassandra sailed large on a course north by northwest on a soldier's wind over the taffrail. By the master's log, they made a steady one hundred and seventy-five to two hundred miles each day, noon to noon. They stayed largely out of sight of land, with rare sightings of Arab traders in their sambuks and baghalas who universally fled pell-mell at their appearance. Cromley's recordings were sparse:

Date	Noon Sighting	Comments
June 9	17 deg 41' N	Wind steady SSE
June 10	20 deg 20" N	Ditto
June 11	22 deg 29' N	Ditto
June 12	25 deg 9' N	Dawn, St John's I. W 3 leagues, wind ditto

Charles was thankful for the constant breeze which hurried them up the sea. He looked skyward frequently for signs of change above the masts with their expanse of canvas. There were small and scattered white puffs, too high and too few for rain, drifting slowly toward the east most days and an increasing humidity which cast a haze off the water and limited their range of vision.

On June twelfth, a Wednesday, he ordered that the sails be shortened to topgallants alone and that the ship heave to precisely at midnight. The following morning he came on deck at dawn. Beechum stood officer of the watch with Sykes his second. Immediately he exchanged "Good morrows" with the two, he opened his long glass and trained it to port, sweeping the surface of the sea. He scarcely needed the instrument in the growing light. Not six miles off the bow he picked out two small islands, mere lumps, barely above the surface of the water. From his study of Cromley's chart, he knew they were the Brothers, so named by the sloop Dolphin on a survey some twenty years before. "Mr. Sykes," Charles called.

The midshipman approached and touched his hat. "Yes, sir?"

"If you would please inform Mr. Jones that I require his presence on deck immediately."

"Aye, aye, sir," answered Sykes, and left.

It was an uncommonly long period before Jones appeared, somewhat bedraggled looking, probably fresh from his bed. "What do you want at this ungodly hour?" Jones said by way of introducing himself.

"It's a fine morning," Charles responded. "Pity to sleep it away." Then, feeling the social amenities had been completed, he said, "Do you see those two islands there?"

"You woke me to look at islands?"

"Do you know what they signify?"

"How would I know that?"

Charles sighed. "Ten leagues due west of this spot is the Egyptian port of Koessir. We must arrange a rendezvous for when your work is done."

"Anywhere will do," Jones snapped.

"No, it won't," Charles said patiently. "The place needs to be a distance from the town, at least thirty miles, and along an unpopulated part of the coast."

"God's balls," Jones grumbled. "All right, choose anyplace you like."

"Would you prefer it be north or south of the port?"

The American tugged at his beard thought. "How long will I have to wait?"

"If all goes well, one night. We'll do it in the small hours, sometime in the middle watch."

"To the north then," Jones answered.

Charles saw Cromley and Bevan coming onto the quarterdeck together. He signaled for them to approach. "Topgallants and topsails aloft, if you please," he ordered. "In three hours we will wear to the west and close with the shore."

As Cassandra resumed her way northward, Charles kept Jones on deck to impress upon him the procedure he must follow if he wished to be taken off. "I will call for you on the night of the twelfth of August. That's sixty days from today. You do have a calendar, don't you?"

The American nodded.

"Listen to me closely," Charles said. "You will show a light at midnight and leave it burning until you are taken off. It should be shielded to landward and on both sides. It's only to be visible from the sea."

"All right," Jones said, showing no concern whatsoever.

"When we see it, there will be an answering signal. This means that we have put out a boat. Do not extinguish your own light, the boat will need it to find you."

"Yes, yes. I'm not stupid, you know."

"Of course," Charles said. "Have you any questions?"

"We shall probably have dromedaries."

"The camels will remain behind," Charles said firmly.

Jones gazed outward at the Brothers, now sliding behind to port. "What if we—or you, for that matter—are unable to attend the rendezvous at the appointed time? What have you dreamed up then?"

"I will return the following two nights to look for your beacon."

"And if it's longer?"

"I hope you have good camels."

At two bells in the forenoon watch, Cassandra's bow fell off to put the wind on her beam, and she started toward the still unseen coast. Charles ordered lookouts all the way to the crosstrees and on all three masts in the event they should be discovered by a French warship. It would not do to be pinned against a reef-strewn shore, especially by the large Raisonnable. If she appeared and took up his wake, he would have to circle around and beat to the south—all the way to Mocha if necessary. If he stayed to windward, he would be forced into the narrow waters of the Gulf of Suez where nothing could save them.

"Land hoy!" the watch in the mainmast shouted down. "Straight on the bow."

"Send a midshipman up each of the masts," Charles said to Bevan. "Remind them to keep an eye out for enemy sail." Having two pairs of eyes at each station could do no harm. He was acutely aware that the approaches to Koessir and the port itself lay just over the horizon.

Cassandra ran easily across the low chop, the yards braced well around, under the strengthening late morning sun. Her wake bubbled and churned behind, leaving a ragged line as the water's surface moved with the currents. Before noon a point of gray-tan land could be seen from the deck. Thankfully, the lookouts above remained silent. The point slowly neared, revealing a small inlet with an arid plain spreading southward toward Koessir and a chain of smallish rock-strewn hills hugging the coastline to the north. Looking through his glass, he saw a dry ravine at the end of the hills descending to meet the sea. A few palm trees sprouted along its banks. It looked a suitable place to land a small boat, Charles thought. He spoke to Bevan again, "Start a lead going forward. And send someone for Jones and Winchester."

Charles saw Stephen Winchester crossing the deck first. The leadsman in the forechains began to call out the depths. "By the mark twenty-two," Charles heard clearly, and breathed somewhat easier. It was still about three miles to the shore. If the seabed shelved at all gradually, they would be able to approach quite close to the landing place.

"You sent for me, sir?" Winchester asked.

Charles handed his lieutenant the glass. "In two months' time I'll be sending you with a ship's boat to collect Jones and his people from this shore. It'll be in the dark of night. Take a look at that small inlet forward and tell me if you're comfortable with it."

Winchester raised the telescope to his eye and trained it landward. Jones appeared on the ladderway and started toward them. "Twenty and a half," called the leadsman. Charles stared intently at the slowly closing coast. He could see a line of surf breaking at about a half mile from the point, with calmer waters beyond. There would be coral there, he guessed, the outcroppings a few feet beneath the surface. The jollyboat should be able to clear that in calm seas. He glanced upward into the masts high above to reassure himself that the lookouts were attentive to their duty. From where he stood he could easily see the figures in the mizzen and mainmast crosstrees; they seemed alert enough. He was becoming nervous about their exposed position in the broad light of day so close to the French-occupied port and about what traffic might by happenstance pass within sight.

"What do you want?" Jones announced himself without preamble. Winchester lowered his glass at the sound.

"Are you comfortable with it, Stephen?" Charles asked.

Winchester nodded. "There's a channel through the reef up to that ravine, I'm sure of it."

"What's this about?" Jones demanded a second time. "I'm a busy man, you know."

Charles looked at Jones, irritated at his tone. How busy could he be, cooped up with two women in a single cabin? Then he took a guess. "I apologize for disturbing you," he said, suppressing a smile. "Do you see that ravine there, just where the line of hills ends?"

"Do you mean the wadi?"

"Wadi?"

"Yes, the wadi," Jones snapped. "It's the bed of a stream; only runs in the wet season."

"I see," Charles said, not caring what it was called. "There's a point that runs into the sea just beside it. That's where we'll take you off."

Jones frowned. "It's a bit far from anyplace, isn't it?"

"You want me to sail into Cairo for you?"

173

Before Jones could respond to this, Charles heard a shout from the mizzenmast, but couldn't decipher the message. The word, "sail," caught his ear and he arched his head back to see Aviemore leap out onto the shrouds to hurry down. "Make sure that Mr. Jones understands where he is to be taken off, and be certain that he will be able to find it from the landward side," he said hurriedly to Winchester, then turned to go to the rail and await Aviemore's descent. As he passed Daniel Bevan, he said, "Put her on the wind, a full suit of canvas. We will make to the north."

The young midshipman came sliding down the topmast backstay at such a speed that Charles was certain he would break something when he collided with the deck. Instead, at the last minute the boy braked with thighs and feet against the heavy cable to light as soft as a bird. "It's a ship, sir," he said excitedly.

"Thank you, Mr. Aviemore," Charles said. "What can you tell me of her?"

"Sir? She's a ship; three masts anyway. Not very large."

"Her course?" Charles prompted.

"Oh. She's tending away from us, but aiming to the land, like."

Charles thought it likely she had been making for Koessir. "Can you tell me if she's a ship of war?" That was his central concern.

Aviemore put a finger to his lips in concentration. "I don't rightly know. I already said she had three masts. Wilson, he could tell you, possibly."

John Wilson, Charles knew, had been the lookout in the mizzen crosstrees. "Just one more thing," he said. "Did she alter her course or do anything else to indicate she might have seen us?"

"Not that I seen."

"Thank you, Mr. Aviemore. You may go." Charles clasped his hands behind his back to walk up the windward side of the quarterdeck, turn, and stride down again. It was possible Cassandra's topgallants had not been spotted at that distance, or that the ship they'd seen wasn't a threat to him. Aviemore had said she had three masts, which ruled out most of the local Arab craft. The boy's description of "not very large" could mean anything, but she was not likely the French frigate or seventy-four. If his presence was reported to the French at Koessir, Cassandra would be well away before any chase could be mounted, and sunset would be in less than an hour. He looked up to see that they had worn around to put the Egyptian coast on the port beam. The topmen in the fore and mainmasts were hurrying to their places along the lower yardarms, fifty feet above the deck, preparing to loose the huge mainsails.

"Daniel," Charles called. He ceased his pacing and crossed to speak with his lieutenant.

"Aye?" Bevan answered.

"If you would be so good as to call all of the lookouts down, I wish a word with them. A single replacement up the mainmast should suffice for now."

"Aye, aye."

Charles saw Cromley standing beside the quartermaster at the wheel. "Set the course for Cape Mohammed at the head of the sea," he directed. "We will enter the Gulf of Suez in the morning, God willing."

"Yes, sir," the master said, touching the brim of his hat.

Charles watched, paying attention with only part of his mind, as the courses dropped like giant curtains, to belly out as the wind filled them and the sheets hauled tight. He felt the movement of the deck quicken beneath his feet. Midshipman Sykes mounted the ladderway, hurrying forward. "Captain, sir," he said.

"Yes, Mr. Sykes."

"You asked to speak to the men on watch aloft. I've assembled them on the gundeck. Do you wish me to bring them here?"

"I'll come down, thank you." In the shade under the break of the quarterdeck three seamen stood passing a ladle from a butt of drinking water among them. They straightened as Charles approached. Charles recognized them as John Wilson, Samuel Tate, and Tim Giles, all topmen. "Do you mind if I have a drink?" he said.

"'Ere, sur. I'll do it," Giles said, dipping the ladle and holding it out.

Charles drank half its contents and handed the remainder back. They were only weeks from Mocha and the water was still reasonably clear. "Wilson, I know you saw that sail off the port beam as we were headed toward the land. Did the rest of you get a look at it?"

The three heads nodded. "Aye, zur," Tate spoke out.

"What manner of barkey did you make her out to be?"

"A polacre, zur," said Tate immediately. "Her masts be all of one piece, wif no tops or such." Giles, who had been in the mainmast nodded in agreement.

Wilson, from the mizzen, the shortest of the three masts, assumed a wounded expression as if Tate had stolen his place at the front of the stage. "No, she weren't no such thing," he protested vehemently. "Yer both addled."

"What were she then?" Tate demanded. "If she weren't no polacre, what?" Turning to Charles he added, "He's a sodding blind bugger. Always has been."

"Ah . . . ," Charles began.

"A xebec is what she be, ye son of a whore. And what ye were birthed out of her arse," offered Wilson, his face reddening.

Tate forced a loud, derisive laugh. "Ye wouldn't know a xebec from a sow's teat, which be where ye were suckled. She ain't had no lay-teen sail."

"Thank you," Charles interrupted loudly. "Remember what I said about fighting."

175

"Oh, they won't be no brawling," Giles said calmly. "They know they'll get no leave if they do. It's just a manner of speaking with them. It's two to one she's a polacre, sur. Couldn't be no xebec, I'm sure."

"I see," Charles said. "Thank you for the drink and for reporting so, er, positively." He turned and left, the sounds of Wilson's continued observations on his mate's ancestry following him to the ladderway. He knew of only one polacre in the Red Sea, and that one far south at Massawa. It was not impossible there was another. On his quarterdeck, the sun almost touching the now distant Egyptian coast, he glanced skyward to see wispy mare's tails feathering the sky, tinted orange in the last of the light.

"There'll be your change in the wind," Cromley said conversationally, following the direction of Charles' gaze.

"Mares' tails signaling a shift in the weather is an old wives' tale," Charles answered. Satisfied that everything was in good order, he went below for his supper.

*****

The wind did not change immediately. Cassandra sighted Cape Mohammed at dawn the next morning. High and forbidding, its deeply ravined scarps gleamed golden in the beams of the rising sun. The sky had changed its mood, turning a deep red to the east. The narrow passage into the Gulf of Suez for the moment lay darkened in the shadow of Mount Sinai. By the end of the morning watch, the cape glided past to starboard, a few small islands and the arid heights of Egypt easily visible on the port side. After cruising the center of the Red Sea with its unbounded horizons, the space seemed dangerously confined with little room for error. Charles ordered a man in the forechains with a lead to take soundings as they went. The depths proved ample, but any veer in the wind would present him with a nasty shore under his lee in the blink of an eye.

The sky turned overcast as the morning wore on, lowering clouds skimming the tops of the mountains to port. Charles looked to Cromley by the wheel and received a confirming nod in return. To Bevan he said, "Get the topgallants and courses in. We'll proceed under the topsails. Have the best bower cast loose and the cable bent on in the event we must come to anchor."

"Aye, aye," the answer came in ready agreement.

With the topmen still aloft, the air deadened, the wind falling away. "Lively there; lively!" Charles heard the boatswain shouting upward. There was a note of anxiety in his voice.

The first gust came across the highlands to the west with surprising force. Charles could actually see it, a dark smudge of dust and grit blown sideways off the ridge tops. "Get all the canvas off except the foretopsail," he said to Bevan.

To Cromley: "Put the helm over. Bring her head into the wind." There was little wind as yet, but there soon would be more. It came as Cassandra was only beginning her turn, a gust like the punch of a fist, carrying a cloud of sand and pieces of brush across the deck with stinging force. The ship heeled sharply with the onslaught and her head immediately began to fall off. Charles turned his back to the wind to protect his face and eyes from the flying debris. The sea surface had churned to a seething froth in an instant. He had to shout to gain Bevan's attention. "Let go the anchor!"

Bevan nodded that he understood and waved his arm repeatedly to Winchester who had gone into the bow with a party of men. Charles did not hear the splash as the heavy hook pierced the sea surface, but he saw the cable race out the hawse. He felt through the deck as the thing bit, dragged, and bit again. Charles stood tensely still, holding his breath while the wind howled around him, feeling with his feet whether it would hold. After a moment he breathed easier.

As soon as it had settled from the west, abating its force, the wind shifted to the south again; then east of south with a feeble gust. Cassandra swung dutifully on her cable in response. By mid-afternoon it dropped altogether and rain began in a thunderous downpour, turning the grit-covered decks a muddy brown, which quickly ran out in small rivers through the scuppers. Charles stayed on the deck in his sodden clothes enjoying the blood-warm tempest, the first precipitation he had experienced since entering the Red Sea. The clouds parted in the late afternoon, and then they vanished, the sun raising trails of steam off the warming deck boards. The wind, when it started up soon after, came just from west of north, straight down the gulf. The change in the seasons had begun. Charles knew that whatever plans the French might have would be put into motion as soon as they found themselves ready.

*****

With a contrary breeze in the narrow waterway it took a full two days of tacking and tacking again to cover the last ninety miles to Zafarana. The landing place proved a desolate little cluster of barely a half dozen huts beside a treeless wadi now running full with water down from the rugged hills behind.

"Remember, Mr. Jones, the twelfth of August at the place we agreed to, and not a day later if you can help it," Charles said. The two women had already been lowered into the cutter waiting alongside, dressed in loose black gowns with headscarves that covered their faces. Jones himself wore his customary baggy white covering and turban. Charles wondered for a moment at the man's mission and his methods and what perils he might expect to encounter.

"And I'll thank you to be prompt," Jones said tersely. "It may be that we'll need to be taken off in a hurry."

"We'll be there," Charles answered. "You may count on it."

Jones swung out onto the sidesteps. He paused before starting down. "One more thing: Do you recall that ship which sighted us while you were dallying unnecessarily at the rendezvous north of Koessir?"

"She may not have picked us out," Charles said. "It's unlikely she did."

Jones assumed an expression as if speaking to a truant child. "But if she did, her captain would have reported it when he came into port."

"I suppose so. What of it?"

"Don't be slow," Jones said. "You must continue up to the port at Suez and make a show of spying out the harbor. Otherwise, if they see you coming back down they'll wonder what you were up to. They're not stupid; they'll put two and two together."

Charles thought that Jones was being cautious to the point of paranoia. Still, it made some sense. He had come this far, it would be useful to be able to report on any French preparations at the very head of the sea. "All right," he said. It came to him that there would be a small problem, but something he could manage.

Jones finally went down the side. "Give way all," Charles heard Beechum order the cutter's crew. On the shore he noticed two men in Arab dress emerge from one of the huts to meet the boat as it was pulled up onto a small strip of sand. Jones stepped out first, then the women. Without looking around they disappeared with their hosts back into the hut. Charles shook his head and returned to the quarterdeck.

"Please see that the cutter is brought inboard and secured as soon as she is alongside," Charles said to Winchester. He turned to the sailing master. "We will resume northward to Suez."

Cromley nodded. "Suez? Yes, sir," he said.

"Suez, Charlie?" Bevan interjected. "Why do you want to go to Suez?"

"To see what the French are up to. Also, Jones requested it."

"What about your promise to the crew?"

"Two days, Daniel. That's all it will take. We'll just have a look into the harbor then turn south. I think we will have a gander at Koessir on our way down the sea so that we can make a complete report to Admiral Blankett in Mocha."

Bevan's eyes narrowed as the cutter was hoisted up over the side to be stowed in its place midships on the beams over the gundeck with the other ship's boats. "I don't know about this," he said. "The crew are expecting . . ."

"I'll fix it," Charles answered.

Augustus appeared a moment later. Charles had sent him to move his belongings back into his own cabin the moment the Joneses had decamped. "They done left all of their things all over the place like they was expectin' to be right back," he said unhappily. "I don't think they thought you'd be usin' it."

"Throw it all in a sack," Charles answered. 'Then have it struck to the hold."

*****

"No, sir. We ain't havin' it; not one bit," Thomas Sherburne insisted. "Ye promised to take us south direct."

"I know, and we will," Charles said, trying to sound reasonable. "But the situation has changed. It's only to look into the port so see what's there." Charles had summoned Sherburne onto the quarterdeck as the spokesman for the crew. He intended to explain what he was about to do, and that it would only delay them for a day or two, so as to forestall any discontent or further refusals of orders.

"I don't know," the able seaman said. "Me mates won't be likin' it. They been too long aboard already. Goin' back is all they talk about."

"I'll make it up to them. It'll just be a quick look from a distance. There'll be no fighting or anything else to delay us after. You tell them I said that."

"Well, I suppose . . ." The words came out with the greatest of reluctance.

"Thank you," Charles said.

Suez proved a heat-baked little port with a few dozen buildings shimmering in a sea of sand all around. A crumbling castle guarded the harbor close in. Through his glass Charles saw the French tricolor fluttering from its single tower. The approaches were a maze of bars and shoals, hardly suitable for deep sea craft. He saw no sign of anything like a buildup of transports for India or, more particularly, any French warships. He doubted that a seventy-four could make her way in if she wanted to.

"We will put to across the mouth of the harbor, if you please, Mr. Cromley," Charles said. "Then you may come about and we shall depart."

"Yes, sir. That's it then, just the look?" Cromley asked.

"It was more to be seen than to see," Charles said with some satisfaction. "Our work here is finished. The next port of call will be Mocha."

Cromley nodded agreeably, then called for the boatswain to have the sails trimmed and the yards hauled. Charles noted signs of animation among the men as they took up the halyards or started aloft, the first he'd seen since putting Jones on land. Cassandra glided slowly across the entrance to the port, a mile from the shore, and what must certainly be in full view of the castle. As if to confirm this, a single puff of smoke appeared from its battlements, followed shortly by the distant report of a cannon and a smallish fountain in the sea a cable's length to port. A six-pounder, Charles thought, from the size of the splash. It would be an army field gun and little threat to him. Disdainfully, his ship turned her stern landward and slipped away.

With a following wind, they made short work of the Gulf of Suez. Cromley had a firm idea of the deep channels and Cassandra sailed large, approaching the straits to the main body of the Red Sea early in the middle watch the next day. Charles felt pleased. If the breeze held constant he could expect to reach Mocha in a week's time. Better, he had resumed sleeping in his own bed, in his own cabin. All was right with the world, or at least as best as could be expected under the circumstances. It came as something of a concern, therefore, when he saw Midshipman Hitch running along the gangway from forward. "There's the Frenchie frigate t'other side of the passage," the boy shouted breathlessly, still a distance away.

"Who sighted her?" Charles said as the boy came to a stop.

"Giles, the lookout in the foremast, sir," Hitch managed. "He says she's hove to, waiting like. The same what we had with all these times."

Charles swore under his breath. The midshipman had made his report loud enough to be heard by half the men on board. He knew immediately why the frigate was there. The polacre they'd seen making for Koessir five days earlier had indeed sighted Cassandra's masts and reported it. L'Agile had been dispatched to search him out, guessed or knew that he'd gone up the gulf, and had bottled up the exit to await his return. Charles realized that he was in trouble. It wasn't the frigate that concerned him—he thought he could contest with her on equal terms if the crew were willing. But would they be willing? He saw the answer marching across the waist toward the ladderway to the quarterdeck; Sherburne and two others with a growing collection of men behind, all scowling angrily and shaking their heads.

"Damnation," he said.

CHAPTER ELEVEN

Charles needed time to think; there was no time. With the wind as it was there would be no going back up the gulf, and no point to it anyway. He'd have to come out sooner or later. Should he press on with as much sail as Cassandra could carry and hope to slip past in a mad race for Mocha? No, L'Agile was the faster ship. He called up in his mind the narrow passage between the gulf and the Red Sea, with reef-encircled islands on one side and reef-encrusted shoals on the other. The straits were too narrow for maneuver. The Frenchman would rake him repeatedly at an ever shortening range as he bore down. If his masts were somehow miraculously undamaged and he slipped by in one direction or another, she would run him down, yawing to fire her broadsides into his stern until he was crippled. They had to fight; it was their best chance; it was their only chance. More than that, it was the opportunity to close, yardarm to yardarm, where gunnery would tell.

He looked again at the men collecting at the ladderway to the gundeck. Ayres' marines held them back from storming upwards. Surely he could reason with them; they would have to see that it was their best course. Damn them all anyway. What did they expect him to do? He went forward to the ladderway.

"We ain't stopping to have at that Frenchie," a man shouted at him before he even reached the forepart of the quarterdeck. Bevan bellowed over the din for order. Winchester had his sword drawn. Charles raised his hands for silence so that he could speak. "Ye give us yer word, no fightin'," a man near the head of the ladderway called out. "We sail past," another yelled, attempting to out shout the first.

"Let me speak," Charles shouted back.

"We've 'ad it wif yer promises," someone else called out. "You don't keep 'em." They were crowded together, so that Charles had difficulty recognizing who was speaking. He couldn't find a pause to get a word in. "Sail past." "Run for it." "We ain't gonna fight." "You promised us," all jumbled together and competed to shout him down. His hopes for reason turned to frustration, his frustration to anger. He raised his hands again with no result. Cassandra had already glided into the head of the narrow passageway, only Cromley and the quartermaster guiding her course. Without the men in the yards there was no way to add sail or shorten it. He had to do something soon; he could make out the tops of the French warship's masts from where he stood.

"Quiet!" Charles screamed at the top of his voice. He drew his own sword and waved it in the air. "Shut your mouths, all of you!" The noise abated marginally, but did not stop. Furious, he snatched the musket from one of the marines protecting the quarterdeck, pointed it skyward, cocked its hammer, and fired. "Cease your jabbering or by God I'll run us upon a rock." He knew that he was on the edge of losing control of himself, of everything. He needed quiet. "We don't want to fight," one seaman said. "We want to go back, just like you said." Charles saw the man clearly.

"I don't give a damn what you want, Hill," he snapped. He stepped toward the head of the ladderway, his sword held out in front. "Get off the ladderway. Back onto the gundeck where you belong. I'll not have this kind of behavior. Who the hell do you think you are?"

The men within the reach is his blade backed part way down, still glaring in defiance at him. "We ain't . . . ," a seaman began.

"Shut your mouth, Tipperman," Charles said. "I'll flog the next man who speaks out of turn. I will talk with you man to man, but I'll not be shouted at. Where's Able Seaman Sherburne?"

Sherburne was pushed forward to the foot of the ladderway. "What's your grievance?" Charles snarled.

"We want ye to sail past and make a run for it," Sherburne said. "There ain't no need for a fight. Ye promised us."

Charles was not in any mood to be reasonable, or in any temper to compromise. Indeed, there were no compromises to make. Cassandra was well into the passage and barreling straight ahead at close to her best speed. "I know what I promised. The situation has changed. We have no choice but to fight. Will you or won't you?"

"That ain't as it is," a man beside Sherburne blurted out. "O' course we got choices. We got the choice to run by."

"No . . . ," Charles began, promptly out-shouted in an uproar of protest.

Sherburne looked around him to a chorus of nays and shaking heads. "We won't do it, sur," he said. There was a finality to it.

Charles glared down at the crew a moment longer, humiliated by the refusal and stung by their insubordination. His eyes settled on Sherburne. "Fine," he said coldly. "You are dismissed; you're all dismissed. The next time you are called to order it will be as prisoners to the French."

"Dismissed, sur?" said Sherburne.

"Yes, dismissed. You may not be willing to fight, but I am. I'll do it myself. All of you get out of my sight. I'm sick of looking at you." He turned on his heel to walk away.

"I beg your pardon?" Bevan said, catching his arm. Charles hadn't realized that his lieutenant had been standing beside him. "Do you know what you're doing? You're going to fight who? What with—a one pistol broadside?"

Charles looked at his friend and saw Winchester and Beechum on his other side. There was also Augustus immediately behind him, and the midshipmen and other petty officers. All were staring at him. "I'm sorry, Daniel," he said. "I should have said, 'we.'"

"We, who?"

Charles felt no need to explain. There was one hope upon hope, his last hope, that the crew would see the inevitably of it and come to their senses. And if not? He knew that he would have to strike as soon as the enemy brought her broadside to bear. At least he would have offered some resistance. They were already in the center of the straights, the open sea beyond. He could easily see the French frigate's masts over the bow, square in the middle at the end of the narrows. "Mr. Baker," he shouted at the boatswain.

"Sir?"

"Loose all of the sheets and let them fly. All of them, do you hear?" He had to get the way off. Since he had no topmen to send aloft to furl the sails, the simplest procedure was to undo the halyards holding their lower corners and let them stand out in the wind like laundry on a line. It wasn't very tidy, but it would have to do.

"Aye, aye, sir," Baker's voice came back.

Charles had already turned to Bevan. "You'll have to go forward and get the anchor down. Put a spring on so that we may direct the guns."

"Bevan's eyes widened, then narrowed. "How?" he said.

"I don't know how; any way you can. Use the petty officers, some of the marines. Afterward the marines will have to man the capstan to bring our broadside to bear."

Bevan looked at him in disbelief. "You're really going to fight? Who'll man the guns?"

"We will," Charles snapped. "The anchor please."

Bevan opened his mouth, then shut it. He started reluctantly forward, limping slightly on his gimpy leg. Charles heard a snapping sound and looked up to see the sails on the mizzenmast lose their bellies as the clews ran free, the foot of each sail flopping lazily forward. Baker and the two boatswain's mates were undoing the mainmast halyards. Forward of the bow, broadside on, he saw L'Agile, the line of her upper deck visible on the horizon. Her captain would certainly see Cassandra's disordered canvas. What would he make of it? A flying sheet was a time-honored signal that a ship was in distress. He wouldn't believe that, would he? He should; it was the truth. It could also be interpreted to mean 'enemy in sight,' as if he were signaling to some unseen reinforcements just over the horizon. The French captain would know that he was bluffing; he might interpret it as an act of desperation. That would be accurate; it was an act of considerable desperation.

Baker and his men had finished their work on the mainmast and were moving to the foremast belaying pins. Charles could feel his ship begin to slow. He picked up his prized glass from the base of the mizzen and trained it forward. He wouldn't have it much longer, he reflected; some French officer would surely covet it. There were figures of men climbing the French ship's shrouds. As he watched, her fore mainsail, which had been laid against the mast, began to turn.

Charles took a deep breath and wondered if maybe it would have been better to run after all. His eyes searched along the gangways and down into the waist. The deck seemed strangely empty except for the boatswain and Bevan's anchor party by the beak. Only Cromley remained with him on the quarterdeck, and he was conning the ship. The crew had evidently taken him at his word when he'd told them to get out of his sight. The foresails ran free. Cassandra lost way rapidly. "Bring her to, Mr. Cromley," Charles said. As the bow began to swing he yelled, "Let go the anchor," to Bevan forward and waved his arms. He heard the splash. L'Agile's canvas expanded as if by magic, braced tight, beating up into the wind toward them. The distance couldn't be more than three miles.

Charles went down into the waist to examine the guns in a state of high agitation. He counted on his fingers what men he could rely on. He had three lieutenants and three midshipmen—Sykes might be useful on a gun, if only just. Aviemore and Hitch could act as powder monkeys. There was Augustus, Cromley, Baker and his two mates, and Burrows, the carpenter, if they were willing. He didn't think Wells, the purser, would be of much use, and the surgeon would soon have better things to do. Two guns. They could probably manage two of the twelve-pounder cannon. It didn't really matter if it were two, three, or four. Out of the corner of his eye he noticed Sherburne, with two others—Hurley and an American named Townes, he thought—move along the far side of the deck to prop themselves casually against one of the port side guns. Charles ignored them. The starboard battery would be employed against the Frenchman; at least the numbers eleven and thirteen guns, he decided.

Cromley came down from the quarterdeck. "You're going to assist?" Charles asked.

"I am," the master answered soberly. "Such as I can. It's years since I served afore the mast."

"Thank you," Charles said. Augustus appeared next, without saying a word. After a few moments Winchester, Beechum, Bevan, and the trio of midshipmen came from forward, followed by Baker and a few others.

"Lieutenant Winchester, you will captain the eleven gun," Charles said formally. "You will have Mr. Baker, his two mates, and Mr. Burrows. Mr. Aviemore will carry the powder."

Winchester nodded, his expression grim.

"Lieutenant Bevan will captain the thirteen gun with the rest of us."

"Why am I the gun captain?" Bevan asked suspiciously.

"Because you're lame and can't haul on the tackle," Charles said.

"I'm not lame, just slow."

"Whichever you prefer."

"Charlie," Bevan said.

"What?"

"You're crazy, you know that don't you? They have a space at Bedlam Hospital already reserved in your name." He sighed in resignation. "Well, we might as well enjoy ourselves."

"Just shut up and run the goddamned gun out," Charles snarled, with all the self-righteousness that only one who knows he is probably making a serious mistake can muster. "And no one is going to enjoy themselves." Augustus and Beechum took up the relieving tackle on one side, Charles, Cromley, and Sykes on the other. Charles threw his weight on the line.

"Open the gunport," Bevan said, taking his watch from his pocket and glancing at it. "No point in doing the Frenchmen's work for them."

Charles muttered an obscenity under his breath and let go the line. He went to the bulwark, unlatched the port, pulled its rope to trice it up, and tied it off. "Now run the thing out," he growled, returning to his place at the gun tackle. He heaved, Sykes in front of him strained manfully, Cromley grunted. The gun inched forward with small thump, thump, thumps as is crossed the deck boards. Christ, the beast weighed a ton—two tons actually, he recalled. With a twist of his head he saw that Winchester's gun was already hard up against its port, waiting for the order to fire. Charles redoubled his effort. In his uniform coat and hat, sweat ran off him in rivers, stinging his eyes. Just when he was certain that a hernia could not be long in coming, he heard a satisfying clunk as the carriage bumped softly against the bulwark. "There," he said breathlessly. "You may fire the damned cannon."

"Out tompkin," Bevan said with a broad smile. The wooden plug to protect the gun barrel from the wet had been left in.

"Bloody hell," Charles swore. "Fire it off anyway. It'll come out on its own." He had done this once by accident when he was a midshipman, much to his captain's displeasure.

"That tompkin's the king's property, I'll remind you," Bevan answered.

"Fire the goddamned, sodding, whoreson's, bloody gun."

"Can't, the Frenchman's still out of range. Beside which, you don't tell me when to fire. I'm the gun captain."

"Hell," Charles said. He knelt to look out the gunport. L'Agile was easily visible, her masts in a line, every stitch of canvas set as she bore up into the wind. She was not more than a mile and a half distant. It would be a very long shot, but what possible difference could it make whether they hit her or not? As he straightened he noticed that more of the crew had come to stand along the far side of the deck to watch their officers struggle with the cannon. No doubt they were greatly amused. He wiped at the sweat on his face with the back of his hand, then stripped off his jacket and hat and threw them over the fifteen gun. "Fire anyway, or I'll make you haul on a line, lame or not."

"Step aside, gentlemen. Stand clear, please," Bevan intoned. Positioned well beyond the limit of the recoil, he pulled the lanyard. The gun exploded with a deafening bang, as did Winchester's, whose crew had been waiting patiently. Charles easily saw the tompkin flutter away from the ship like a spinning coin, to land in the sea forty yards out. The ball went farther, sending up a geyser a quarter-mile short and well to starboard of L'Agile's relentlessly approaching bow. The second gun was also short, but on line.

"Well, that was certainly satisfying," Bevan said, looking again at his watch. "Only six-and-a-half minutes so far, not at all bad. Of course, we haven't completed the full sequence yet. Tompkin removed? Oh, yes. Sponge out, if you please."

Muttering every obscenity he could think of under his breath, Charles took up the five-foot length of stiff cable, unraveled into a brush-like ball at one end, dipped it into a tub of water, then rammed it into the cannon barrel. Because of the restricted distance to the bulwark, it was necessary to slide the long handle of the sponge out of the gunport. It caught against the side, slipped from his grasp, and dropped into the sea. He swore loudly. Sykes tactfully handed him the one for the fifteen gun. Charles struggled to push the awkward, flexible instrument in the full length of the barrel, twisting it around to be certain that all of the embers and bits of burnt cartridge were extinguished. Satisfied, he pulled it out.

"Load with cartridge. No hurry, whenever you're in the mood," Bevan continued. Charles glared at him in annoyance. Midshipman Hitch handed him the felt bag with its four pounds of black powder. Charles fisted it into the mouth of the gun then heaved to ram it in with the reverse end of the sponge. His hands came away blackened from the filth on the sponge end.

"Wad," Bevan said. "You know, as in 'wad' you want for supper?"

Beechum laughed, then struggled to smother his mirth. Charles angrily tossed the rammer to him. "Here, see if you can do any better." The lieutenant quickly rammed the wad in place, Sykes rolled in the twelve-pound ball, followed by another wad, which Beechum quickly jammed home. Charles saw that the other working cannon had been pulled up against the bulwarks and was awaiting orders to fire.

"Run out," said Bevan with an anticipatory chuckle.

Charles took up his place on the line and heaved. Sweat ran from his scalp and down his back and chest. The line was slippery in his hands. The monstrous brute inched forward. He looked at the gun crew in frustration. Augustus seemed to be making barely any effort. "Goddamnit, pull," he growled at his servant.

"Yes, Cap'n," Augustus answered with a hint of irritation. He threw his weight on the tackle, his muscles bulging. Immediately the carriage slewed to the left, the barrel jammed against the side of the gunport. The movement caught Charles off balance. As he sidestepped, his sword caught between his legs and he crashed to the deck.

"You there, no taking a break now," Bevan said. "Get back on that line or it will go hard on you." Then he burst into laughter.

Charles fumed in embarrassment.

Bevan took out his watch and looked at it. "Eleven minutes between broadsides so far," he managed between guffaws. "I imagine we got that Frenchman shaking in his boots. Come on, if we apply ourselves, we can get the full evolution done within the quarter-hour. That'll show him English gunnery."

Silently, Charles picked himself up and took the line in his hands. "Pull back a little so we can straighten her out," he said to the others, not daring to look at any of them. Something tapped on his shoulder. "Begging yer pardon, sur," a voice said.

Charles turned his head, then let go the line and turned fully around. He saw Sherburne's open face, struggling unsuccessfully to assume a serious expression. Others of his seamen stood just behind. Charles stared, holding his breath.

"This be my gun, sur," Sherburne said. "Ye'r in my way."

"Of course," Charles said. In spite of himself he grinned. "Thank you."

"Ain't but naught, sur." The regular gun crew levered the cannon into position with practiced ease. Charles looked out the gunport again. The French frigate was a mile away, making slow but steady progress into the breeze. It came to him that she had not returned any of Cassandra's fire (such as it was) with guns that could surely have been moved into the bow by now. The remainder of his crew were loosening their cannon and removing tompkins.

Charles turned toward Bevan. "Don't open any more gun ports or employ additional guns," he said. "Just these two."

"Why not?"

"I'm still thinking," Charles said. He turned back to Sherburne. "Keep up a steady fire, if you will. Aim is more important than how fast you go. In fact, take your time. Try to hit her beak."

"Aye, aye, sur," the gun captain said.

A flood of thoughts came into Charles' head. Why hadn't L'Agile fired? What had her captain witnessed so far? What would he deduce from this? He looked upward at the untended canvas snapping loosely from their yards. The disorder offended him, then it didn't. Only two guns had managed to be brought into action; and those, he admitted, were sloppily handled. The French commander could easily conclude that the English ship was in some dire difficulty. What would he do then? If it were himself, Charles knew, he would come close alongside to demand surrender, or, even better, he would board straightaway. Gunplay would merely damage an already certain prize.

The two cannon went off nearly together. Charles came to a decision. "Stephen," he called to Winchester. "No one is allowed above this deck but by my order. I want the quarterdeck and forecastle kept clear."

"Aye, aye," Winchester answered.

"Mr. Beechum," Charles said next, "if you would see to it that my cabin is struck below and that the gundeck only is cleared for action. Do it quickly." Without waiting for a reply, he waved at Sykes to approach.

"Sir?" Sykes said.

"Go topside. Stay below the gunwales so you won't be seen. I want you to report to me what you can make out of any activity on the frigate's deck." The boy left.

"What are you thinking?" Bevan asked as soon as Charles was alone. The two twelve-pounders fired again, one a few seconds ahead of the other.

"I'm thinking, hoping, that they will decide that we are in some way incapacitated and will bring her bow right up to our side."

"And then?"

"At half a cable's length we will disabuse her."

Bevan smiled.

Charles looked out the gunport again, the merest glance. L'Agile came on, as close to the wind as she would lie, a thin wash of white curling back from her stem. One of the twelve-pounder cannon lurched inward, accompanied by a pall of smoke. In an instant, the second belched fire. A cheer went up from the latter gun's crew as their shot struck home.

Charles considered the effect. It could hardly have done crippling damage and it wouldn't discourage the French captain. It might annoy him enough, however, to override any caution he retained. He would want to get the thing done as quickly as possible.

One-half mile, Charles judged. Four cable lengths.

"Lieutenant Winchester. You have command of the gundeck. See that the armament is double shotted and you may position your men beside their weapons. I needn't remind you to make every shot count." Winchester began bellowing the orders.

"Mr. Beechum," Charles called. He felt a thrill of anticipation up his spine at what was about to happen. "You will assemble the forecastle gun crews at the forward ladderway."

"Aye, aye, sir," Beechum said.

"They may go up on my command. The first broadside will be as the guns are currently loaded. The second will be grape on ball. After that grape or canister only. Aim to clear any men preparing to board."

Beechum touched his hat gravely and went to call his men around him. Charles stole a look outward: a cable's length and a half; L'Agile's bow almost filling the gunport.

Sykes came scrambling down the forward ladderway. "She's nearly on us, sir," he said with some excitement. "There's a mass of men at her forecastle."

"Thank you," Charles said, swallowing to relieve a sudden dryness in his mouth. "Collect the quarterdeck gun crews, if you will. We'll go up in a minute."

The two operating cannon continued to hammer regularly away, connecting in the rapidly narrowing range with every shot. Another glance at the oncoming Frenchman. It was time. "Open your gun ports," he yelled loud enough to be heard the length of the deck. "Stephen, you may commence firing. To your weapons!" he shouted at the others.

The gundeck exploded, the line of black cannon flinging themselves inboard in a resounding crash. Charles raced for the stairs to the quarterdeck. He looked to starboard as soon as his head cleared the coaming. The French frigate filled his view. L'Agile came on, but her bowsprit had broken, tilting downward, her head shattered. There were indeed a very large number of men at her forecastle, confused, staring around them.

In a thrice the quarterdeck and forecastle guns boomed out, including the carronades with their heavy twenty-four pound balls. Two at least sliced through the Frenchmen on the forecastle, parting them like wind through a field of wheat. Her foremast cracked, angled forward, and swept down, pulling the main topgallant mast with it. The frigate's head began to fall off on the wind as Cassandra's gundeck thundered out again, a dense cloud of smoke drifting across the gap. She was close enough that Charles could have thrown a stone all the way across her, if he had one. She had not yet opened her gun ports.

It ended almost as soon as it had begun. With her foremast and bowsprit useless, L'Agile lost steerage and steerageway. Her men, those that remained from preparing to board, ran toward their battle stations, or for cover. Ball and grape scythed her decks, punching in her bulwarks at point blank range. The remainder of her mainmast collapsed, falling to port. As she drifted sideways her broadside came to bear. Charles held his breath. Three gun ports levered open, then one fell shut. Two cannon poked out and fired.

Cassandra's guns replied in a savage outpouring, beating in gun ports, chasing those still living above decks down her ladderways. Her quarterdeck had been abandoned, her forecastle a shambles. L'Agile continued her uncontrolled turn, drifting on the wind, her stern windows coming into view.

"Baker! Where's the boatswain?" Charles called. To Bevan he said, "Slip the anchor cable. We'll come back for it."

The boatswain arrived. "Refasten the sheets, then take in the courses. Draft as many men as you need. Mr. Cromley, as soon as we are under sail we will bear down on her."

Cromley signaled his understanding. The moment Cassandra's sails filled and her head began to turn, someone on the frigate braved the quarterdeck to cut a halyard on the mizzenmast, the only mast remaining, and the flag of France fluttered to the deck. "Cease firing," Charles said to Bevan. "Send Winchester with Ayres and the marines across. I should think the surgeon and his assistant would be useful as well."

Alone for a moment, he stared soberly at the battered opponent, not believing that it was over so quickly. He smiled tightly. Through no intention on his part she had been caught wrong-footed, overconfident at Cassandra's apparent floundering—and she had paid.

*****

Having captured the French frigate, the problem was what to do with her and her crew. She had no prospect as a prize, battered and slowly settling as she was, even had there been a friendly port within two thousand miles where she might be towed. L'Agile's crew, those that remained, would have to be taken off and the ship scuttled. Where to put them? Charles had given much thought to this. He suspected that if transferred to the mainland, their existence would be short-lived. The local inhabitants would have little love for their European conquerors. It would be possible to carry them on board Cassandra to Mocha for Admiral Blankett to decide their fate. The small squadron had no facilities to tend to such a number however, and Charles sensed that Blankett would not be pleased by the imposition. There was one remaining possibility. He called Bevan from across the quarterdeck.

"You want to have another go with the guns? I'm more than happy to serve as captain," Bevan greeted him. "We did so well that last time."

"That will not be necessary, thank you," Charles answered, not wanting to be reminded of the incident. "I want the French crew put on that little island over there." He pointed toward a low-lying lump of sand with a few palm trees, two miles to the south. The place was about a mile and a half long, baked by the sun, and clearly uninhabited.

"You're going to maroon them?" There's no water or shelter. They'll die."

"I'm hoping they won't be there long. I'll let them take off their own water and food, canvas for tents, whatever they want."

"Why won't they be there long?"

"We will inform the authorities at Koessir of their whereabouts as we pass by."

"And the ship?"

"Run a length of fuse down to her magazine. It should be a spectacle."

Bevan left to put his orders into motion. Cassandra's boats would have to be employed, since L'Agile's had been beaten into matchwood. The unwounded remnants of the French crew would do the heavy lifting and rowing. Charles had one further duty to attend to before his ship could resume her course southward. He had also considered this carefully. He pushed himself off the railing where he had been leaning and went down into the gundeck.

"Sherburne," Charles called to get the man's attention. "A word if you please." The hands were largely occupied with replacing the partitions to his cabin and otherwise putting the ship back into order after she had been cleared for action. There was not a scratch of damage from the battle.

The seaman approached cautiously and knuckled his forehead. "Sur?" A number of others gathered nearby, close enough that they might overhear what was said. Charles gestured that they were welcome to come closer.

"I wanted to thank you, all of you, for stepping up when you did. I'll make it up to you as best I can."

Sherburne looked uncertain. "'Twarn't nothin', sur," he mumbled. Then his eyes narrowed to slits and he smiled. "I'm sure ye and t'other officers could have did it yerselfs if we'd let ye be." There was laughter at this, and more when Charles said, "It would have taken us a trifle longer."

He turned serious. "I will increase everyone's ration of spirits at supper this evening by half. That's little enough." Some nodded and there were murmurs of appreciation. He waited for silence. "I want all you to know what I am going to do next, so that you may be prepared for it." He spoke for several minutes about transporting the French crew ashore; the necessity of sailing by Koessir to spy out any preparations there and to pass on a message as to where the frigate's crew could be found. After that he promised to make directly for

Mocha, if they met no further obstacles, and if no other event occurred that their duty would require them to attend to. The gathering around him grew in number. Charles explained matter-of-factly that Admiral Blankett had expressly forbidden their presence on shore at their last visit. "I will request it again, in the strongest terms," he said. "If he refuses, I will resign my commission in protest and he will have to appoint someone else to captain you. That is all I can do."

Heads nodded soberly at this. No one spoke. "You tell your fellows what I have said," Charles concluded. "I know that you have doubts about my honesty, but I mean every word on my sacred honor."

The silence among those around him seemed magnified by others passing by and the work still going on. "If there is nothing further, I will return to my duties." He held out his hand. A surprised Sherburne dusted his own against his trousers and shook it.

"Thank ye, sur," the seaman said.

*****

Charles watched from his quarterdeck at the jollyboat as it fairly skimmed across the water away from the broken French frigate. The morning sun had risen a quarter toward its zenith, dancing glitter reflecting off the bright blue sea. L'Agile wallowed two cable lengths off the stern, her waterline about four feet closer to her gun ports than it had been before the battle. He had regrets about what was to occur. He could have left her as she was; she would probably sink in any case before the day was out. This way, however, he would be certain.

He checked his watch; it had been seventeen minutes since the boat's crew climbed down her side and hurriedly cast off. Charles had ordered the ship thoroughly searched from stem to stern; several kegs of powder breached in the powder room; and a half-hour's length of slow fuse suitably inserted and lit. He glanced at the small island where the French were now in occupation. It had taken all night for them to ferry everything and everybody across, and he could just see the piles of casks on the beach, and several already erected canvas shelters on the higher ground. They'd even fastened a tricolor flag near the top of a palm tree. He heard Bevan's hail as the boat neared and Beechum's reply. He pulled out his watch again to check the time. Twenty-three minutes. Before he raised his eyes he sensed more than saw the flash.

L'Agile's forepart, just behind the foremast, erupted in a glowing ball of flame and smoke. The blast came to him an instant later. He'd seen a ship of war blow up once before. This wasn't a particularly large explosion as these things could be, but it was more than enough. The fore half of the hull abruptly vanished, blown upward and outward in pieces of broken timber. The center, open to the sea, dipped as if exhausted. The stern lifted, the rudder in its entire exposed to view, then slipped forward and downward. For a moment only the mizzenmast could be seen, rapidly shortening until just six feet of the topgallant mast remained visible. She had struck bottom. A cheer went up from the waist. Charles didn't see what there was to cheer about; she had already been defeated.

He turned toward the helm. "Have the hands piped aloft, Mr. Baker; all plain sail. Mr. Cromley, we will make east by south, if you please."

Both men acknowledged their orders. Charles saw the jollyboat being secured in its place midships, nested inside the launch. Beechum appeared from along the gangway. "We did as you said, sir," the young lieutenant reported.

"I saw," Charles said. "In fact I could hardly have missed it. You're sure she was empty?"

"Yes, sir. I checked the hold myself. There was nobody left; I'm certain of it."

"Thank you," Charles said. He had once, almost by accident, found a small child on a French ship about to be similarly destroyed. Little Claudette now lived with Penny at their home in Cheshire. "If you would be so good as to inform Lieutenant Bevan that I anticipate looking into Koessir tomorrow morning."

"Aye, aye, sir." Beechum touched his hat and left.

Charles stayed where he was a few moments longer in a reflective mood. If he'd guessed right, somewhere in the sea was the seventy-four gun Raisonnable. Winchester had queried the frigate's surviving officers, but they had been uncommunicative. It was possible he would find her at Koessir.

*****

The Egyptian coast emerged slowly in the stillness of the morning gloom. Cassandra glided effortlessly under topsails and topgallants, an easy northwesterly wind on her stern quarter, the dark line of the shore three miles off the port beam. Ting-ting-ting, the ship's bell broke the quiet.

It was not unusual for him to be on deck at this hour, but it wasn't normal either. There was nothing he wouldn't have entrusted Beechum as officer of the watch to attend to. He had slept poorly during the night, and when he attempted to recall Penny's expressions and features to compose himself, the dark-haired Italian woman's face intruded. After being away from home for longer than eight months, he suspected that this was not unusual, but knew it was something he'd best not dwell on. Being on his own quarterdeck helped.

"Hoy the tops!" he shouted upward through cupped hands. "Anything? Anything at all?"

"Naught, sir," the answering call came down. "I can see the surface well enough, but she's bare." There was a pause. "There's a point of land, mebby two leagues ahead."

"Thank you," Charles said in an almost normal voice. That would be Koessir Point. From the chart, it was a low headland projecting a mile or so into the sea with a wide band of coral around its base. There should be an old Turkish fort on its southern side overlooking the town and harbor.

"Mr. Dill," he said to the quartermaster standing behind the wheel, his hands resting easily on its spokes. "Please make our course two points to port."

"Aye, aye, sir. Two points it is. I make it to be south-by-southeast, less a half."

"Very good."

The wheel came over a few spokes. After a moment Charles felt the movement of the deck change almost imperceptibly as Cassandra sliced across the easy seas at an altered angle. The sun showed, a sliver of orange on the horizon to the east, looking for all the world, he thought, like the yoke of a frying egg as seen from the side. The distant shore turned a radiant yellow. Charles went to the binnacle, opened the cabinet beneath, and removed his long glass. The point of land just to starboard of the bow showed starkly in the strengthening light. He snapped open the telescope and trained it forward. He soon found a foreshortened rectangle of stone projecting from behind the headland—the blunt upper battlements of Koessir's fort. A flag flew above; he couldn't make out the colors, but he knew well enough.

"Mr. Beechum," he said as he closed the glass.

"Yes, sir."

"At the next bell we will alter course to starboard to weather the point. After that is accomplished, you may clear the ship for action."

"Yes, sir."

"I would like fresh eyes in the mastheads as well, please."

"Yes, sir."

Charles pulled open the telescope again. He guessed that if the French seventy-four were in the roads beyond the headland, her masts would reach at least as high as the fort, probably higher. He saw nothing. "Tops," he shouted upward.

"Naught, sir," came the immediate reply. "I'll tell ye on the instant."

"Thank you," Charles muttered to himself. Despite his impatience, he breathed a little easier. It looked to be unlikely Raisonnable was in the port, nor any other sizable warships. The usual early morning life of the ship began around him: cleaning the decks, flaking down disordered lines, running the log to measure their speed, the carpenter and boatswain making their rounds to see what repairs or maintenance might be required. Charles could see the wood smoke wafting forward from the galley chimney, indicating that the cook had begun preparations for the crew's breakfast.

At four bells, Bevan came onto the deck with Sykes. Winchester and Aviemore would be asleep, having stood watch during the graveyard shift from midnight to four in the morning. Beechum promptly gave orders for the ship to be prepared for battle and the waisters be called to trim the sails.

"Good morning, Charlie," said Bevan. "Anything yet?"

"Nothing so far," Charles answered. "No sign of the seventy-four. We'll know for sure soon enough."

Bevan seemed satisfied with this and turned his attention to the set of the sails aloft. Charles noticed the carpenter on the gangway and went to speak with him. "Mr. Burrows, I have a request," he said.

"Aye, sir?" He touched his hat.

"I require an empty keg to be made watertight, with a weight in the bottom, and a four-foot staff with a flag fixed at the top. It's to be put in the water with a message for the French."

"Aye, we can do that. When do you want it?"

"Before the watch is out, if you please."

In time, the point before Koessir neared to starboard. Charles kept Cassandra two miles out, well clear of any of the submerged coral closer to land. The lookout high in the mainmast reported a large number of local bottoms in the harbor and a polacre at anchor just outside, but no warships of any consequence. As they passed the headlands, Charles ordered Cromley to angle in toward the shore. The fort showed itself on the southern slope, a modest town beneath its walls, and a mole protecting the harbor from the sea. The ship's bell rang again——this time eight strokes, the end of the morning watch. The crew should have just finished their breakfast.

"Beat to quarters," Charles said to Bevan. "Have the starboard guns run out." He turned to Sykes: "The colors, if you will, and hoist a white flag from the foremast."

"A white flag, sir?"

"To show that we won't fire on them if they don't fire on us first."

"Yes, sir.

At that moment, a puff of gray-black smoke showed from the fort. The distant bang and a spout in the sea, well short, came an instant later. "Carry on as you bear, Mr. Cromley," Charles said. His keg with the flag on it, almost a marker buoy, had been placed by the entry port midships. A canvas envelope containing a precise description of the whereabouts of L'Agile's crew was affixed just below the flag. Two men and Midshipman Hitch stood beside it.

The mole came into clear view. Charles took up his glass and saw that the inner harbor was crowded to its capacity with small shipping, almost entirely single-masted sambuks and a few only slightly larger baghalas. A three-gun battery of six-pounder field artillery had been set up on the end of the breakwater, and he saw a party of French artillerymen running along the stones to man them. Beyond the battery, as he had been told, a single European polacre rode at anchor. He lowered the glass and looked upward to see that the union flag had broken out on the mainmast; the white banner requesting a truce running up its halyard.

"Mr. Cromley, steer to run alongside the mole from fifty yards out."

The master acknowledged. Cassandra bore down at a goodly speed toward the harbor, its contents coming into easy view by the unaided eye. Charles thought the craft inside were a curious collection. Except for the polacre, they were adequate for running up and down the sea but too frail for fetching India. He counted fully fifty of them before he gave up. The foot of the mole showed alongside. The fort had not fired after its initial warning. The battery at the mole's head was manned, the guns presumably loaded, the gun-servers standing beside their weapons. It would take courage, Charles decided, for them to stand like that. In any exchange with his own much heavier and more numerous broadside they would be annihilated in an instant. As Cassandra swept past unmolested, the French artillery captain raised his plumed hat in salute. Charles returned the greeting, then gestured to Hitch that the keg be lowered over the side and released. "We will stand off the shore, Mr. Cromley," he said. "Make for the center channel of the sea."

"Mocha, sir?"

"Mocha, Mr. Cromley, with all speed. Daniel, you may dismiss the men from quarters and house the guns."

Charles paused by the rail to look over the polacre. She flew no identifying flag. A lighter lay in the water alongside as some of her cargo was swung down in a net. He squinted into the reflected glare. Black men, barely clothed, huddled on the lighter's boards. Other men stood over them—European men in broad-brimmed hats with muskets. The cargo net was a jumble of black arms, legs, torsos. More blacks crowded the merchantman's deck waiting to be lifted down. He turned away in disgust.

Charles saw Bevan staring through narrowed eyes at the polacre. "Jesus," Bevan said.

"It's not our concern, Daniel," Charles answered.

Bevan looked at him seriously. "Don't you find all this more than a little strange, Charlie?"

"What, the slavery? It's a foul practice, but not strange."

"No. I mean that they let us sail blithely by, taking in all the sights we cared to see. You'd think that if this was their staging area for the assault on British

India, they'd go a little out of their way to shoo us off. They might at least have fired on us."

"We had a flag of truce," Charles observed.

"The French have been known to overlook such niceties before."

"They had no way to stop us. The battery on the mole was a joke."

"Then where's their heavy ship? They must know Blankett and his frigates are encamped at the foot of the sea. Why isn't the seventy-four here to protect the harbor from the likes of us?"

"I don't know," Charles said.

"I didn't ask for an answer," Bevan asserted. "I just said it was strange."

"All right, it's strange."

CHAPTER TWELVE

Cassandra raced southward down the long, empty sea under every strip of canvas she would carry, including her studdingsails and royals. By Cromley's accountings, she logged eleven and twelve knots, once averaging twelve and a half from noon to noon. Charles paced his quarterdeck during the daylight, twelve paces precisely in each direction as the limit of the deck would allow, up and down and down and up again, until he had every knot and imperfection of every deck board underfoot memorized.

He found it unsettling that the lookouts sighted no sails of any kind, friend or foe; not even the meanest dhow. He attributed it to the thoroughness with which the French had scoured the sea. Where were they, particularly the larger ocean-going baghalas? Not at Suez or Koessir, he was sure of that. As to where else they might be secreted away he had no idea. His other thoughts were of his meeting with Admiral Blankett, requesting leave for his crew, and the repercussions if it were refused. He did not want to quit the navy, nor did he resent the promise he'd made to the crew. They deserved whatever consideration he could offer them. It would be the Admiral's attitude that determined the outcome, and Charles would be deeply saddened to leave Bevan, Winchester, and the others behind while he made his way somehow to Bombay and from thence to home.

At least then he would be able to return home. In the evenings, after his supper, he resumed adding to the long letter it was his custom to write to Penny. He did this dutifully, although he too frequently found his attention straying to the small Italian settlement at Massawa and the woman Teresa. He would welcome seeing her again, if only to speak. He remembered her eyes and smile, the earthy tone of her voice and its foreign rhythms. He could talk to her about his doubts and troubles. She would sympathize, he knew. It wore on him that he was practically alone in his efforts to uncover French intentions, in his upcoming confrontation with Blankett, in being so far from home in his wife's time of difficulty. He needed sympathy.

On such an evening, the fifth since passing Koessir, Charles sat at his table chewing at the end of a fresh quill while struggling with his letter to his wife. Augustus approached the table with a tray to collect the remains of his supper. Charles lay the pen down and raised his head. "Do you ever think about going home?" he said. "How would you feel if we did that?"

"Me, Cap'n?" Augustus answered good-naturedly. "That depend on which home you speakin' of."

"I mean Tattenall, in England, with Mrs. Edgemont and Miss Viola." Charles pushed out an adjacent chair. "Please, sit."

Augustus lowered himself and sat carefully erect. "Yes. I think on it. I'd be pleased, if it were the time."

"The time might be sooner than you'd think."

The steward met Charles' eyes. "Because you quit?" Augustus said.

"Where'd you hear that?"

"I speak with some."

"I might have to," Charles said. "You would return with me, of course."

Augustus was still for a moment. "It be best to finish what you start," he said slowly. "You got to go on if you can. It eat you up inside otherwise. I be pleased to see Miss Viola when we done with what we come to do."

Charles did not find this advice to be immediately helpful. Nevertheless, when his steward had gone and he resumed his letter to Penny, he inserted a line that, "Augustus related that he will be pleased when he is able to visit with Miss Viola again."

The meridian attitudes the following noon showed them to have reached the sixteenth latitude. The outermost islands of the Dahlak Archipelago appeared as small specks to starboard on the barely ruffled sea. Charles stood alone, staring outward over the rail. Beyond those islands was the little colony of Italians and the woman. Over the bow, less than a full day's sail at their present progress, lay Mocha and whatever awaited there. He would have preferred their course to be westward toward the African shore.

"Captain, sir." Beechum announced himself from a respectful distance.

Charles turned. "Yes, Mr. Beechum?"

"I apologize for intruding, sir," the young lieutenant said. "But there're three seamen who have requested permission to speak with you personally. I can tell them you're occupied at the moment."

Charles looked and saw no one beside Beechum, or anywhere near him. "Who are they?"

"Sherburne, Willits, and Giles, sir. They're at the foot of the ladderway."

"Do you know what they want?"

"No, sir. They only asked for a moment of your time."

"Thank you," Charles said. "I'll go down." He turned from the railing and started forward. What was it now? The three were all able seamen. He'd thought they would be satisfied with his promise. Perhaps it would be better if he were to resign and leave his troublesome crew to some other captain's methods; his had clearly failed. He passed the marine sentry at the head of the ladderway with barely a nod and descended. "You wished to see me?"

All three removed their hats. Sherburne spoke. "We beg yer pardon, sur, but we 'ave been speakin' among the 'ands. We 'ave a request to make."

Charles frowned. "Of course you do. What do you want this time, feather beds, maid service?"

Sherburne glanced at his mates, then shuffled his feet. "It ain't nothin' like that, sur. We're satisfied for ourselves. We ain't desirin' ye to quit. We don't want no other captain."

Charles swallowed, looking from face to face. Willits and Giles nodded in agreement. "What if I cannot obtain leave for you ashore in Mocha?" he said.

"We'd like to have it, sure enough," Ben Willits said. "But if we can't, we'll have it somewhere else."

Charles wasn't sure what to say. A lump rose in his throat. "Thank you," he offered. "I sincerely appreciate your sentiments."

"We know there been troubles at times," Sherburne said. "We got it sorted out now. It won't be that way no more."

Charles knew what that meant. It was significant that all three spokesmen were senior seamen. It meant that their type had come to an agreement and asserted their authority over the remainder of the crew. He imagined there were some bruises below decks. "Thank you again for your confidence," he said. "I will still do my utmost to give you time ashore."

*****

The dusty pink battlements of Mocha showed along the Yemeni coast to port at mid-morning the next day. Cassandra's lookout in the mainmast had long since reported two British warships at anchor in the roads. With the aid of his glass, Charles made them to be Blankett's small two-decked, fifty-gun flagship, Leopard, and the frigate Daedalus. Both wavered in his lens from the shimmering heat rising off the water. He assumed this indicated that Fox and Hellebore were out keeping watch at the foot of the sea.

"Run up the colors and our number," Charles said to Sykes. "We will prepare to salute the flagship as we are closer to. Take care to do it smartly so as not to displease the admiral." He guessed Blankett would find some reason to be displeased anyway; he just seemed that kind of person.

Charles turned to Bevan. "As soon as we get the anchor down, we will put all of our boats into the water. The jollyboat will go over on the side nearest Leopard, the launch and cutters on the off side."

"You have a plan?" Bevan said. The two had discussed Charles' intention to gain leave for the crew.

Charles nodded. "Load a few water casks into each, and as many of the men as they'll carry. We'll make a show of replenishing the supplies while allowing a number to roam the town. It's possible Blankett won't notice. If we can drag it out for a few days we might give them all a spell on shore."

"And if the admiral does notice?"

"Then I shall have to think of something else."

"You're not going to resign your commission, are you?"

"Not if I can help it."

"Good; see that you don't."

Cassandra began her salute as she rounded the spit of land with its crumbling fort protecting the northern edge of the harbor. Leopard returned the courtesy then promptly ran up the signal, Captain report on board flagship.

Charles climbed down into the waiting jollyboat, uncomfortably hot in his heavy uniform coat and hat. In his pocket was the report he had prepared on his engagement with L'Agile, and the results of his looking into Koessir and Suez.

He was met at the entry port on Leopard's gundeck by Lieutenant Danforth. "The admiral anticipated your return before now," he greeted him.

"Really?" Charles said. "I can't imagine why." He wondered if the lieutenant had been instructed to be intentionally rude in order to keep visiting captains off balance.

"In future you should attempt to be more timely in the execution of your orders," said Danforth.

"In future you should show more respect when addressing a superior officer," answered Charles.

Danforth frowned, then turned to lead the way aft to Blankett's cabin.

"Captain Edgemont," Rear Admiral John Blankett said from behind a small desk in a cabin not much larger than Charles' on Cassandra. He was without his uniform coat and had removed his stock. The top several buttons of his shirt were also undone in deference to the roasting heat. He did not rise, but nodded for Charles to sit in a chair opposite. "I trust you have completed your meanderings up and down the sea," he said testily. "You have certainly taken your time."

"Yes, sir," Charles said, biting back the urge to say anything more. He wondered if Blankett knew how long it actually took to sail to Suez and return.

"You have deposited this spy Jones in Egypt, I presume."

"Yes, sir. I am to return to take him off north of Koessir in a little over a month's time. We will sail as soon as our supplies are replenished."

"I will return to the subject of Jones and what you will or will not do for him in a moment. First, you have been to the head of the sea. I assume you have formed an impression of French intentions, should they have any. What have you found?"

What did he mean by "what you will or will not do?" Charles thought. The Admiralty had ordered him to both deliver and recover the man and his companions. There was no question about this. "I have investigated both the ports of Suez and Koessir, sir," he said, attempting to read Blankett's attitude. "Suez is for all purposes empty. There are a sizable number of dhows and coastal craft at Koessir, being collected for some purpose. I have it in my report." He removed the envelope from his pocket and laid it on the desk.

Blankett did not touch or even look at the document. "So there is no evidence of any armada of sea-going transports for India. I knew it was an Admiralty pipe dream."

"Sir," Charles said, "I found no such transports in the Egyptian ports. That does not mean the French couldn't be keeping them somewhere else. The Red Sea is bare of the larger Arab shipping. They've disappeared to someplace. We also encountered the French national thirty-two-gun frigate L'Agile on two occasions, the second at the entrance to the Gulf of Suez. We were fortunate enough to carry her."

"A frigate?" Blankett said. His mood lightened. "Did you really? Where is she?"

"I put the crew ashore and touched off her magazine, sir."

"How much damage did you sustain?"

"Minimal, sir. We caught her in circumstances favorable to ourselves." He would have said "none," but he didn't think the admiral would believe him.

"A frigate," Blankett repeated. "I owe you an apology. I remember your mentioning something like that when you first arrived. If I recall correctly, you speculated on the possibility of two sets of sail. Have you seen any sign of the other?"

Charles steeled himself. "No, sir. But I have reason to believe the second to be the seventy-four-gun Raisonnable that accompanied L'Agile into the sea."

Blankett actually laughed. "That's ridiculous, captain. It's not possible; not possible at all. The resident, Mr. Underwood, is very well informed of goings on the length of the Red Sea. He would certainly have informed me if there were the slightest hint of an enemy ship of the line in these waters. She'd be too big for somebody not to have noticed. I have had my own craft patrolling in the south. They've reported nothing like that."

"But, sir," Charles said.

Blankett scowled. "Oh, come now," he said. "We mustn't allow ourselves to see perils behind every headland." He held up hand to forestall Charles' protest. "You haven't actually seen this warship. What evidence have you that she has come onto the scene? Mind you, I want hard facts, no ghosts or demons."

The muscles of Charles' stomach tightened. He knew in his gut

Raisonnable was nearby. She would be with the transports the French had assembled—wherever they were—protecting them from discovery and preparing to clear a path for them when it came time to exit the sea. It wouldn't be difficult. He looked around him at Blankett's cabin and the four canvas-shrouded eighteen-pounder cannon. With Raisonnable's thirty-six pounders on her lower gundeck, it would hardly be a fair contest. The only fact he possessed was that she had been in consort with the frigate in the Atlantic. It was enough for him to go on; he knew it would not be enough for Blankett. "I have nothing concrete, sir," he said.

"Then we are agreed," Blankett said with a forced smile. "There'll be no more nonsense about that."

"No, sir," Charles said. "But there was the frigate."

"Could have been any number of reasons for her presence. In any event, she's no threat to us now."

"No, sir." Charles' mind returned to the earlier subject. "What are your concerns about Jones and his party?"

Blankett sighed as if to deliver some unpleasant news. "I regret to tell you that all of your efforts have been wasted. I have discovered from reliable sources that this Jones fellow is in the employ of the French. His object was to determine the strength of my squadron and report it to Cairo. In the circumstances, I imagine this to have been accomplished. I don't hold you responsible, of course. There is no way you could have known. Still, as it happens, you've ended up doing his work for him. Very clever on Jones's part. There's no point in your going north to take him off. I'm certain he won't be at the rendezvous in any event."

Charles felt his face flush. The cabin became unbearably close. "May I ask how you came by this information, sir?"

Blankett glanced at the deck beams above, then at the desktop before meeting Charles' eyes. "I really shouldn't say. It is of a most confidential nature."

"I can well understand that," Charles said, choosing his words carefully. "I must insist. I am, after all, answerable to the Admiralty for his transportation and may be called upon to justify any inaction." He could guess the answer, but wanted it confirmed. If the source was Gladfridus Underwood, he was going to have to make some difficult decisions.

"You will recall, Mr. Underwood, the local representative, I believe," Blankett said, lowering his voice as if they might be overheard.

"I do, sir," Charles said, his heart sinking.

"He has been of invaluable service to the government for many years, and to myself in particular since I took this command. Don't know what I would have done without him."

"I see," Charles said.

"I tell you this in the strictest secrecy. Mr. Underwood and Mr. Jones have, shall we say, crossed paths several times. I have been informed, with details and particulars, of Jones's unsavory character and untrustworthy nature. The man and his two cohorts are well known to serve the master with the most gold and will switch allegiances at the drop of a purse."

Charles held himself expressionless. He recalled the evident rivalry between the two men, and he wondered again at Underwood's relationship with Blankett and the influence he exerted over him. "I must admit that I am shocked at this revelation," he said carefully. "I would never have guessed otherwise. Where is Mr. Underwood, is he in the town?"

"I've found you can't take everything at face value, young man," Blankett said paternalistically. "You'll learn as you gain more experience. To answer your question, Gladfridus is on a commercial mission. To Jeddah, I believe."

"It is a most unfortunate turn of events," Charles said, moving to stand. "If that is all, sir, I have responsibilities on board my own ship." Since the admiral seemed in an agreeable mood, he had thought to make a formal request for leave for his crew. Now he decided against it. He was about to incur Blankett's extreme displeasure anyway. It wouldn't matter if the doings of his men were discovered or not.

"Of course," Blankett said. "I am sure you are aware that your orders from the Admiralty specify you are to place yourself under my command once the Jones business had been completed. Since we are in agreement that this condition has been fulfilled, I will have new orders drawn up within the next several days."

"Thank you, sir," Charles said. "There's no hurry on my part." With that, and a few additional niceties, he removed himself.

*****

"Daniel," Charles said the moment he set foot on Cassandra's deck. "We need to get a number of things done very quickly."

"What things?"

"Revictualing and watering as much as possible and getting the crew their leave. Forget about the subterfuge with the water casks. All of those who weren't put ashore today will go tomorrow. We sail the night after."

"I don't know where to start. Do you have the admiral's permission?"

"It's neither been approved nor denied. I didn't ask."

Bevan was silent for a moment while he thought this through. "Then why the hurry?" he said.

"Because the local resident is on a vendetta to exact revenge against Jones," Charles answered. "I am soon to be officially forbidden to sail up the sea to take him off. I don't wish to be charged with willful disobedience to orders at my court martial. I would prefer the charges be something with a less permanent penalty. Hopefully, we will be gone before any written orders are forthcoming."

"Death is rather inflexible," Bevan observed philosophically. "Either way it would resolve your conflict over resigning your commission. We won't get the watering and resupply done in two days, you know."

"Collect as much food as you can. We'll water someplace else. I am thinking to call on the Italians at Massawa again. Nobody would think to look for us there and they've offered to help with supplies."

*****

At two bells in the middle watch two nights later, Charles stood tensely by the mainmast in the dark listening to forty pairs of padded footfalls as the capstan pushed round. Its axel was newly greased and nearly silent. There was no tic-tic-tic as the pawl was tripped, since it had been removed. He could hear the anchor cable as it rubbed in through the hawse, uncomfortably loud to his ears. He looked to starboard and saw the single lantern hung on Leopard's mizzenmast, a pinprick in the night. If he stared hard he could just make out a similar beacon on Daedalus at anchor on the flagship's far side. Cassandra showed no light beyond that shielded from outside view in the binnacle. This would not be remarkable, she had shown no light the night before either. The tide was on the make, such tides as there were in the almost enclosed sea. A soft groan came from the ship's timbers forward as the cable tautened. Movement on the capstan slowed, then ceased.

"The bower's hove short, Charlie," Bevan's voice said, a little more than a whisper. With Leopard only a hundred yards upwind, Charles thought his friend's caution prudent.

"Sheet home the fore and main topsails, if you please," Charles ordered. "Steady on the bars," he said to the men at the capstan. "She'll come atrip in a minute." The word to release the sails was relayed to the topmen in the yards by Aviemore and Hitch, racing up the ratlines. The sounds of the heavy canvas unfolding as it descended seemed almost deafening. "Brace up," he said to Winchester, supervising the men on the falls. "Mr. Cromley, we will make due west, if you please."

Charles felt the deck beneath him begin to move. Someone on the bars slipped and fell with a curse, caught unprepared as the strain came off the anchor cable and the capstan began to turn. "Smartly, now," Charles said. "Get her up." Beechum would see to having the smaller of the two bow anchors catted home once they were out of earshot.

Leopard's lantern faded sternward, then in time blinked out. There had been no outcry at Cassandra's departure, in fact no sign that anyone on board had noticed at all. Blankett would be called in the morning to find the space empty where one of his frigates had been the day before. Charles gritted his teeth, then took in a deep breath and breathed it out slowly.

Daylight found them entering Beylul Bay across the sea from Mocha. Cassandra came about to tack northward until the Hanish Islands were sighted forward of the bow shortly before dinner time, then tacked again to west-by-northwest, slowly clawing her way to windward and up the sea. On the third day they rounded to the west into the Dahlak Archipelago on the same path they had followed on their first visit to Massawa. Toward evening Cassandra passed carefully between the recently named Ellie's and Penny's Islands, then put down a stream anchor to wait out the night.

"You know the course?" Charles said to Cromley the next morning as preparations were being made to get under way.

"Aye, sir. It's straightforward enough from here. With the breeze on her beam, I reckon we'll be there in the early afternoon."

"Very good," Charles said. In spite of himself, he felt a thrill of anticipation at reaching the town. Teresa would be there. It was only a friendship, of course, nothing more. But he would welcome the opportunity to speak "intimamente," as she had put it, and escape from the weight of his responsibilities, at least for a time.

The rugged coast of the Abyssinian highlands slowly rose and took form over the starboard bow, the last of the archipelago diminishing behind. What an out of the way and curiously sheltered place, Charles thought. It was like a sea unto itself. A fleet could be hidden in these waters and no one sailing up or down would ever suspect. The familiar mouth of Massawa's bay showed to the southwest. With his glass, Charles could see the stone redoubt at the end of the point and the newly completed quay in front of the settlement. The harbor was bare of shipping save a single Arab sambuk.

"Show the colors," Charles said to Sykes, close by his side awaiting instructions.

"Do we fire a salute, sir?" Sykes asked. "We did t'other time."

Charles thought of his now seriously diminished supply of gunpowder. "No," he said. "The colors will do."

Cassandra glided toward the harbor under a breeze that barely ruffled the sea's surface. The figures of people appeared from the buildings along the waterfront, tiny in the distance. Charles raised his glass again to examine them. He soon picked out what he was looking for, a petite woman in a full-length skirt holding an umbrella for shelter from the sun. It was hard to be certain, even magnified in the lens, but he thought her to be Teresa. His heart beat quickened. She was speaking with three men, one of whom, he was certain, he recognized as the governor of the colony, Bellagio. Charles transited the glass the length of the quay to the redoubt. He was surprised to see the muzzles of a number of small cannon in its embrasures.

"Let go the anchor," Charles said. Cassandra came to rest at almost the same space she had occupied during her previous call. The topmen aloft fisted in the canvas to furl the sails and tie them against their yards. He looked shoreward and saw a cluster of people gathered along the quay. Almost immediately he picked out Teresa, standing a little apart and waiving a handkerchief at him. Charles lifted his hat and waived back. He noticed some of the crew staring out at the settlement. Leave might be arranged for them on shore, he thought. There was no reason not to; it would be several days before he was required to start north to find Jones.

"Anchor's down, Charlie," Bevan announced.

"Hoist out the jollyboat. I'll go across."

"Do you want a few of the marines?"

"Not this time," Charles said. "I don't think it will be necessary. I plan to inquire about completing our water and stores and liberty for the men while we're in port."

"Two ports of call in a row. They'll hardly know what to make of it," Bevan said.

"God knows what they'll find to do. Speak with them about respect for the local women, if you will. I don't want any incidents."

Charles climbed down over the side and settled into the sternsheets of his boat. A glance told him that Augustus was at his place on the stroke oar. In spite of himself, he took comfort in having him close by. It was something he was becoming accustomed to. "Make for that near ladderway on the quay wall," he said to Malvern.

"Out oars," the coxswain ordered. "Push off."

Charles looked up at the top of the wharf for Teresa to see if she might be watching. He found her right away, her side to him. She was listening to a man speaking volubly, gesturing urgently with his hands. The man turned for an instant to look at the approaching boat. Charles recognized the sun-darkened features of Gladfridus Underwood, the British representative at Mocha. "Put your backs into it," he snapped at the boat's crew.

They soon came alongside the ladderway, securing it with a boat hook and pulling close. "Augustus, come with me," Charles said, stepping over the gunwale and starting quickly upwards.

Teresa came forward as Charles climbed onto the quay's surface. "Capitan Edgemont," she began.

Charles saw Underwood's back, in the company of two others, hurrying away. "In a minute," he said and started after them. "Wait," he shouted. "I want a word with you." Underwood's pace quickened, aiming toward a second ladder with an open-decked dhow waiting below. Charles broke into a run. "God damnit, Underwood. Stop!"

The British representative reached the head of the ladder and paused to stare malevolently at his pursuer. The two men in his company turned. Charles saw they were the large doormen he had encountered at Underwood's house in Mocha. He came to a halt in order to avoid running into them. Augustus arrived to stand beside him. The two bodyguards stood their ground. Underwood went down the ladder.

Charles moved to the edge of the wharf as the bodyguards followed their master into the boat. "I know your game, you bastard," he called down. "It won't work, do you hear? It's a despicable thing to turn on an agent of your own country. It doesn't matter what grudge you carry."

At this Underwood looked up. "It would have been better for you to have followed orders and remained at Mocha, Captain Edgemont," he said.

"I'm not finished with you," Charles shouted back. "We have a score to settle."

Underwood shrugged, then he gestured to the dhow's crew to cast off.

Teresa caught up a moment later with the governor and several others close behind. Slightly breathless, she said, "Capitan, Carlo, what is this? Why have you so angered with Signore Underwood?" She laid her hands on his arm, alarmed by the confrontation. "He is you countryman, no?"

"Yes, he's my countryman," Charles said, his anger still high. "He's also betrayed a man I'm responsible for. I am on my way north, all the way to Koss . . . ," he caught himself, ". . . to Egypt, to take him on board. Underwood would rather I left him there to die at the hands of the French."

"I didn't know," Teresa said. "What a very bad thing."

Charles watched as the dhow came alongside a sambuk, larger than usual with two masts. Underwood boarded and went immediately below. The crew set about pulling her small bow anchor and loosening the sails. If Charles had wished to, he could have the craft stopped and the representative detained, but on what charge? He let the idea go. "Why was that man here?" he asked.

"He comes often on the affairs of trade," Teresa said. "It is normale, no?"

"Yes, I suppose so," Charles said. He looked into her eyes and saw she was upset. "I apologize for my behavior. This is no way for a gentleman to call on one's friends." He noticed she was wearing a loose blouse, scooped modestly in front, and a full black skirt reaching down to her shoes. She looked altogether beautiful.

She took his arm in hers, pressing it against her side. He could feel the warmth of her body through the fabric of his jacket. "Come," Teresa said. "For myself, I am very pleased you have come, but you must be respectable to Signore Bellagio."

Charles saw the governor waiting impatiently a few paces away. The man glowered unhappily, but then he remembered Bellagio always seem unhappy. Teresa spoke at some length in Italian. Bellagio reluctantly half bowed; Charles half bowed in return. Bellagio spoke a terse sentence which Charles did not understand. He looked to Teresa.

"Governatore Bellagio welcomes you again warmly to our small colony," she said. "Of course our hospitality is open to you. He asks how he may be of service." She ended with a dazzling smile.

"Please thank the governor on my behalf, and on the behalf of my king, for his courtesy," Charles said, searching for the correct diplomatic niceties.

Teresa translated.

Bellagio half bowed.

Charles bowed back. "We wish to complete our stores of water, a small part of our foodstuffs, and firewood. This was agreed on our last visit. We will pay, of course."

This provoked an unexpectedly lengthy exchange between the governor and the woman, spoken in rapid staccato sentences. Bellagio seemed to be insisting on something which Teresa found unwelcome. In the end she nodded her acceptance. The governor's expression softened. He almost smiled.

"We are most hopeful to serve your every need," Teresa said to Charles. She seemed for a moment to be distracted, then spoke with a renewed smile. "Water is plentifully available by the aqueduct at the end of the harbor. Signore Bellagio is only concerned that time will pass before sufficient food can be obtained. What was the other?"

"Firewood for cooking," Charles said. He wondered what the discussion had been about and what she might have agreed to.

"This will take a few days only," Teresa said. "It must be gathered, you understand."

"I will have my men do it."

"No, no. We are pleasant to perform every service for you."

"Thank you," Charles said. "We will do it ourselves. I do not want to impose on you more than necessary." He still wanted to get his men some time on the land under any guise. "I have one additional request."

"Si?"

"Would it be permitted to allow my crew leave to come ashore? They would benefit from the experience."

Her face reddened. "I have spoken before, we have no such facilities," she said in a low voice.

"For seeing the local sights only," Charles said. "They would come in small groups so as not to be disruptive."

There was a brief exchange. The governor shook his head vehemently. "It is not possible," she said. "We have concern for the honor of the women. I am sure you understand."

"I will vouch for their behavior," Charles said. "This is important to me. I would consider it a personal favor." He was sure that at least a few of Massawa's ladies would receive offers to which they were unaccustomed, no matter what he said to his men. Still, he thought no real damage would be done.

Teresa looked doubtful. Charles decided that Bellagio was simply being disagreeable. There was clearly no good reason to keep his men confined on board. If he decided to put them ashore anyway, there was little the Italians could do to stop him. "I must insist," he said firmly.

She translated this at such length that additional arguments must have been made. Bellagio shrugged his approval. After a few additional bows, he and his lieutenants marched away. The two found themselves alone except for Augustus, standing resolutely close by.

Teresa stood silent for a moment, tight lipped. Then her expression softened and she turned. "Come, mio Carlo," she said warmly, taking up Charles' arm again. "Let us find a little shade, there is a place nearby. I have so many questions and so little news of the civilized world. We may have some time alone to speak intimamente. You must tell me everything." Her eyes darted meaningfully at Charles' steward.

"I would enjoy that," Charles answered, pleased that he had her attention to himself. "Augustus, you may return to the ship. Please inform Lieutenant Bevan that he may begin the watering parties and that the men are allowed on shore. I will return in due time."

"I'll tell Mr. Malvern, Cap'n," Augustus answered firmly. "Then I just stay close by."

Charles did not want to argue with his servant in front of the woman. "Fine," he said, "but not too close. Tell Malvern that he may return to the ship with the message for Lieutenant Bevan." He could guess what Augustus was concerned about. The man had appointed himself Charles' chaperone as well as bodyguard.

Momentarily alone, Teresa took his arm loosely in hers and guided him in the opposite direction down the waterfront until they came to the end of the buildings. There a pair of long benches were set among a stand of palms. It was a pleasant, quiet place with a view of the harbor and Cassandra riding placidly at anchor. They sat, she close beside him, still with her arm in his. "You must to tell me for how long you may remain with us. For my person, I am hoping a long visit."

Charles answered, "Three days," thinking that was the most he could wait before starting north to pick up Jones.

"Why must you leave so quickly? We are friendly, no? It is my wish to entertain you. What can be so important that you may not stay?" She squeezed his arm.

Charles felt flattered by her attention, welcome in her presence, and stimulated by her intimacy and closeness. He answered vaguely about having orders to sail to the north. He might return when that was complete. As they talked, the heat of the day diminishing quickly, she showed great interest in his career as a naval officer, the places he had been, and his battles with the Spanish and French. She often touched his hand when she spoke, to emphasize some point, or caressed his arm, or squeezed it against her side. Charles assumed these were her normal gestures. Italians were known to be expressive. He relished the contact between them. Augustus returned to sit on the second bench, a respectable distance away. Teresa did not ask if Charles was married (a question he had answered evasively on their first meeting) or refer in any way to his life in England. As the sun neared the tops of the mountains to the west, he realized that he must return sooner or later to his ship. He had already remained ashore, in full view of Cassandra's quarterdeck, too long—a circumstance which he suspected would not go unremarked upon by certain of his officers.

"I must go," he said softly, patting her hand.

"So soon?" She twisted to face him so that his arm pressed against the side of her breast, yielding and firm.

Charles' heart pounded. He stood, taking her hands to help her up. "I'm sorry," he said with a huskiness in his throat. "I must. My officers expect me to return. They won't know what to do without me."

"I am sure you are very commanding," she said with a large smile. "And domani? May I see you tomorrow?"

"Yes, tomorrow," Charles said. "I have duties to attend to. I will come in the afternoon when it is cooler."

"That is good," she said. "I will make for you a supper in my home. You will enjoy to be with me, no?"

"Yes," Charles said, reflecting momentarily on the several possible meanings of the words, "to be with." She pointed out the small building that was her residence. Reluctantly he parted from her and walked with Augustus back up the harbor front. Neither spoke, but Charles sensed his steward's disapproval. The sun had gone, the last of the day lingering. He saw one of the ship's cutters tied up to the ladderway. Bevan had not wasted any time; there were numbers of his crew wandering in threes and fours along Massawa's few streets and alleys in hopeful pursuit of what they were unlikely to find. The town's residents had closed themselves inside their buildings, locked the doors, and shuttered the windows. Armed men guarded the warehouses. Charles ordered one of the marines standing guard over the boat to find its crew to take him back to his ship.

Lieutenant Winchester stood at the entry port as Charles climbed on board, his expression one of suspicion and disapproval. "Oh, for Christ's sake, Stephen," Charles said. "I haven't done anything improper, nor do I intend to." He did not want any discussion with his younger brother-in-law about what his intentions might or might not be. Winchester had already made his views on Charles' deportment toward the Italian woman well known.

Winchester remained silent, his expression unchanged.

"It's none of your concern in any event," Charles asserted brusquely. "If you will excuse me." He shouldered his way past.

Almost before he reached the quarterdeck he was approached by Bevan. "Have an enjoyable afternoon?"

"I do not wish to discuss it. It's a private matter," Charles answered in a tone to end any further commentary.

"It's not private anymore," Bevan said agreeably. "We've all been watching. I could have charged good money for the use of the telescopes. I watched myself. She's quite a handsome woman."

Charles flushed. He knew he and Teresa had been within view of the ship, but had no idea they'd been watched so closely. "It's nothing, Daniel," he said. "I've been invited to supper tomorrow is all. She's just someone I can talk to."

"Sure, I can well believe that," Bevan said. "I'm certain it's all quite innocent. Let me ask you this: What does she want?"

"Only the pleasure of my company," Charles answered.

"Of course that must be the reason. But with her looks, I'd have thought she could do better. As for your dalliance with this person, child-like friendship though it may be, I will say only that I've never known you to do anything more than your workaday stupid, Charlie. My advice is, don't start now."

The next morning Charles busied himself with his usual shipboard routine. Bevan sent two of the ship's boats to Massawa's aqueduct to refill empty water casks and another with a wooding party further inland to collect fuel for the galley stove. The jollyboat ferried off-duty seamen back and forth to the quayside where they might examine the town. As the day wore on, he found himself with little to do and a growing edge of anticipation toward the evening's arrangement. As the time drew near, he washed and shaved carefully, then dressed in a fresh shirt and stock. At the end of the first dog watch he requested the jollyboat to take him across.

"A word, if you please," Bevan said as Charles was about to climb down into the boat.

"If you're going to start up again about my possible wanderings," Charles began.

"No," Bevan said seriously. "I want you to take two marines with you to stand guard. They can wait outside the entrance."

"Why?"

"I don't know. I'm not comfortable. There's something about this place I don't trust. I've already spoken to Ayres. There's two of them in the boat."

Charles looked over the side and saw two redcoats with their muskets in the bow, as well as the boat's crew with his steward at his accustomed place. "Did Winchester put you up to this?" he asked. "I'm surprised he didn't offer to come himself."

"No, it was my idea. He agrees that something's amiss. We just can't put our finger on what it is."

"I'm sure I'll be perfectly safe," Charles said. "I'll keep the marines. If nothing else, they'll provide Augustus with company. If you're so concerned, perhaps you should post extra sentries around the ship."

"I already have," Bevan said.

Charles went across in the boat, the sweltering heat beginning to cool with the coming of night. He studied the neatly aligned rows of European buildings behind the stone wharf. How had these people, refugees from Napoleon, found their way here? There was something odd about it, improbable. He dismissed the notion. The Italians were friendly enough, or at least Teresa was. Stranger things had happened in the world, all with perfectly logical explanations.

At the quay ladderway, Charles climbed up, followed by Augustus and the marines. He had not actually ordered Augustus to accompany him, but he would have been surprised if he hadn't. "I'll have the boat wait, if you please," he said to Malvern. "I don't expect to be more than a couple of hours. The crew may loiter along the waterfront. Don't let them stray too far."

"Aye, aye, sir," the coxswain replied.

Charles started across the nearly empty flagged surface, his steward beside him, the two marines marching in step behind. He thought there was an air of the ridiculous about paying a call on a woman with a military force in tow. He saw the house she had pointed out to him with a small garden in front behind a low wall. He stopped by the gate, made sure his hat was on straight and adjusted his sword. "You will wait here. I'll call if I need anything."

"Aye, aye, sir," said the senior of the marines. Augustus stood silent.

"You have nothing to worry about," he said to his steward.

Augustus nodded.

Charles approached the solid wooden entrance, took a breath, and knocked. The door swung back to reveal a thin, rather tall African woman and a room beyond. "Signore Capitan Inglese," she announced. Teresa appeared at once. Charles stared, then caught himself. She had dressed in a fetching blouse, as a peasant woman might wear to a village festival, with flowers embroidered in the edging around the neck and sleeves. It stretched across her chest, below her shoulders on both sides, scooped low to reveal a large amount of rising cream-colored chest and an impressive cleavage. Rich dark tresses curled down to rest on bare flesh.

"Mio Carlo," Teresa greeted him. "I am so pleased to receive you." She stepped forward to lead him inside and saw the marines with Augustus by the gate. "Why is this?" she said.

"A precaution," Charles answered. "In the event I require protection."

"From me?"

Charles appraised her with an admiring expression. "Possibly," he said. He removed his hat and stepped inside. The door closed. It was a clean room with spartan furnishings: a table, several chairs, a dresser, a cupboard, and a bed in an alcove. It was about the same size as his own cabin, he realized. A doorway led to a room beyond.

"You will pardon my poor house. We are not so wealthy here," Teresa said, taking his hat from him. "Here, give me your sword. You must be at your ease. I will not attack you. I promise, I will cross my heart." She did so and Charles broke into a sweat. She laid his hat and sword on the bed. "And your coat. It is too warm." He did not protest.

The table in the room's center was laid for two with pewter dishes, knives, forks, and wine goblets. He noticed a bottle wrapped in straw on the cupboard. "And now you must to sit. I have small business first, then we may eat," she said. She wrinkled her nose prettily to indicate the subject of business was distasteful to her. Charles helped her into a chair and then sat himself across the table. Teresa spoke to the maid in Italian, of which he understood the word vino. He had an impression that she was nervous, ordering and directing things to cover it up. It was possible that the presence of the bed accounted for that. Glancing at it made Charles nervous as well. The maid unstoppered the wine and poured it out, a rich, dark-red, almost purple liquid. A single candle flickered on its stick in the middle of the table.

"You mentioned some business?" Charles said when they were alone. He sipped at his wine and found it full bodied and rough. It burned its way down to his stomach. He began to relax.

Teresa settled herself and smiled warmly. "Si, I am to tell you that the food we are to send to you is a little delayed. It must come from the farms in the mountains, you understand. All is arranged; it will be assembled in some few days." She reached across and touched his hand as was her customary way when speaking to him. "But there is no hurry, no? You can wait, your ship, perhaps to visit with me?" A fingernail scratched lightly across his skin, leaving a thin white trail.

In spite of himself, Charles' pulse quickened. "A few days?" he said. "It may be possible."

"Good," she said. "Now we may eat. I have prepared this myself, speciale for you." She clapped her hands. The maid soon reappeared with a bowl of steaming pasta, a plate of greens, and another with some kind of fish. There was a tub of butter, a small bowl of salt, and a quantity of grated cheese.

Charles paid little attention to the meal before him. They ate, mostly in silence with short exchanges of conversation. She filled his plate herself and kept his wine glass full. He watched her while they ate, her lips as she chewed, her lowered eyes, the movement of her hands, and the tops of her breasts as she sliced her portions and raised them to her mouth. Despite the wine, he felt the tension in the room rise until it became stifling. She was a desirable woman, firm and soft at the same time, and enchantingly attractive. He allowed himself to imagine what she would be like on the bed, her inhibitions gone, her bare breast against his own . . .

"Basta cosi, enough," Teresa said at length, putting down her utensils and dabbing a cloth to her lips. "But you have eaten nothing. You will be too thin."

Charles glanced at his plate, about half of his serving remaining. "I'm satisfied, honestly," he said and pushed his chair back from the table to stretch his legs. "It was a fine meal. Thank you."

Teresa rose and moved toward him. Charles watched every step; he thought to rise himself. "Stay," she said, placing her hand on his shoulder. She lowered herself into his lap, her arm around his neck. "Cara mia," she breathed, her face close to his. His arms went instinctively around her, strands of hair brushed through his fingers. Her lips parted, close, closer, until they were on his. Charles pressed his mouth against hers, he breathed her breath, warm, sweet, moist.

Teresa responded with passion. "We have so little time, my heart, my lover. Please, you may stay one night, two nights, a week only that we may be together. I am so alone in this place." She kissed his lips, his eyes; her breath now in his ear. Her teeth pulled on the lobe, hard enough for pain, exquisite pain. Charles' mind churned with a confusion of racing emotions. He knew himself to be as aroused as he had ever been, a fact of which she must certainly be aware. He struggled to suppress a thought that would not go away. He couldn't. Well, he could; he wanted to; God knew he wanted to. Of its own volition, his hand found her breast and caressed its fullness, her nipple under the thin cloth. Teresa's fingers opened the buttons of his shirt, pulled the garment up, its shirttails free. Her nails raked his bare skin, her lips again on his. Charles found it difficult to think, or even breathe. Who would know? No one would know. He remembered that Augustus waited outside the door with the marines. He would have to be sent back to the ship. He remembered Winchester's icy disapproval that Charles had even sat alone with the woman outside on a bench. Everyone would know.

Another image came into his head, unbidden, unwanted: Penny's face, clear in every detail to the tan flecks in her clear gray eyes; fine strands of fawn-colored hair wind-blown across trusting lips. She might never know, but Charles knew that he would know. He could not lie to her, even if she never asked. He couldn't.

"No," he said. "It's not possible. All right, it's possible, but I can't. I'm sorry." He removed his hand, pushing her gently back.

Teresa stared at him in bewilderment, then hurt. "No? But why? We would . . ."

"I have a wife and a child at home."

"Oh, it is nothing to me. She is so far away," she said, attempting to pull him close. "There is no need for her to know."

"No," he repeated more firmly. He removed her arms.

"You cannot be serious."

"I assure you, I have never been more serious, nor regretted it more deeply. I wish the circumstances were otherwise."

Teresa's eyes hardened, her mouth a tight line. She rose to her feet, her face flushed. "I am sorry you do not find me attractive. Bastardo Inglese, you are not a man."

Charles stood, dismayed at her sudden change in attitude. He had assumed, to the extent that he had thought about it at all, that she would be more understanding. "I'd better go," he said.

"Yes, you go." She began an uninterrupted string of shrill Italian which he was grateful he did not comprehend. Quickly, he retrieved his things from the bed. Without waiting to put them on, he made for the door. She picked up his half-empty plate and threw it at him, which struck the wall with a loud clatter. Charles yanked on the door latch in time for the second platter to sail past, out into the night. He hurried through and closed the panel behind him. Something substantial, possibly the butter tub, crashed against its other side.

The two marines stood by the gate staring at him. Augustus retrieved the dinner platter from the pathway. "You all right, Cap'n?" he said.

"Yes. Fine," Charles answered. "You may leave that by the entrance. A small disappointment, is all."

"Yes, Cap'n. I know that kind of thing myself."

"Do you?" Charles said. "We can discuss it another time. I think it best we return to the ship for now. Possibly we should hurry."

Winchester stood stiffly by the entry port as Charles came onto the deck, his expression cast in a rigid scowl. The sight of his brother-in-law caused him a moment of guilt at what he had almost done, wanted so badly to do, that he reacted angrily. "For Christ's sake, Stephen," he snapped. "Nothing untoward happened. I am disappointed that you would even entertain such a suspicion." He hurried past toward the quarterdeck. He found Bevan standing under a lantern hung from the mizzen.

"Oh, my," his friend said.

"Oh, my, what?" Charles answered, his tone carrying every indication that he did not wish to discuss the subject.

Bevan persisted, undeterred. "For starters, your shirttail is out, shirt undone, stock gone, holding your jacket. I take it you boarded and carried her successfully."

"I did not," Charles asserted hotly. "I resisted every approach. Well, almost every approach."

"You fended her off? How quaint. What did she want?"

"How specific do you want me to be?"

"That, I can guess. No, what did she want in return?"

Charles had to think. "Nothing really. She said our foodstuffs would be delayed a few days. Something about it having to come down from the farms in mountains. She hoped we could remain in the harbor for a week or so."

"So that you might enjoy her, ah, company?"

"That was the gist of it."

"Charlie," Bevan said seriously. "There'll be no victuals from here. I've had the midshipmen keeping watch every minute. One horseman went galloping north along the coast yesterday, but no one has gone into the hills at all. They'd have to do that in order to request the provisions."

Charles was silent for a moment. There was something seriously out of place. "Is everyone back from their time ashore?"

Bevan nodded.

"Roust out the hands. Do it quietly, it would be impolite to wake the town. It's not too early to start up the sea for Jones."

CHAPTER THIRTEEN

The Brothers, the same two low-lying islands Charles had pointed out to Jones before selecting their rendezvous, lay fine off the port beam, froth-ringed lumps on the water under a searing mid-morning sun. It proved fortunate that Cassandra sailed from Massawa at the time she did. Contrary winds and sudden squalls had slowed their progress. Still, on Sunday, the eleventh of August, Charles felt they had time in hand to look into Koessir to see if the contents of the harbor had changed in any way.

"Daniel, I'll have the topgallants taken in, if you please, and their yards struck to the deck." Bare mast poles would be harder to see at a great distance than broad sheets of canvas. He wanted to look into Koessir; he would prefer not to be seen doing it. Bevan relayed the orders.

"Mr. Beechum, do you have a glass?" Charles said.

"I'll just get one," the lieutenant answered.

"Here, take mine." Charles held out his own personal telescope, the same he had received as a gift from his wife when they were together at Liverpool, those many months before. It was the finest on the ship. Since he intended to remain at as great a distance as possible, its superior optics would be helpful.

"Oh, thank you, sir," Beechum said.

"Get you up to the main topgallant mast, as high as you can go. Take careful note of what you see in the harbor. Mr. Sykes will accompany you as far as the crosstrees to pass your report down."

"Yes, sir. I understand."

"Signal as soon as you are satisfied, and we will stand out to sea again."

"I'll wave my arm, sir," Beechum offered.

"That will do," Charles said. "Mr. Sykes, you will relay Lieutenant Beechum's intelligence onward by way of Misters Hitch and Aviemore."

"Aye, aye, sir," said Sykes. The younger midshipmen nodded agreeably. It was a complex business communicating quickly from the highest point on the ship down to the deck, one hundred and thirty feet below.

"Aloft then, all of you." Charles nodded to Cromley, who had already been informed as to the coming maneuver. The master looked upward to see that the topgallant yards were well down their masts. He then ordered the helm to be put over. Cassandra stood in cautiously toward the Egyptian shore.

"You do know, don't you," Bevan observed. "With all this relaying, Beechum is going to report an enemy fleet in sight. Aviemore will happily inform you that enema heat is slight."

Charles grinned. "I only want to know if Raisonnable is in the port. She has to be somewhere. As for the rest of it, I don't think if of much importance." As Bevan turned away, Charles' smile faded. It was true, the French seventy-four had to be somewhere, but that somewhere did not have to include the Red Sea. He only knew for certain that she'd come into the Indian Ocean. She could have been bound for Mauritius, or Batavia, even off Annam where the French were said to have interests. There were dozens of possibilities. What if the lookout was wrong about seeing two sets of sail entering the Straits of Mandeb? He had, after all, been looking into the sun. What if Admiral Blankett and St. Legier in Cape Town and all the others were correct—that the French did not have, and had never had, any intention of invading India? In that event, if he was lucky, he would be replaced and never receive another command. If he were unlucky, and if Blankett cared to make a point of it, he would be dismissed from the service in disgrace, or worse.

Charles arched his head back and watched anxiously as Beechum climbed the mainmast, Sykes close behind. At the crosstrees at the foot of the topgallant mast section, the lieutenant paused and extended the telescope, pointing it forward. Apparently dissatisfied, he closed it again and resumed his progress upward, half shimmying and half pulling himself by the stays. There were no ratlines to climb or any platform to rest on this high in the mast. It must be dizzying to look down to the deck from there. At length, Beechum reached almost to the truck at the very top of the mast. He found a tenuous foothold on the collar to the stays, one leg and one arm wrapped tightly around the pole. Awkwardly, he pulled the glass to its full length and braced it to his eye.

Almost at once, Beechum half-lowered his instrument and bent his head downward, which he would have to do to speak to Sykes below him. Sykes shouted to Hitch on the topmast shrouds, Hitch to Aviemore at the tops. Charles heard Hitch's voice, but couldn't make out the words. He could guess though; it had to be something important. Aviemore immediately leapt for a backstay to ride down to the deck. "There's a ship of the line off the harbor. The same what we saw afore," the boy squeaked.

Charles felt a wave of relief wash over him, followed quickly by apprehension. "What's her attitude?" he asked. "Has she any sails set?"

"I dunna know," Aviemore answered. "I'll just ask." With that he ran toward the shrouds and scurried upwards.

That was enough, Charles thought. It was unlikely Cassandra's bare poles had been seen and it was time to leave. He looked up for Beechum again to see him lower the glass, transfer it to the arm clinging to the mast, and wave. At that instant the foot on the stay collar slipped. The lieutenant gripped the mast section with both arms. The telescope came free, rotating lazily as it fell until it struck the topmast yard, then spun like a spoke on a wheel. Charles felt sick. It met the deck boards with a shattering crash.

"Oh, my," Bevan said.

"Mr. Cromley," Charles said. "We will wear ship immediately to stand away from the land. Daniel, get the topgallant yards back up and their sails bent on." Then he went to retrieve the shattered pieces that had been his telescope. He was holding them regretfully when Beechum arrived back on deck.

"I'm sorry, sir," Beechum said. "It was my fault."

"I saw," Charles answered. "I'm only pleased that you didn't slip along with it. Please tell me what you saw."

Beechum took a deep breath. "It was Raisonnable, sir. I'm sure of it. She's at anchor just off the mole. I saw no sign that she'd spotted us."

Charles was grateful for that. "And what else is in the harbor?" he asked.

"About the same as before, as far as I could tell. A mass of small bottoms. A few was coming or going."

"Thank you," Charles said. Once Beechum left, he gently unscrewed the eyepiece, still intact, from his instrument and slipped it into his pocket as a memento. The remainder he roughly folded in half and replaced in its wooden case.

*****

A half moon showed through wispy clouds. Sufficient light filtered down for Charles to see the dark line of the coast off the rendezvous he had agreed to with Adolphus Jones sixty-three days before. The ship's bell dinged five times in the middle watch. The eyes of the lookouts in every mast, and most of those of the watch on deck, were fixed on the shore. No one had seen any light. It was the third consecutive night Cassandra lay hove to, backing and filling, in the same patch of sea.

"Damnation," Charles muttered, as he had at every turning of the glass and ringing of the bell since midnight.

"It doesn't look like they're going to be here," Bevan said.

"We'll wait," Charles said. "We must give them every chance."

"You know that it's possible something else could have happened. They might have been discovered. Spying is a dangerous business, I'm told."

"We'll give them every chance," Charles repeated. "We'll stay a little past daylight to see if that tells us anything." It really didn't matter, he knew, whether the Joneses were delayed longer than expected, or were captured or killed, or even if they'd simply gotten lost. If for any reason they did not appear, Blankett would still have cause for court martial and Charles would have no defense. Blankett might still do it even if he returned with his quarry, but he didn't think he would. In that case, a board of inquiry might well go harder on the short-sighted admiral who overruled Admiralty orders than on the disobedient captain attempting to fulfill them. The ship's timbers creaked gently in the easy sea. They waited.

The first light of the day came hard and gray over the water, the land an indistinct wash to the south, the uneven outline of hills running northward. Charles stretched his arms and yawned. He was worn from the long night and the tension of waiting. His fingers tapped endlessly on the rail cap in front of him. The long, long journey from Chatham to Cape Town to Mocha and back and forth along the infernally hot sea had finally come to nothing. The bell rang twice for the morning watch. "Damnation," he muttered.

"Deck there!" the lookout in the mizzen tops called down. "There's some what's moving about on the shore."

Charles strained his eyes over the features of the land.

"Where away?" Bevan shouted up.

"Jus' by that bit of a run."

"Look, sir," Beechum said. He had a ship's telescope to his eye, pointed more or less toward a small spit of land where the hills trailed away into desert. There was a riverbed there, running down from the heights, exactly the place where Charles had arranged to take the Joneses off. It was just growing light enough for him to make it out. He saw nothing moving on the sandy beach.

"Is it Jones? There should be three of them."

"No, sir," Beechum said. "It's soldiers. Here, look."

Charles took the glass and raised it. He soon saw the figures of men with muskets in dark uniforms and shakos moving deliberately across the riverbed and fanning out in a line. They must be looking for something, and he could guess what.

The lookout shouted down, "Deck, them's more sodgers to the south a league or so." Charles swung the lens, transiting the shore. Immediately he picked out a small column of cavalry, about twenty, cantering up along a track from the direction of Koessir, a thin mist of dust rising behind. The newly risen sun glinted off weapons held aloft. Lancers, he decided. Then he saw a second unit, larger, riding a distance behind. He couldn't tell how many; maybe a hundred.

"Brace the foresail around," Charles said to anyone who might be listening. "Daniel, put a pair of leadsmen in the bow. Mr. Cromley, we will close with the land as near as we dare." He tried to think of what he must do. The French weren't searching for nothing. They had to have been given reason to believe Jones and his companions were in the area. He cupped his hands to yell up to the tops and the length of the ship, "There's a guinea for the first man who spies a party of civilians along the shore."

"Ten fathoms," came the call from a leadsman. Cassandra began to move toward the shore, still a mile out.

"How close to you reckon we can come, Mr. Cromley?" Charles said.

"Half mile, if we're lucky," the master replied tersely. "Not more."

"Stephen," Charles called.

The lookout in the foremast bent over the edge of the tops to shout something down. Charles couldn't hear what it was.

"Sir?" Winchester said.

Charles looked out at the approaching cavalry. They had closed noticeably. They would, he reasoned; horses are faster than ships, at least over short distances. "There's been a change of plans," he said. "Have the launch and a cutter hoisted out to port, if you please. We'll tow them alongside for now. You may assemble their crews."

"By the mark, eight," cried the leadsman, starting a regular chant.

"Sir." Sykes came running from forward. "There's someone a piece up the coast. A woman it looks like. She's waving a cloth at us."

Charles ran to the far side of the deck where he could look northward. He raised the glass and saw something moving on the shore. He transited the lens in both directions, then focused on the figure again. Whoever it was wore a black gown. That would likely be Constance or the other Mrs. Jones. Where the hell was Mr. Jones? "Mr. Sykes," Charles said. "Pass the word . . . , no, find Lieutenant Ayres and have him report to me immediately. Afterward I will want the name of the seaman who spotted her." He turned, looking for Cromley. "Bend to the north. As close in as you consider prudent."

"The wheel's already over," Cromley answered.

"By the mark, five and a quarter."

Charles looked for the French. The foot soldiers were too far from the woman to present a problem. The horsemen were not.

"You asked for me, sir?" Ayres reported. His eyes too were on the line of horses.

"I'm going to put you and your men on the shore between that first squad of lancers and a woman just up the coast from here. You must delay them long enough for us to take away her and her companions. Can you do that?"

"Give me your glass," Ayres said. He scanned slowly along the shoreline. Charles looked for the cavalry and found them not two miles from the riverbed, moving quickly. "There's a track running along under the bluffs," Ayres said calmly, lowering the lens. "That's how they'll come, seeing as we're tied to the sea. Just by that outcropping, a hundred yards short of where she is, it appears to be some cover. We'll land there."

"Can you stop them?" Charles asked. "Only the first. I want you away before that larger body catches up."

Ayres stroked his chin. "It depends on how much courage they have," he said. "We'll stop some."

"I'm sure you will do your best. Assemble your men. They will go down into the launch within the half-hour."

"By the mark, four, less an eighth." The edge of the land lay a quarter mile to the north. It was a close as they were going to get.

"The launch and cutter are alongside," Winchester said, appearing at his side. "Shall I send the crews down?"

"In a minute." Charles called for Bevan and Beechum. When his lieutenants were assembled, he said, "Stephen, you will command the launch with the marines. If it goes badly, take them off and return to the ship. Lieutenant Ayres knows where he wants to land."

Winchester touched his hat and left. Charles took a quick look at the slowly passing terrain. A glance told him that the first group of horsemen had closed on the wadi, the leading riders just then crossing. He realized that they would use Cassandra's progress to locate their prey. It would be a near thing. "We will take the cutter to collect whoever is on the shore," he said, a note of urgency in his voice. "Beechum and Sykes will accompany with a half dozen fit seamen in addition to the boat's crew. Arm them with muskets. Bring a few litters in the case there are any injured. Mr. Beechum, you will captain the cutter; I will go ashore."

The marines filed over the side with their muskets; the launch cast off, pulling hard for the land. The leading horsemen were on the track, slowed by the uneven terrain, perhaps a mile away. Charles could see their blue jackets with yellow frogging and the vermilion plumes on their caps. Forward, the woman was easily visible. She had stopped gesturing to watch as Cassandra approached. He recognized her as Constance. Augustus came with Charles' pistols and had armed himself with his cutlass. Charles took the guns and stuck them in his belt, then pulled on the hilt of his sword to test that it was free. The cutter began to fill. Charles went down last.

"Shove off," Beechum ordered. "All ahead, pull. Quickly, please." The cutter rapidly picked up speed as the oarsmen strained. No one needed reminding that time was precious. The view from the sea's surface was not as good as the vantage from his quarterdeck. Charles saw that the launch had landed and the marines debarked. He could not see the enemy horsemen. Constance stood by the water's edge alternately watching the nearing cutter and staring apprehensively southward down the track.

"Hurry," she called. "For God's sake hurry."

Charles distinctly heard the crackle of musket fire just as the cutter grounded on the gravelly beach. He made his way forward and jumped into the surf with the others of the landing party. The stone and sand underfoot made progress difficult. Immediately, he heard a pounding of hoofs to the left. Four horsemen, lances leveled, galloped toward them at incredible speed. It happened too quickly. A seaman who had gained dry ground cocked his musket, only to be ridden down and impaled before he could raise it to his shoulder. Charles snatched at the grip of a pistol, jerked the hammer back, aimed, and fired at another charging toward him. The mount stumbled, collapsing forward, shot in the neck. Someone smashed the butt of his musket into the rider's head. Two muskets went off, a horse reared, neighing in terror as the lancer fell to the side, his foot trapped in the stirrup. The panicked steed bolted, dragging its burden along the ground. The forth rider flashed through. Another seaman fell in agony, a lance through his chest.

Charles stumbled onto the dry ground. The two remaining cavalrymen wheeled their mounts thirty yards beyond and drew sabers. "Whose muskets are still loaded?" he snapped. Three men raised their weapons. "Shoulder them; wait; steady. Aim, Goddamnit." The riders charged. Charles pulled his second pistol. "Fire!"

One Frenchman fell, the second came on, his sword high. Charles sighted along the hand gun's barrel at the man's chest and prayed it didn't misfire. The pistol kicked in a puff of smoke, the rider jerked back, the horse raced past. He took a deep breath and looked at the carnage around him—six or eight dead in the small level space; a horse thrashing feebly half in the water, tinting the surf red.

"Come, hurry, come!" Constance pulled on his arm, her eyes wild. "This way; he's injured."

Charles tried to take stock. He could see the marines forming into a line on the track a hundred yards away. The second troop of cavalry could not be long in coming. He could already hear the growing rumble of onrushing hooves. "Sykes," he shouted. The boy turned toward him. "Run as fast as you can down to Lieutenant Ayres and tell him to clear out. I'm ordering him back to the ship now. Run!" Sykes ran, his coattails flying.

"You three—Jenkins, Wilson, Giles. Collect the stretchers and follow me. Hurry up about it." Charles looked at Constance. "Where are they?"

She scrambled toward a pile of boulders. Charles followed. Behind the stones he saw Jones lying on the ground, his head propped on a bundle of cloth. The front of his shirt was brown with dried blood, flies swarming over it. "Is he dead?" he asked.

Constance shook her head. "Shot. Lost blood," she managed.

"Where's the other, er, Mrs. Jones?"

"Euthellia is killed. They were waiting."

"Who is, they?" Charles began, then forgot the question. His seamen arrived with the litter. "Hurry," he ordered. "Get him into the boat." To Constance: "Go." He heard the thunder of horses, growing rapidly more urgent, then musket fire. He hoped Ayres was firing at them from the launch. "All of you, into the cutter," he shouted. Jones's litter was on board, Constance being pulled in. He saw an unending line of cavalry on the track pounding toward him, the noise deafening. "Shove off!" he screamed.

"Come, Cap'n," Augustus's voice said from beside him. Charles looked around. Everyone was in the cutter except for themselves. Beechum yelled something at him. The craft bobbed five yards off shore, oars extended. Augustus pulled; Charles ran. Thigh-deep in the surf, a horse and rider splashed after them, saber pointed forward like a spear. A bang came from the boat as Beechum's pistol fired. Waist-deep in the sea, a milling, shouting melee of cavalry, two pushing their mounts into the surf. Charles stumbled on something on the seabed and fell, the water closing over his head. Powerful arms grabbed him around the middle, thrusting him upward, out of the water into a clutch of outstretched hands, which dragged him over the cutter's stern boards.

"Away all!" Beechum screeched.

"Wait!" Charles snapped. He brought himself to his knees and reached out to grab Augustus's jacket to keep him afloat. "Malvern, give me a hand. " The two men took firm hold. "Away all!" he shouted at the boat's crew and heaved Augustus bodily on board. Still on his knees, Charles looked back. To his surprise, they were well off the shore, a half-cable or more. The mass of French milled aimlessly in the space he had so recently occupied. To starboard he saw Winchester's launch making steadily back to the ship. At least most of the red coats seemed to be present.

Charles climbed up Cassandra's side first, immensely pleased to be back in own world. "Rig a whip to sway Jones on board," he said to Bevan. "He's in a bad way. Have him taken directly below decks to the surgeon." He pulled off his sodden jacket. "I am going to my cabin to change. Have Lieutenant Ayres call on me as he is available. After that I will see the second Mrs. Jones. You may start south as soon as the boats are secured; we will look into Koessir again as we pass. You needn't be secret about it; a few miles out should do." Before Bevan could answer, he turned and left.

In his cabin, Charles threw his sodden coat across a chair, then leaned against the bulkhead to collect himself. He was still on edge, almost giddy from the flurry of excitement on shore. After a moment he unbuckled his sword belt and hung it on its peg. He was pulling off his shirt when Augustus entered the cabin in his own dripping clothing.

"Do you require help, Cap'n?" he asked.

"No," Charles said with a grin. "Go find yourself some dry clothes. You've done more than enough for a day's work."

Augustus smiled. "It wasn't nothing."

"I owe my life, or at least my freedom, to you. You may be assured I will report as much to Miss Viola." Augustus had no answer for this. He put Charles' coat on a hanger to dry and then departed.

"Lieutenant Ayres for you, sir," the sentry announced after knocking at the door and sticking his head inside.

Charles had already donned fresh breeches and was buttoning up a dry shirt. "Have him come in."

"Are you whole?" Ayres said.

"Yes, thanks to you and your efforts. How many did you lose?"

"I had to leave eight behind. Some wounded, some dead; I don't know how many of which."

"I appreciate all that your men have done," Charles said. "It was a devilish close thing. I'll authorize an extra measure of spirits with their supper."

"I'm sure they will appreciate it after what they've been through, sir. French cavalry have a way of focusing one's attentions."

"Missus Jones, sir," the sentry announced.

"Invite her in as you leave, will you?" Charles said, stuffing his shirt tails into his pants. "Again, my sincere thanks for your efforts."

Constance entered as Ayres departed. She looked around her. "Where are my things?" were her first words.

"I had them stored below," Charles said. "I'll send someone for them. Please be seated. May I offer you some refreshment?"

Her hair was disheveled; her face pinched and stained, the black dress filthy. "Tea would be lovely," she said. "Why are you in my cabin?"

"It's not your cabin anymore," Charles said. "I'll arrange someplace else for you. Mr. Jones will remain with the surgeon for the time being. Please sit." He'd dismissed Augustus; how was he going to arrange tea? "Pass the word for Midshipman Hitch," he shouted at the door. Constance seated herself at the table. "Tell me what happened," Charles said, sitting opposite her.

Constance wiped a hand across her forehead and attempted to pull her fingers through the tangles of her hair without success. "I need to bathe."

"Soon," Charles said. "I promise. What did Mr. Jones learn?"

"I don't know. I wasn't present at these discussions. From Zafarana we traveled to Cairo and then Alexandria. Adolphus has acquaintances there. He does not confide in anyone what he uncovers. I know he was concerned though, I could see it."

Hitch arrived. "A pot of tea, if you please," Charles ordered. "Also a cup and saucer, sugar, you know what to do."

"Me, sir?" Hitch protested. "No, I don't know. Tea just comes ready to drink."

Charles sighed. "The fixings are in my larder. The cook will know how to prepare it."

"I like Ceylonese tea," Constance said. "From Ceylon."

"How interesting," Charles said. He had no idea what kind of tea he had, he rarely drank the stuff. "Hurry, if you please," he said to Hitch. "So you don't know anything about French intentions to go down the sea?" he said as soon as the boy had left.

"But, I do. I'm not a flower in a vase, you know. I have my own resources."

"You do? What do you know?"

"I have entertained two French officers. Separately, you understand. Men are too easy. They feel obligated to talk."

"I see," Charles said. "And what did they talk about?"

"There is another place, not Koessir. Transports are at this moment gathering there. They know the British are asleep at Mocha. One said there is a surprise for them."

"What place?"

Constance fell silent as Hitch entered noisily into the cabin with a tray and a large tin teapot. He placed it on the table and laid out the saucer and sugar and a container of goat's milk. "What place?" Charles repeated.

She blew across her cup and sipped carefully. "I don't know, neither man could say. How many such places can there be?"

Suddenly, Charles knew where the place was, he was sure of it. There were only two that would be suitable, and Blankett was anchored in one of them. Everything made sense when one looked at it that way. Constance took a second sip, and a third. She drained the cup. Charles refilled it. "Help yourself," he said. "What happened on your return to the rendezvous?"

She was silent for a moment, stirring the sugar and milk into her drink. "We were betrayed by someone," she said softly. "They were already searching for us."

Charles also knew, or at least could make a very good guess, as to who had provided the information about the rendezvous. Indirectly, it was himself to Teresa, who must have gotten word to Underwood. He remembered Bevan saying something about a horseman galloping north along the coast from Massawa. "Mr. Gladfridus Underwood," he said. "Men can be loosened up just at the thought of sex, I've recently discovered. He received that information from me by way of an intermediary. I'm sorry."

Constance's eyes met his. The corners of her mouth tilted upwards. "Thank you," she said. "That explains everything. I'll cut his balls off, first just one, and then the other. Then I'll kill him." She reached inside the folds of her dress, came out with her dagger and nonchalantly laid it on the table. "Now I need to pee," she added.

"The quarter gallery," Charles said, which was his own personal toilet. "You know where it is." As she rose, a knock sounded at the door. "Come," he said.

Beechum entered in a state of some excitement. "Lieutenant Bevan's respects, sir." He stopped. "I apologize for intruding."

"It's all right. Do you remember Mrs. Jones?"

"Oh, yes, sir." He removed his hat. "I am pleased that you are well, ma'am."

"Thank you kind sir," Constance replied, batting her lashes. "No small thanks are due to you."

Beechum blushed to his toes. "Oh, no. It was . . ."

"And, what of Mr. Bevan's respects?" Charles asked to regain the lieutenant's attention.

"Oh, yes. We're within sight of Koessir, sir. From the masthead, that is. The seventy-four is not in the harbor. She's nowhere to be seen."

*****

"There's three, sir," Sykes reported, having just returned from the foremast tops. "Two frigates and a brig, from their masts. They've altered course to intercept us."

Charles was relieved that it was not Raisonnable, which had been his first thought since they were only one day south of Koessir. "Have you any guess as to their nationality?" he asked.

"Tate, he's the lookout, he thinks they're ours," Sykes offered. "The brig and one of the frigates he claims he remembers from Mocha."

"Thank you, Mr. Sykes," Charles said. "You might have the colors and our recognition number close to hand." If he was relieved that it was not the French battleship, he was less sanguine about an encounter with any officers sent north to find him by Admiral Blankett.

Within the hour all three vessels were within easy sight from the deck—the northbound squadron braced tight and beating into the wind, Cassandra sailing large with it on her stern quarter. They were indeed two frigates and a brig-sloop, all with the blue ensign run up their mizzens indicating they were under Rear Admiral Blankett's command. Charles had ordered the union flag run up his own mainmast to assert that he was under Admiralty orders. Just below flew his recognition signal. He recognized the thirty-two-gun Fox and the sloop Hellebore. The second frigate was a new thirty-six-gun eighteen-pounder. Her recognition signal translated to Hotspur, Captain George Bland, with seventeen years seniority. A second string of flags ran up her halyards. Charles could read them.

"Heave to to windward for boarding, it says, sir," Sykes reported dutifully. "Why do they want to board?"

"Her captain wishes a word with me. If you would hoist the acknowledge. Also, inform Lieutenant Ayres that I would appreciate his presence."

"Sir," Ayres said, coming to a halt in front of him a little more smartly than usual.

He knows why we are about to be boarded. The more usual would have been for Charles to have been called to report on board Hotspur. "I am about to be visited by a superior officer," he said to the marine lieutenant. "I would like all the men you have to be turned out in respect."

"Aye, aye, sir. I see," said Ayres, not seeing yet.

"It is possible that I am going to refuse orders, Mr. Ayres. If that occurs, you are under no obligation out of honor to my person or rank. Is that clear?"

"Yes, sir," Ayres said. Charles guessed that it wasn't quite clear, but he knew it soon would be.

Cassandra turned her beam to the wind and backed her foresail to lie still in the water fifty yards upwind of Hotspur. The larger frigate smartly hove to herself and lowered a cutter over the side. Charles watched from his quarterdeck as the boat's crew-four marines, a naval lieutenant, and last her captain-climbed down. The boat spread her oars in perfect unison.

Charles decided to greet his visitors on his quarterdeck, just abaft the mainmast, with Ayres's now twenty-four marines smartly aligned along the lee rail. Winchester and Beechum stood beside him. Bevan went to the entry port to escort the party aft. Hotspur's marines came onto the deck first. To the shrill of the boatswain's call, Captain Bland in his full dress uniform coat and hat followed. Charles watched as he and Bevan exchanged greetings. The party started toward him.

"Sir," Captain Bland said. "You are Captain Edgemont of His Majesty's Frigate Cassandra?"

"At your service, sir," said Charles with a small bow. "To what do I owe the honor of this visit?" He knew.

Bland, a short, lean man, wore an unhappy expression. "I have orders for your arrest, sir, from Admiral Blankett." He took a folded sheet of paper from his pocket and held it out.

Charles did not take it. "On what charge?"

"On the charge of willful disobedience to orders, as stipulated under Article Eleven of the Articles of War, as passed by Parliament in the year 1757. I am to take you into custody on board my own ship for transport to Mocha as soon as our other business is complete."

"Captain Bland, I am not under Admiral Blankett's orders. Until I return to Mocha, I sail at the direction of the Admiralty. Therefore, I cannot have broken any lawful orders."

Bland frowned. "I have been forewarned of this argument and it does not hold. Your obligations to the Admiralty have been satisfied. It does not answer in any event; my own orders still apply. A court martial will decide the right of it. I must ask for the surrender of your sword and person, sir."

Charles looked at Bland and his four marines, then at Lieutenant Ayres with his own redcoats behind him, and finally at Bevan who met his eyes. "My apologies to the admiral and to yourself, sir," he said slowly. "Circumstances are such that I cannot comply. May I acquaint you with the latest intelligence regarding French operations?"

"No, you may not," Bland blustered. "If you refuse to come willingly, I am prepared to use force." He turned to his marines.

Bevan nodded to Ayres. "Present arms!" the lieutenant of the marines shouted loudly. Charles was also surprised to see Winchester and Beechum move forward, their hands on their sword hilts. Bevan leaned casually against the base of the mainmast, his hand also resting on his weapon.

"This is beyond an Article Eleven," Bland sputtered, his lips quivering with fury. "You'll hang for this."

"Sir," Charles said. "I am doing what I must for the good of the country and the conduct of the war. May I please tell you what information I possess? It will surely influence your own actions."

"No. I will not listen to any excuses until you submit as ordered." Bland steamed with anger, his face red.

"Aside from arresting me, may I ask the reason for your squadron's presence so far from Mocha?" It didn't take two frigates and a brig-sloop to collect a single captain.

Bland produced a strained smile. "I am sure our purpose will answer your so-called intelligence. We are to destroy the port of Koessir, and all the shipping there. That will settle any possibility of French transport to India once and for all. Cassandra is to follow and participate in the action." He paused. "I will offer you a compromise. You may remain in command for the time being, sail with me to Koessir, then return to Mocha. Admiral Blankett will deal with you himself as he sees fit."

Charles thought he saw Underwood's influence behind this rather pointless exercise. It might mean that time was running short. "I cannot accept your offer. There will be a French expedition to India, but not from Koessir. A flotilla is now assembling at the port of Massawa, farther south. In addition, the seventy-four-gun French ship of the line Raisonnable will lead. That is where you are needed, and urgently so. I will happily accompany you there."

"Blankett said you had some fixation about an imaginary seventy-four. As for this Massawa, I've never even heard of it." The captain drew himself up as best he could. "No," he said strongly. "Orders are orders. I, sir, will obey mine. I demand that you do the same."

"I won't," Charles said. "Daniel, we will resume our course southward with all speed, if you please. Captain Bland and his company are to remain as our guests until we are past the squadron. If Hotspur's cutter cannot keep up, you may come alongside Hellebore to put them off." He turned back to Bland. "May I offer you some refreshment, sir? I hope not to detain you long." It occurred to him that Mocha and the exit to the sea would now be guarded by only one, or at most two, relatively small warships.

CHAPTER FOURTEEN

"Does anyone care for a wager?" said Charles. Cassandra ran down the deep-water channel between the Dahlak Archipelago and the serrated highlands of Abyssinia, mottled in grays and greens in the early morning light.

"On what?" Bevan offered. "Are you asking whether Blankett hangs you by the neck from the nearest yardarm or whether he builds a gallows to do the job on shore?"

Charles did not see the humor in this. "No. About what we'll find at Massawa. In particular, is Raisonnable there?"

"She probably is," Bevan said. "I can't think where else she'd be. What do we do then?"

Charles had thought about this; he had no good answer. He should inform the admiral, and recommend he take his squadron to Bombay where a British ship of the line or two could be enlisted for support. But in all probability, Blankett would not believe him. Charles would be arrested on the spot and held in confinement until Captain Bland and the others returned from Koessir to form a court martial. By then it would be too late; and even if all of Blankett's frigates could be assembled, Cassandra could hardly play a role in any battle. He had been informed that she had exhausted better than four parts in five of her supplies of powder and shot. "I don't know," he said.

"We'll have to decide soon, Charlie," Bevan said.

Charles recognized the bluff point of land in the far distance that marked the entrance to Massawa harbor. The lookout at his post in the foremast should have something to say before long. As if on cue, he saw the man lean out over the edge of the tops to shout down. Aviemore, waiting at the foot of the mast to relay messages, started aft at a run. Charles' heart quickened.

"There's masts in yon harbor, sir," the boy burbled. "A mess of them."

"Is there any sign of a ship of the line, Mr. Aviemore?" Charles said.

"Not as yet. I inquired particular about it."

Charles thought this an improvement on the more usual, "Don't know; just a moment, I'll ask." "Thank you," he said. "Please keep me informed."

"Aye, aye, sir," Aviemore answered, touched his hat, and commenced to skip forward along the gangway.

"Clear the ship for action," Charles said to Bevan. "We will beat to quarters as we approach the point." Cassandra closed at a goodly pace. He would have to begin taking in the canvas soon. Through one of the nav's telescopes, he could see the small redoubt at the tip of the peninsula on which the Italians had built their settlement and the roofs of the town itself. In the low scrub desert inland had sprung up sprawling cities of white canvas army tents; behind the redoubt was a forest of masts. Aviemore arrived regularly with revised estimates of their number—forty, sixty, seventy-five, and up. There was no sign of the overarching masts and crossed yards of a seventy-four. Charles did see that the yellow-blue flag of the Genovese over the fortification had been replaced by the tricolor of France.

"Ship is cleared for action, sir," Winchester reported.

Charles nodded. Where was Raisonnable? "Begin taking in the sails, if you will. We'll keep the topsails for now."

"Aye, aye, sir," Winchester said and turned away. The boatswain's shrill call sounded, and shouted orders for "all hands to shorten sail" came up and down the deck. Men hurried aloft and to the bunt lines.

"More than a hundred bottoms now, sir,'"Aviemore said, relaying the lookout's message.

"The seventy-four?"

"Naught, sir."

"Thank you," Charles said.

Bevan came from across the quarterdeck. "My God, they've left themselves unguarded."

"Probably the frigate was to cover the embarkation," Charles answered. "She is now in no position to do that. They had to gamble."

"It's going to cost them."

"You can't win every wager," Charles muttered. It was curious, he thought. He took no joy, no sense of triumph or vindication that he'd been right and Blankett wrong. Through blind luck he had found the French invasion fleet at its most vulnerable. He knew what his duty required. It would not be so much a great victory as wanton destruction. There was no joy to be taken in that. He looked upward. The courses and topgallants were neatly taken in and bound to their yards. He could feel that the ship's progress had slowed. "Beat to quarters, if you please. We will show our colors."

The drum roll rattled loudly across the decks. They could probably hear it in the settlement, Charles decided. He could see the redoubt clearly now, ahead off the starboard bow. There were men there, the smallish noses of six-pounder field artillery poked out. One, the only one that would bear on the approaching frigate at the moment, gave off a cloud of smoke. The ball struck the water twenty yards short, skipped, and bounced off Cassandra's side then sank into the sea. "Starboard battery," he said to Bevan. "We will salute the fort in passing."

Charles could see into the outer limits of the harbor. All manner of shipping lay moored together, beam to beam: Arab sambuks and baghalas, small dhows, and behind the point the taller masts of the Italian's pinks and polacre merchant ships. Their number had grown. It was a jumbled crush of sea craft—a hundred and fifty, maybe more. The small fortification fired again, two guns, as Cassandra bore down. A ball sang low through the rigging; the second punched the side with a loud crack, then a splash. At thirty yards they came abreast. "You may fire," Charles said.

The broadside crashed outward in a ripping string of explosions, covering the decks in smoke. As it cleared, he saw the stone ramparts broken and crumbled, three of the guns dismounted, one artillerymen standing stunned in shock among the wreckage. The quay came into view behind the redoubt as they glided past. The inner harbor appeared a carpet of shipping, crafts tied up five and six deep along the wharf side. The waterfront itself was a crowd of sailors, soldiers, and civilians all hurrying in different directions. The doors to the large warehouses stood open. Charles could see barrels and casks piled to the ceilings where the sunlight angled in. Numbers of seamen ran, jumping from deck to deck, to reach their craft, hopefully to cut them free and somehow escape. Cassandra entered the mouth of the harbor between the Arab island and the Italian settlement. "Back the foresail," Charles ordered. "Get an anchor in the water with a spring on."

He stood for a moment in awe of the audacity of it. Under the very noses of the British squadron guarding the exit to the sea, the French—this Napoleon Bonaparte—had assembled his invasion fleet almost entirely from local resources to strike at the heart of British wealth. It bespoke of both strategic genius and ruthless determination. And it had almost succeeded.

The anchor cable rasped out through the port side hawse at the bow of the ship, accompanied by a loud splash. Charles saw the second cablet attached to the bower's shank being fished in through an after gunport to be wound around the capstan barrel. Hands in the waist took up the bars and heaved; slowly, Cassandra turned her broadside toward the mass of tethered vessels.

"The spring is rigged," Bevan reported.

"Fire into them," Charles said.

The cannon exploded, rebounded inward, were cleaned and reloaded, and exploded again. The French seamen who had gone on board their boats hurried back to shore in a panic, tumbling over bulwarks as their frail merchantmen shattered around them; masts fell, bows and sterns gaped. One ball might pass through two or three of the tightly packed, frail scantlinged ships. The difficulty was that there were just too many.

A battalion of infantry, organized by their officers, marched in perfect order onto the nearly empty quay. What the hell did they think they were they going to do? To shouted orders, the body formed smartly into a line. The front ranks knelt and all raised their muskets to their shoulders. The weapons popped and banged along the line with tiny puffs of smoke. Musket balls ripped through the air with the sound of swarming bees. Several at least entered through gun ports, and he saw a seaman clutch at his arm, his shirtsleeve turning red. "Cease firing," Charles said to Bevan. "Haul on the spring."

The guns fell silent and hands fell to the capstan bars with a will, feet shuffling and the pawl clicking as the axel turned. Cassandra's broadside pivoted toward the quay. "Avast! Cease hauling," Bevan shouted. A second volley sounded from the French muskets, disciplined, accurate. Lead shot flew across the air or came up with a smack against bulwarks or masts.

Charles looked at the infantry in annoyance. More an irritation than a threat, they were powerless to damage his frigate's thick wooden sides. "Mr. Sykes," he said. "If you would be so good as to direct that the carronades be loaded with grape."

Sykes grinned and touched his hat, then spoke to the carronades' crews. Charles did not smile. He knew that he was about to kill a great many men because of some officer's stupidity. Doubtless, that officer thought himself courageous.

"Ready, sir," Sykes reported.

"Run them out," Charles said. The three twenty-four-pound quarterdeck carronades, each charged with a canvas bag filled with perhaps a hundred cast-iron balls, ran forward on their slides.

"Fire."

The barks of the guns sounded across the waterfront, startlingly loud after the prolonged silence. Broad swathes scythed through the tightly aligned infantry in three places. How many were killed or injured, Charles could only guess to be in the many dozens. The remainder broke their ranks and fled to the cover of the buildings, some dragging wounded comrades across the flags.

"Shall we resume with the shipping?" Bevan asked.

Charles needed to think. It was difficult to sink a wooden ship with cannon balls. It could be done if they were struck below the waterline often enough, but it would take hours for them to actually slip beneath the surface. Cassandra would expend all of her remaining powder and shot before even a fraction would be destroyed. There was a quicker, cheaper, surer way. He should have thought of it earlier. "Keep her trained as she is. Fire at any organized force that presents itself. As for the shipping, we'll burn them. Mr.

Sykes," he called.

"Yes, sir?" Sykes.

"You will relieve Lieutenant Winchester on the gundeck. Say that I require his presence. Inform Mr. Hitch similarly to replace Lieutenant Beechum."

"The gundeck? Me, sir? Thank you," Sykes said.

"Don't forget my messages to Winchester and Beechum on the forecastle."

"No, sir, of course not." Sykes hurried for the ladderway.

Winchester arrived first, then Beechum. "Stephen," Charles said. "I'm sending the ship's boats out. You will be pleased to command the operation. I suggest you divide your force into two units with Beechum in charge of the second. Your object is to set fire to as much of the shipping as you are able."

"Yes, sir," Winchester touched his hat then looked to Beechum who nodded seriously.

"Divide up the marines among the boats as you see fit, and a small work party in each to accomplish the task. The way they're packed, it should spread by itself if you give it a good start."

Winchester nodded.

"Don't endanger yourselves trying for every last one; the majority will do," Charles said. The lieutenants left, talking between themselves.

The boats were hoisted over on the off side from the town. Their crews and the others went down; the craft set off across the ripples on the harbor surface, their oars dipped and flashed leaving tiny pools like a centipede's footprints on either side of the wakes. The launch and jollyboat approached the choked mass reaching out from the waterfront while the cutters angled toward the clusters of bottoms moored further out. Charles watched with interest as the launch came alongside the nearest baghala, three-masted and broad-beamed in the Arab fashion. She was abandoned and already much cut up by Cassandra's broadsides. Winchester, his seamen, and marines climbed aboard, the lieutenant and work party immediately going below. Within five minutes they were up again, and in another minute back in the launch. A thin trail of gray smoke started up from her midships. They did not go to the next, a pink moored bow to stern, but to the third down where the process was repeated. By this time the smoke from the baghala had become thick and dark, drifting through the bare masts of the boats tied up closer to the shore. There was a crackle of musket fire as the launch and jollyboat neared its next target. The marines boarded first to chase some of her few remaining crew away.

In the outer harbor Charles saw a collection of three Arab craft tied up together, one smoking like a volcano. Beechum's cutters were approaching a second group. The closer baghala, the first ignited, erupted in orange-yellow flame from her middle, tongues reaching for her rigging. A wooden vessel, for all the time it lies on the water, burns gleefully. Fire engulfed the thing in an instant, running up the masts like flaming spires and spreading readily to those closest alongside. Charles could feel the heat on his exposed skin. Farther down, the second that Winchester had visited billowed its own pall of smoke. The inner harbor began to cloud over with it. On the waterfront, he saw a few brave souls emerge from behind the buildings to witness the growing inferno. He also noticed again the warehouse doors standing ajar. "Daniel." He said it twice to get his friend's attention.

"Yes?"

"I wonder what's in those warehouses?"

"Ship's stores, I should imagine. To get them to India."

"Let's find out."

"How? I'm not going ashore. They'll be impolite after what we've done."

"You'll see. Run up a signal to recall the boats; they've done enough. We'll fire off a gun to call attention to the flags."

Bevan spoke to Aviemore, and then opened the signal book to show him what to do. Charles approached the captain of one of the quarterdeck six-pounders. "Do you think you could put a ball right inside that warehouse entrance?"

The burly man, Tully by name, rubbed at his forehead. "Zure I can, zur."

"Let's see you do it then."

"We've loaded with grape."

"Withdraw it and put in solid shot."

The gun crew hauled their weapon inboard, extracted the bag of grapeshot with a hook, then placed a ball down its mouth and a wad. All was rammed home. They ran the gun out.

"Whenever you're ready," Charles said.

Tully made a show of sighting along the barrel and having the carriage levered around. He adjusted the quoin for elevation then adjusted it again. "Clear," he said, finally satisfied. He stepped well back with his lanyard and pulled. The cannon leapt backward with a loud bang to be brought up against its breeching. The few people on the quay jumped and ran for cover. Charles saw no sign of the ball striking anything until a gush of bright red liquid flowed outward through the doorway, forming a large pool on the flagstones.

"Very good shooting, Tully," Charles said. "I couldn't have done better myself." At this Tully struggled to suppress a smile.

"What did you find?" Bevan said, having satisfied himself that Aviemore could manage with the signal halyards. "My word," he said as he saw the bright pool in front of the warehouse.

"That's right," Charles said happily. "Wine, barrels and barrels of it."

"Pity to let it go to waste," Bevan said.

The flotilla of transports burned fiercely, devouring ship after ship to their waterlines. The sky to the west turned dark with smoke, flames showing farther and farther in the distance as the inferno spread. Winchester's boats returned first. Charles ordered the launch left in the water alongside, the jollyboat hoisted onboard. Beechum and the cutters, who had a greater distance to row, arrived within the hour and the boats stowed away. The sun, watery through the blackened haze, glared from overhead. The once full harbor of seagoing ships lay oddly bare, a vast floor of charred ribs and planking only inches above the water. Every few minutes the remnants of one would slip under the surface with a hiss of steam. The rest, still smoking, presented a scene from Dante's Inferno. There were a few still whole craft at odd places on the periphery that had escaped the conflagration, but the collection was nothing anyone was going to transport an army with.

"Are we finished?" Bevan asked.

Charles had two questions he wanted answers to. He knew whom to ask. "Not yet. Send up a white flag, if you please. Have the launch manned and brought around to the starboard side."

The signal for parley ran up Cassandra's halyards. There was at first no response from the town. With his guns trained to sweep the quayside, the space remained empty except for the forms of the dead infantry cut down in their ranks. "It's no good, Charlie," Bevan said. "We've hurt their feelings, and now they won't speak to us. It's how people get when you destroy their invasion fleet. I know I'd feel the same."

"Fire another gun into that warehouse. That might encourage them."

"Sir, look," Sykes said, pointing with his arm. Charles looked. Several figures advanced across the waterfront. One held a white cloth tied to a standard. He recognized the others as Governor Bellagio and his translator, Signora Teresa de Correglia. A lump came to Charles' throat in spite of himself. "Send the marines into the launch. I am going across."

The marines climbed the ladderway onto the wharf first, Lieutenant Ayers in the lead. Charles followed, Augustus behind. Seen close up, the carnage on the quay's surface turned his stomach. The hundreds of iron balls had cut through the French with horrible effect, pulverizing some into unidentifiable hash. Dark swarms of flies covered the flesh and drying pools of blood. He had no feeling of triumph. Charles looked to Bellagio, who returned his gaze with a kind of belligerent resignation, then to Teresa. She stood, head bowed, with her hands clasped in front of her. The blouse she wore was buttoned to the neck. Charles could find no feeling in his heart for her. Her eyes rose to meet his. "What do you want? Everything is destroyed. There is nothing more," she said.

"I have come for Mr. Gladfridus Underwood, to arrest him on the charge of treason against his king and country."

Bellagio turned, awaiting a translation. Teresa answered in English instead. "He is not present in Massawa."

"I have it in my power to bombard the town, in particular the warehouses, if he is not delivered to me," Charles said coldly. "Tell the governor that I demand his surrender." He knew it to be a bluff; Cassandra had expended all but a few broadsides of her powder and shot, but the Italians could not know this.

Teresa shrugged defiantly. "Do what you must. You have burned our boats. Now you will destroy our food, our houses." Her expression hardened into anger. "You may even wait here in the harbor to see us starve. That should please you."

The words stung. "You have no right to such a statement. You betrayed me," Charles said.

Bellagio looked from speaker to speaker without comprehension. "Di che lei parla?" he demanded.

Teresa ignored him. "It is my duty. I did not do so happily," she said.

Charles looked closely at her. Her expression was one of distress; he had to steel himself. "It doesn't matter now. I want Mr. Underwood."

"He is not present. You have my promise on this."

"Che dice?" Bellagio said loudly.

"Tell him to shut up," Charles said. "Where is he?"

"He has gone away to Mocha," Teresa said reluctantly. "I should not say this to you. You must not follow." She turned to the governor and spoke sharply to him in her language. Bellagio scowled, but did not speak. Charles thought he must have understood some of the exchange—words like Underwood and Mocha.

"Why must I not follow?" Charles said softly. But he already knew.

Teresa brushed a strand of hair back from her eyes. She glanced uneasily at Bellagio then returned to Charles. "Because Signore Underwood is transported on a very large warship. Much larger than yours, more powerful than any Inglese boat with cannons in the Red Sea. She left here only yesterday. If you meet her, you will surely be defeated. You shall swear to me that you will not do such a thing."

"I'm sorry," Charles said. "It is my duty."

*****

Charles bent over the form of Adolphus Jones, lying on the cot in what had formerly been Beechum's cabin adjoining the wardroom. Constance stood anxiously beside him. Jones appeared to be asleep, his breathing regular if shallow. "Does he have much pain?" he asked.

"Not these past few days," Constance said. "At least, he doesn't complain of it. He eats better also."

Charles had been informed by Mr. Owens that Jones had been shot, probably by a pistol, probably at close range. The ball struck the clavicle, shattered it, and traveled downward into the torso. There was no exit wound and exactly where it rested, no one knew. The injury was two weeks old. The surgeon entered the now full cabin. "What are his chances?" Charles said.

"If he's lived this long, it's likely he'll live longer," Owens answered. "There's no sign of putrefaction and he improves daily. Yesterday's bombardment didn't help. He needs rest and quiet."

Jones's eyes blinked open. They moved from Constance to Owens and rested on Charles. "You have knowledge of Gladfridus Underwood's whereabouts, I understand," he rasped.

"I do," Charles answered.

"What are you going to do about him?"

"I don't know yet."

Jones shook his head as if it didn't matter. He beckoned Constance to bend close. "Kill the bastard," Charles overheard him whisper. "You'll find a way."

"Of course I shall, my darling," Constance answered, her lips touching his forehead. "I'd already decided on it."

Charles found the intimacy both touching and frightening.

"You must both leave," Owens ordered. "I am about to change the dressing."

Instead of returning to his quarterdeck, Charles went forward through the crew's mess and down by the ladderway to the magazine. There he found Benjamin Willis, the gunner, who was responsible for Cassandra's supply of powder and shot.

"We've no more powder in the keg," Mr. Willis responded to Charles' query. "Every last grain is made up into cartridges. After that, there ain't no more."

"I see, Charles said. "And how many cartridges would that be?"

"I've made 'em up in proportion for each size o' gun. In addition to what's in 'em now, there's sixty-two for the twelves, sixteen for the six-pounders, and twenty-one to the carronades. By St. Cuthbert's bones, that's the truth of it."

"Thank you for such a precise report."

"Given what it is, it weren't hard to count, sir."

Including the cannon as they were presently loaded, he could fire off six broadsides from one side of the ship, seven if he drew the charges from the unengaged side. He muttered an obscenity as he turned to go topside.

*****

241

At first light the lookout called down that masts were visible forward of the bow—tall masts, ship-rigged masts, masts that might well be those of a French seventy-four-gun ship of the line. Cassandra, being the faster under all the canvas she could carry, had made up ground on the more cumbersome Raisonnable, which Charles judged to be not more than twenty miles ahead. An already merciless sun inched skyward over the harsh Yemeni highlands in the distance to port. The Mocha roads, and whatever force Blankett had retained there, lay just over the horizon southward. They would be visible from the French ship's mastheads by now.

Charles knew that Raisonnable was committed to either attacking the English ships off the port or passing them by. Cassandra firmly held the wind gage, and the French ship could not turn to attack. If she hove to or came about to challenge, Charles would heave to and wait at a respectful distance, or come about and flee into the wind. He alone would decide when, how, or indeed if the two ships would engage. Guessing what Blankett would decide at Raisonnable's unexpected appearance was more difficult. He hoped the admiral would cut his cables and run to the south, but he doubted it. Blankett could not know there was no invasion fleet following in the seventy-four's wake. He would also not know that Cassandra had almost no powder and shot remaining.

Charles' fingers beat a relentless tattoo on the railing cap. Perhaps the greatest service he could render would be to maintain a safe distance until the confrontation and its inevitable result was over, or he could sail past to Bombay or Cape Town to report the danger of invasion past. The mission for which he had been dispatched by the Admiralty had been achieved, and the fate of Blankett and his squadron no longer mattered. There was no point in sacrificing his own practically defenseless ship to no purpose.

"Sir," Sykes said, coming from the foremast shrouds.

"Yes?"

"The fort north of Mocha Bay is visible from the masthead. The lookout says he can just see two sets of masts off the harbor. He thinks one might be dropping her sails."

"Thank you. I would appreciate regular reports as we progress."

"Aye, aye, sir." Sykes returned to his station.

Charles clasped his hands behind his back and paced the length of the windward side of the quarterdeck, then back again. "Christ," he muttered. He stopped his walk. "Daniel," he called.

"Aye?" Bevan said.

"Have the sergeant at arms set up his wheel in the waist. We will sharpen all of the hand weapons."

"You're planning to board her?"

"I have no plan at the moment, except to keep every option open. If you would see to this." He withdrew his sword and handed it over. Boarding the two-decker was not a promising prospect. She would have a crew at least twice, maybe three times the size of his own. He looked up at the spread of canvas above. Cassandra was making as much speed as she was capable of.

"The lookout can see fair well into the harbor, sir," Sykes voice said excitedly.

"Charles turned. "What does he see?"

The midshipman screwed up his face in concentration. "Leopard and Daedalus are present. Daedalus has put on her canvas to come into the wind, he says. Leopard appears to be at anchor. The Frenchie's almost up to them."

What did that mean? The frail Daedalus was the same size as Cassandra. Was she moving to attack or escape? Did Blankett intend that Leopard fight from anchor? Maneuver was his only hope. "Thank you," Charles said. "Send for Hitch and Aviemore. You may report in turns."

Looking forward along the coast he made out the old fort on its low peninsula marking the northern edge of the harbor. If he squinted he could see the masts of three ships. The sea air proved hazy close to the surface. Better visibility would be had by the lookout higher up. Ten miles, he guessed. He would be on them in an hour's time, more or less. He distinctly heard the distant crash of a heavy broadside, long and drawn out as it reached across the water. Sykes came running toward him.

"The seventy-four has fired into Daedalus. She's lost a foremast."

"Thank you," Charles said. A second rumble like distant thunder reached his ears. Sykes turned to run forward. Charles saw Hitch coming aft. He also saw Mocha's north fort clear on the port bow and two sets of masts in the roadstead.

Bevan arrived at the same moment as Hitch, who cannoned into him, then held on to keep from falling down. "Daedalus has lost her masts! All of 'em! Frenchie's making for Leopard!"

What the hell had Captain Ball, Daedalus's commander, been thinking? "Thank you, Mr. Hitch. You may approach more slowly next time."

"Aye, aye," said Hitch, saluting, then ran forward.

"The weapons are ready," Bevan said, handing Charles his blade. "Your orders?"

"Clear for action, please."

"Have you a plan yet?"

"Not a notion."

"You'll have to have one soon, you know."

Midshipman Aviemore interrupted. "The flagship is signaled, sir," the boy said calmly.

Charles thought he had probably benefited from Hitch's example. "What does she say?"

"Engage the enemy more closely, it says. With an imperative."

"I'll bet he put an imperative with it," Bevan observed. Then he said, "All right, all right, we'll clear for action."

"You may acknowledge the flagship's signal, Mr. Aviemore," Charles said. "In fact, you may acknowledge any signal she flies."

Charles stared upward again. He should begin to shorten sail. Then he decided it would be better to wait until the very last minute. What was he going to do? The fort passed by on the port beam. He could see the walled Arab city and the dismasted frigate Daedalus, her guns silent, listing to port. The fifty-gun, two decked Leopard had anchors down fore and aft in precisely the position he had last seen her a month and a half before. As he watched, the flagship's ports triced upward and her cannon ran out. Raisonnable bore down like a charging bull whale, taking in her sails. Leopard's broadside blasted outward in a cloud of smoke. Orange fire flashed in a double line.

The effect was hardly noticeable. The French seventy-four glided irresistibly forward. Charles saw her anchor let go to fall into the sea with a splash, not fifty yards from Leopard. She began to swing, her own broadside coming to bear. He noticed a second cable veered aft from the anchor to enter a lower gunport toward the stern. The spring came taut as the larger ship loosed her own guns in a thunderous roar. Cassandra raced across the anchorage. Charles searched desperately for some opportunity, anything he could do that would make the slightest difference.

"Cleared for action, Charlie," Bevan reported.

"Beat to quarters," Charles said. That was the next logical order, but for what? He had to do something; his mind turned over option after option, rejecting each in rapid succession. He looked at Daedalus, dead in the water, and at Raisonnable on her spring and close to Leopard. "Wait!" he shouted after Bevan. "Beat to quarters, then get all of the ship's boats over the side to starboard. Tether them bow to stern, the jollyboat first, and send a crew down into her."

Bevan's brow furrowed. A question on his lips.

"Do it now," Charles said. "We'll tow them behind for the moment. Get some men aloft to start furling the courses; take in the studdingsails. We've too much speed."

Bevan shrugged his acquiescence and began bellowing the orders.

"Pass the word for Malvern," Charles said to Sykes, who had returned to the quarterdeck. In a moment the coxswain appeared at the head of the ladderway. A mile ahead, Leopard kept up a respectable rate of fire, faster with her guns than the Frenchman but suffering more anyway. Her foremast had gone by the board; her bulwarks were pummeled.

"You sent for me, sir?" Malvern said, touching his forehead.

Charles paused to put order to his thoughts. "I want you to take the launch and cutters in tow behind the jollyboat. In a short time, Cassandra will turn sharply to port. You will cast off the moment we do and pull as hard as you can for Daedalus. Speed is everything. Do you have that?"

"Aye, sir."

"Please inform Captain Bell that he may use the boats to make for the French warship and board her. Are you clear on this?"

"Yes, sir. He's to attempt to carry the seventy-four in our boats."

"Convey to him my sincerest regards and request that he do so with all possible dispatch."

"Yes, sir."

"And find someone to replace my steward in the boat's crew, if you will."

The ship became alive with activity. The drummer rolled out his tat-tat-tat-tat; men ran to their cannon or into the masts. The last of the boats went over the side. Raisonnable's guns exploded outward yet again, the sound immediate and menacing. Leopard appeared pitiful, her mainmast now broken at the tops. Not all her guns answered as she fired back.

"Run out the port side battery," Charles said to Bevan.

Bevan immediately shouted down the order to Winchester. "Do you plan to come across her stern and rake her?" he said to Charles. "We haven't much shot to send across."

Charles shook his head, his eyes never leaving the towering ship of the line, not more than a half-mile away. "I plan to have her think we're going to rake her." In particular, he focused on Raisonnable's anchor cable and its spring. He saw that her gun ports on the near side remained closed. "Mr. Cromley, we will turn hard to port in a moment. If you would see to it that the sails are braced around, we must keep our way on."

"Aye, aye, sir," Cromley answered.

Charles turned back to Bevan. "As soon as we have turned, you may man the starboard guns. Forget the ones to port. Fire as you bear."

"So you do have a plan after all."

Charles struggled to present a sense of inner calm he did not possess. "I am in hopes of running upon her anchor cable and parting it. We will then board by the bow. With any luck we'll both drift down on Leopard and they can do the same. Daedalus has also been invited to participate. See that the men are prepared."

"And if the cable doesn't part?"

"We will be at leisure as prisoners of the French to debate other possible approaches." Charles moved to stand beside the sailing master. "Do you see her cable with its spring?"

"Aye," Cromley said evenly.

"I want to run our bow over it as close to her side as you can."

"Aye, aye, sir," Cromley answered. Charles saw his Adam's apple bob up and down as he swallowed.

Charles gauged the rapidly closing distance. Cassandra's bowsprit presently aimed to shave the Frenchman's transom from an oblique angle. Raisonnable's near broadside cannon could not yet reach him and their ports remained closed. Those for her two stern chasers opened, their barrels sliding out. He was close enough. "Mr. Cromley, put the helm over, if you please. Hard aport."

Two quartermasters threw their weight onto the wheel, the spokes spinning. Charles felt the deck heel as the rudder bit. "Mr. Sykes, run to the taffrail to see if the boats are cast loose. Shout for them to do so if they haven't already."

He saw Lieutenant Ayres close by, awaiting his attention. "Do you want my boys aloft as sharpshooters, sir?"

Charles scratched at his cheek to buy a moment's thought. "No, bring them to the forecastle." Sharpshooters in the tops could serve to good advantage, but if Raisonnable's anchor cable proved stubborn and did not part, it was likely all of his masts would go by the board.

Cassandra increased her speed as the sails pivoted to catch the wind. She settled on her new course angling toward the two-decked ship's towering side. Charles started along the gangway toward the bow. He saw the heads and shoulders of the officers on the French quarterdeck staring at him. There must be confusion on her decks as she rushed to man her offside cannon. The gun ports remained closed for the moment as the bowsprit swept past Raisonnable's stern at fifty yards distance, angling sharply closer. Beechum's guns exploded as he reached the forecastle. A long rippling thunder followed as the remainder of his cannon bore. The twelve-pounder shot would be pinpricks, but it at least announced their presence. One by one, the enemy gun ports jerked open; too late, Charles thought. He would be on them before the cannon could be untethered and heaved outward. He saw the hard line of the cable, with its spring tilting downward from the bow and stern at a low angle into the sea. It disappeared from his view as Cassandra's bow rushed onward. A yardarm from the French warship tore through his foresail, snapping lines directly overhead. Raisonnable's side loomed above. Ten yards away, he could see inside her gun ports, the crewmen frantically casting off the tackles and breechings to free their weapons.

"Here, Cap'n." Augustus appeared behind him thrusting two pistols into Charles' hands. "I didn't know we was goin' on board."

He pushed them into his belt. "Stay close by me, please," he said.

A loud, screeching protest of stressed timbers and cables came from beneath his feet. Cassandra slowed precipitously, her bow riding up on the obstacle. Charles clutched at a foremast shroud to keep from falling. She seemed to hang, frozen, the downward force on the cable pulling the ships closer. An unearthly rending sounded, then a snap as loud as a musket. Cassandra's beak settled back toward the sea, the remainder of her diminished momentum pushing toward Raisonnable's bow. His own starboard cathead and anchor smashed against the seventy-four's sideboards in a grinding crash and carried away.

Charles drew his sword and flourished it in the air. "Boarders away!" he yelled at the top of his lungs. He jumped onto the breeching of a six-pounder cannon, then to the top of the hammock netting. The rail for Raisonnable's beak came within grasp and he heaved himself up. The space was clear; he had caught the French unprepared, rushing to man her guns. He suspected it wouldn't be clear for very long. Already, others of his men were clambering up behind him.

Charles jumped for the ladderway to the forecastle and ran upward. Immediately two men confronted him from beside a nearby cannon. One held the gun's rammer, which he thrust forward in defense. Charles grabbed the object in his left hand and slashed down with the sword in his right. The blade bit into the seaman's shoulder, slicing muscle and shattering bone. The second, in a lieutenant's uniform, screamed out a warning, drawing his own blade. Charles thrust, the lieutenant parried expertly and jumped back. Other English, shouting insanely, rushed up onto the deck with cutlasses and pikes. The French officer looked around him wide-eyed, hesitating, his guard momentarily lowered. Charles lunged for the man's middle before he could recover, pushed the sword point into soft belly and wrenched it free as the man fell. English seamen and marines swept past. The air filled with cries and shouts in two languages; muskets fired; steel rang on steel. He saw Augustus close beside him and the blue coats of Bevan and Winchester among the seamen a short way ahead. Raisonnable's forecastle was almost won in the initial rush. His own men continued across onto the beak, and up the ladderway. He noted that the French cannon had fallen silent.

Charles started forward, looking for an opening in the mass of men. Cries of "Repell l' anglais!" reached him above the din of battle. A loud, "Horra!" sounded. He saw scores, if not hundreds of French pouring up from Raisonnable's gundecks, surging toward the ladderways. Overwhelmed by the sheer weight of numbers, the line in front of him faltered. Step by step, his men fell back, yielding precious space only recently won.

Charles threw himself toward a knot of British, nearly surrounded by French seamen, slashing and hacking with his sword. Two men fell; a third came at him inside the arc of his blade with a cutlass. They locked swords, chest to chest, wrestling and pushing in a struggle for space to swing their weapons. Augustus wrenched the man off and threw him over the side. Still the hoard of French advanced across the forecastle in overwhelming numbers. All coherence to the battle evaporated into a general melee of isolated islands of English in a sea of the enemy. The decks became slippery with blood, the footing treacherous with fallen bodies and discarded weapons.

Charles knew that he must regroup his men. A Frenchman lunged forward with an outthrust pike. He jumped to the side to avoid the strike, pulled a pistol and fired, then used its butt to smash the face of another. "Fall back! Fall back!" he shouted in desperation. He doubted the words could be heard over the uproar; there was nowhere to fall back to.

"HUZZAH!" A loud cry bellowed out from somewhere close by. Charles saw the broken stub of a ship's mast just beyond the starboard rail. Men swarmed over, rushing at the defenders. The tide turned again. Dozens, scores, uncountable numbers of Leopard's seamen came across, beating down the French. Those of Raisonnable's men still on the forecastle retreated toward the ladderways, dropping weapons in their haste, or raising their hands in surrender.

Charles gasped in lungsful of air to catch his breath. His heart hammered. He knew himself to be nearly spent. The resistance stiffened in the gundeck below and along the gangways where the French retreated grudgingly toward the quarterdeck. Augustus stood beside him, his face twisted in pain. One hand clutched his arm; blood seeped between its fingers.

"Is it serious?" Charles said.

Augustus shook his head.

"Let me see,"

The hand moved. Charles saw a deep slash across the bicep. He reached into his pocket for a handkerchief. "Hold this over it," he said. "Go back to Cassandra and have Owens tend to it."

Augustus shook his head again. "I follow."

"No. Go back," Charles said. There was no time to argue. He turned and started aft to the gangway. He guessed that the numbers of English and French were about equal. Whoever controlled the quarterdeck would control the ship. He needed only a final effort from his flagging body. Out of the corner of his eye he noticed the form of a French seaman lying on his back amid the carnage, his eyes unfocused in death. Then he saw that the man had fallen on his stomach, his head twisted grotesquely backwards. He found this curious; it reminded him of something..., what? He cast the thought away.

A tightly packed group of Frenchmen ahead held off a smaller number of attackers. Charles saw Bevan in their midst. Beyond he could see Raisonnable's captain, near the wheel, with a number of others. A small collection of exhausted English seamen leaned heavily against the bulwarks or sat on the deck. All were bloodied from injuries. He recognized Sherburne and Roberts from Cassandra and two of the marines. "Come with me," he ordered. "One last push and it will be over."

Almost to his surprise, a half-dozen men rose and straightened. Sherburne grinned, wiping at a wound to his forehead. "Do ye promise?" he said.

Charles grinned back. "We'll soon know, won't we?" He moved toward the seething struggle on spent legs, into the crowd of men, pushing, heaving to get through. He saw Augustus's bulk beside him. The line bowed, broke into individual skirmishes. More French came from somewhere, the result of shouted orders from their captain to stem the breech. A cheer went up from the far side of the deck. A space cleared in front of him and Charles saw new figures climbing over the side rail onto the deck. His fogged mind told him they must be Daedalus's crew, finally arrived on Cassandra's boats. He moved unmolested toward Raisonnable's commander, a white-haired man standing rigidly erect beside several of his younger midshipmen. The French captain eyed him warily.

"Vous rendez, s'il vous plait?" Charles said. "Will you surrender?"

The man nodded somberly. "Yes, I will strike," he said. "Arrete!" he ordered sharply. "Arrete, c'est fini." He gestured to one of the midshipmen, who went to the mainmast and lowered the French flag.

It ended. Shouts for surrender echoed up and down the decks. The fighting trailed away to isolated knots of men too absorbed to hear the commands. Out of the corner of his eye, Charles noticed a group near the ladderway still grappling with each other. He went to stop it. As he neared, he saw that one of his seamen—he recognized him as the harelip Roberts—had taken the unusual tactic of circling around behind an otherwise occupied opponent, grabbing his head in an arm lock and twisting viciously. An irrational glee showed in his expression.

"Stop that," Charles rasped at them. "Stand down, all of you." The other English relaxed, realizing that he battle had been won. Roberts stared wide-eyed at Charles, uncomprehending. A French seaman, his head still in Robert's grip, jerked himself free and flashed a knife upward into his assailant's belly.

"Enough!" Charles shouted. He raised the tip of the sword and touched it to the French seaman's neck. "Step back," he growled. It was in English, but the man understood. To the others, he said, "Disarm them; the thing is done." He looked at Roberts's writhing body on the deck boards, blood bubbling at his mouth. The wound was surely fatal. At least, Charles reflected, he knew who had killed Stimson all those months past. The why of it he would never know.

Winchester and Bevan stood together on Raisonnable's quarterdeck, with a growing number of others. Admiral Blankett, with the still perfectly attired and unruffled Lieutenant Danforth, had arrived to receive the French captain's sword. Charles saw Mr. Gladfridus Underwood standing alone near the far rail, between two eight-pounder cannon. The two men's eyes met. Charles started toward him.

"Captain Edgemont," Blankett said, noticing Charles' approach. "It seems I owe you . . ."

"Come with me, please," Charles said as he passed. He focused on the British representative for Mocha. "Mr. Underwood, I arrest you in the name of the king."

"On what charge?" Underwood replied. He stepped backward against the rail and looked to the admiral. "This is absurd. I have been held prisoner on board against my will. This fool doesn't know what he's talking about."

"On the charge of treason against your country and providing aid to her enemies," Charles said. "I can prove it, as you know well."

Underwood reached beneath a fold in his shirt. His hand came out with a pistol, already cocked.

A shot rang out, deafening, just behind Charles' ear. Underwood stared sightlessly, a red dot the size of a farthing coin on his forehead. The body fell backward against the rail and sagged to the deck. Charles turned. Constance stood with a still smoking gun in her hand. "Damn, I wanted to use my knife," she said.

THE END

AFTERWORD

In the weeks following the Battle of Mocha Roads, 22 August, 1799, the British squadron guarding the exit to the Red Sea was broken up. Cassandra and Leopard remained at anchor off the harbor with their prize until rejoined by Hotspur, Fox and Hellebore, who had been sent north to bombard Koessir on Underwood's "intelligence" that the French invasion fleet was harbored there. Daedalus was declared irreparable, her officers and ratings distributed to make up for other ships' losses and the remainder transferred into Raisonnable to serve as her prize crew. Admiral Blankett assumed a forgiving attitude toward the independence occasionally exercised by Captain Charles Edgemont—the more so after the duplicitous role played by Mr. Gladfridus Underwood was fully explained to him—and overrode Captain Bland's repeated demands for a court martial.

In early September, Leopard, Fox and Raisonnable sailed for Bombay, Hotspur, Cassandra, and Hellebore to return to England. In mid-November, the three reached Cape Town, where crews were given leave ashore and their stores replenished. Edgemont had his jollyboat lowered into the water to call on the port admiral almost before Cassandra's anchor found the harbor bottom. "Captain Edgemont to see Admiral Cobbham," he said to the first clerk he saw.

"I'm sorry, sir," the clerk answered. "The admiral has gone to his residence for his dinner. Do you wish me to send a messenger?"

"No, thank you. Have you any mail waiting to be called for by the frigate Cassandra?"

"Yes, I believe we do. Quite a bit of it. Just a moment and I'll see what I can find." The clerk returned a moment later with a canvas sack, rounded at the bottom from the bulk of its contents.

Edgemont took the bundle. "May I?" he said and, without waiting for a reply, emptied the contents onto a table. He shuffled impatiently thorough the jumble of envelopes, setting a number aside. Most of it proved to be for Lieutenant Winchester, addressed in Edgemont's sister's hand. There were nine addressed to himself, in a precise script from, "Mrs. Charles Edgemont, Tattenall, Cheshire." The most recent carried the date, Twelfth Day, Ninth Month, 1799. The captain tore it open, his eyes running down the lines until he found what he wanted.

". . . young Charlie has tested his first strained vegetables and was not immediately pleased by this addition to his normal diet. He reminds me of thee in many ways and shares thy space in the closest part of my heart."

Captain Edgemont refolded the page and replaced it in its envelope. He put the letters from his wife into his jacket pocket and the remainder back into the bag. "Thank you kindly," he said to the clerk, choking on the words.

*****

General Napoleon Bonaparte, who had pinned his career on the emancipation of British India, secretly abandoned his army in Egypt. He departed Alexandria on the frigate Muiron, in the dead of night on the same day he learned of the destruction of the flotilla of transports at the port of Massawa. Fearing that he would be imprisoned by the Directory in Paris on his return for the failure of his greater mission, he was instead greeted by frenzied crowds at Frejus on the ninth of October 1799, as the conqueror of Egypt. The leading French political factions vied for his endorsement. Never one to miss an opportunity, he had established himself as effective dictator of his country before the year was out.

Great Britain's war with revolutionary France, already seven years in duration, would soon come to an end. The Napoleonic Wars had only just begun.

AUTHOR'S NOTE

The reader is reminded that this is a work of fiction, and the author has taken certain liberties. In particular, my conscience nags at the treatment afforded Rear Admiral Sir John Blankett. The actual Admiral Blankett was in fact dispatched to the foot of the Red Sea by the Admiralty to forestall any French intention to descend on India. His squadron was very much as described, although most historians have omitted Hellebore and Cassandra from the list for reasons I do not fully understand. Despite what my children will tell you, I have never personally met the admiral, nor have I corresponded with him. The character attributed is perforce a product of my imagination. He does, however, seem to have been less than aggressive in the performance of his military duties during this period, preferring commercial and diplomatic activities on shore. He died not far from Mocha from natural causes during a subsequent expedition into the Red Sea two years later.

--Jay Worrall

ABOUT THE AUTHOR
JAY WORRALL

Jay Worrall was born in Walter Reed Army Hospital in Washington, DC, in the middle of World War II. Raised as a Quaker and in a military family he grew up in a variety of places around the world, living in six countries on four continents. He speaks English, French, German, Italian, Japanese and Vietnamese with varying degrees of fluency. At Earlham College, a Quaker school in Indiana, he received a BA with a major in Physics, and later an MA and ABD in Anthropology from the University of Virginia. He also studied at the University of London in England. As a pacifist and conscientious objector during the Viet Nam War he worked for two years in refugee camps in the Central Highlands of that country. Afterward he taught English in Japan.

Jay worked for many years in the area of social science research in and around Washington, DC, eventually specializing in developing innovative and humane prison programs, policies and administration. He has also managed his own construction company as well collaborative programs on Soviet-American literature and Chinese-American business relations. Most recently he worked for a major Quaker organization in Philadelphia, Pennsylvania, as director of historical interpretation. His principal lifelong interest, both from an academic perspective and personal experience, has been the intersection of history and technology and their influence on the values, social systems and daily lives of ordinary people across time.

Jay's first two efforts at historical fiction—_Sails on the Horizon_ and _Any Approaching Enemy_—were published by Random House in 2005 and 2006. Set during the Napoleonic Wars they follow the life of Royal Navy Captain Charles Edgemont and his Quaker wife, Penelope Brown Edgemont. The series focuses on the adventures of Charles (and sometimes Penny) during the long conflict, but also explores the tensions between the two and their very different attitudes about war. Jay is very pleased to have the third volume in this series, *A Sea Unto Itself*, published by Fireship Press. He currently lives and writes in Downingtown, Pennsylvania, not far from Philadelphia, is married and the very proud father of five grown children and seven grandchildren.

———

If You Enjoyed This Book
You'll Love Everything
That Has Ever Been Printed
Or Ever Will Be Printed
by

FIRESHIP PRESS
www.fireshippress.com

All Fireship Press books are available directly through our website,
amazon.com, Barnes and Noble and Nook, Sony Reader, Apple iTunes,
Kobo books and via leading bookshops across the United States,
Canada, the UK, Australia and Europe.

Lonestar Rising

The Voyage of the Wasp

by

Jason Vale

Fans of Alternative History celebrate! Jason Vail's compelling novel, Lonestar Rising: The Voyage of the Wasp, is must-read literature.

The American rebellion has failed. George Washington is dead. The surviving revolutionaries have retreated to Tennessee, only to be routed again. In 1819, John Paul Jones, Jr., a smuggler, plies the waters off the coast of New Spain, while a new generation of rebels have settled in Spanish territories and the wasteland called Texas. But Andrew Jackson is not content to be a Spanish subject. He dreams large. Texas must be free and independent from the corrupt old empires of Europe. But with no army other than the Texas Rangers, and no navy, Texas has no hope of opposing the mighty forces of Spain. No hope, that is, until David Crockett recruits the sardonic John Paul Jones. Together they buy and refit a broken down warship to become the first ship of the Texas Navy. With a handful of Crockett's men, the blessing of a voodoo queen, and a dubious crew of French pirates, they set sail to seize Spanish treasure and remake history in a ship called the Wasp.

Fireship Press
www.FireshipPress.com

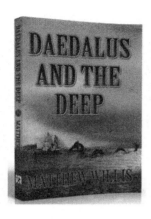

Daedalus And The Deep
By
Matthew Willis

For Midshipman Colyer of the corvette HMS Daedalus, life is a constant struggle: savage pirates in the South China Sea, an erratic Captain, and a perfectionist First Lieutenant. Things are made no easier by the need to guard a personal secret at all costs. But the voyage of the Daedalus takes a stranger turn when the ship encounters a giant sea-serpent in the South Atlantic, and is plunged into a headlong pursuit of the creature in the name of science, personal glory, and the promise of fortune. But as the quest leads further into the cold wastes of the Southern Ocean, becoming ever more dangerous, Colyer begins to wonder just who is hunting whom? The sea-serpent's purpose could turn out to be more sinister than anyone on board the Daedalus imagined

Fireship Press
www.FireshipPress.com

www.Fireshippress.com
Found in all leading Booksellers and on line
eBook distributors

"OLD IRONSIDES" AND HMS JAVA
A STORY OF 1812

A highly recommended must-read for every naval enthusiast—indeed, for every American!

Stephen Coonts
NY Times best-selling author

HMS *Java* and the USS *Constitution* (the famous "Old Ironsides") face off in the War of 1812's most spectacular blue-water frigate action. Their separate stories begin in August 1812—one in England and the other in New England. Then, the tension and suspense rise, week-by-week, as the ships cruise the Atlantic, slowly and inevitably coming together for the final life-and-death climax.

The Perfect Wreck is not only the first full-length book ever written about the battle between the USS *Constitution* and HMS *Java*, it is a gem of Creative Nonfiction. It has the exhaustive research of a scholarly history book; but it is beautifully presented in the form of a novel.

WWW.FIRESHIPPRESS.COM
Interesting • Informative • Authoritative

THE PATRIOT'S FATE
BY
ALARIC BOND

"In his new novel, The Patriot's Fate, Alaric Bond joins the ranks of well-known Age of Sail authors C.S. Forester and Patrick O'Brien in his skillful combining of historical fact with compelling fiction to produce another gripping novel in his Fighting Sail series.

It is 1798 and Ireland rises up against years of repression and injustice. Rebels, supported by a mighty French invasion fleet, prepare to claim their land but find themselves countered by a powerful British battle squadron. Two friends and former allies, separated by chance and circumstance, witness developments from opposing sides while storms, political intrigue and personal dynamics abound. In The Patriot's Fate Bond maintains a relentless pace that climaxes in thrilling naval action and noble sacrifice."

Fireship Press
www.FireshipPress.com

WWW.FIRESHIPPRESS.COM
HISTORICAL FICTION AND NONFICTION
PAPERBACK AVAILABLE FOR ORDER ON LINE
AND AS EBOOK WITH ALL MAJOR DISTRIBUTERS

**For the Finest in
Nautical and Historical
Fiction and Nonfiction**

WWW.FIRESHIPPRESS.COM

Interesting • Informative • Authoritative

Lightning Source UK Ltd.
Milton Keynes UK
UKOW05f0333021216
289050UK00019B/960/P